Praise for RM Johnson
and
The Harris Men

"First novelist Johnson's writing is clear and straight-forward. . . . Readers will root for the underdog and welcome the subtle messages. . . . RM Johnson is an author to watch."

—*Library Journal*

"Johnson proves that the key to a good story is in its telling. . . . *THE HARRIS MEN*'s strength is in its honesty, which speaks volumes to readers who, in some way, shape, or form, carry the baggage of struggles with family."

—*Mosaic Literary Magazine*

"Johnson's novel reminds us that the importance of men as a presence in the lives of their sons cannot be understated. Hopefully, as more male authors tackle the issue of absentee fathers, we will find our way to preempt the blame we seem to prefer with a measure of understanding. Perhaps together we can find ways to aid a father's return to his children. After all, we are in need."

—*The Black Book Review*

"*THE HARRIS MEN* is an insightful novel that reaches into the deepest recesses of a man's heart. It dispels the rumors of why we sometimes do what we do: abandon our children, leave our wives, run from commitment."

—E. Lynn Harris

THE HARRIS MEN

a novel

RM JOHNSON

WASHINGTON SQUARE PRESS
PUBLISHED BY POCKET BOOKS

New York   London   Toronto   Sydney   Singapore

A Washington Square Press Publication of
POCKET BOOKS, a division of Simon & Schuster Inc.
1230 Avenue of the Americas, New York, NY 10020

Copyright © 1999 by R. Marcus Johnson

All rights reserved, including the right to reproduce
this book or portions thereof in any form whatsoever.
For information address Simon & Schuster Inc.
1230 Avenue of the Americas, New York, NY 10020

ISBN 978-0-7434-0059-6

First Washington Square Press trade paperback printing April 2000

10 9 8 7 6 5 4 3 2 1

WASHINGTON SQUARE PRESS and colophon are registered trademarks of
Simon & Schuster Inc.

Cover design by Matt Galemmo
Front cover photo by Barry Marcus

Printed in the U.S.A.

ACKNOWLEDGMENTS

I would like to thank my agent, Elizabeth Ziemska, for getting her hands dirty, digging through the slush piles, and seeing value in my writing when others were blind or did not care to acknowledge me. I am so grateful. I want to thank my editor, Laurie Chittenden, for using her expertise, understanding, and intuition to improve the quality of my work, even when we disagreed. I also want to thank Laurie's assistant, Nicole Graev, for handling the smallest details in the biggest way. I would like to thank my friend E. Lynn Harris for sharing his talent, knowledge, and experience, and for opening doors that I would've been standing outside of, banging on for years before getting an answer. To Adrienne Upchurch, my dear friend to the end: You believed in me from the start. That means so much. To Randy Crumpton: Thanks for all your help, and the discussions on what writing really should be. To my favorite writing instructor, Bill Ryan: You are the single person I've learned the most from. Thank you. To my dear friend and adviser in all things gray to me, Sheila Sumners, whom I not only know now, but knew in a past lifetime: Your presence has made all the difference.

Acknowledgments

Thanks, Tammy McCann, for all your enthusiasm and your criticism regarding my work. Most of the time you were dead-on. To my friends Raymond Ross, Dion Blassengame, and Reggie O'Donoghue: Surprise! You guys will be my buddies forever. Last, and most important, I must thank my family. To my mother, the most wonderful woman walking this earth: There would be no me without you. To my brother Irvin: I've idolized you since childhood. You will always be my big brother. To Renee, my dear little sister: You are more important to me than you'll ever know. And to my brother Reggie, who has forever beaten a path to make my way a little easier than his—I'll be there, right behind you, always.

For My Mother—
and all the boys who grew into men without their fathers.

ONE

"**M**r. Harris, I'm sorry, but you have cancer," the thin, white-haired doctor had told him. The man said it without emotion, without sympathy, without the slightest look of sadness in his eyes. Julius had to let it sink in a moment and decide whether his doctor was telling him the truth or not. He remembered sitting in the chair, stone-faced, unable to move.

Julius Harris shook the old thought out of his head, knowing he shouldn't dwell on the past. He pushed open the bathroom door, and there, sitting in the middle of the antiseptic room, was the toilet. He walked cautiously up to it as though it might snap at him like a small angry terrier. He unzipped his pants and stood poised above the bowl. He stood there holding himself, the bright bathroom light splashing across his slumping head and shoulders as he waited for the flow of urine to make its way toward his urethra.

It will be a while, he told himself, and when it finally comes it will hurt like hell. Julius took deep breaths. Deep cleansing breaths, hoping the action would trigger something inside him, release the old dam gates and let the fluid flow. He tilted his head back, closed his eyes, and tried to relax.

Come on, dammit, he urged himself. I don't want to be here all day, not again. The thought of just saying "screw it" ran across his mind. He'd zip his fly back up and busy himself with some simple task, just forget about it. But past experiences told him that wouldn't work. Even though he didn't have to urinate that minute, it sure as hell felt as though he did, and that feeling would remain with him until he let his contents out. So he stood and waited.

Then he felt it. It was coming, and he was able to relax for the most part and just let it flow. He always felt normal at this point, like he was a kid again, when pissing was something that you never thought two seconds about—feel your bladder getting tight, whip it out, piss all over the side of a tree and push it back in. One, two, three. Didn't even have to worry about shaking it, because dried piss stains in the front of your Fruit of the Looms were commonplace at that age.

But, like always, he soon realized it wasn't just like normal. The flow of urine was approaching its exit when Julius felt an extreme pain. It was like a bolt of lighting striking the tip of his penis, then flowing up his urethra and exploding somewhere just behind the center of his pelvis, very close to his anus. He shrugged, gritted his teeth, then relaxed a little as the pain subsided. The urine shot out in spurts at first, two streams flowing in different directions, one stream stronger than the other.

A lot of blood came out this time and the water was pink from the quantity. Some had managed to land on the rim of the toilet and the floor, speckling it like a weird abstract painting; pink drops on an all-white canvas. He rolled out some more toilet tissue, dropped to his knees and began to wipe it clean. He inspected the floor, and it was clear of all droplets. But wait. There was one . . . and another, he thought. But the droplets were not urine and blood, but tears. Two fell quickly from the corners of his eyes and splashed to the floor before he even realized he was crying. He sat up, pushed himself against the vanity, and smoothed the tears away with the heels of his hands.

"No. Don't let it get to you," he told himself in a hushed voice. He had to accept it. That was all. There was nothing he could do. Nothing would change, the disease would take its course whether he filled himself with self-pity and dreaded waking up every morning, or took each remaining day as a blessing. His doctor had told him that. But what the hell did he know, he wasn't the one dying.

Julius stood, telling himself he was stronger than his actions displayed. He looked in the mirror and a man of fifty-five years stared back at him, dark under the eyes; two days of hair growth dirtied his face. "Pull yourself together," he told himself. The doctor was right, and he knew it.

"Two years, thirty months on the outside," the doctor had said. That was all he had left to live. Julius had swallowed hard and tried to stop himself from breaking down. He had tried instead to focus on the man who had just condensed the rest of his life into a number of months. He looked in the doctor's eyes, and the doctor looked back, a blank stare, not *at* him but past him. Julius understood. The old guy couldn't get too involved with each individual poor sap that happened to be dying in two years. It would be too much to take.

Outside of the hell that was taking place in Julius's head, he had heard Cathy, his girlfriend of twenty years, crying. She was grabbing both of his hands, had pushed her chair very close to his and was bawling, sobbing heavily on his shoulder, a combination of tears and mascara falling to his sweater. Julius wrapped an arm around her. The sight of her experiencing so much pain made him furious.

That was a couple of months ago, and the memory still devastated him. To think that in a matter of months he would no longer exist. Julius reached for the sink, bracing himself there for fear he would fall. He looked up at himself in the mirror again, a desperate look on his face. Why me? he wanted to cry out. He wanted to yell at the top of his lungs, look toward the heavens and demand an answer from the so-called God that lived there in relative comfort while he suffered like an animal beneath him. He wanted to feel pity for himself, but he had done that so many times over the past two months that he knew it would do no good. It would just increase the despair he was already feeling, and pitch him into a deeper hole.

Julius heard footsteps above him, Cathy's gentle movements about the house, which signaled that she had awakened. She had probably reached a hand across the bed, felt that he wasn't there, and immediately become worried, wondering if something tragic had happened to her dearest friend. She cared the world for Julius and he knew that. She would have gladly taken the pain for him, taken the death sentence that he had received just so he could go on living. It was one of the hardest things about accepting the knowledge of his dying—knowing he would be leaving her behind to grieve painfully for probably the rest of her life.

Julius heard her descending the stairs, making her way just outside the bathroom door; he could feel her weight, her presence there waiting. He turned on the water to mask any sounds that would betray the fact that he had been wallowing in self-pity again.

"Jay, are you in there, sweetheart?" Cathy called. Her voice seemed tentative, as if she hadn't known the man she was speaking to for the past twenty years, but had met him yesterday and now found him in her bathroom.

Julius didn't answer, just rubbed his face with a hand towel, peeked in the mirror, and slipped on the most authentic smile he could manage. She'll never buy it, he thought, as he heard her voice again, more frantic this time.

"Jay!"

"Right here." He opened the door. "Just washing the old mug before breakfast." He smiled, feeling unnatural. Cathy looked up at him and didn't say a word. She stared in his face as if trying to decode some puzzle that was hidden there.

"What?" Julius asked, extending his arms out to his sides in animated bewilderment. She threw herself into him, her arms around his neck. He closed his arms around her small body and could feel her trembling within his embrace. He felt how her heart was rapidly pounding in her chest. Her grasp on him was tight, and he knew she knew exactly what had gone on in the bathroom, could read it in his face like she could read everything he was thinking. He squeezed her tight, rubbing his cheek against the soft curls of her hair, smelling the natural sweetness of her scent. The love he felt for her at that moment was too intense to bear.

"I'll fix you a big breakfast. Pancakes, sausages, eggs, grits, everything, well, not sausage. That's bad—turkey sausage. I'll call off from work, and we can—"

"No. Don't. I'll be fine," Julius said, pulling her hands away from his face, holding them in his hands. "I'm fine, really." He tried the plastic smile again, feeling just as phony as before.

She stared into his face with her big brown-orange eyes. She always did that, as though she couldn't say anything without first really thinking it over.

"Why didn't you wake me when you got up?"

"Because you were up with me late last night, and you needed to get your sleep."

"I thought you said you'd wake me if you weren't feeling well."

Julius let go of her hands and took a couple of steps back. "Yes, I did agree on that, but I'm feeling fine. I'm fine, Cathy."

"Then why—"

"Cathy, stop. I'm dying. I accepted that. But I'm not dead yet. I don't even feel that bad. I'm all right, and I'm going to be all right for who knows how long. Now, I love you to death, but I don't think I'll be able to handle you on my case like you are now for the next couple of years. I'll go crazy before it's time for me to check out. You wouldn't want that, would you?" He laughed a little, feeling more genuine.

"I'm sorry, Jay. It's just I don't want you to feel alone with this thing. I want you to know that it's not just your problem, but ours. I'm here, whatever you need. Whatever you want."

"What I want is for us not to dwell so much on my, I mean, our problem. Can we just live like we have been for the past twenty years, huh?"

"Okay. I'll . . . I'll try that." She smiled, giving him a small kiss on the lips. "I'll go to work, but I'm still going to fix you that breakfast."

"No. That's all right. I have a lot on my mind. I was really just planning on going out and finding somewhere nice to sit. You know, something beautiful to look at."

Cathy didn't say anything, but he could see her making an effort to try not to ask to accompany him.

"Okay, sweetheart. I'll eat all by myself, but don't complain when you miss out on the best breakfast I've ever made."

Julius parked his car, a 1970 Mercedes two-door coupe, on the bank of the Pacific Ocean. It was spotless. He had just washed and waxed it two days ago and it looked brand new. He looked back at it as he walked toward the water, remembering when he had first purchased it so many years back. Fifteen years to be exact, from some old guy. It was spotless then, and looked just as good now, if not better.

It was his gift to himself for making it, for doing what he set out to do and accomplishing it, even though he had to sacrifice a wife and three sons. He stood, the water to his back, a gentle breeze in the air, looking at the car. A solemn look covered his face. What a gift. He had bought the car in celebration of leaving his old life, venturing out in the cruel world where no one knew him, and making a new life. Yes, he had bought the car five years after he left his family, to commemorate the year his business was finally in the black, and he could feel accomplished.

The car had meant so much to him then. It helped mask the pain he was feeling for abandoning his family, helped him forget that he was still a married man with three boys that were probably missing him as he drove through the streets in the small two-seater, declaring how single and carefree he was. It had meant so much to him then, but now it really wouldn't matter to him if the brake slipped and the thing slowly started rolling toward the water. He would let it roll. He'd probably even give it a nudge and watch the water eat his car, leaving behind only ripples and bubbles, then nothing. It would only be fitting. But then he would have nothing, neither the car nor his family. He would only have his diseased shell of a body, and soon that too would be gone.

TWO

Austin Harris sat at his desk. His coat was on, his briefcase sitting before him, waiting to be picked up and toted home. Austin looked at his watch. It read 5:35 P.M. He could have gone home long ago, he just didn't want to. He pushed away from the large oak desk and stood up from the executive chair. He walked from behind the desk and started to pace about the plush carpeting. His coat on, tied at the waist, he walked abut the room, the only light coming from a small halogen desk lamp, set on low. He paced back and forth, stopping in front of his desk. He picked up the long triangular block of wood, his name stenciled across in gold letters: Austin H. Harris, Attorney at Law.

"Yeah," he blew sarcastically, walking another line across the room. He stopped again, this time picking up the picture of his wife. She stared back at him, holding his son and daughter, as if to say, "Hurry home, we're waiting for you." The thought made him shudder. Fairly attractive woman, he thought, but she gave me beautiful kids. He touched each child with his finger, not regarding his wife, then put the picture down. A knock at the door startled him.

"Come in," he answered.

A woman peeked in. She was holding a manila folder against the breast of her pink blazer. Her hair was cropped short, but very stylish. Her eyes were big black circles.

"What are you still doing here? You should've been gone an hour ago. And why are you walking around in the dark?" she asked.

"I'm about to go home. There were just a couple of things I needed to finish, that's all. Is there a reason I'm looking at you?"

"Oh, yeah. I just wanted to drop this case file on your desk for to-morrow morning, that's all."

"Well," Austin prompted.

She walked over and laid the folder on his desk.

"Very well done, Reecie. Sometimes I think I don't pay you enough."

"Well, I think that all the time, Mr. Harris." She turned around and was about to walk out the door. "Is everything all right, Mr. Harris?"

"Yeah. Why do you ask?" He felt defensive all of a sudden, as though he had something to hide.

"I don't know, just something. I don't know." She smiled, then closed the door behind her.

Austin walked behind his desk and slumped into his chair. She read me just like that. That shouldn't happen, he thought. Obviously he was becoming too emotional about the problem, and that meant he needed to either become more detached or resolve the problem altogether. But for now, he'd forget about it. He was tired after putting in a hard day's work at his firm. He just wanted to go home, get dinner, and relax in relative peace and quiet.

Austin sat outside in his car, parked in the driveway. He hoped no one had heard him pull up, and they probably hadn't, for he saw no little faces peeping out between the curtains of the front room. The radio was playing softly, and the soft green light colored his face in the dark.

I'll go in there in just five more minutes. Like, after this song goes off, he told himself. He wasn't quite sure what kept him from opening the door of his car and walking in the house and greeting his family like he did every night. He just wasn't sure. Or was he? Was it the every night part that bothered him? Could it be the wife, the house, the kids? Could it be that what he had worked so hard for had somehow become mundane to him? He looked at the house. A very nice house in many respects, in a very nice Chicago neighborhood. He looked at the garage standing plainly in front of him.

"The garage," he said aloud, for no other reason than to identify it. He looked down the block and saw all the other houses and garages, then looked in his rearview mirror and saw the houses that lined the other side of the street. My house is just like theirs, he thought, save for the minor physical differences that fool us into thinking that we have something unique. My house is the same, and my life is probably the same, too. I'll be walking in my house, greeting my family just like every other guy on this block probably did an hour ago. And I'm not only doing the same thing everyone else is doing, but I'm doing it after them.

He placed the thought into the "unimportant things to worry about" file in his head. He snapped the radio off and made his way to the house.

He walked in and it was quiet. The front room was empty. The light was turned down overhead, and the place was clean. No stuffed animals thrown about the couch or floor. Elmo, the orange Muppet thing, was not crumpled into a pretzel in front of the TV where Bethany usually left him. No trucks, no footballs, and no superhuman action figures suctioned to the walls. Obviously his son had been made to clean up his mess.

It wasn't as bad as he thought it was going to be, and he almost wanted to kick himself for devoting so much negative thought to what wasn't even there.

Austin took off his coat, opened the closet door, and hung it up. The door wouldn't close all the way because there at his feet, lodged in the doorway, was Elmo. He picked him up and shook him. "What are you doing in there?" he said. He smiled and thought of his daughter.

He tucked the doll under his arm, grabbed his briefcase and listened as the rumbling in his stomach became louder.

"Honey, I'm—" He laughed to himself at how routine that sounded. "Darling, I'm back." Ricky Ricardo never said that. "Where is everybody, I'm starving."

"We're in the kitchen," he heard his wife call to him.

The kitchen. That meant dinner, and he hoped she had cooked something good, because he could have eaten a small mammal the way he was feeling. He walked into the doorway of the kitchen and was greeted by Bethany. "Daddy!" she yelled, jumping into his arms. Quite a load at five years old, he thought, catching her, forced to drop Elmo and his briefcase.

"What did you bring me from work, Daddy? Did you bring me a doll?" she asked, gleaming.

"No. Buutttt . . . I brought you . . ." He searched through his pants pocket for anything he could pass off as a gift. "A stick of GUM!" he said triumphantly. "How's that?" She grabbed it, tore off the wrapper and gobbled it.

"It'll do for today," she said, around her chewing.

He gave one to his son who was sitting in his mother's lap, patted him on the head, then kissed his wife on the cheek. She kissed him back. His son, Troy, yanked on his tie.

"Hey," Austin said. "You want me pulling on your tie?"

"I don't have no tie, nah," Troy said, reaching for the dangling brightly colored fabric again.

"That's all right, you might be four now, but the day you make five, you're getting a job." His son laughed, and he laughed, too, thinking that things weren't that bad after all. After all, they were rather nice.

"What's for dinner, sweetie? I'm starving," he said, patting his stomach.

"Aw, baby, we already ate."

"You did what?"

"Yeah, you hadn't gotten home and the kids were getting hungry so I fed them. I thought you were going to get something out," she said, readjusting Troy on her lap.

"Well, what did you make?" he said, feeling slightly left out.

"We had McDonald's, Daddy. Happy Meals! Want to see my toy?" Bethany held up at ant-sized blue-faced doll with a bushel of blond hair attached. Troy pulled a little green truck out of the pocket of his Incredible Hulk shirt.

"You mean you didn't even cook."

"I told you, I thought you were eating out. The kids were getting hungry and you know they don't mind McDonald's, so that's what I got. Besides, I didn't feel like cooking. I was tired."

"Tired from what?"

Trace didn't answer the question, just looked at him. "Don't even go there, Austin. You act like you never ate out before. Last time I waited for you, the kids almost tore the house up trying to eat the furniture they were so hungry. Then you saunter in the house with a full belly wondering why I was losing my mind. You even told me next time you were late to go ahead and feed the kids. Remember?"

Yes. He did remember, but it didn't matter at that moment. He was hungry and that was all that mattered. And besides, all she had to do was take care of the kids all day. She could've prepared dinner *and* gone to McDonald's. And how tired she was had nothing to do with it.

"Yeah I remember," he said, defeated.

"I can always see if we have something left over from a couple of nights ago. I think there's some—"

"Don't worry about it. Don't put yourself out. I'm going to go upstairs and take a shower first, then I'll fix something myself."

He saw his kids looking up at him as he bent down to grab his case. Their big eyes were on him, and he knew Bethany was wondering if she should say something or not. He kicked Elmo. The Muppet slid across the floor and rebounded against the wall. Austin turned and slowly walked toward the stairs.

"Daddy's mad, isn't he?" he heard Bethany asking her mother.

"No, Daddy isn't mad," Trace replied.

But she's wrong, Daddy *is* mad, Austin thought to himself. Daddy's mad and he shouldn't be. He should be glad to be home among his family after a long day. And Daddy is also hungry, and he shouldn't be. He should be full, eating a wonderful meal that his wife so lovingly prepared for him, while she awaited his arrival.

Austin stepped out of the shower, beads of water running down his body. He pulled a towel from the rack and started to pat himself dry, looking at himself in the mirror. His hair was getting a bit long on the sides. He needed a cut. He didn't want to be like so many other people—get married, then just let yourself go. Grab someone, legally obligate them to you for life, then start eating Twinkies, stop shaving, and never pick up a book again in life.

He wasn't like that, married or not. Appearance was paramount to him, and he would take care of the puffs of hair that had started to grow out of control on the sides of his skull first thing in the morning. He danced on one foot as he dried the opposite leg, wrapped the towel around him, and stared plainly in the mirror. He straightened his back, turned his palms outward—perfect anatomical position—then looked over his body. Outside of the misshapen hair, he was in pretty good condition. The muscles in his shoulders and arms were still tight and well defined. He took a deep breath, flexing the muscles in his chest; they jumped mildly at his command. He looked at his stomach, ran his hand down the ripples, then pinched the tiny pocket of skin just to the side. Usually he could always pinch about half an inch, feeling the little bit of fat that was stored there, but when he pulled this time, there was nothing but skin.

"Damn," he said. He yanked on the other side. Same thing. That meant he was losing weight, and that meant he wasn't eating right. And why was that? he asked himself as though he didn't know. I'm not eating right because my wife isn't cooking right. Simple enough. He threw on his bathrobe and walked into the bedroom. Trace was not there and he figured she was probably putting the kids to bed. Well, at least she's doing something, he thought.

Austin stood in front of the fridge. A tiny scrap of paper was stuck to it by a magnet in the shape of a smiling slice of bread. Marcus called—6:00. Call him back, it read. He pulled the door open.

Trace hadn't found the time to shop this week. There was really nothing worth eating inside. A deflated bag of bread, two slices remaining—both ends. A bowl of cream-style corn covered with plastic wrap. Half a slab of ribs wrapped in foil from a week ago; he didn't even consider it. A small blue plastic bowl of milk, two soggy Cheerios doing a synchronized swimming routine, compliments of his son, he was sure.

He pulled out a half-eaten sandwich, the bowl of corn, and the bowl of two Cheerios. He dumped the cereal in the sink, then slid the corn into the microwave. He punched 5:00 minutes. Standing over the microwave, he unwrapped the sandwich, noticed the rough edges from where it was last bitten, then took a bite himself. He didn't know how old it was, but it didn't matter. Considering how hungry he was at that moment, he could have clubbed the neighbor's dog over the head and eaten it.

The bread was hard and stale, the meat tasted rubbery and artificial, and the vegetables, if they were once that, were wilted and devoid of taste. The continuous beeps of the microwave insisted that he remove his corn. He sat at the table in his dark blue pajamas, eating his dinner of stale mystery meat sandwich and lukewarm cream-style corn, straight from the big refrigerator storage bowl.

He tried to calm himself, but it did no good. He was seething each time he took a bite out of the tasteless sandwich and each time the little spoon slipped down the bowl and slid into the thick gook that was his corn, forcing him to dig his fingers into the soup to retrieve it.

"So, how's dinner, master chef?" Trace was coming down the stairs, a grin on her face as though she took great pleasure out of what she was seeing.

Austin didn't say a word, just put his face farther into the big bowl and continued spooning the slop into his mouth.

"Mmmmm, sure smells good," she said. She was now behind him, both hands on his shoulders, leaning over him, examining his food. She even had the nerve to stick her fingers in his sandwich to look at its contents.

"Boy, now that's a sandwich. Do you think I can have a bite? Pleeease."

Austin put down his spoon. It slid down the curved insides of the bowl and drowned in his corn again.

"What's with you?" Austin asked in a voice of suppressed anger.

Trace practically jumped backward. "Nothing, I was making a joke, that's all. Thought you would like a little company with dinner." She chuckled a bit at the use of the word "dinner." Austin didn't smile, and Trace's smile quickly drained.

"My goodness, what's with *you*? You come in late, then you try to bite my head off." She opened the fridge and pulled out a yogurt. She popped the cap on it, sat down with a spoon, and began to eat. What she was eating looked so much more appetizing than what Austin had.

"Well," she said, the creamy pink stuff in her mouth made visible as she spoke.

"Well, what?" Austin replied, knowing what she was talking about but wanting her to devote more effort to asking the question.

"Why are you so irritable? Was it a rough day at work? Did any of your clients give you a problem?"

Austin couldn't believe it. They had been married for six years now, and she couldn't even tell what was bothering him. Or could she? She was so into that little cup of yogurt, twisting and turning that spoon so not an ounce of the stuff would escape her, that she probably wasn't even paying any attention to what she was talking about. He wanted to tell her straight out, let her have it, blast her for the meal that was unmade when he got home, but as she had informed him earlier, she really had done no wrong.

"Well," she said once again, finishing the yogurt. She put the empty cup down and it fell over due to the weight of the spoon inside it. She licked her lips and folded her hands before her, giving him her full attention.

"I had a hard day at work, and I come home to this." Austin picked up the sandwich, shook it a little. A limp slice of tomato fell to the table.

Trace just looked at him till he put the sandwich down.

"We talked about this earlier, I thought."

"We did, and you were right about feeding the kids early, but do I have to eat this?"

"Austin, didn't I try to offer to fix you something earlier? But you refused. You said no." She did her Austin impression she was so proud of, lowering her voice. "I'm gonna go upstairs and take a shower, then I'm gonna fix it myself." She stood in front of him, her hands on her hips, a mock-angry mask on her face.

The gesture was kind of cute, and if Austin hadn't been so pissed he probably would have cracked a smile, but that would have been exactly what she wanted. She was right again, as she so often was, and Austin could do nothing but sit among the mess of disgusting old food he had prepared and listen to her mocking him.

"Don't worry, sweetheart. I'll fix you something." She moved about him, clearing away the damage he had done, leaning over him, brushing against his face with her hair, leaving a bit of her scent in the air for him to take in. She brushed against his shoulder and back with her breast, as though it was purely accidental.

He knew it wasn't. He watched her as she prepared his food. She was actually beautiful. Short, petite, and she had managed to gain only a few pounds after being pregnant with their two children. She turned to look at him, probably realizing he was staring, then she smiled. A beautiful bright smile, a loving smile, and it made him wonder how he could feel the way he sometimes felt about her, his life, their life together. The anger seemed to drain from his body as he gazed at his wife, watching her do for him. He resolved not to think any more of the thoughts that came to him when he was angry. Everything is fine and it will remain that way, as long as she does what she's supposed to do, he thought. She looked at Austin again, a spatula in her hand. He simply smiled back at her.

THREE

Marcus Harris woke from a deep sleep and moved from his bed in slow, dragging steps. As he walked out of his room he noticed the clock read 11:35 in the morning. He wasn't very alert till he washed his face and had his first glass of orange juice.

He had been up all night working on some illustrations for a publisher friend of his. She had to have the illustrations by Friday, so he put in extra work so she'd have it on time. He really didn't mind because he set his own hours. He decided when he did and didn't want to work, and when he didn't want to, he ended up working anyway.

The second bedroom of his house had been converted into his studio and office. His drafting table was there, and the paints, pens, pencils and everything else he used in his trade were neatly stacked on top. On the walls were tacked pictures of the many children's book characters he had drawn over the last three years, some finished, brightly colored with markers or paint, some only outlined in pencil waiting to be completed.

Marcus walked into the office still in his pajama bottoms. He sat down at the table and picked up what he had been working on so late into the night. It wasn't bad, and he was satisfied with the time he had spent on it. He considered picking up his pens again and finishing the project, but his heart wasn't in it. He yawned, stretching his arms wide above his head. He wanted to get out and do something. He looked toward the window and saw how the sun was trying to find its way in through the thin curtain. It would be a nice day to be out, but the problem was, with whom?

He was thirty-three years old and he was alone. He had never been married, and had no kids. He shied away from relationships. People get hurt, he told himself, and it's a terrible kind of hurt. Not like a scratch, or a bump on the head; not a physical pain, something far worse. A dull, heart-aching pain that makes you want to roll over and die. When you're in love and the relationship ends for whatever reason, the loss of it leaves a void, a gaping hole from which all your heart and soul and guts seep out.

Of course it had never happened to Marcus, not directly, because he wouldn't let it. But he had seen it happen to someone else—his mother, and that was as close to the pain as he needed to be. It was twenty years ago or so, and his father, for some reason or another, decided it would be best for all parties concerned if he just split. He did just that, without any explanation whatsoever.

Marcus wasn't sure what that man told his mother the day he left, but she cried hard all day, like a woman who had lost her children in a fire. It seemed as though she cried every day until she died of breast cancer. Whenever he thought about his father he could never stop thinking that his departure was what actually killed her. Marcus imagined that if he ever saw his father again he would kill him. When he envisioned the man standing before him, his hand extended, a smile on his face, as though they had never lost a day, he knew he would kill him. He would simply blow him away with a shotgun for taking his mother away.

After his mother died, Marcus had no one. His big brother Austin had gone to law school, even though Marcus begged him to stay. Austin told him that he had to get on with his life. "Mother would've wanted me to go." And to this day, Marcus had never forgiven him for that. With his mother's death and Austin's departure for school, the youngest brother,

Caleb, was put in Marcus's care. He was more than a handful, bordering on a troublemaker, and Marcus did his best for him as long as he could. But Caleb had no intention of taking orders from a brother who was only three years older than himself. He got a two-bit job as a custodian, quit high school, and moved in with some woman ten years older than himself. Caleb didn't even make it there with the woman a year.

His brothers were still around, and he saw them on occasion, but they were not the family they should have been, the family Marcus wanted them to be. Austin and Caleb never seemed to get along, not even when they were children. They rarely spoke or saw each other and the responsibility was left to Marcus to keep them civil and acting like brothers.

Marcus yawned and stretched, picked up a blue pen, realizing that there was nothing else to do but finish the work he had started the night before, but first he'd grab a glass of orange juice. He had started toward the kitchen when the phone rang.

"Marcus Harris speaking," he answered, grogginess still in his voice.

"Wake up, it's almost noon." A voice came over the phone a little too loud and energetic, forcing Marcus to pull away from the receiver. It was his older brother, Austin.

"Do you ever do any work, or do you just sleep all day?"

"Good morning, Austin. And yes, I do do work. I was up all night doing some as a matter of fact, and I was just about to do some more. You finally found time in your busy schedule to call me back," Marcus said, pacing his office with the cordless phone.

"I have important things to take care of, Marcus. I just can't pick up the phone whenever you call just to chat. What did you want, anyway?"

"Nothing in particular, just wanted to talk, you know."

"About what?"

"I don't know. Just talk. See how you were doing. It's not like I talk to you every day."

"Marcus, you have too much time on your hands. You find a woman desperate enough to date you yet?"

"That's none of your business, and that's not what I called to talk about."

"Okay, talk. But make it quick. I can't just sit around my house all day, scribbling on the flaps of cardboard boxes like you do."

Marcus heard Austin laugh a little, but he didn't take offense. That was what Austin had always thought of Marcus's livelihood. "When was the last time you talked to Caleb?" Marcus asked.

"I don't know, a couple of weeks, maybe longer. Why?"

"I just think maybe you could make more of an effort to keep in touch with him. He is your younger brother, you know."

"Well, he's your younger brother, too."

"I keep in touch with him," Marcus replied.

"Why can't he call me? He has a phone just like I do, if it hasn't been turned off yet."

"I know he does, Austin. But that's beside the point."

There was a long pause on Austin's end of the phone. "Well, can you get to the point, Marcus? I'm busy, all right?"

"I was wondering if you want to get together sometime soon. The three of us, do some bowling or something?" Marcus could sense the answer even before it came.

There was another long moment of silence.

"Marcus, don't you think you're trying a little too hard with this?"

"With what?"

"With this Three Musketeers crap. We're brothers, Marcus. I think we all know that. I'll even say it for you—we are brothers. But just because we are doesn't mean we have to walk arm in arm everywhere we go."

"I know that. I didn't say that. I just thought it wouldn't be a bad idea if—"

"When do you want to get together? Do you want to meet for drinks tomorrow evening or something?"

"I don't know if I'll be able to get in touch with Caleb that soon."

"Then just come yourself," Austin said.

"What do you mean, just come myself?"

"You heard me."

"The whole idea was to get the three of us together."

"No, Marcus, the idea was to get Caleb and myself together. Look, I don't know what you want from the two of us, but I don't think you're going to find it. Face it, we just aren't each other's favorite people."

"But you're brothers."

"Marcus, so what. Do you hear me? So what! I know we're brothers.

I care for the man, I never want anything bad to happen to him, and if he ever needs me, I'll be around for him, and that pretty much fulfills my brotherly duties. Hold on a minute," Austin said.

What an ass my brother is, Marcus thought. He heard a woman's voice in the background, then his brother's voice giving her orders of some sort.

"Look, I've got to go. Do you want to have drinks or not?"

"Do you mind if Caleb comes?"

"Marcus, I never said I didn't want him to come."

"Do you mind if Caleb comes?" Marcus asked again.

"I don't care. If you find him, bring him. If you don't—don't. All right. See you later."

"Bye," Marcus said. "What an ass."

He didn't understand why his brother felt the way he did about Caleb. They were different, yes, but that didn't mean he had to shun him like some homeless dreg begging for money. It was wrong, and that was the long and short of it. If this continued, they would be strangers, and Marcus couldn't let that happen.

Marcus remembered one night when he was a child watching his mother lying ill on her bed. She was well into her sickness, very close to the end. She lay there, her eyes half open, the long painful fight with cancer evident on her face. Marcus sat on the floor by her bed. The two of them were having a slow, soft-spoken conversation in the dark.

"Nobody should be alone." She spoke slowly, pulling in air when she needed it, making long, thin wheezing sounds with the effort.

"Everyone needs someone, no matter how strong they believe themselves to be. Your brothers have never really gotten along, not even when they were little boys. They always found something to argue about. Always." She laughed a little, but it sounded more like a short series of coughs. There was a distant look on her face as if remembering something. "I don't want you to see it as a burden, and if you don't think that you want to be bothered with it, don't be, but they won't come together by themselves."

"I know, Ma," Marcus said, caressing her hand in his.

"I want you to try and keep the three of you together. It would be nice." She smiled absently again. "You'll have no one but yourselves after . . . after I'm gone." She tightened the grip on her son's hand.

"Ma, don't say that." Marcus moved closer to her. She placed her arms around him. He could barely feel the weight of them.

"I'm not going to be here forever, Marcus. You know that. It's not bad to talk about it."

He was aware of what she was asking him to do, but he had no way of knowing how to do it. If they didn't want to be together, then they just didn't want to be, and there was really nothing he could do about it. That was how he really felt then, but he couldn't tell his mother that. He couldn't tell her anything like that, because she was near her death, he could feel it, and he didn't want to put anything on her mind that would disturb her peaceful passing.

Marcus immediately picked up the phone and dialed his younger brother.

"Hello," the voice on the other end of the phone said.

"Hello," Marcus answered. "Sonya?"

"Yeah."

"This is Marcus. Is Caleb there?"

"No, Marcus, he's not. He's supposed to be out looking for a job, but you know what that means. There's no telling where he could be."

"Well, please tell him I called, and if he gets in anytime before five, can you tell him to call me back?"

"Yeah, I'll tell him. Bye, Marcus."

"Hey, hey, hold it," Marcus said quickly.

"Yeah?"

"How are you doing?"

"Huh?"

"How are you doing? Is everything all right?" he asked, wondering why she sounded surprised by a simple question like that.

"Aw, yeah, everything is fine. We're making it. You know, one day at a time, every day." She laughed a little.

Her response was thin. Marcus could tell it was phony. "Yeah, I know. And how is little Jahlil? He's all right?"

"Yeah, he's fine, with his bad self."

Marcus paused for a moment, feeling that there was something weird about the way Sonya was responding to his questions.

"Everything is fine, right?" he asked with some concern.

There was a long pause, and he had to speak her name before she responded again.

"Oh, well, there is this problem with the . . . uh . . ."

"With the what, Sonya?"

"Uh . . . with the . . . never mind," she came back quickly. "No, everything is fine."

"You were about to tell me something. What was it?"

"Nothing. I forgot. It was nothing, all right, Marcus?"

"It had to be something, or you wouldn't have mentioned it." He could feel himself becoming irritated with her childish behavior. She was twenty-seven years old, far too old to be playing games like that.

"Marcus, I'll tell your brother you called. I'm sure he's out there finding a job, and he should be home soon, okay?"

"But—"

"Bye, Marcus." She hung up the phone.

Marcus's first thought was to call her back, but he realized she probably wouldn't pick up the phone. He needed to know what she was talking about. He knew that something was up, he could hear it in her voice. It bothered him that she wouldn't tell him. She should have known that he would do anything within his power to help them. He dialed the number again, then after thinking for a moment, disconnected the call before it went through. Sometimes he wished he could just not care, distance himself as Austin did, but that wasn't the type of person he was.

FOUR

Caleb sat on a slab of rock and watched two old men play chess. One had a beard, and one was wearing an old fishing hat. They were both filthy. It was an interesting game, so Caleb couldn't just get up and leave in the middle of it, he had to see who won. He looked down at his watch and it read 11:52 A.M. He had gotten out of the house at eight o'clock, telling Sonya that today would be the day that he would find a job. He had even put on his only pair of real pants, a pair of cotton Levi's Dockers. They were a little big and a little long because he had bought them at a discount store, but they still looked kind of professional. Stuffed in his pants pocket was a clip-on tie that he had taken off during the intense chess game.

When the game was over Caleb moved to a park bench and opened the paper to the job section. He started to glance over the tiny blocks of advertisements. "Computer Analyst," one announced, and the ten blocks under it marked positions. Sales Manager, Nurses, Engineers wanted, Electricians, Marketing Executives. These were the ads that caught his attention and all they did was discourage him. There was no way in the world he could qualify for one of those positions with his limited education. He hadn't even graduated from high school for God's sake.

He sank his face in his hands and wondered why he was even going through the trouble. It didn't make sense to look, get all dressed up and walk around like a fool panhandling for a damn job. Something would come along eventually, it always did. Somebody who knew somebody else would offer him a job, didn't really matter what it was, but he'd take it and everything would be cool. And if that didn't happen, he'd hit Sonya up again. She worked at the unemployment office, and she'd get him a couple of inside tracks just like she had last time, even though he screwed those up.

Happy with himself, his actions all planned for finding a job, he tossed the job section in the trash can near where he was sitting, and folded the rest under his arm. It was too beautiful a day to be out begging for a job. He looked at his watch again and it was only 12:15. Sonya wouldn't expect him back till at least three, so he would find something to do.

He hopped on the bus, showing the driver the crinkled little piece of paper he used to transfer from one bus to the next. He had to squeeze his way through the people because the bus was crowded with the lunchtime rush. A woman was getting up and he took the seat, even though another woman seemed to have been waiting patiently for the vacancy.

The bus was heading in the direction of the inner city housing projects, the many tall identical buildings that lined one of the major highways of Chicago. They stood there, hundreds of feet tall, as a constant reminder of how poor black folks were in this city. They were like building-sized billboards, Caleb thought, screaming "Blacks folks be po'! Hey, just look where we live!"

The crowd on the bus started to thin because of the direction the bus was traveling. No one wanted to end up among the project buildings if they didn't belong there.

Across the aisle from Caleb was a man wearing one of those fancy business suits like Austin always wore, the kind Caleb hated so much. But he had to admit, of all the ones he had seen, this was one of the nicest. He was a man of about forty-five or fifty, Caleb figured, and on his lap rested, of course, a briefcase. The man was black, neat-looking, clean-shaven, with shiny shoes and those thin little black socks that you can see through. He wore a diamond ring on his right hand, a wedding band on

his left, and on his wrist was a very nice watch. He sat facing Caleb, looking out the window behind him. Caleb looked him up and down; the attention didn't seem to bother the man. He reminded Caleb of Austin, so
damn caught up with his suits and ties, watches and rings. He would have
bet anything that this guy was just as much a joke as Austin was.

He looked him over again, and wondered what the man was still doing on the bus—they were closing in on the outskirts of the danger zone,
and looking the way he was, Caleb figured he should've gotten off the
bus long ago. But the man just continued looking out the window as if
the surroundings were nothing new to him. Caleb wondered how much
money he made, what he did, and what the hell he was doing so damn
far away from the suburbs where all the other un-black black folks lived.
The man must have felt Caleb's stare. He smiled slightly and nodded.
Caleb nodded back, feeling the man was as phony as a three-dollar bill.

"Hey, what's your name?" Caleb asked, not feeling at all out of place.

The man looked up, raising his eyebrows as if to ask, "me?"

"Joseph Benning," he said, seeming comfortable speaking to a
stranger. "And what's your name, young man?"

Caleb thought about not answering, not liking the "young man" remark, but he figured compared to his old ass, he was a young man.

"Caleb. My name is Caleb Harris."

"Nice to meet you, Caleb Harris. Nice day, isn't it?" He smiled,
looking out the window. Caleb looked out the window behind him, the
same one Benning was looking out, as if it was the only one with the
view of the nice day.

"Yeah, I guess so." Caleb looked over the man again, paying close
attention to the watch, the big diamond that was where the twelve
should have been, the shiny gold of the rings, and the expensive look of
the briefcase. He wondered what the street value would be for all that
stuff. That is, if he were still into robbing, which he wasn't. But he was
sure it would've been reason enough to risk taking it off the old guy. Besides, he probably had it insured, and if he didn't, Caleb was sure he
made enough to run out and buy replacements.

"Hey, how much you make?"

"Excuse me," the man smiled, seeming embarrassed by the question.

"You know what I mean. How much money you bringing in? I
know it has to be a lot if you're walking around with all that on," Caleb

pointed a finger in the general direction of the man's hands and wrist.

"That's not the sort of question you ask someone you've just met. That's really not the sort of question you even ask a friend."

"Yeah, I know all that, but I wanted to know, so I asked. All you can do is say no, right? I'd just be right back where I started. So how much?"

The man laughed. He looked at Caleb, appearing to consider the question.

"I make enough," he finally replied.

"All right then, you don't have to tell me. All the people making the big money don't want the little folks to know how much it is, like they're ashamed of their big salaries 'cause they know we aren't making nothing."

"Well, how much do you make, Caleb? If you don't mind me asking."

"No. I don't mind you asking." Caleb paused for a moment, feeling a bit ashamed of himself. "I don't make anything. I don't have a job. I'm out here looking, that's why I got the schoolboy getup on." He reached in his pants pocket and pulled the tie out a bit so Benning could see.

"And how is it going?"

"It ain't. It's tight, man. I been all through this paper, and ain't nothing in here for me to do." He tossed the paper to the seat next to his.

"And what is it you do?"

"Damn, you ask a lot of questions."

"If I'm prying, just ask me to stop." He placed his briefcase to his side and crossed his legs.

"Yeah, well, I do the basic stuff, you know, hands work. Lifting boxes, washing dishes. Stuff like that." Caleb looked away.

"So do you think—"

"What do you do?" Caleb interrupted, taking the spotlight off himself.

"I'm a manager and partial owner of a large computer software supplier downtown. Main Frame Software, you heard of it?"

"Yeah, I think so." Never hearing the name before in his life. "So what you doing on this side of town? You a bit far from the Gold Coast, don't you think?"

"I'm visiting a friend, she's sick."

"Don't you have a car, making all the money you do?"

"Yes, I do, making all the money I do." He smiled. "It's in the shop getting the window replaced. Someone broke into it."

"Mercedes, Lexus, BMW, something like that, right?" Caleb asked.

"Something like that."

"Well, if you keep coming around places like this, it's going to stay in the shop. You don't belong out here, you think?" Caleb asked.

Benning looked out the window at what was passing outside.

"Why don't I?"

"'Cause you . . . you know. You rich. You got all that. These people out here, we don't have nothing. You never know, man. They might try and knock you over the head. If I were you, I'd be scared."

"Why, are you scared?"

"Naw, hell no," Caleb said. "I ain't scared. Besides, I don't have nothing. I'm referring to you." He pointed a finger.

"Well, I'm sorry to say, but I disagree. I don't think that a man should fear places that his own people live in just because he has nice things. Besides you make it appear as though everyone here, or individuals without money, are bad people and can't be trusted."

"Well, I almost want to say that's right," Caleb said.

"I don't think you're a bad person, Caleb Harris. Are you?" He looked intently in Caleb's eyes.

Caleb looked back, then smiled and laughed a little. "Very funny, I see your point, but I'm just telling you, you should watch your back, that's all. I'm just looking out for an old guy," Caleb said, joking. "You know, you're out of your element. It's rough around here."

"I'm not as old as you think, but thanks for the gesture." Benning stood, grabbed his briefcase, then looked out the window. "Well, this is my stop. Interesting conversation. I wish we had more time to continue it."

"Yeah, me too," Caleb said, nodding his head.

"I tell you what." Benning reached into his jacket pocket, took out a tiny leather folder, and pulled out a little white card. "This is my business card. If you would really like to continue this conversation, give me a call and we can meet somewhere for lunch or something."

Caleb took the card, looked it over. "Main Frame Software, Joseph Benning, Dept. Manager." "Yeah, okay, I'll do that."

"Good." Benning extended his hand and Caleb shook it vigorously.

"Good-bye, Mr. Harris." Benning walked toward the front of the bus, but stopped. "Oh, yeah, and the remark you made about me being out of my element—I'm not. This is where I grew up." He smiled at the look on Caleb's face and stepped off the bus.

He grew up here? Caleb thought. He's lying. He's making too much money to come from this. It couldn't be. He looked down at the card again. He held it with both hands, almost caressing it. Department manager grew up in the projects, that's something. Caleb felt good that he had met someone that had actually made it out of the wretched place, that is if the old guy was telling the truth. He was a cool old guy, and he had a lot to say. Caleb was genuinely sorry that they couldn't keep talking. He could have learned a lot from the man, or at least found out how much money he made. But he had already decided that he would call him. He would call him and they would do lunch. He really didn't have much else to do during the day. Caleb Harris and this important, rich, money-making old dude that grew up in the projects would talk.

Caleb felt good about himself, felt proud, as though he had accomplished a great deal. He wanted to tell someone, but he didn't feel like going back home. He wanted to celebrate, get a forty-ounce bottle of beer or something. He got off the bus, stepped into the liquor store, and grabbed a bottle of beer. Miller High Life, his favorite. He paid for it with loose change, then set off to find a couple of his friends. He knew they'd be hanging out on a nice day like this, because they had no jobs either.

He took off down the street, carrying the bottle of beer, small paper bag covering it halfway, exposing the neck. It was almost two o'clock and the sun was getting warmer. It was pretty bright and it seemed to improve the looks of everything. Even the streets of the projects didn't look that bad. The abandoned cars, the bits of trash that grew along the curbs as if they were flowers that belonged there, the areas of hard-packed gray dirt where grass used to grow. Nothing looked as bad as it did on glum, dull days when the sun wasn't out. When Caleb saw his friend Blue sitting on a park bench with a couple of other guys, he said loudly, "Hey, man, what's up with your black ass?" They called him Blue because he was so black—so black that he was blue.

Blue looked at him weirdly, as if he had never seen Caleb happy. "What's up with you? Finally win the Lotto or something?" He had a bottle of beer himself. He was sitting on the backrest of the bench, his feet planted on the seat. He reached down and grabbed the forty-ounce bottle from between his legs.

Caleb had known Blue since they were kids, the better part of his life, and like Caleb's, Blue's life seemed to be moving in every direction but the correct one. Blue's father hadn't cut out on him, but he was gunned down on his way home from work one day. Wrong place wrong time. So Blue knew what it was like to grow up without a father, and that was one reason the two of them were so tight. Whatever it was they were missing by not having fathers around, they found in each other, and Caleb could no longer count how many times they had saved each other's asses from sticky situations. Blue had always been there for him, just like a brother, even when Caleb's real brothers weren't.

"What you doing all spiffed up, looking like you coming from church?" Blue said, taking a swig from the bottle of beer. The remark provoked a chuckle from the two other guys, one standing and one sitting.

"Been looking for a job, man. Had to," Caleb said, slapping Blue's hand.

"Sonya been riding that ass again, huh?" He did his Sonya impression, raising the sound of his voice. "You better get your ass out there and find you a nine to five, or don't think about bringing your butt back in this house!" He took another swig from his bottle, this time a longer one. Caleb could see the tight little ball in his neck go up and down as the beer slid down his throat. Blue pulled the bottle away and smiled, the gold tooth in the front of his mouth reflecting sunlight.

"Naw, it ain't nothing like that. I got responsibilities, that's all," Caleb said.

"Well, did you get one? You find a job?"

"Naw, but I met this dude. Real cool dude. Grew up in the projects, got this software company, and make big cash. We talked on the bus. He got a lot to say, and I'm going to listen. I'm going to get a job from him, just listen to what I'm saying."

"Yeah, all right, that's cool," Blue said, with little enthusiasm.

"I'm for real. Look at this." Caleb reached in his pocket and pulled out the card. He held it in front of Blue's face, not allowing him to grab it.

"Let me hold it," Blue said.

"Naw, you going to get it dirty, bend it all up, just look."

Blue took a quick glance, then dismissed it. "All right, man, that's great. Happy birthday. Now why don't you put your toy away and crack that brew, 'cause if you ain't, you can pass it this way."

Caleb did what he was asked, and decided that his friend would never make more of himself than what he was at that moment: one more brother sitting on a bench, swigging on a forty. Sure Caleb was doing the same thing at that moment, but he wouldn't be there for the rest of his life.

They sat and talked, the four of them. They talked about life and women and the white man keeping them down, lack of job opportunities, the destruction of the world, and whatever else floated into their heads. One of the other guys that Caleb didn't know—his name was Pete—took out a small, crumpled piece of aluminum foil. He opened it up, then pulled out of his pocket a small booklet of thin papers. He proceeded to roll the contents of the foil into the paper, licked it a couple of times, then lit it.

"Now you talking," Ray Ray said. That was the other guy, big afro on his head. He was a huge lethargic guy. Pete passed Ray Ray the joint, and he took a long drag from it.

"See, the white man want us to work a nine to five. That's where he want us, see," Ray Ray said, already high. "Because if we work a nine to five, he'd have control over us. He'd be monitoring us, you see. Have us piss in a bottle to see if we be enhancing. They don't want us enhancing our minds with the herb, because they know that it gives us knowledge, it clarifies shit." He took another puff, pulled the joint from his mouth, and held it before him, staring at it, marveling as if it was the cure for cancer. "I'll fuck a motherfucker up, he try and take this from me."

"Just pass the shit and stop tripping!" Blue said. "I ain't working that shit, 'cause it's just like slavery. They want you to sweat, break your back for them, and what do they give you? Some money so you can run out and buy some insignificant shit on credit. Then they have you paying them, not just one time but for two years, or three years, or five years." He took a hit of the blunt and held the smoke in as he finished talking, his voice sounding strangled. "And then don't just have you paying them for years and years, but have you paying for more than the shit actually cost—interest and shit." He blew the smoke out through his nose and mouth. "Black folks think they arrived when they get a credit card and a car note, but they don't realize, they just jumped into a funnel, and it goes nowhere but down." He passed the joint to Pete.

"But what do you have?" Pete asked. "You ain't got shit but them gym shoes on your feet, and you need to be buying a new pair real soon, 'cause those starting to talk."

Everyone laughed a little, except Blue.

"That's cool, too. I ain't got no car, and I don't have no credit card either, but you know what else I ain't got? Debt. I don't owe no one shit. You hear me. Shit! Big fat zero. So yeah, I ain't making no money, but I sure as hell ain't spending none, either. Am I right, or what, Caleb?"

Caleb looked over at Blue and considered what he had said. "You right, man, for the most part. I don't like it either. I don't like no one telling me what to do, sizing me up, condemning me 'cause I put the square peg in the circle hole. And you right about folks being so far in debt that they never going to see they way out. They going to die still paying off that TV that they renting to own. But if you got responsibilities, if you going to live, you got to make money. That's just the way life is. White folks made it that way so we got to work, and that brings us back to them controlling us."

"I don't care what you say, I'm living, and I ain't working. I'm living, smoking this here joint, and it's what I'm going to continue to do until I find out what it is I really want to do," Blue said.

"And when is that going to be, when you fifty?" Ray Ray said.

"That's going to be when that's going to be. I ain't rushing for nobody."

"I'm glad you got it like that, but some of us can't be taking our time," Caleb said. He wanted to continue, letting them know that some of them, speaking of himself, had a girlfriend that practically was his wife, and a child to raise, plus rent to pay and food to buy, but they wouldn't have understood. All they thought about was sitting out, talking shit, and getting high.

There was a time when that was all that interested him as well, but lately he had been getting ridiculed from all sides. Sonya had done everything but come out and call him a complete loser. She'd leave the day's paper on the table with the job section open, things circled, things that she thought he should check out. She'd always ask him how things were going, had he found a job yet? It all seemed like gentle nudging, something that she referred to as "support," but he found it painfully annoying. Like she had to remind him every day that he had no job, that he brought no money into the household. He needed no one for that. He could simply dig in his pockets, and the lint there spoke loud and clear.

Caleb downed the last of his beer and looked at his watch. It was a little after four o'clock and he figured it was time he got home. He said good-bye to his friends. "Yeah, better get that ass home before you get in trouble," was Blue's farewell.

Caleb only had to wait about five minutes before he saw the bus slowly roll down the street.

He didn't like the pressure, not just from his girlfriend but also from his brothers. Marcus kept telling him that he should do this and do that. Maybe enroll in school, take the GED, and maybe he'd find out that he had a new liking for school. That shit would never happen. First of all, he wasn't the slightest bit interested. Secondly, he was scared as hell of all the book stuff. He could never get it. The math, the science, it was too far above his head, and he just felt like a fool even attempting to make an effort. It was just easier if he didn't have to bother with it at all, so he dropped out, and he would not return, no matter what Marcus said.

Then there was Austin. Caleb realized that Austin really didn't give a damn anyway, but he still felt pressure. Not pressure directly from Austin, but pressure from himself to do something, if for no other reason than to prove his brother wrong. It seemed from as far back as he could remember, Austin had written him off as a loser. He didn't know why, and it was something that had bothered him even as a child. He could remember his father would give him the same loser treatment, as if he wasn't as deserving as his older brothers, or as if he always got in the way of their time together. Caleb just figured that Austin's treatment of him stemmed from his father's treatment, considering how much Austin looked up to the man.

Caleb would do something. He would have to. He couldn't just continue to live the way he was living, freeloading off his girlfriend, not being able to contribute a single dime toward their expenses. He pulled out the card again and held it before him. "Mr. Joseph Benning," he said softly to himself. He smiled, then put the card safely back in his pocket.

FIVE

Austin sat at the head of a long table occupied by the attorneys he employed at his firm. Next to him sat his friend and second in charge, Chad Dubois. Chad was a good-looking, square-jawed, confident guy, and the two had been best friends for years. The only major difference between the two was that Austin was married and Chad was not. Although they were only a year apart, Chad felt there was a time for everything and this just wasn't the time for marriage. He was more than a bit of a flirt, and he felt marriage would just make him, and all the women that he would have to deny, miserable.

Austin's secretary, Reecie, was at the table as well, taking notes. There were papers spread out all across the table, and coffee mugs with silly sayings and comics scribbled on the front before each person except Austin. He didn't drink coffee. The few times he had drunk it, he had caught an awful case of the shakes.

Jessica was arguing with Chad. "Well, if it wasn't for the woman, he wouldn't have made all the money that he did, so she's entitled to more than what he wants to give her."

"One thing you fail to realize is that the man is the same man now as he was before he got married. He would've been just as successful had he not gotten married in the first place. It wasn't as though she guided and trained and taught the poor bastard everything he knows. She's lucky he's willing to give her anything." Chad raised his mug—a comic of Bart Simpson on the front flashing his middle finger to the world—and took a sip, peeking over the rim to see Jessica's reaction to what he had said.

"Well, that's why it's a good thing you have nothing to do with this case, and your opinion is nothing more than your opinion. I'm going to push for five hundred a month alimony."

"I would try six," Patti said.

"I would go six-fifty," Fresca said, pulling her pencil from in between her teeth.

"And you'll get it, too."

"Money hungry, all of ya'll. That's why—"

"We know, Chad. That's why you aren't getting married," Reecie finished for him.

"That's right. What do you think, boss man?"

Austin looked up from a sheet of paper he was doodling on. He was drawing a stick person with a huge head standing in a grass field, a stick house in the distance, like something one of his children would draw. He thought a moment. The stick man could have been him, and the house was probably his own. He was a long way from their conversation, as he usually was when they decided to start babbling among themselves. This was good for them though, got their minds working, so he would let them continue while he sorted out whatever problems were on his mind for the day.

"I think this meeting was over twenty minutes ago, and you guys are just talking about nonsense so you don't have to go to work. That's what I think, Chad," Austin said.

"Now that's a man who knows his employees," Fresca said as she gathered her things. The others picked up their papers and cleared out, except for Chad. He sat there, drinking from his Bart mug, watching as they filed out.

"Oh, yeah, Jessica." Austin caught her attention before she got out of the room.

"Yeah?"

"Five-fifty a month, okay? The man has got to live, too."

"Right," she said, smiling. "I knew you'd say that."

Austin sat rubbing the inside corners of his eyes with his fingers.

"Nice haircut, man. Who cut you up, Gerrell?"

"Yeah, he did a decent job," Austin said, his mind still a million miles away. "It was sticking all out on the sides, and you know I hate that." Austin took a sip from his cup of orange juice. "I don't know how you drink that stuff," referring to Chad's coffee.

"Got to, man. It keeps the mind and body alert." He took another sip, and let out an exaggerated "aaahhhh" to prove it. "What's up, man? You weren't all here this morning, is everything all right at home?"

Austin didn't answer right away, just looked at Chad for a moment. "Why does something have to be wrong at home, something can't be wrong somewhere else?"

"No. Nothing has to be wrong at home. I mean . . . that's why I'm asking, I don't want anything to be wrong at home, or anywhere else."

"But you didn't ask about anywhere else. You didn't say, 'is everything all right at home and everywhere else?' Like my situation at home is all there is—is all that can go wrong." Austin felt himself becoming angry and didn't try to contain it.

Chad cocked his head to the side, a questioning look on his face. "I was just asking a question. I don't know what you're talking about. Is there a little vodka in that juice? If so, give me a sip, buddy."

Austin tilted the cup slightly, looked inside, then cracked what he considered a smile. "Never mind, Chad. I didn't mean anything. Sometimes I take myself a little too seriously, you know what I mean?" Chad nodded.

"What do you have going this morning?" Austin asked.

"Nothing that can't wait a while. Why?"

"Because I'm hungry. I skipped breakfast so I could get my hair cut this morning. Did you eat?" Chad raised his mug, letting him know the coffee was his breakfast.

"Let's grab some breakfast then, my treat," Austin said.

Chad hit the switch on the alarm remote attached to his key ring. There was a chirping sound announcing the disabling of the alarm, and then the unlocking of the doors. Chad and Austin jumped into the car, a bright red Audi coupe, the license plates reading "LAW MAN." The car was spotless and even the dull overhead lamps of the parking garage reflected brilliantly off its metal skin.

The two men slid into the gray leather seats and buckled up. From the glove compartment Chad pulled out a pair of expensive sunglasses and put them on. He adjusted the rearview mirror so he could see himself, then ran a hand over the shiny black waves that lined the top of his head.

"Simply marvelous," Austin heard him say. He threw the stick shift in reverse, pulled out a little too fast for Austin's taste, and they were on their way.

Chad was working the stick on the car like a crazed man, changing gears up and down, the car speeding up then slowing down, braking then speeding up again. He switched lanes as if Austin was a pregnant woman beside him about to give birth, spilling his insides all over Chad's fine leather seats. He did all this while humming along very calmly to one of his favorite jazz CDs.

"Driving a little wild, don't you think? Alive is a nice way to eat breakfast," Austin said, sitting up very straight in the seat, his sunglasses now on.

"Gotta drive like this, boss man. This is a performance car. Wouldn't be getting all my nickels and dimes' worth if I didn't. Watch this." He looked over his sunglasses at Austin and cracked a wicked smile, then grabbed the steering wheel firmly and yanked it hard to the right. He cut across two lanes of traffic to make a right turn and practically hit a bicycle delivery boy in the process. "Almost made a sticky surface out of that little guy." Austin shook his head and paid little attention to Chad's antics.

Actually, Austin could have been having a good time, if only he had allowed himself. The sun was out, it was shining in his eyes, the wind was blowing in his face, they were doing what seemed to be ninety miles per hour down a residential street, and for some reason his mind was still filled with his problems, even though he felt less burdened than he had in quite some time. He looked over at Chad, who was shaking his head to the beat of the music and driving as if his car was a new bike he had just received for Christmas and this was the first day warm enough to take it out for a spin.

He led his life with such abandon, and Austin often ridiculed him for it. For someone as old as Chad, he shouldn't act in such a way, or he should use more common sense with this, and pay more attention to that.

But being driven about town at racing car speeds went far beyond common sense, and the fact that Austin was actually enjoying himself a little made him realize that there might be something to the way Chad behaved. The man never seemed to have too much more on his mind than which car accessory he would buy next. And that was because he had so few responsibilities. He didn't have a family at home, wife, kids, and all the other restrictions that went with it, so he didn't have to worry about getting himself wrapped around a pole, leaving no one at home to raise his fatherless children and take care of his widowed wife. It must be nice, Austin thought as they pulled into the restaurant parking lot. He almost felt himself admiring Chad. But that was foolish, because the way Chad behaved was careless and without regard to the future.

"We're here. In record time and all in one piece," Chad said. He hit a switch and the roof closed above them, blotting out the sun. They walked into the restaurant and were greeted by the hostess at the door. She held a couple of menus in her hands and looked approvingly at both men as they walked up to her.

"Table for two?"

"Unless you'd like to join us," Chad said.

She smiled. "Smoking or non?"

"Nonsmoking, please," Austin said.

"Right this way." She led them to a table, placed the menus before them, smiled again at Chad, and went off on her way.

"You don't stop, do you?"

"What?" Chad said, looking as if he knew exactly what Austin was talking about. "I made one remark. C'mon, she left herself open for that one. Besides, she was checking you out."

"I don't think so," Austin said dryly.

"Yeah, I'm telling you, she was." He opened his menu and glanced at it, then closed it. "Ah, I know what I'm getting. You?" Chad asked.

"Oatmeal, some fruit; juice."

"Sounds good to me."

The waitress came. An older, thin white woman with white hair and too much makeup. They ordered and she took their menus.

"So what's up, man? What was with you this morning?" Chad asked.

"I don't know. Just thinking."

"'Bout what?"

Austin didn't want to get into what he was really thinking. They were thoughts that he wasn't really sure about, nothing that should be openly discussed, at least not now.

"Nothing, it's not important."

"Okay, whatever you say, but when it is important, I'm here, man." Chad took a sip of his water.

"How come you aren't married yet?" Austin leaned back in the booth.

"Not this again. C'mon, man, I told you, it's just not my time."

"Pretty good life, huh? No worries, few responsibilities, date a new girl every night."

"Hey, you make it sound like it's easy being single. I gotta wash my own clothes you know." He laughed. Austin didn't think it was funny. His hands rested flat on the table as he looked intently at Chad.

"Really, pretty nice, huh? No need for commitment, or responsibility to anyone."

"What do you want me to say?" Chad said, looking exasperated. "No, I don't have the responsibilities like you do, and yeah, I date pretty much when and who I want to, but . . ."

"But what?" Austin sat up.

"But . . . umm, it can get lonely, a little—sometimes," Chad defended.

Austin shook his head as if the poor response was the exact answer he had expected. "I think I would call that privacy, and that wouldn't be that bad of a thing."

"Let me tell you, it's really not all you think it is. Sometimes it would be nice to have that special person there to do for me, you know cook for me, share special things with." Austin thought he sounded clumsy speaking those words, as if he were reading them from a greeting card and had no experience whatsoever with what he was talking about.

"Sometimes that special person can get on your last nerve, and sometimes that special person doesn't cook you dinner when you expect it. Let me tell you, it's really not all *you* think it is. I don't know, sometimes I look at my life and then I look at yours and I almost envy you. Almost. I just wish I had taken the time to at least sit down and give thought to what I was going to do before I did it."

"Whoa, ho, ho, hold it. What are you talking about? Is everything cool with you and Trace?"

"Yeah, everything is fine. Just thinking, that's all. Just harmless thoughts."

Their breakfast came. The waitress set both plates on the table and asked them if there was anything else they needed. Both men shook their heads.

"You just don't think about things if there's no reason to think about them," Chad said, stirring a spoon around in his oatmeal.

"Like I said, it's nothing, but over the last few months I've just been taking account of my situation. Am I really happy or not? And if not, what are the reasons for my unhappiness?"

"And you think Trace has something to do with that?"

Austin picked a grape from the plate of fresh fruit sitting before him and played with it a minute, rolling it between two fingers. "I didn't say that, and I don't know. I don't want to jump to all kinds of conclusions. I'm almost afraid to think about it, because what if it is her? I'd have to do something about it. And our lives are tied together, with the kids, the things we've acquired over the six years of our marriage—it just wouldn't be a good thing if it was her."

"Then make it not her," Chad said.

"What do you mean?"

"Do you still love Trace?"

"Yes, I believe so."

"Then just don't think about it anymore. Just forget about the fact that something's bothering you and concentrate on all the other things, the good things, man."

"I would really like to do that, but . . ."

"But what? Do you think everything about marriage is supposed to be wonderful? You take the good with the bad, and you make it work. That's if the bad isn't greater than the good. Look, you're married, all right. For better or for worse, through thick and thin, sickness and in health and all that crap. I just think you should really try sticking it out. You know, for the sake of the marriage."

"Is that what you'd do?" Austin quickly countered. "If you're unhappy in a relationship, you just stick it out, right? You say to yourself that the good comes with the bad and you'll just accept that, even though you aren't happy anymore. That's what you do?"

"That's different. It's not a marriage," Chad defended.

"It's not different. It's different to you, because you aren't in a marriage. But to me, a relationship is a relationship to whatever extent, and happiness is happiness. Just because I'm married doesn't mean I should put up with or accept more drama. Doesn't mean I have any less of a right to be happy, or if I'm not, have any less of a right to try and change things so that I am. Do you see what I mean?"

Chad nodded silently, as if he understood perfectly but didn't agree. "That's not what I'm saying. I just mean that you're married. You go into that situation with the intention of never coming out. It's not the same with a relationship. Those things start and end every day. Trust me, I know." Chad winked at Austin.

"I know you know, Chad, that's one of the problems with you."

Chad was about to load another spoonful of oatmeal into his mouth, but stopped in response to the comment. The spoon was floating in air not two inches from his face.

"Hold it. I didn't tell you to get married, all right? And if I remember correctly, I think I advised you not to. But you were so hung up on it being the right thing to do. The right move to make for a successful future, and all that. I'm not going to apologize or feel bad that I'm single. Hell, I enjoy it. I'm taking advantage of it. Is that such a bad thing?"

"No." Austin spoke softly, but loud enough to be heard from across the table. "Just foolish."

Chad let his still elevated spoon fall to his oatmeal with a plop. "Foolish, huh? Well, forgive me for not being as much of a prude as you are."

"You're going to get yourself in the same situation as that guy we're talking about with the child support. Do you want that?" Austin was leaning over the table pointing a finger in Chad's direction.

"Hey, this is my life. So what business is it of yours?" Chad leaned forward as well, placing his face not far from Austin's accusing finger.

"I know you're sleeping with Fresca," Austin said, out of the blue.

A look of surprise flashed across Chad's face, then quickly faded. "So what? Is there a reg saying I can't sleep with someone I work with?"

Austin pulled away, took a sip of his juice, then settled back into the booth. "I didn't say that. I just wouldn't consider it a favorable or advisable practice."

Austin continued eating and so did Chad. The only noise from the two was the sound of their utensils hitting their plates, and sipping sounds as they drank. The waitress came and asked if everything was all right. Chad grunted a yes, Austin didn't even look up.

"What the hell is wrong with you, man? You want me to fucking get married?" Chad asked. "Pick the one you want me to marry. Pick any one of my women except Sheri or Anna, and I'll marry them if that'll make you happy."

"Really?" Austin asked.

"No. Not really. But we shouldn't be going on like this. We're supposed to be partners. C'mon, man, we go back a ways, right?" Austin nodded his head in agreement. "You and Trace aren't happy anymore?" Chad asked.

Austin didn't answer right away. He looked out the window for a moment, then scratched his face a little, his eyes focused on nothing more than his thoughts.

"I don't know how I feel. I don't know anything, and that's the part that's making me insane. There's nothing wrong that she's done, she hasn't cheated on me, we haven't been arguing, nothing, but this . . . this feeling I'm getting."

"And what feeling is that?"

Austin brought his attention back to his friend and looked at him as if shocked by the question. "Cramped, I guess. Pressured, maybe. Caged in. I don't know, and I don't really expect you to understand. It's something I'm going to have to deal with." Austin's stare faded away into his thoughts again.

"Well, Trace is a good woman. I hope—"

"I don't need you to tell me that, Chad. I'm the one that married her, remember?"

"Austin. Hey, it's me, remember—your best friend. I was just saying

I want things to work out, that's all." He picked up the check the waitress had left on the table. He reached in his wallet and fingered out a few bills and threw them on the table, appearing a little hurt.

"I told you I'd get that," Austin said, reaching into his jacket.

"Look, we've been friends for a long time, a very long time, and to tell you the truth, it hasn't been that easy. You're a tactless say-whatever-you-think son of a bitch sometimes, and not many people can relate to that kind of interacting, but I can. I have, and I will. But you need to drop that one-man-island crap. I'm on your side, man, whatever it is. Now, I don't know what's happening at home and I sure don't know what my marital status has to do with it, but whatever you decide, be it stay with Trace or something else, we're still partners, you know."

Austin looked at Chad for a long moment and smiled an over-worked, halfway smile.

"Sure."

It was 5:00 P.M. and Austin sat at a table in a darkened bar, listening to jazz coming softly from speakers placed in the corners of the large room. He smoothed his finger around the edge of a short round glass of cognac. He was thinking about his conversation with Chad and how he almost resented the man for his situation. It wasn't as though he wanted to trade places; he still thought Chad was somewhat foolish with some of his choices. But if Chad had to, he could turn around, start all over and not affect anyone but himself.

Trace had called his office and left two messages while he was at breakfast. They were on his desk pad written in red, the ink she told Reecie to write in so he wouldn't overlook them. He hadn't returned her calls upon seeing them so she called again, interrupting his work to remind him to stop at the grocery store and bring home some lettuce for the salad they were having tonight. She was at the store earlier and forgot it and didn't feel like going back out. Austin accepted the task just to get off the phone, and thought that it wasn't his fault she forgot the lettuce; he wasn't going to any store. They would just have to do without.

He drained the last of the cognac. It was hot going down his throat. He put the glass down and called for another, feeling bad about his recent thoughts.

"Seat taken?"

Austin looked up and it was Marcus standing before him, a wide smile on his face.

"Yeah, it's yours."

Marcus pulled the seat out and sat down. "So, how you been? Haven't seen you in a while."

"That's because you're cramped in that house of yours drawing your make-believe friends all the time." A young woman came with Austin's drink. "What are you having, Marcus?"

"Club soda," Marcus answered.

"Get him a beer, please." The young woman nodded, and Marcus gave Austin a look which he ignored.

"So how is everything? Things been all right with you?"

"Everything is everything, Marcus. How are things with you?" Austin replied, sniffing the alcohol before he took a swallow.

"I can't complain. Business is steady, which is always a good thing, and I have my health and my family." He slapped a hand on his brother's shoulder. "So things are good, I guess."

"Is that it? Things are good. As long as you keep busy and healthy life is good for you. That's very good, Marcus—simple."

"Well, what else is there?" Marcus's beer arrived. Marcus looked at the bottle a bit strangely, then politely thanked the waitress.

"You find you a woman yet?"

Marcus didn't answer, just continued swallowing from the bottle of beer. When he set the bottle down, he took a moment to think. "No. But I'm not looking for one. I'm too busy with what I'm doing to be bothered right now, all right?"

"Sure," Austin agreed. "When you coming to see your niece and nephew? Too busy for them, too?"

"Naw, I'm going to get over there. Just trying to finish this last project, that's all." He took another swallow from the beer. "So, I couldn't find Caleb."

Austin nodded, rolling the round glass between his palms.

"Well?" Marcus asked.

"Well, what?" Austin replied.

"Well, don't you have anything to say about that?"

"What am I supposed to say?"

"You could've at least asked where he was, considering he's not here, and I said I was going to try and contact him."

Austin set the glass down and dragged a hand down the length of his face. "I know he's not here, and that's all that matters. Why is it always the same thing with you, Marcus?"

"Doesn't it at least matter where he is? Don't you care to ask? Something?"

"All right, Marcus. Where is he? Where is Caleb since I should be aware of his whereabouts every second of the day?"

Marcus let out a long exasperated sigh. "I'm not saying that, but . . . I don't know where he is. It's no big deal. I just think that you would at least want to know what's going on with him. I spoke to Sonya the other day, and she sounded strange, like something was going on. I asked her about it, but she wouldn't tell me. I just hope everything is all right."

Austin looked over at his brother and could see that he was plagued with genuine concern. He couldn't understand why he let something out of his control pull down on him so. "And if it's not, what are you going to do, little brother? It's their problem. Would you just let them handle it? Caleb is a grown man—what he has to deal with, he has to deal with. Are you planning on holding his hand every step of the way for the rest of his life?"

"That's not what I'm doing. He's my brother, Austin, and he's yours too. Are you aware of that?"

"Yes. I am aware of that. Painfully so, sometimes. He is my brother, okay."

"Well, you sure don't act like it. The least you can do is wonder if he needs help and if he does, lend a hand once in a while."

"Marcus." Austin dug his fingers into the corners of his eyes to illustrate how fed up he was with his brother's behavior. "I can't care for the man like that. I *have* children already, and I don't feel like adopting any more. I'm sorry that the man can't afford some things."

"What's with this 'the man' thing? He's your brother, he has a name," Marcus informed him.

"I'm sorry *Caleb* can't afford some things, but that's his problem. If he wishes to put himself in a position where he can provide for his family, well, that's something he'll have to deal with himself as well. What

I'm trying to say is, if he can't afford food, he'll go hungry, can't afford clothing, he'll be cold, and can't afford shelter, he'll eventually die. It's called survival of the fittest. Natural selection, Marcus. I'm sure you learned that in school, and if Caleb would've finished he would've learned it too."

Marcus just sat there looking surprised at what had come out of Austin's mouth. "I'm sorry he's not as fortunate as you are. It's a damn shame that he didn't have all the opportunities you did, and wasn't smart enough to take advantage of the ones he did have. He really should be disowned for that."

"It's not my fault—"

"It's not his either! Sometimes you can't be accountable for every single thing that happens in your life before you're even sixteen. He didn't get the attention that we got, and you know it. He didn't have all that we did." Austin knew he was talking about the relationship that he had had with his father and Marcus had had with his mother.

"You act as though we had a monopoly on Ma and Dad," Austin said. "Caleb was their son just like you and I."

"Maybe you should've tried telling *your* father that," Marcus said.

"My father? What the hell is that supposed to mean? He was there for all of us."

"Was he? All I can remember is him doing for you, being concerned for only your problems, and devoting all his time to you. So don't be surprised if Caleb is resenting you for that."

"Well, that's not my fault either," Austin said smugly, taking another drink.

"Why must you look at this in terms of who's to blame? The important thing is that you should realize that something's keeping the two of you apart and you should do something about it."

"Do something about it," Austin said, as if shocked by the suggestion. "I've tried that, and it's like throwing stones in the air, looking up, and expecting them to grow wings and fly away. It just ain't going to happen."

"I see what you're saying," Marcus said sarcastically. "I gave it a couple of tries. It didn't work, so the hell with him. Yeah, he's my brother, but if he doesn't get with the program, who needs him. Right."

"That's right," Austin said. "I think you're finally getting it."

"You can't do that. It's not his fault that he's where he is. He's not to blame."

Austin looked in Marcus's eyes and saw that they were filled with guilt. "You think it's your fault, don't you?" Austin said.

"What?"

"You heard me. You think it's your fault he's going through what he is. You think because you raised him after Mother died, it's your fault his life is the way it is."

"I don't think that," Marcus said, turning his chair a bit away from his brother.

"It's not your fault, Marcus. You did what you could. It's not your fault he turned out the way he did. He was like that when Ma was still alive and to tell the truth, he was destined for it before he was even born. That's just how life is. He's been on that path, and that's the path he'll continue to stay on."

"I don't think that's true, and if you stopped believing that, your feelings about him would change. All you do is ridicule him. Why can't you just accept him?"

"Marcus, why can't you just accept the fact that it's not going to happen for us? Okay, we're brothers, but that's about the extent of it. I care for the man, I even love him, but he's just not one of my best buddies, that's all. If something really happens to him that warrants my attention, I'll be there. Guaranteed. But before that, I really have no desire to see him, so I wish you'd just lay off it and give me a break. I don't know why you continue to push the issue."

"Because it's what Mother wanted." Marcus was looking directly in Austin's eyes. Austin tilted his head and fiddled with the glass again. There was nothing Austin could say about that, it was true, but this would be just one more wish of his mother's that would go unfulfilled.

"If he really needs me, I'll be there, okay? That's all I can do for you."

They sat quietly for a few minutes. "I'm not going to continue to push this point," Marcus started, "but it would be nice—things would be nicer between the three of us if you just put forth some effort."

"Well, things would be a lot nicer between the two of us if you *wouldn't* put forth so much effort," Austin said. "Marcus, I think you have too much time on your hands and maybe it's because you don't have a woman to occupy your time. Let me do you a favor." Austin reached into his pocket and brought out a business card and a pen. "Here, take this. This is the number of my secretary. Her name is Reecie and she's a very nice lady. Give her a call sometime. Maybe she'll have pity for you and let you take her out."

"I don't want it," Marcus said.

"Take it anyway."

"No," Marcus insisted.

Austin took the card, placed it in Marcus's breast pocket, and patted it twice. "I'll tell her to expect your call." He tilted his glass up to let the last of the cognac slide into his mouth, put some money on the table, and grabbed his coat. "See you later, little brother."

SIX

Caleb sat slumped into the couch. His feet were kicked up on the coffee table in front of him. He was watching an afternoon cartoon and picking at one of the many holes that spotted the sofa. Benning's card lay on top of the TV. He was trying to decide if he was going to call him today or not.

"I'm tired of that old man," Sonya said, walking in the door, Jahlil's small four-year-old body attached to one hand, a sack of groceries in the other. "Always bugging me about the damn rent. Don't he know people got to eat around here? I told him we was going to be a little late this month." Sonya released the child's hand and he ran over to his father.

Caleb grabbed his son and hoisted him up on the sofa beside him. "Well, why is he still bothering you about it then?"

"I don't know. That's what I'm talking about. He ought to be paying *us* to live up in this ratty-ass apartment." She pulled the contents of the brown bag out and started to put things away as she complained. "I told the man the sink doesn't work. He didn't fix it till a month later." She put a jar of peanut butter into the cabinet.

"Don't nothing but hot air blow out the air conditioner." She placed a loaf of bread over the refrigerator. "And I told him a million times about these damn roaches, but does he do anything?" She threw a gallon of milk in the fridge then slammed the door. "Caleb, I'm tired of living like this." She was facing him, both her hands on her slender hips. She looked exhausted. Her hair was pulled back in a knot at the back of her head, a single rubber band holding it in place, strands managing to find their way loose all about her head. "Did you find a job yet?"

"What?" Caleb asked.

"C'mon, Caleb, you know you heard me. Did you find a job yet?"

"No. Not yet, but I'm still looking." He wanted to tell her about the talk he had with Benning, but he didn't want it to seem like one more prospect that would turn into a dead end like all the rest. He'd wait until something came of it before he let her in on anything.

"Well, I hope you're still looking if you haven't found anything yet." She walked over toward him, undoing the buttons of her blouse. She pulled the tails out from the waist of her skirt. The blouse opened up, exposing her flat belly and the upper curves of her breasts.

"So how was work today?" Caleb asked, lifting Jahlil to his lap so Sonya could sit.

"It's like it is every day. A lot of out-of-work folks stacked up like sardines, trying to collect unemployment or trying to get jobs 'cause they unemployment ran out. It's no joke, Caleb."

"Don't you think I know that. Why do you think it's taking me so long to find a job."

"Because you probably aren't looking as hard as you can. 'Cause you probably out there messing around with your friends. Aren't you?"

"That's not even right for you to accuse me of something like that. I hit the pavement hard every day. I go up to every place I can and ask, with my saddest, sorriest face on." He saddened his face and poked out his lips. "Do you have a job for a poor old guy like me, suh?" Sonya laughed. Jahlil saw her laughing and began to laugh too. "I'm telling you, sweetheart, I'm on it. No rest for the weary, no sleep for the tired, no money for the poor and all that, till a job is found. I'm on it," Caleb said, winking.

"My ass you are. But I tell you what, you need to be, 'cause I don't think your sense of humor is going to pay the rent." She stood up, running her hands through her hair.

"I'm going to take a shower, that is if the hot water is working. I feel like I've been playing in the mud all day, all those filthy people I been dealing with." She turned and went into the bathroom. "Oh, yeah, your brother called a couple of days ago. It slipped my mind," she called out from the bathroom.

Caleb knew it wasn't Austin, but he asked just for the hell of it. "Which one?"

"Yeah, right. It was Marcus, Caleb. Who do you think," she called over the running water.

He wondered what Marcus wanted. He was probably trying to get the three of them to do some family thing, and Caleb had no intention of participating in any crap like that. One day Marcus would get the picture and give it up. Caleb felt a tugging on his shirt and looked down to see Jahlil pulling at his sleeve. "What's up, little man?"

"I'm hungry, Daddy."

"You're hungry! Your Aunt Tara didn't get you any lunch?" The child shook his head. "Well, we're going to just have to see what we can scrounge up for the kid." He stood up, grabbed for the remote off the top of the TV, noticing Benning's card staring him in the face again. He gave the controller to his son. "I tell you what. You sit right here and watch cartoons while I fix you lunch. How's that?"

"That's cool," he said, not moving his eyes away from the action on the screen.

"I'm glad to see you're so excited about that. What do you want?"

"Peanut butter and jelly." Jahlil waved Caleb to the right because he was standing in front of the screen.

"Yes, sir. Peanut butter and jelly it is."

Caleb pulled down the loaf of bread Sonya had just bought. Cheap bread. Caleb hated cheap bread. It was a good thing Jahlil didn't know the difference because it was all they could afford. He reached into the cabinet and got the cheap peanut butter, reached into the fridge and got the cheap jelly, and started to make the sandwich.

He really should call Marcus back. It could be something important, but even if it wasn't, he should call him back anyway, and he should also call Benning. But he really hadn't come to a conclusion about that. "It's no joke, Caleb." That's what Sonya said about the job situation, and she should know because she worked at the damn unemployment office. The one spot you should be able to go to get a job. But there were just no jobs to give. So maybe he should call the man. He really needed a job, because he was tired of having Sonya nagging him like he was a child, tired of eating cheap food, and on top of all that, the rent was due.

All that was playing around in Caleb's head while he put his son's sandwich together. But it was nothing new to him. His head was always filled with what he had to do, or what he wasn't doing, or how things could be if he did what he was supposed to. It was something that he had grown accustomed to. He wouldn't know what it would be like to walk around without the weight of the world spinning on his head like a giant pointed top.

First things first. He learned that from somewhere, he couldn't remember where, but it had been what kept him from going crazy for as long as he could remember. With all the crap that he had to worry about, actually worrying about it all would surely have torn him to pieces ages ago. So his method had been to concentrate on the immediate, what was most important at that moment, and put all his effort into that.

"Wha-lah! Your sandwich is finished," he said, standing before Jahlil. "Just the way you like it. Peanut butter on one slice, jelly on the other, then smacked together."

"Thanks, Dad." And those were the words that made all the worrying worth worrying about. He placed a tall glass of milk on the coffee table for his son to wash down the spongy sandwich with. Jahlil took a bite of the sandwich and jelly spread across the side of his mouth. "This is good, Dad." He tore the sandwich in half and offered a small jelly-bleeding half to his father.

"Uh, that's okay. I've been eating peanut butter and jelly sandwiches all day," he joked. His son continued to munch on the sandwich and Caleb just sat there and watched, in awe of how wonderful the child truly was.

He looked down at Jahlil to catch him fingering the last smudge of jelly from the plate before sticking the finger into his mouth. The boy reached for the milk and took long gulps till the glass was drained. He put the glass down, leaving the remnants of the fluid on his top lip.

"So, is everything cool, little man?"

"Yeah, Dad, everything is cool," he answered.

For four years old, the boy could surely snore. Jahlil lay between Caleb and Sonya. She was stretched out on the bed too, both of them soundly sleeping. She had only a pair of panties and a tank top on because the air conditioner was on the blink again; Jahlil just wore Superman underwear. Caleb nudged the boy, rolling him over to his stomach to stop him from snoring. It worked.

Caleb went back to staring at the ceiling because he couldn't sleep. He slept all night and didn't do anything all day, so he wasn't tired. Besides, he had too much on his damn mind to sleep. He needed a job and he needed it now. He squirmed around in bed and pulled out the business card from the back pocket of his jeans. It was now dog-eared on the right upper corner. He made an effort to straighten the tiny crease.

I'll call the man, he finally decided, but for some reason he was scared, scared out of his mind. For one reason, the man had never said anything about offering him a job, just said he would like to finish his conversation.

Second, even if he did have a job for Caleb to do, what made him think he was capable? If Caleb could remember right, he said he did something with computers, and the last time he checked, he had problems even spelling the word right. Third, what made him think it was something he'd even want to do? It went against everything he believed. He would be one of those fools out there hustling to work every day to do what? Make back the money he spent when he was out treating himself to something nice simply because he was making money. It was a cycle, that's all, and it just sucked folks in without them even knowing it, and once you're in—that's it, you'll be there for the rest of your life. He didn't want it, he really didn't, but he had a son to worry about. He stroked the boy's hair. And a girl that one day, maybe, he would make an honest woman of.

And last but not least, who was this guy? He could actually be some clown that escaped from the county mental institution, stole some poor guy's suit, and was parading around town calling himself Joe Benning, selling dreams to poor suckers like Caleb. That could be the case, but Caleb felt compelled to phone the man anyway. Someone like him could not afford to be casual about anything that could be an opportunity.

It was 4:00 P.M. the next afternoon, and the streets weren't really that loud considering everyone was about to get off work. Caleb would make the call from the pay phone that was standing on the corner, because he didn't want Sonya around when he was rejected. He didn't want her staring at his mouth asking him what was wrong. He stood outside by the phone and fished in his pockets for a quarter, slipped it in the phone, then dialed the number. He noticed his hand was shaking as he punched the small squares. He told himself to calm down.

"Main Frame Software, Mr. Benning's office, how may I help you?" A high-pitched voice. Caleb froze, couldn't speak for a moment.

"Hello," the voice called.

"Yeah, uh . . . Mr. Benning. Can I speak to Mr. Benning . . . please," Caleb stuttered.

"And who may I say is calling?"

He was caught again, wondering if he should just hang up the phone and run home, wondering if his name was important enough to say over the phone and not be hung up on. "Caleb Harris." He shuddered as he spoke his name.

"Just a moment, please."

"Hello?" He spoke into the empty line, wondering what was happening, but felt a bit of confidence funneling his way when he realized he had not been hung up on.

"Caleb Harris, how are you doing?" Benning asked.

"I'm doing good," he responded nervously.

"I'm glad that you called back, young man. I was starting to wonder."

There he went with the young man remark again, but Caleb was glad to hear his voice and glad that the tone was friendly and familiar. It allowed him to relax.

"Well, I knew you were making all that money, so I didn't want to get in your way, you know," Caleb said, smiling.

"Yes, I know. So, how is the job hunting going, did you find anything yet?"

"No, I'm starting to think people just don't want me to work."

"I wouldn't think that to be the case, but then again I wouldn't know firsthand. But stick with it, persistence is the key. I'm sure someone will recognize your potential and take advantage of it soon enough," Benning said.

"Well, even though you're probably the only one that feels that way, thanks for the vote of confidence."

"Anytime," the man said. "So what are you doing for lunch tomorrow, Mr. Harris?"

Caleb was stunned, and had to gather himself before answering. "Uh, nothing. I ain't doing nothing. Why?"

"I'm looking at my schedule and I see I have an opening tomorrow at 11:15. Would you be available so we can talk some more?"

"Hold on, let me check *my* schedule." He paused for a moment. "I think I'll be able to swing that, Mr. Benning," he said, joking, excited.

"Good. You know where our building is, right?" Benning asked.

"Yeah, no problem," knowing he didn't have a clue, but not wanting to seem ignorant. "I'll be there."

"Great. Terrific. It was good talking to you, and I'll see you tomorrow, all right?"

"You got it," Caleb said, confidently.

SEVEN

Julius watched as Cathy steered his Mercedes through the congestion of late morning traffic. She was buckled in tight, her hands were at ten and two o'clock, and she had adjusted the seat and mirrors to her short height as she always did before driving his car. Even though she took such precautions, Julius still felt a little apprehensive about her being behind the wheel of his classic. He sat quietly and tried to contain himself each time he thought she was riding the brake too much or not keeping the car steady enough in the lane. Normally he wouldn't let her drive, but in this case she had insisted.

They had just come from the hospital, his three-month check-up, and for some reason she felt it wasn't good for him to drive after the visit, even though he had driven there before the visit.

"So what do you think about it?" Cathy asked Julius as she flipped on the turn signal.

"Think about what, darling?"

"The group. The support group the nurse was talking about. I think it's a good idea." She turned briefly and showed a smile to Julius. He smiled back politely, then let the smile go as soon as she turned her eyes back to the road.

"Well?" she asked again.

"If you want to know the truth, I'm not crazy about it. I don't see the need for me to sit in a room full of people with the same problem as I have and mope and cry about it. Sweetheart, there are a million and one other things I could do, like mope around in the comfort of my own home."

"The idea isn't to mope. It's not designed to depress you, its purpose is to lift your spirits, to let you know that you're not alone and other people are coping with it just like you. You can draw strength from them." They were sitting at a red light, and her hand wandered over to his and gave it a squeeze.

"I know that I'm not alone. I realize that there are thousands of other people going through the same thing I am, but I just feel that I don't need to be reminded of it every week, or every two weeks, or however often the meetings are." He flipped through the pamphlet the nurse had given him, then tossed it up on the dash. "What difference would it make anyway? It's not like during one of these meetings some graying old man will come up with the cure. It's not like just going to these things will make me feel so much better that I'll live years and years past the time that the stupid doctor prescribed. I don't see the good in it, so I don't even know why it's such an issue that we go."

"It's not an issue," Cathy said. "But you said it wouldn't make a difference either way, so why don't you just go? You know it couldn't hurt. And you never know, you might just get something out of it. You might meet someone who's dealing with it a certain way that you could learn from, or there might be some information that you may find beneficial, and you would miss it if you don't go. All I'm saying is, it wouldn't hurt to try."

"And all I'm saying is it would." Julius reached over and clicked off the radio, feeling it was taking away from the importance of what he was saying. "I can't surround myself with people like that because I don't want it to be a constant reminder that I have cancer and that I might die soon. Do you think that's a pleasant thought, do you think that's something that I wake up in the morning with and smile about? Every night I think it's a dream and when I wake up and realize it's the truth I don't know what to do. I don't know if I even want to get out of the bed. I can't embrace something like that, and I can't use it as some kind of motivation or turn it into a damn positive. There's nothing positive about dying, nothing. And to sit around with a number of people and talk about it like it's worth discussing is beyond me. That's the main thing I'm trying not to do. It makes me feel sick even if I was feeling fine a moment before. When it's not on my mind, I feel fine. Sometimes I almost forget that I have it, till something comes up, or someone feels they have to mention it to me, and then I realize again, I have it and because of it I'm going to die someday soon. That's why I don't want to go."

Cathy didn't say a word, just pulled the car over to the side of the road even though they were only five minutes from their house. Julius looked around and wondered why they had stopped. She turned the ignition off, unbuckled her seat belt, and turned to face Julius.

"What did you mean by that?" Cathy asked.

"By what?"

"You said, 'And someone feels they have to mention it to me.' I'm the only one that knows, Julius. Were you talking about me?"

He knew the answer and so did she, but he really didn't want to hurt her feelings. "Sometimes you tend to go a little overboard," Julius said mildly.

"Julius, what do you mean by that?"

"It's . . . it seems like it's not even me you're dealing with anymore. It's like I'm the 'man with the cancer' and you have to care for me because you cared for me before I had cancer and it would be wrong for you to run out now, even though it's such a pain in the ass." He heard what he said, and couldn't believe he let that escape. He wished he could recall every word he had said, but it was too late, it was already out there, and by the look on Cathy's face, the damage had already been done.

"That's what you think of me, Julius? When I ask you to eat right, you think all I'm doing is reminding you that you have cancer. Or when I tell you to be careful, or get your rest, or put on more clothes so you won't catch cold, you think I'm doing all that just so you know and won't forget that you have cancer. That's what you think, huh?" A tear rolled down her cheek and she quickly brushed it away, as though it were a sign of weakness. "And even worse, you think I'm doing it because I feel some sense of obligation to you. You think I feel as though I have to be here. For what, Julius? For what? Why do you think I think I have to be here?"

He tried to answer, but she cut him off. "Julius, I don't have to be here. I don't. I'm doing this because I love you, I have since the day I met you, and I will as long as you live. I just want that to be as long as we can possibly make it. That's why I do what I do, that's why I ask you to take care of yourself and if you aren't willing to do it, I'll run behind you like you're a child until you do. That's why I asked you to go to these meetings, not because I think it'll bring you one step closer to death, but that I think it'll take you one step further away."

She pulled the keys out of the ignition and threw them into Julius's lap, then got out and slammed the door behind her. He watched as she walked down the middle of the street, a hand up to her face, probably wiping away tears. He got out of the car and ran to her.

"I didn't mean that. It wasn't supposed to come out that way," he said, grabbing her by the shoulders.

"What way was it supposed to come out, Jay?" Her face was covered with tears, her nose was a soft shade of pink. "You said what you thought. It wouldn't have made a difference if you were more polite."

"I know, I just don't know what to do about this. You've got to understand me. One day I think I'm in perfect health and the next someone is telling me I have two years to live. Do you know how that makes me feel? Everything I have will be gone. And you." He held her face in his hands. "I won't have you to love anymore. That's the scariest part. I'm just trying to hang on, that's all, and not let this get the best of me. I know all you're doing is helping me, but sometimes I'm too stupid to recognize that. I'm sorry, baby. I'm sorry." He started to walk her back to the car, his arm wrapped tightly around her. "If you think the meetings will help me, I'll go."

Cathy paused for a moment and looked into his eyes. "You do what you want, Julius, since you know what's best for you."

Julius escorted Cathy into the house. It seemed she expended all her energy when she cried like that. Julius could feel by how much she was resting on him that she was pretty worn out. It could have been from the argument they had, or from all the time she spent up late at night worrying about him, then going to work the next morning. He walked her upstairs, laid her down on the bed, and pulled off her shoes. He covered her with a blanket and kissed her on the forehead. "I love you, darling," he said.

"Is there anything you need?" she asked, her voice filled with exhaustion.

"You. All I need is you." She smiled a little, then let her eyes close.

He stood in the doorway and looked at her as she fell into sleep. He felt both content and anguished. Content at the thought that she loved him as much as she did, but anguished because he would leave her soon, and there was nothing he could do about it. He closed the door slowly, not allowing it to make a sound. He slid his hands in his pockets and walked down the stairs, his head slumped into his chest. He wanted to forget, just get it out of his mind, but it wouldn't let him.

He went outside to the car and started it up. He looked up to their bedroom window and thought about going in the house and telling Cathy he'd be gone for a while, but figured it would be best to let her sleep. He put the car in drive and sped off. He took turns tighter than he should have and weaved through traffic more recklessly than he normally did. He was trying to get to the ocean. The destination he referred to as "somewhere beautiful." He had to go there to get everything out of his head, dump it out into the water and let the waves carry it all away. It was evening now, and the sun would be going down soon. He knew it would be beautiful, the oranges, yellows, and deep reds bleeding together, reflecting off the vastness of the water.

He pulled the Mercedes into the parking lot, got out, and sat on the large rocks that bordered the ocean. There were only a few people there and he was thankful for that. He needed to be alone with his thoughts, sort things out, plan the rest of his life, and even the sight of too many people would make him feel uneasy. Julius pulled his knees into his chest, roped his arms around them and buried his face into the privacy of his body. Self-pity was what he was feeling, and it was the hardest thing to deal with. No one but himself was making him feel that pain and no one but himself could take it away, but he let it loom anyway.

He wanted to cry out "why me?" But he had done that already and no answer had made itself available. Besides, he knew the answer, he just didn't want to face it. He tilted his head up and looked to the sky. The sun was descending into the horizon, and the brilliant colors that streaked the clouds began to darken. It was all so beautiful, he thought. He looked deeper into the clouds, into the space where God was supposed to live. He wanted to know why God would take his life like this, why he would take it now. But there was no reason to ask any longer. It was because he had left his wife and children. He knew it, even the day he walked out of the house, he knew something terrible would follow him and make him pay for such an evil, thoughtless act.

"I can't, I just can't stay anymore." That's what Julius had told his wife so many years ago at three o'clock in the morning. They had gotten married right after high school because she was pregnant. It was the only respectable thing to do, so Julius married her for the sake of the child. Then she miscarried and was so distraught that all she wanted to do was become pregnant again. Julius agreed, hoping it would relieve some of her pain. A year or so later she gave birth to their first child, Austin. Three years after that they had another son, and another three years after him.

Julius had a wife and three children and had not even been married ten years. At the age of twenty-eight he had already begun to feel trapped, pressured to make certain decisions and carry out certain actions, not because they were what was best for him, but for everyone but him. He told himself it would get better, but if it didn't he would consider leaving. He thought about it for six years after that until the night he couldn't bear it any longer.

They were lying in bed, the lights off, Mary turning beside him, trying to fall asleep. Julius wanted to wait, wanted to see if he could tolerate being there any longer, put his life on hold another day for the sake of his sons, but he couldn't. "I can't, I just can't stay anymore." He said it out of the blue, as if he was already in mid-conversation. His wife turned in bed.

"What did you say?"

"I . . . I have to go. I can't stay here anymore."

Mary reached over and clicked on the lamp. She had been almost asleep, and her eyes were slits. "What are you talking about, Julius?"

He took the time to explain how he was feeling, how he had felt over the last sixteen years of his life. Mary looked as though it all came as a huge surprise, as though she had no idea it was coming, there were no clues that her husband felt that way. But Julius had made a point of displaying how unhappy he was for some time. She started to cry.

"Why are you just telling me this now? Why are you telling me this the night before you're supposed to be leaving?" She was angry, Julius could see that, but she spoke in a hushed voice in order not to wake her sons just down the hall.

"I don't know," he said. But the reason was very simple. He knew how he felt and there was no reason for discussion. There was no need to talk about whether he would be staying or whether they could work things out, because the answer to both of those questions was no.

"So that's it," she said. "Just like that you're going to walk out. What about the boys? Don't you even care about them?"

"I told you they're the reason I stayed as long as I did," Julius said, sitting up in bed.

Mary just stared at him. "Well, don't let me keep you."

"What?" Julius knew what she had said. It was Mary trying to call his bluff, as though it was one. She always played that game, and for some reason it had always worked to her advantage, but not this time. She would realize that after he was gone.

"You heard me. If you're going to leave, don't let me keep you any longer than you need to be here, since it was so terrible for you."

"Mary, I didn't—"

"Just take your things and leave!" She threw her face into her hands, her hair falling wild about her arms. "Just leave."

Julius pulled two suitcases from under the bed. They were already packed, waiting for his departure in the morning. All he had to do was gather a few things from the closet and out of the drawers, say good-bye to his sons, and he would leave. He moved awkwardly about the room, pulling his things together as his wife sat there on the edge of the bed and cried. She had gotten up and covered herself with her bathrobe as if to say that since he was leaving, he could no longer see her bare arms or legs. He didn't say a word to her, just busied himself with trying to get out of there as fast as he could.

He slipped on some jeans and shoes and tucked his pajama top into his pants. "Can you go and wake the boys so they'll be up by the time I'm ready to go?"

Mary didn't respond. She continued to sit, her face still in her hands, the crying sounds decreased to sniffles.

"Mary, did you hear me? Can you wake the boys?"

She pulled her face up from her hands and looked at him. Her eyes were streaked with red, and the area around them was puffy and irritated from her crying. She smoothed away the last remaining tears with her hand, then spoke.

"Wake them up for what?" she asked plainly.

"So I can talk to them. So I can say good-bye."

"Say good-bye. It's not enough to pull me out of my sleep and tell me that you're leaving me, but you have to do the same to them. Isn't it enough to just hurt me? Isn't that enough for you? Must you hurt your sons too?"

"What am I supposed to do? Leave and not say anything to them?"

"I'll tell them something. I'll tell them that you're away on a long trip, or that you're visiting relatives, or better yet, that you were involved in a bad car accident."

"What are you talking about?" he demanded.

"This way there will be no stress, Julius. You're not going to see them again." She sat on the edge of the bed looking as bad as he had ever seen her. She was looking through him, as if there wasn't another single person that she hated more.

He couldn't believe she'd suggest something like that. That she would be willing to tell their children that he was dead just because he no longer wanted to be with her.

"Go wake them up, because if you don't, I will," he said.

"You aren't waking those children up," she said, moving over to the door, placing herself before it and spreading her arms wide. "Why don't you just take your things and leave? I'll tell them that you'll call them."

Julius sat down on the bed, the very spot his wife had gotten up from. "Mary, get out of the way. I just want to tell my sons good-bye."

"I don't want you to hurt those boys like you're hurting me. They don't deserve this, Julius, and you know it." She started to cry again.

He took his suitcases over to where she was standing and placed them before her. He stood between them. "Just let me go. I'm not asking you again."

She stood there, wide-eyed with fear. She was shaking, and although she was still guarding the door, she had slumped down considerably, one hand grabbing weakly at the doorknob, the other grasping for something to hold on to. Julius felt sorry for her. She thinks I'm going to hurt her, he thought, but I would never do that. Never.

"Why don't you stay? Why don't we just try to work it out?" she pleaded. She extended one hand, trying to caress his face, but she was shaking so badly that her hand just floated there two inches from his cheek. "I still love you."

"Mary, get out of the way!" he yelled. He was beyond anger. He grabbed her hand off the doorknob and tried pulling the door open.

"No, Julius," she screamed. She threw herself into him, wrapping her arms tightly around his neck and clasping them together. He pulled at her hands to try and release himself, but she was stronger than he had ever imagined. He continued to pull at her hands until he felt her grip weaken. He pulled until they broke apart, but she was still fighting him, putting forth everything not to let go. Her fingernails dug into the back of his neck, opening up long thin wounds. Julius felt the cold air as it hit the blood on his neck.

He grabbed her by her sides and threw her out of the way, harder than he intended. She fell back, knocking over a floor lamp. The bulb exploded with a loud pop. She lay crumpled in the corner of the room. He looked down at her, feeling bad that it had to go that far. He walked over and extended a hand, but she swiped at it like an angry alley cat. "Just get out!" she spat.

He shouldered his bag, grabbed his suitcases, then looked back at his wife. "I'm leaving now," he said. She did not respond.

He opened the door, and to his shock, there stood his sons, all three of them standing before him in their pajamas. They looked up at him, then past him to their mother, and immediately Caleb started to cry. Marcus ran over to his mother, but Austin just stood there, looking up at his father with his big circle eyes, a questioning look on his face. Julius wanted to say something to him, tell him that it wasn't what it seemed, but there was no way the boy would have believed that. His mother was lying on the floor and his father was standing, bags in his hands. It would have been like telling the boy that his eyes were lying to him. He walked past him, placing a hand on his head in silent good-bye.

When Julius looked up, the sky was dark. He didn't bother to smooth away the tears that rolled down his face.

It wasn't supposed to happen like that, he thought, pulling his knees closer to his chest, bracing himself against the slight chill in the air. It wasn't supposed to happen that way.

And what my wife must've thought about me at that moment, Julius sadly thought. That I didn't love her, that I never had. How untrue that was. But what difference did it make now? He would never be able to convince her otherwise, for she was dead, and Julius felt a sharp pain of regret in his heart.

And about his sons. They must have thought the same, must still think so, but they were still alive. They could be told that what they saw happen before them was not what he felt in his heart. Julius felt a slight bit of hope. The only question was, would they listen?

EIGHT

"**C**an you tell me what floor Main Frame Software is on?" Caleb asked. He had gotten up early that morning, pressed his clothes, and taken the bus downtown to see Benning. A copper-brown security guard with salt-and-pepper hair looked up at Caleb and smiled. "Sixth floor, sir. You can take these elevators right here." He pointed behind him.

"Sir," Caleb said softly to himself, in the elevator alone. "He called me sir, God dammit!" Sir Caleb Harris, he thought proudly as he got off the elevator and walked down the long hallway looking for Main Frame Software on one of the doors. Door 603. He pushed it open and was greeted by a secretary. She wore a practiced smile on her face, a pair of glasses pushed into her hair, and a scarf tied around her neck. It looked odd dangling there, like a fashionable infant's bib.

"And how may I help you, sir?" she said. It made Caleb feel good to hear himself called "sir" again, but she didn't seem as sincere as the guard.

"I'm here to see Mr. Benning," Caleb said, smiling at the woman but feeling a bit uncomfortable.

"Just a moment, I'll see if he's available." She pushed away from her desk as if it were a major bother, then walked toward the back of the office, stopping before she disappeared to take another look at Caleb. "I'm sorry, your name, sir?" she asked.

"Caleb Harris."

She nodded and displayed the plastic smile again. Caleb hated her.

"I'm sorry Mr. . . . ." The secretary was standing before him now, her hands clasped together.

"Harris. My name is Mr. Harris," Caleb said.

"Yes, Mr. Harris." She said it as though the name was not fit to be said from her lips. "I'm sorry, but Mr. Benning will not be able to keep his appointment with you today. Something very important has come up this morning and he must attend to it. But he wants me to let you know that he deeply regrets canceling, and wants you to make another appointment as soon as it can fit your schedule."

Caleb felt that she was simply lying to him. "I don't believe you," he said plainly.

"I'm sorry?" the secretary said.

"I—don't—believe—you. Which word didn't you get, I'll say it over for you."

"I'm sorry, sir. I have no reason to lie to you about such a matter. He will have to see you another time."

"Bullshit," Caleb said. The secretary looked astonished. "You acted like you didn't want me here from the minute I walked in that door, looking at me like I'm some criminal. Don't worry, lady, I don't want your job. I'm just here to talk to Mr. Benning. You don't have to lie and say something came up. I told you I got an appointment with the man. Hold it a minute." He went in his pocket and pulled out the card, now looking tattered. He held it up so the woman could see. "See, I told you."

"That's fine, Mr. Harris, but that doesn't change things. You will still have to reschedule," she said, her voice now more firm.

"Why you doing this?" Caleb asked, starting to feel grief.

"I'm sorry, sir."

"Stop saying that 'cause you ain't sorry. You ain't sorry at all. You're loving this!" A security guard walked in the door. It wasn't the same one from downstairs, but a white man. Someone must have heard the commotion and called for him. He was tall, and big, and he walked in slowly, placing himself next to the secretary, a hand on his billy club. "May I help you with something, sir?" He said it in a polite but threatening tone.

There was that "sir" shit again, and it no way did the same that it did for him earlier. He just laughed a little, a hurt laugh. "Ya'll motherfuckers are a trip, you know that. Always sticking together."

"Sir, I'm going to have to ask you to leave."

"Or what?" Caleb said. "You going to have to pull out your stick and beat me over the head with it a few times. Is that what you're going to have to do? Well, don't worry about it, I'm not going to give you the pleasure. And for you—" he shifted his stare toward the secretary— "you can take that scheduling book and shove it right up your tight ass."

The secretary gasped in humiliation, which made Caleb feel some form of redemption. He turned and walked out the door.

After all that, he didn't know how to feel about anything anymore. He had thought that his luck was starting to change for the better, but now he realized that he had no luck whatsoever. He wondered why it had taken him so long to see that, because his experiences had been similar since childhood. He wondered if the secretary was telling the truth; he really doubted it. But even if she was, she still acted like an asshole and she deserved what he told her.

Caleb found himself standing on a bridge, leaning over the rail, looking down on the tracks below. All that he did today—for what? A waste of time. He decided right there that he was through. Through with trying to meet expectations and through with trying to conform and do the right thing and everything else; just through. He snatched the tie from his shirt, looked at it in his hand, then tossed it over the bridge, watching it float down, twisting and turning, to the dirty tracks below.

He felt deceived. Not just by Benning, but by life. It was a shame, because he felt that he could have really learned from that man. And if nothing else, they could have probably been friends, that wouldn't have been that bad at all. Things just never wanted to go his way, and they never would. So, now that he was done, now that he had given up on everything, he would go home and . . . and do what? He would go home and see Sonya and tell her what? That another opportunity had fallen through again, but not to worry, something else would come up. But she wouldn't understand. She never really understood how things went.

He would share his pain with Jahlil. The boy wouldn't know what his pain was, but his love was unconditional. He had no expectations of Caleb outside of being loved. But what would happen when the boy got sick, or got hungry again? What would Caleb do? He would go in the kitchen and pull out all the cheap shit again, and make a cheap sandwich and give it to his son to choke down again, because he couldn't afford anything else, because he gave up on everything.

He couldn't do, or not do, just for himself anymore, but had to consider others. He was pushed along and made to move by what others needed. He felt controlled, felt like a damn puppet, and whether he liked it or not, he couldn't just give up.

He looked down at the tie, twisted and crumpled on the tracks below like a fallen body, and he thought if it was, all the bones would have surely been broken in a million pieces, kind of like his ego. He looked around for some means of getting down there. He found some stairs and walked down briskly, then moved slowly toward the tie, as if it might take off running, never to return. He kneeled down and picked up the thing gently. There was some dirt on the knot and some on the tip. He tried brushing it off with his hand, but it wouldn't clear. He dabbed two fingers on his tongue, then tried again. Some of the dirt came off, and he felt better knowing that he could take it home and restore it to the way it had been. He folded it twice and slipped it into his pants pocket, then made his way home.

NINE

Austin sat in his office behind his large oak desk, all the lights turned off save for the small halogen desk lamp. He sat there, elbows propped on the desk, hands folded together, his chin resting on his intertwined fingers. He wasn't thinking; he was doing the opposite, just trying to clear his mind of everything. He had made his way into his office not more than a half hour ago, escaping the chattering, bickering, and arguing that happened on a consistent basis outside his door. There were times when he wanted nothing to do with it, and this was one of them. He didn't worry about business being taken care of; he knew Chad could handle that. Even though the man behaved very much like a child outside the office, he was the most professional, competent, and talented attorney Austin knew. So many times when he didn't feel like being bothered, he would retire to his office and let Chad know that the ship was in his command.

Austin rubbed his temples gently, trying to relieve himself of the tension there. He looked over at the clock: 3:30 P.M. The day should be winding down now, and he could return home soon, unfortunately. No need to dwell on that now, he told himself. He was trying not to think about bothersome things.

A knock came at the door. He didn't ask who it was, just closed his eyes, hoping the person would go away. The knock came again, and he wished he was anywhere else but there.

"Who is it?" he called.

The door cracked open. Reecie stuck her head in. "I need your John Hancock on these for tomorrow." She held up a small stack of papers.

Austin nodded his head, then prompted her in with a wave of his hand. She walked up to the desk, looking as smart and snazzy as usual, smelling of expensive perfume.

"So how are things, Reecie?" Austin asked, lacking enthusiasm, while he signed the papers.

"I'm fine. My brother was supposed to get married next week, but he got into a fight with the girl and now they broke up and I think they're calling off the whole thing. I tell you, people just need to make up their minds. If they're going to do something then they should just do it."

Austin wondered if she had insight into what he was thinking; was she somehow prompting him to take care of his business? Nonsense. "Yes, I agree," he said. "So how long have they known each other?"

"Not long enough. Six months. I tried to tell him to wait. He's only twenty-five. I told him he has the rest of his life to make that decision, but he wouldn't listen."

"I'm sure he'll make the right decision, whatever that may be," Austin said. "Is there anything else?"

"Um, no. Thanks," Reecie said. She turned to walk out the door, then turned back around.

"Well, yeah. Do you have a minute?" she asked.

Austin looked at the clock. It read ten minutes to four. "Sure," he said.

"Like I said before, I've been here for a few years, and we talk on occasion. I bring you my problems sometimes and you gave me pretty sound advice every time except once, but I'm not going to get into that. What I'm trying to say is that I consider us to be friends. You think?" she asked.

"Yes, okay," Austin answered.

"So, it shouldn't sound too out of line if I ask you what's up?"

Austin thought for a moment and didn't understand the question. "Excuse me?"

"What I mean is, is everything all right?" she asked.

At that moment, Austin felt transparent, naked, as though he had a plate glass window where his forehead should have been and people could just look in on what he was thinking and feeling whenever they felt the urge.

"What do you mean, Reecie?"

"Well, you've been acting kind of strange lately. Not really strange—like crazy, but just a little out of the ordinary. I mean, I know you're usually pretty quiet and keep to yourself, but this is different, and it's been lasting a little longer."

"What, have you been monitoring me lately?" He felt himself becoming defensive.

"No. It was just something I noticed, and I just wanted to know if everything was all right. I mean, I'm not the only one."

"What's that?" Austin asked, somewhat alarmed. He could become angry if he let himself go there, but he wouldn't do that, he told himself.

"It's just a few people noticed the same thing I noticed, that's all."

"I see." He pulled himself together, and realized people seemed to be reading him easily enough as it was. If he tried to explain himself, or defend his behavior, he might just be opening the book a little wider. "Well, it's nothing. It's just the Brown case. I've been thinking a lot about it."

"Oh," she said simply. "Well, if you need any help, you know that's why I get paid the big bucks." She winked at him, grabbing the papers off his desk. He managed a tortured wink back.

"Thanks again, Mr. Harris," she said, then walked out.

Immediately after his conversation with Reecie, Austin decided that he couldn't stay at work a minute longer. He gathered up his things and prepared to leave. He walked through the department looking for Chad, wondering if people were staring at him and asking themselves, "What's wrong with him?" He found Chad and told him he was going. "Is everything all right?" Chad asked.

Austin wanted to blow up in his face right there, but he realized that the question was in no relation to his conversation with Reecie. The question could have just as easily been worded, "Why are you leaving early?" Austin didn't respond, just walked out, leaving Chad there with a stupid look on his face.

Twenty minutes later Austin was on his way home. It was raining out, and the day looked just how Austin felt: dreary. Big raindrops crashed against his windshield, making it hard for him to see as he drove through the wet streets. He was really rather angry. Not at the people at work for realizing that he had something on his mind that seemed to occupy every minute of his day, but at the reason. He was angry at the cause of his walking around so troubled. But what *was* the cause? he asked himself. He wasn't sure, but he thought that it had something to do with his situation at home. He thought about his kids. Could they be causing his anguish? No, don't be silly, he told himself, they're what I live and breathe for. Then it had to be Trace. He didn't know for what reason in particular, but he felt it could have very well been her.

He stopped at the liquor store not far from his house and picked up a bottle of cognac. He felt he not only deserved it but needed it. About to turn onto his street, he felt a bit apprehensive, unsure about going home at just that moment. He thought about turning the car around and finding a bar to crash at till Chad made it home. Maybe he would hang out with Chad until he felt better about coming back home.

He pushed the thought out of his head, and told himself he couldn't run from whatever it was that was bothering him. But he could hope that his wife just happened to be out. Yes he could, and that was what he did. He turned the corner slowly and looked down the street to see if the blue Volvo station wagon was parked in its usual spot. It wasn't, and he felt a little better. He cruised down the street a little slower than he normally would have and pulled into the driveway. If her car wasn't parked in the garage then he would have some desperately needed time to himself.

He clicked the opener that was clipped to his visor, and focused his attention on the increasing space under the garage door, looking for the first sign of the black tires of her car. As he sat there outside the garage, gripping the steering wheel, almost holding his breath, he realized how ridiculously he was behaving. He had to stop. He had to take care of his business, whatever it was, and stop behaving like a lunatic.

The only things in the garage were a few tools tacked to the walls, a couple of rakes standing in the corner, and their barbecue grill. He felt at ease.

He grabbed the brown paper bag and went to the house. He slipped his key in the door, opened it and stepped in quietly. He looked around the house as if he were an intruder there, then called out. "Hello. Trace, are you here?" No one answered. He took a few steps into the living room and called out again. "Anybody home?" There was nothing but the silence his voice left.

Austin looked through his CD collection, trying to find something that would help him relax and forget about things even if it was just for a little while. He pulled out Miles Davis and slipped it into the machine. There was a moment of mechanical clicking, then the faint sound of a horn came distantly from the four speakers that hung in the corners of the room.

He grabbed his round glass, the brown liquid swooshing around inside, then sat down in his leather recliner. He pushed the chair back to a reclining position, took a sip of cognac and closed his eyes. Why couldn't it just be this, he asked himself. Why couldn't life just be beautiful music, exquisite cognac, a fine leather chair, privacy and peace of mind?

He took another sip of cognac, letting it stay in his mouth for a moment, reaching all areas of his palate. He placed the glass on the table beside his chair, then picked up the picture that was sitting there. It was a framed snapshot of Trace and himself, from years ago, and he noticed how young they looked, how innocent. He saw the happy expression on his face, and thought that he hadn't felt like that in so long, too long.

He touched the picture with a finger, wishing he was back there, that he had never left, and placed it back on the table. He lifted his drink, tilted back the glass, finishing it off.

He had been asleep for two hours when he felt a gentle tugging on his wrist. Still sleeping, he brushed it off like a pesky fly in his dream. The tugging continued, forcing him to slowly open his eyes. His wife came into focus, standing before him, a smile on her face. He didn't know why, but he was shocked to see her there, and for a moment he was without words.

"Hey, sleepyhead," she said, bending to kiss him on the cheek. "Rough day at work, huh?"

"Uh, yeah," Austin said, stretching in the chair. He looked around to make sure there were no telltale signs of what he had been thinking, as if he'd been constructing some dreadful device he didn't want her to know about, and might have left out a pair of pliers or a screwdriver. There was nothing but his empty glass and the old snapshot of the two of them.

As he looked up at Trace, he was not necessarily sorry to see her, and he even felt a little glad. But he realized it was because he had grown accustomed to seeing her. She made him feel safe, that things were in order, that the puzzle was complete when she was placed next to him. Unfortunately, it wasn't as though he was missing her and counting the hours till her return. On the other hand, he did miss his children, and when she was gone, he was always happy when she returned so he could see his kids.

"The kids downstairs?" he asked, ready to greet them.

"No. But that was supposed to be a surprise," Trace said. "I dropped them off at Margaret's. I thought we could use just a little time to ourselves. You've been seeming a bit uptight lately, and I was thinking you just needed a little space." She moved close to him and brushed up against him. Unknowingly, contradicting what she had just said.

Austin was disappointed, not only because he couldn't see his children but because he would be isolated with his wife. It had been so long since they had been alone together without the kids. He knew the evening would be filled with nothing but conversation pertaining to the two of them. He gritted his teeth and tried to look excited. "Well, what did you have in mind?"

"I hope you're hungry because I bought some things for a special dinner tonight. All I have to do is put it in the oven. It'll take a while so we'll have to think of something to do until then." She grinned wickedly.

He lay across the bed with nothing but his bathrobe on, smelling like soap. He had taken his shower first, and his wife was now in the bathtub. He could hear her splashing around, cupping water with her hands, pouring it over her body, and humming a tune. Austin looked up at the ceiling, his hands crossed behind his head, thinking about nothing in particular, and he felt somewhat sad about that. There used to be a time when he would wait impatiently for his wife to come out of the bathroom, clean and smelling like roses. She would come to him, walk into his embrace, and he would take her. Then, it was very emotional, very spiritual. But now it was nothing but sex, and if it wasn't something that he had become so accustomed to getting, he probably wouldn't have done it with her at all.

He heard Trace step out of the tub, pull a towel from the rack, and dry herself off.

"You aren't asleep out there, are you?" she called into the bedroom.

"No, I'm not." He tried to duplicate her cheerful tone, but failed.

She walked out of the bathroom, the towel wrapped tightly around her body. She was still very attractive, Austin thought as he raised his head to get a look. Her hair was damp from the steam and plastered in some places to her face, giving her a very seductive, primal look. Her skin was a flawless tan, almost gold, and it shined from the baby oil she covered herself with.

"Are you ready for this?" she asked him, smiling wide.

Austin nodded his head and didn't say a thing. He just thought that it had been quite a while since he saw his wife like that, and he found himself wanting her very badly. She unfastened the towel and opened it up wide behind her as if it was a cape. Austin was surprised to see that she wasn't naked. She was wearing a pair of panties and a bra, both black. They were of a sheer see-through material and he could see the tiny triangle shape of the hair on her crotch and the circular nipples behind the bra. He leaned up on his elbows and motioned for her to come to him.

She walked to him, a very sexy walk. "Do you like what you see?" she asked softly.

"Yes," he replied. "I want you."

"I know." She bent down and kissed him passionately on the lips. She kissed him like that for a while and when he reached for her breast, she moved slightly, just out of his reach. He reached for her again, her thigh, and she sidestepped him. He heard her giggle after she did it. She's teasing me, he told himself, but for some reason he didn't mind. It was exciting to him, something that he hadn't felt in a long time.

Trace continued kissing him, and Austin kissed her back. She reached behind her and undid the clasp on her bra. Her breast fell out and dangled before him. She took his hand and placed it on her right breast. He felt a shock flash through his body. She then reached down and slid down her panties. Austin watched the painted toenails on her feet as she stepped out of the black underwear.

"How are you doing?" she asked, her voice sounding very throaty now.

"Fine," he said.

She opened up her husband's bathrobe and grabbed him tight, pulling gently. The feeling drove him crazy. He felt like a boy in her grasp.

"How are you feeling now?" she asked again.

Austin couldn't speak; all he knew was that he felt great. He wanted her so bad, and he knew she knew that. He overlooked the fact that they had been married six years and she practically knew everything about him. She moved even closer to him, straddled him, then pushed herself down on him. They both moaned in ecstasy.

Austin looked up at her sensually moving about on him. She was a vision. He had all but forgotten how beautiful she really was. He wanted to kick himself for behaving the way he had, for thinking the things he had thought about her.

She swayed back and forth above him, her face displaying her pleasure. Her eyes were closed. She always closed her eyes when they made love and Austin thought that was so sexy. She rubbed his chest, caressed his neck, then placed her hands on his face. "You're a beautiful man, Austin Harris," she said, as she rotated about him harder, quicker.

Austin felt the tingling building all about his body. He grabbed her breasts and massaged them. He let his hands slide down the silkiness of her skin to her wide hips, and caressed her round behind. He was in heaven, and he never wanted to stop feeling like that.

Trace quickened her pace even more when she saw that he was moving to the point of no return. "I love you, Austin. I love you so much," she cried, tilting her head back, a tear dropping from the corner of her eye.

"I love you too." His entire body was trembling. It was like he was being electrocuted. He tried holding back. All his muscles contracted, almost painfully so, then the release. He grabbed on to his wife, who had dug her fingernails into his shoulders, and held on as they both let out cries of extreme pleasure. She collapsed onto his chest, her body twitching uncontrollably. Sweat covered their bodies, and they were both breathing heavily. She pulled herself off him and laid her face on his chest, kissing him there. "I love you, Austin," she said again.

Austin played with the moist curls in her hair. "I love you too," he heard himself say.

They remained there for some time, Trace falling in and out of light sleep, Austin trying to get his thoughts straight about what had just happened. He was looking for the feeling that had overtaken him just before and during their lovemaking, but it managed to escape him. He didn't want to think that it was something transitory, that the feeling was strictly sexual and didn't last past the physical. But maybe it was. He felt strange and vulnerable, and he could feel himself resenting her for that, as if she had tricked him, stolen his power to make him weak.

None of it made sense to him. The feelings were unfounded, and he had no reason to think like that, but he did. He had told her that he loved her. He had told her in a fit of passion, but he knew that he meant it, or he would not have said it. He could tell by her deep breathing that she had fallen asleep again. He didn't know what to do. He shouldn't have made love with her. It just made things more complicated, he thought.

But the truth was, he thought a moment later, that it actually clarified things. Even after the act, he still felt as unsure about her as he did before she walked into the room. He had thought that the sex would remind him, reacquaint him with his feelings for her, but he realized that he would probably yell out his love for any woman if she were rolling around on his penis the way Trace was.

"Wake up, honey." He gently shook her by the shoulder. "Do you want to check on dinner?"

"Oh, I almost forgot," she said, coming out of her sleep. "Have I been asleep long?"

"No. Just a few minutes."

"That's because of you, big guy. You wore me out." She tapped him on the lips with her finger. She got up from bed, reached in the closet for her robe, and put it on.

"You can just come on down in a few minutes. Dinner should be ready, I just have to put it on a plate."

Austin nodded and watched her leave. He pulled himself up from bed, feeling a bit sorry for her, but told himself he wouldn't think about it. Not until he was ready to do something. He took a shower, then stood staring into the mirror. She doesn't even have a clue, he told himself.

Trace was standing in front of the table when Austin came down the stairs. The lights were low and two tall candles burned at the center of the table. Trace had prepared a dinner of lobster tail, zucchini, and some sort of rice pilaf. There was also a bottle of wine on ice, and fresh-baked bread cut into thick slices. It was all very romantic.

"Well, sit down," Trace said. She looked proud of herself, and she had reason to be, Austin thought.

"It looks good," he said.

"Thank you, sir." She smiled. "Look around you, is there anything else you need, before I sit down?"

Austin shook his head. He reached for the wine and poured their glasses full, then began to eat. He was chewing when he felt his wife staring at him. She had her hands crossed, looking at him in anticipation.

"Well, what do you think?" She was excited, and Austin didn't know why she was making such a big deal over a dinner.

"It's delicious," he said. She nodded her head, smiled, then picked up her own fork.

There was very little conversation. It wasn't because of Trace, though. She tried starting up small talk about everything under the sun, from the kids to possible vacations to ideas about redecorating a couple of rooms in the house. The problem was that her topics of conversation all had to do with the two of them sometime in the future, and Austin didn't really know if there was going to be a future for them, so he gave one-word answers and avoided some subjects altogether.

By the time they had finished dinner, Trace had gotten the idea that something was wrong. They both sat picking at their food, fishing for something to say.

"Dessert," she said, no enthusiasm at all in her voice.

"No. I'm pretty full." He didn't even raise his head to look at her when he spoke.

"What's wrong with you, Austin?" she asked. She had a worried look on her face.

"Austin," his wife called to him again.

"I think we need a break," he said.

"What did you say?" Trace asked. Her fork clattered onto the plate.

"I said, I think we need a break."

"I heard what you said, I just don't think I understand what you mean," Trace said.

"It's not working, Trace. It's just not," Austin said, sounding exhausted by the argument he was boxing himself into.

"And what about tonight? I thought tonight was good. It was like it used to be. I thought it would help."

"Is that what you thought?" He hated how his wife could make a situation seem so simple. It was one of the things he had never learned to like about her. "We had sex, Trace." He lowered his head and continued picking at his food. He could tell his use of the word "sex" cut into her like a knife. She would have preferred "make love," so it wouldn't seem as though there was nothing between them but the exchange of sexual fluids. But for the most part, that's all there was for Austin. "Having sex and making dinner can't cure all the ills of a mediocre marriage all the time," Austin said. The words slipped out before he had an opportunity to judge them and he regretted their harshness.

"So that's what this is, a mediocre marriage," Trace said. She grabbed her plate, grabbed Austin's from in front of him, carried them to the sink, and slammed them there. It was a wonder they didn't shatter into a million pieces.

"If that's how you felt, I wish you could've told me earlier. We could've saved, what, three or four years of having to deal with this mediocre marriage. Or did you start feeling this way before then, maybe a week or two after we were married?"

"Trace, I didn't mean exactly that."

"Then what, Austin? What did you mean?" Trace moved about the table, clearing the dishes as if making some sort of statement. She grabbed the candles, blew them out with more force than needed, then chucked them into the trash.

Austin looked down at his hands. He wanted to tell her how he felt, but whatever he said came out the wrong way, too hard, too much to the point, and he didn't want to hurt her feelings more than he had already.

"It's not what I thought it'd be like with you," he said cautiously.

Trace stopped in front of him. She was holding the bottle of champagne, and Austin was hoping she wouldn't knock him over the head with it.

"Well, I'm sorry I didn't live up to your expectations, sir. I'm sorry I can't be perfect and have dinner on the table for you, steam floating from it every time you walk in the house," she said, making airy gestures with one hand. "I'm sorry I'm not the type that walks around in an apron all day and washes walls, does laundry, and vacuums. I'm really sorry about that, Austin, but I didn't think the quality of our marriage was based on things like that."

"It's not that," Austin said, feeling himself losing ground.

"Then what is it?"

"You don't do shit!" Austin said, and was not sorry about the way that came out. Trace looked as if he had slapped her across the face.

"What do you mean?" Trace said. "What do you call all this?"

"Why did you quit school?" Austin said.

Trace blew out a sigh. "We went through that years ago."

"Why did you?" he asked again.

"Because I didn't want to do it. Dammit, why can't you understand that?" Trace said.

"But you could've been successful."

Trace gave him a long look. Then she went to the trash, took a swig from the bottle of champagne she was holding and dropped it in the can.

"So I'm not successful as your wife, is that it, Austin? I can't just love you, and be a good mother and a good wife, but I have to have a law degree or something hanging from the damn wall as well."

"I didn't say that," Austin said.

"Then what are you saying?"

"It just seems to me that you gave up way before you even got started. I come in from work and I see you here sitting in the kitchen watching some worthless talk show, and I see so much more in you than that. You had so much potential and you just threw it all away. It just makes me sick to know that, to see that."

Trace just shook her head and laughed sarcastically. "You're a trip, Austin. A motherfucking trip! Telling me what I threw away in my life. If you can't accept me for who I am, obviously I threw away my life when I married you. There were no conditions, Austin. I don't remember hearing anything about, 'to have, to hold, and finish law school' in our marriage vows."

"Well, maybe it should've been in there," Austin said.

"You are a bastard sometimes, Austin," Trace said, shaking with anger. "Everything just has to be perfect with you. It's not even about school, is it?"

"What are you talking about?" Austin demanded.

"Nothing. Nothing at all. So what are you planning on doing?" Trace turned her back on him to go to the sink, as if his response didn't matter.

"I need . . . I need a break," Austin said softly. "I need for us to be apart for some time so I can get my head together. I want to see you in a better light, try and understand why I'm doing what I'm doing, and see if I can come to terms with it, maybe try and make us work."

Trace tried the sarcastic carefree laugh again, but it sounded more like she was about to cry. "Don't do me any favors, Austin. Please. If I'm not the person you think I should be, then I'm just not that person. But let me tell you something. I really think you have a problem if you measure me solely on what I accomplished and not who I am. This is bullshit, Austin, and you know it. Me finishing school has nothing to do with this. I would've been the same person that I am now, I just would've been a lawyer. It wouldn't have really made a difference either way, would it?"

Austin didn't answer the question. It was better not to because he really didn't know the honest answer. Her eyes were intense as she looked back at him; he could feel the resentment in her stare.

"I'm sorry I can't reach perfection, Austin, but that's not everything. Maybe one day you'll realize that." She turned and went to the sink. She squeezed some soap into the running water and started washing dishes.

Austin didn't say a word. He went upstairs, threw on some clothes, threw some things into a bag and carried them back downstairs.

"I'm leaving now," he said to his wife. She didn't turn her head from the dishes.

"I said, I'm leaving now!" he said louder, to be heard over the running water.

Trace turned and nodded her head without speaking, her face emotionless. Austin took a last look at her, then walked toward the door.

"Austin," Trace called. She turned off the water. She looked pathetic. A defeated look on her face, soapsuds climbing up her forearms. "What about the children?"

Austin was almost offended by the question, but he tried not to show it. "They'll still have a father, Trace. I'll be there for them."

Trace nodded, then mechanically returned to the dishes.

TEN

After the failed meeting with Benning, Caleb roamed the streets for hours trying to avoid going home, because he didn't want to appear as a loser in Sonya's eyes yet again. It had happened far too many times, and to stand there and tell her that he had failed again was the last thing he wanted to do. Caleb stepped off the bus and walked down the darkened street that led to Blue's apartment. Some people were standing on the corner, their hands in their pockets, looking to the sky as if expecting money to fall from it in neatly bound bundles. Others sat on their porches and drank or smoked and talked loudly and laughed even louder, as the night moved closer to the morning.

Blue was right where Caleb knew he'd be. Propped right out on his front porch, smoking the last bit of a joint, an unopened forty-ounce bottle of malt liquor in between his legs. Blue caught a glimpse of Caleb coming up the street. "What the fuck you still doing in that outfit? If you selling encyclopedias, I don't want none." He took a long pull of the expiring joint, then put it out on the stair next to him.

"Shut up, Blue," Caleb said. "I'm not in the mood for shit right now. Besides, I'd be surprised if you could even spell encyclopedia."

"Well, excuse me," Blue said, flicking the spent butt into the street.

Caleb sat down on the stair under him. He hiked his knees up, stuck his elbows on them, then let his face fall into his hands. At that point he didn't even know why he had come to see Blue. He had thought it would do him some good to be around his friend, but Blue's pitiful situation just seemed to make him feel worse.

"What's your problem?" Blue asked. He nudged him on the shoulder with the toe of his boot. "You can't be coming over here with all that depressing shit, trying to bring me down. I got problems of my own, if you don't mind."

Caleb turned around to look up at his friend. His black face was floating above him like a patch of midnight; then he smiled and the gold tooth sparkled like the penetrating signal from a lighthouse. "What problems do you got?" Caleb asked, annoyed.

"Where am I going to get my next beer after I finish this one? That's my problem." He lifted the fat bottle of malt liquor and twisted the cap. A fizzing sound pushed out from under it as he lifted it off. He put the bottle to his lips, tilted it back, then took a few long swigs. "Ahhh," he breathed, as he pulled the bottle down and wiped his mouth with the back of his hand.

"You really got problems, man. I'll see you." Caleb picked himself up, ready to leave. He had had enough of feeling like he was the only one who had problems and the only one who cared. But Blue called after him.

"Yo, Caleb. Chill the fuck out. I'm just trippin', man. Don't take off, I'll listen."

Caleb looked back at him. He looked as though he was telling the truth; he had even put down the bottle of beer and was screwing the top back on. There was no one else to talk to, or at least that would understand him like Blue would. Caleb sat back down on the stairs, this time beside Blue.

"Now what's the problem, brotha? White man kicking your ass again?" Blue said.

Caleb sighed. He was exhausted and hadn't realized how much till that moment.

"Naw, it ain't the white man this time. It's a black man who thinks he's white. Remember that guy I told you about the other day?"

Blue nodded.

"He said he wanted me to come downtown and have lunch with him so we could talk. I thought I'd be able to work a job out of it, but turns out when I get down there, that dude doesn't even keep his end up. He tells his secretary that something came up, and I have to reschedule."

"That's foul shit," Blue said, looking upset. "And you say this is a brotha."

"Yeah. I get all dressed up like a fool, take the bus all the way down there, just to be made a bigger fool of by his secretary and all the other people in the building." Caleb shook his head in disgust. "They called damn security to throw me out!"

"You can't even trust your own kind no more, man. Once they get in the system, once they get to the point where they think they successful, or the white man tricks them into believing that they are, they forget all about who they are and where they came from. That pisses me off!" Blue slammed a fist into the palm of his other hand. "They act like they got there all by themselves. They forget about all the little black people that helped them, like their teachers or their brothers or their friends. They get out there in the mainstream, start to liking that money, start to enjoying those white people smiling in their face like they accept them as one of their own, and they just lose their black mind. It's a damn shame. I need a drink behind this shit." He screwed the cap off and took a swallow, then handed the bottle to Caleb. "So what you going to do?" Blue asked.

Caleb held the bottle, smoothing one hand up and down the length of it, as if it was giving him some insight into his problem. "I don't know. I'm tired is all I know. I'm tired of being poor and broke. But I'm tired of doing fucking jigs, jumping through hoops just to impress the white man so he might toss me a few scraps from the dinner table. I don't know what I want to do." He took a swallow from the bottle. It was a short one, one that he didn't enjoy very much. "Sometimes I just want to quit. Just lay the fuck down and give in, not care anymore about what happens and who it affects. But I can't do that. I got responsibilities." He said the word like it brought a sour taste to his mouth. "I got too much stuff. I got a girl, and a kid." He took another swig from the bottle, this one not seeming to bother him as much. "That shit seems to always be there, hovering over me, like some boulder threatening to fall on my head if I don't take care of my business. Sometimes it comes close to driving me crazy."

Blue didn't say anything right away. He just sat there, and when Caleb didn't say anything for quite a while, Blue finally spoke. "You got to do something, but nobody said you got to walk around trying to chase the white man's dream. That shit is dead, man," he said softly, as if it was their secret. "It ain't made for us. 'Cause if it was, there would be a lot more black folks making it. We got to do our own thing sometimes. We got to do what we can to survive. You know what I'm saying?" He put a hand on Caleb's shoulder.

Caleb turned to him. "No, what are you saying?"

"You ever think about selling drugs? I don't do the shit myself. Personally, I think it's some foul, genocidal shit, but I'd understand, considering, and I got hook-ups."

"Naw," Caleb said. "I could never do nothing like that."

"Don't never say never. It's rough out there, and you got mouths to feed. It'd only be for a little bit," Blue said.

"Naw, that ain't me," Caleb insisted.

"Well, you going to have to do something. Ain't nobody going to stick their hand out and give you no money. You know that."

Caleb shook his head, understanding very well the point Blue was making.

"I'm not trying to put you in no shit, man. I mean, you're my man. You're my main man." He put his fist to his heart. "But you know how it goes, drastic measures for drastic times. You might have to take what you want. I'm not saying do that shit now, but it's always an option. If nothing else comes through, just look at it as a last resort. Besides, I wouldn't let you do it yourself. I'd be right there with you covering your back." Blue put his hand back on Caleb's shoulder, near his neck, gripping it firmly, almost painfully. Blue looked into his eyes, more serious than he had ever been.

"Think about this shit, man. Every time you get wronged, that's the white man keeping you from making money, and if he keeping you from making it, it's just like he's taking it from you—stealing it from you.

And when he does that, he denies you the opportunity to feed your family. That's foul shit any way you look at it. And the only way that wrong can be made right is to throw it back in their faces. Take *their* money away, take *their* opportunity away. You get what I'm saying." He spoke in a low but firm voice, droning on in a hypnotic way, never releasing the hand from Caleb's shoulder, as if he was steadying him somehow, strengthening him for what he must do. "I'm not saying this is something that got to be done now, but just stick it in your head until you can wrap your brain around it and see what you think, all right?"

Caleb thought back to a time when he had stolen an old lady's purse. He was running down the street, that purse in his hand, the police on his ass, the wind crashing against his face as he bumped into people, knocking them to the ground, hearing them scream out in pain. It was horrible. For some reason, he thought he was going to die that day. He kept envisioning a bullet speeding up behind him, directing itself for his back, right between his shoulder blades. As he ran, the thundering of his heavy breathing was banging in his ears. He saw himself crashing to the ground after the bullet struck him. His body landing hard, the pavement not giving an inch, a thin fountain of deep red blood squirting out of his body into the air.

He wouldn't do that again, he told himself, as he focused on Blue's dark face and intense stare. He wouldn't go to prison again, even if it was for six months. Sonya had said she would leave him if that ever happened again, and there was no way he would risk losing her and his son. No, he couldn't do it. So much to lose, so much to fear. The only way he would do it would be if his life or his family's lives depended on it, and he hoped to God that wouldn't happen. He didn't answer Blue's question, didn't even comment on it at all, just let it float out there like a heavy gray cloud, pregnant with rain, threatening to storm bad luck all over him.

"I have to go," Caleb said solemnly. He picked himself up off the stairs and moped out toward the street. He looked back at his friend, almost frightened by all that Blue had said.

"You think about that, you hear me?" Blue said.

Caleb rode the bus home, feeling a lot worse on this trip than the one he had taken from downtown. Now he not only felt betrayed but cornered as well.

His head bobbed and swayed with the gentle movement of the bus as it pushed its way down the potholed streets of Chicago. There was no one on the bus but him, and he was only now considering how truly alone he was. He wanted to disappear, hide himself somewhere, then come out years later and hope things had taken care of themselves. Life would have moved on without him, and he would no longer be responsible for anything, anything at all.

Caleb looked out the window at the run-down neighborhood. He looked out at the people, just as run-down, as he passed them. It was amazing how many of them stood out on the streets so late at night. Some sat in chairs outside their front doors, some stood on the corners, others stood in large groups, laughing and playing, running about as if they had no care in the world. Caleb wondered how they could behave like that. They should be just as burdened as he was. He knew they had to be as poor, if not poorer, or they wouldn't be standing in the places they were. He pulled his attention away from the depressing streets and back into the bus. He looked across the aisle to where the man had been sitting. The man he had met the other day that seemed so nice, that seemed to care about people like him, because in essence, he was a person like him. From the projects, he said, but that was bullshit.

Caleb reached into his pocket and pulled out the worn card. Out with it fell the clip-on necktie that he used to think so much of. It fell to the floor. He picked it up and draped it over one knee, not caring if it was covered with dirt or not. He thought about how excited he had been when he received the card, how he had hoped that something would come of it, and how much of a fool he felt like when he was kicked out of the office. He didn't know what to do. Maybe he should call the man back, maybe there was some misunderstanding. He didn't know. He balanced the card on his other knee, then relaxed back into the hard plastic chair, feeling sleepy as the bus made its way closer to his home.

"Hey. Hey!" Caleb heard a voice yelling at him—pulling him out of his sleep. It was the bus driver yelling from the front of the bus. "End of the line, gotta get off here."

Caleb wiped his eyes clear, then stretched a little. He looked down and saw the card and tie on his knees and everything came back to him, the depressed feeling and all. He lifted the things, stood, and was about to put them in his pocket, but then he thought, thought about every-thing.

"You gettin' off the bus or you going to stand there and look stupid all night?" the bus driver barked.

Caleb snapped out of his thought, then looked toward the bus dri-ver. His mean face was in the mirror keeping an eye on him. Caleb dropped the card and the tie to the chair where he had been sitting, then got off the bus, only stopping once to look back.

Caleb walked in the house at fifteen minutes after eleven o'clock. He closed the door gently so as not to make any noise if Sonya was asleep. All the lights were out, save for an intermittent blue glow that came out of the bedroom. It was Sonya watching TV, he thought. He walked into the bedroom. She was on her side, twisted into the sheet, a pillow balled up, pressed in half and stuck under her head.

Caleb unbuttoned his shirt, pulled it off and draped it over the back of a chair. Then he sat down on the edge of the bed, pulled off the dirty, scuffed black shoes, peeled off his socks along with them, then kicked his feet onto the bed and relaxed, exhausted from the trials of the day.

"So what happened?" a soft voice said, coming from the other side of the bed. Caleb was startled, having thought she was asleep. "It fell through," he said, not realizing how hurt he felt till that very moment. It was like confessing that he was a loser. It was like the real question Sonya was asking was, "Have you made anything out of yourself yet?" And his answer was, "No, I didn't. It fell through. I fell through," and it was like letting her down for the millionth time. But he wanted her to ask him why. This time it wasn't his fault and she needed to know that, so she would know that she wasn't involved with someone who would never succeed.

He held his breath, hoping that she would choose to ask him what went wrong. He looked at it as a sort of test, knowing that if she didn't ask him, that meant she no longer cared. She used to ask all the time in the past, and when he told her, even if it was his fault, she would reas-sure him that it would be better next time. So he waited with bated breath for her response.

"Oh," is what she said. It was all she said, and Caleb's heart sank. He wanted to explain to her about the man, how he had turned on him, but he couldn't. He couldn't offer her an explanation if she didn't ask for one, because it would make him appear more of a loser, trying to shift the blame from himself, if he volunteered the information.

"That damn landlord came banging at the door again looking for his rent. He said we're two weeks behind already, and if he doesn't get his money by the end of this week, he's going to put us out." She said the words in a very plain way, as if she'd been through it a thousand times before—not that she didn't care, but that there was nothing she could do about it.

Caleb didn't say a word, just sank even lower, realizing that she really had lost her faith in him. She changed the subject entirely, no longer wanting to talk about him, or even to ask what had happened.

"Oh, yeah, and your brother called about three times," she said, still on her side, her back to Caleb. "I didn't pick up the phone because I knew he was calling for you, and besides, sometimes he gets a little too nosy."

"Thanks," Caleb said, feeling distraught and not caring what she had said. He walked into the kitchen, clicked on the light switch, and the fluorescent lights overhead came on with a flicker. The countertops seemed to move, but it was just the scattering of a million roaches startled by the light. It happened almost every time he turned on the lights in there, and at one time he could overlook it, but now it angered him beyond belief. This entire poor thing had gotten a bit out of control. He had been doing it since he was a teenager and now he was just fed up. He felt like walking up the stairs, banging on the old, bald, fat-assed landlord's apartment, and telling him he could have his stinking, roach-infested apartment back, because he didn't have any money to give him anyway. He didn't have any money and he didn't have any means of making any money, so the landlord would just have to come down there and kick them out, put them on the street.

He picked up the phone and dialed Marcus's number, letting it ring a few times till the machine picked up.

"Where are you, man?" Caleb said, trying to sound as cheerful as possible. Marcus would rush right over the moment he got the message if he thought something was wrong with his brother. "Well, I'm just returning your phone call, I mean calls. Ring me back. Oh, yeah, and there's something I have to talk to you about." He hung up the phone.

He let his hand rest on it, thinking about his brother, regretting that he wasn't there. Marcus was always able to make him feel better about anything. He was the one person that was truly there for him.

Caleb smoothed the table space before him clear, folded his arms there, then rested his head on top of them. He would just rest there, slumped over on the kitchen table, exhausted, the bright light beaming down on his bare back, as he decided what he would do with his life.

ELEVEN

Marcus checked his messages the next day.

"The boy has finally found out how to use the phone," he said to himself. The voice on the machine didn't sound very good, and immediately Marcus became concerned. He had no idea what Caleb wanted to talk to him about, but he picked up the phone and dialed his number right away. *It has something to do with the other day when I spoke to Sonya, I know it,* he told himself, wishing he had pressed the issue further.

"Hello?" Sonya answered.

"Hello, Sonya? What are you doing home?"

There was a brief pause. "It's really none of your business, but I have the day off. Caleb isn't here, Marcus, and I don't know where he is," she said curtly.

"Are you sure?" Marcus thought about the question after he had asked it, and realized it was the wrong thing to say. He knew she'd take it the wrong way.

"I don't have to lie to you, Marcus. If he was here, I'd tell you, and if I didn't want him to talk to you, I'd just tell you that too."

"I'm sorry, but he called me, and I'm just returning his phone call."

"I know. I told him you called, and I'll tell him you called again. Okay?" Sonya said.

"But there seemed to be something wrong when he called me. Is everything all right over there? I mean, is he in any trouble? Can I help in any way?" Marcus asked. He could almost see her on the other end of the phone becoming infuriated with his questions, but he didn't care. He had to know what was going on.

"Marcus, look. There is nothing going on, there is nothing wrong, and if there is, it's something that me and Caleb can handle, all right? You have to understand that he doesn't need you every time there's a little trouble. He's a grown man. Now, I'll tell him that you called like I always do, and if he returns your phone call, that's up to him. Bye, Marcus." She hung up the phone.

"But Sonya . . . Sonya?" Marcus called into the phone. His first thought was to call her back, tell her that he wasn't finished talking to her, then make her apologize for being so rude, but he didn't want to get into it with her. Besides, she probably wouldn't pick up the phone anyway. She would stand there and let it ring, knowing it was him. That made him angry. He was trying to speak with his brother, trying to find out if his family needed him, and she was trying to come between them. He couldn't allow her to do that. She wasn't even his wife, just some woman whom he happened to get pregnant. He dropped the phone, grabbed his shirt, and left the house.

Marcus pulled up in front of the building that Caleb lived in. It had been a while since he was there and he had almost forgotten how bad the place looked. It was an old brick building, maybe housing thirty or forty units. It looked as though it had been standing there since the beginning of time. The cement in between the bricks was corroded and crumbling away, and some bricks had fallen, like decaying teeth falling from an old man's mouth. The window sashes were rotted and warped, and covered with paint that was faded and chipped. The panes themselves were so dirty that Marcus could hardly see the towels and bedsheets and newspapers that the tenants had hung to maintain their privacy.

He stepped out of the car, made sure the door was locked, then walked toward the building. The lot the building sat on was covered with trash, beer bottles, cigarette cartons, an empty jelly jar, a plastic milk container, a crushed box of Pampers filled with folded soiled diapers, and a pair of children's jeans, one leg ripped to shreds. These discarded items lay across the dirt-covered path, growing there like grass. He stepped down the path toward the door, kicking a soda can out of his way. Two kids stuck their heads out of a window high up and called down to him.

"Hey, mista. You got some candy?" one of the dirty-faced boys said. He was hanging out the window, exposing almost his entire upper body. The other child, obviously younger, peeked from around the older boy, sticking his head in the little space that was available.

"You shouldn't hang out that window like that. You might fall," Marcus called up to him.

"I ain't gonna fall. You got some candy, though?" he asked again, smashing his hand in the younger boy's face, pushing him back inside.

"Sorry." Marcus held out both his hands, illustrating that he had nothing. The boy smiled, showing a wide gap where his two front teeth should have been, then disappeared back into the window. An old white curtain blew out the window and flapped in the wind, taking his place. Marcus shook his head. He hoped they weren't alone. He hoped that the mother or the grandmother or aunt or older cousin, or whichever elder should have been taking care of them, was just in the kitchen cooking, or in the bedroom watching TV.

Marcus opened the door and walked into the building. The stink of old trash, urine, and different foods cooking hit him in the face. He walked up the stairs and heard loud music beating up against the doors of some apartments, trying to get out. He heard people arguing at the top of their voices behind a couple of other doors, the theme song from a familiar cartoon behind another, and sounds of two people going insane, or having very intense sex, behind yet another door. He continued climbing the stairs to the third floor, where Caleb lived—apartment 313.

He heard a man's voice yelling, followed by pounding on a door. "Ain't nobody living here for free, I tell you. You give me my damn money or get the hell out!" Again the loud pounding following the thunderous yelling. Marcus climbed the last stair that put him on the third floor, and saw the man who was obviously behind all the yelling and pounding. He was an old round figure, looking like an extra-wide bowling pin, covered with a sleeveless t-shirt and sagging black pants.

"I want my money!" he yelled again, and banged only twice. He seemed to be getting tired, and rested against the door.

Marcus walked past 319, then 317, and realized that the big, balding, sweaty man was standing in front of Caleb's apartment. His face was dirty from a few days' beard growth. His shoulders slumped, his t-shirt rose to expose a chunk of fat from his mid-section, and he chewed on an unlit half of a cigar as he smoothed the three strands of hair atop his head, making himself more presentable.

"You know these people here?" he barked at Marcus.

"Yes, I do. Mr. Harris is my brother. Is there a problem?" Marcus asked in a respectful tone, even though he felt the last thing the man deserved was respect.

"Damn right. They owe me money. They're behind on their rent two weeks," he said. "Him and that deadbeat wife of his."

Even though he was angry at Sonya he didn't feel she deserved that. Marcus looked at the man's mouth, at his grimy cigar-stained teeth as he spoke. "She's not a deadbeat, and I'd appreciate if you keep your comments to yourself," Marcus said.

"Whatever," he said, waving Marcus off. "You just tell them that I want my money, and if they don't have it by the end of this week, they can start looking for a new spot on the street. You hear me, boy?" He gave Marcus an evil look. "If you have any problems with that, my number is 565." The man was standing very close to Marcus. He looked him slowly up and down, still gumming the old cigar.

"I hear you," Marcus said, wanting to drill him right in his soft gut. The old man gave him another long hard look, then walked off toward the stairs.

Marcus turned and banged on the door. No one answered, so he banged again.

"Sonya, open the door. It's me, Marcus." Still no answer came. He banged again, then put his ear to the door. He heard someone move, then a bump. "Come on, I hear you in there. Open the door, I'm alone." He waited for a moment, then the door cracked open, and Sonya peeked out from the small space, her eyes floating around in her head, looking in all directions.

"All right, come on," she said, in a loud whisper. Marcus walked in and she closed the door behind him, fastening the chain on it.

"What was all that about, Sonya?"

She walked about the room, her arms wrapped about her body, hugging herself.

"That man scares me." She paced the floor back and forth a few more times then settled herself against the table.

"Sonya, what's going on?" Marcus asked again.

"Why are you asking me? He filled you in on everything. We're late on the rent, and don't have no money to pay him, okay? Happy now?" She hugged herself again, turned her back on him, and began to pace.

"This is what you were trying to tell me on the phone that time, isn't it?" Marcus asked.

"Look at the baby genius," Sonya said.

"I'm going to the bank," Marcus said, turning for the door.

Sonya ran across the room, grabbing him by the arm. "What? What do you think you're doing?"

"I'm going to the bank. I'm going to take out some money so you can pay your rent," Marcus said. He looked into Sonya's eyes. She was scared, but she looked as though she was considering what he said, and wondering if she should let him go.

"You can't," she said.

"Well, I'm going to."

She pulled Marcus again by his arm. "You can't. How do you think that's going to make Caleb feel, finding out that his older brother had to come here and rescue him again because he can't seem to do it himself? How do you think he's going to feel to know that I took money from you to take care of his problems, to take care of his child? Marcus, that's the last thing he wants to do is go running to you, and to tell you the truth, I feel the same way. Damn, we need the money, but we just can't get it from you. You can't step in here every time we have a problem and save us from it. If we can't do it ourselves then how are we ever going to learn how? Can you tell me that?" She was grabbing him with a trembling hand, pleading with him to understand. But he wasn't hearing her.

"How is little Jahlil going to feel? Sleeping on the street when he has no home to go to. Can you tell me that?" Sonya didn't say a word.

"I'm going to the bank. I'll be right back, and you better be here." He looked down at her hands still attached to his jacket. "If you don't mind," Marcus said. Sonya released her hands and they reluctantly slid down the length of his arm.

Marcus rushed to the bank, driving as fast as he could, almost hitting a car that failed to display a turn signal. He wanted to get back and take care of everything before his younger brother got back. He knew Caleb would rather live on the street in a large cardboard box than take another handout from Marcus.

With the money in his breast pocket, Marcus rushed up the stairs, taking them two at a time. He stopped in front of Caleb's door. He wondered if he should go in, but he didn't want to take a chance on Caleb's being there. Then he thought about the landlord. He could take the money directly to him.

Marcus stopped in front of apartment 565 and pressed his ear to the door. He heard the low chatter of a television set, then stepped back and banged his fist against the door as hard as he could. He heard a crash from within the apartment, as if dishes had fallen and shattered. "Who the hell is it?" the old round man's voice thundered from behind the door. Marcus didn't answer, just knocked again, three hard raps, harder than before.

"Who is it, I said?" The big man opened the door and stood filling the doorway, a huge red tomato soup stain on his t-shirt, a menacing look on his face.

"What do you want, knocking on my door like a damn maniac?"

"I only knocked on your door like you knocked on my brother's. So if I'm a maniac, well . . ." Marcus looked dead into the man's evil, tired-looking eyes, expecting anything. Marcus wanted an excuse to give him a good shot to the jaw for the way he had harassed Sonya.

"Well, what do you want? Do you have my money?" he said, lowering his tone a bit.

"I have it," Marcus said, patting his breast pocket.

The round man watched the gesture, seeming to salivate at the idea of getting his money. "Well, give it to me," he said impatiently.

"I'm not going to conduct business in the hallway," Marcus said. "You want the money, we'll take care of it inside."

The landlord swung the door open and Marcus walked past him

into the apartment. The place was filthy, just as he had expected. "Nice place you keep, but then again, I figured it to be like this," Marcus said, walking over to a table as the man directed him.

"I don't have time for your smart-ass mouth. Just give me my money, then get the hell out." They were standing on opposite sides of the table. Marcus didn't say anything and didn't move an inch. Just stood there, his hand frozen in the act of retrieving the money from his pocket, and stared at the landlord. The landlord stared back, looking more evil than before. Marcus could see the muscle in his jaws jump as he clenched his teeth.

Marcus pulled out the money. "How much is rent for this . . ?" He held back his comment on the condition of the building.

"Three-sixty," the man said. "Plus forty dollars late fee."

Marcus counted out the money, laying it on the table. "Three-forty, three-sixty. First month's rent." He counted out two more twenties. "Late fee." Then he counted out another $360. "Next month's rent," he said, laying the crisp, clean bills on the table. He pushed them in the direction of the man. "Here's your money. And do me a favor, don't ever go down there harassing them like that again. If there's a problem with the rent you contact me." Marcus threw one of his cards at the man; it bounced harmlessly off his large gut and landed on the table. The old guy picked it up and looked at it with disgust.

"Considering your deadbeat brother and his wife, there will be a problem, and I will be calling you. Now get out."

Marcus restrained his urge to slam the man in the face. He walked back downstairs and knocked on Caleb's door. Sonya let him in.

"Well?" she said, staring wide-eyed into Marcus's face.

"Well, nothing. I went up to pay him, and let me tell you, he's a complete asshole."

"You did what? Why did you go up there?" Sonya asked.

"I saw how shaken up you were. I figured you didn't want to do it yourself so I did. Is there something wrong?"

Sonya blew out a long sigh. "No." She put her fingers to her temples, then walked a nervous little circle. "You can't tell Caleb that I knew about you giving him that money. If he were to find out, he wouldn't forgive me for letting you do that."

"I think you underestimate my little brother," Marcus smiled.

"I think you overestimate him," Sonya replied. The smiled dissolved from Marcus's face.

"I'll talk to you later, Sonya," he said, reaching for the door.

"Marcus, he's just a man, and one with problems at that," Sonya tried to explain. "I know he's your brother, and because of that, you feel that some of whatever you and your big-time lawyer brother have should've rubbed off on him, but it didn't. The biggest problem is that I think you have Caleb thinking the same thing. He's just Caleb, plain old Caleb, and he's doing the best he can."

"Don't you think I know that? He's my brother," Marcus said, taking offense at her comment.

"I don't know. I really don't. You call here all the time checking up on him like he's supposed to be doing something. Like he's supposed to be making some sort of progress or something from where he is right now, like where he is ain't good enough. It's good enough, Marcus. At least for right now. Do you ever wonder how that makes him feel, do you think about how that makes me feel?"

Marcus had to admit to himself that he never did. He looked at Sonya, her lip starting to quiver. Then she clenched her jaws, blinked her eyes a few times, and regained her composure.

"Even though he's not making a lot of money, Marcus, your brother is still a proud person. He never feels what he's doing is enough, he always feels as though he's falling short of what people expect of him. You probably don't know that about him, because you think he's probably out just fucking around, but he's really trying."

"Sonya, why are you telling me all this? I know this, that's why I'm trying to help," Marcus said.

Sonya shook her head. "That's why you can't help. He needs to know he can do it on his own. If he makes a little progress, starts to see any sign of light, you'll call and tell him you can help, making what he's done look like nothing. I'm tired of him feeling like he's not capable of nothing, that he's not worth nothing. I know it's hard to stand back and not stick your hand out when you think your own brother is drowning, but that's what you have to do. That's why I've been mean to you. I don't think you're a bad person, Marcus. But sometimes I think you talking to him just works for *you*, makes you feel good because you think you're helping him out when all you're really doing is hurting him. Sometimes I think he'd be better off if he didn't talk to you at all."

"So what am I supposed to do, just leave him alone? Stop calling him, stop talking to my brother?"

Sonya looked down at the floor. "Could you do that, just for a little while?"

Marcus couldn't believe what she was asking him to do. If she only knew what he had sacrificed for Caleb, what he had gone through to try and finish raising him after their mother died. "No, I can't do that. Not even for a little while, and if you really knew what you were asking of me, it would've never come out of your mouth."

"Marcus, I didn't mean anything by it," Sonya said. "I just . . ." She didn't explain any further. Marcus wasn't listening.

He was angry, very angry, but he reached into his pocket anyway and pulled out the remainder of the money he had withdrawn from the bank. He grabbed Sonya's hand, slapped the money in her palm, and closed her fingers around it.

"I can't take this. You already gave us enough money." She held the money out to him.

"Take it. Buy yourselves something nice for a change." He was so angry at her that he couldn't even look at her when he spoke. Sonya walked up to him and hugged him.

"You aren't going to tell him about this, are you?"

Marcus shook his head.

"I only said those things because I'm trying to do what I think is best for Caleb. Everything I do is for that reason."

Marcus reached around his neck and gently undid her arms from around him. "I know, that's why I haven't tried to convince him to leave you," he said, solemnly. "I'll talk to you later, Sonya." Still without looking at her, he kissed her on the cheek, then walked out the door before she could respond.

TWELVE

When Julius finally walked in the house, it was late. He went upstairs to the bedroom and wasn't surprised to see Cathy sleeping.
He leaned over, kissed her on the cheek, and got undressed.

Julius had been out thinking about his sons again, letting them
dominate his thoughts. Didn't he have enough on his mind without
thinking about them? Of course he did. So he could not let that continue to bother him, he thought, as he gently slid under the covers next
to Cathy's warm body. He just wouldn't think about it anymore, at least
for right now.

He reached over, clicked off the bedside lamp, and patiently waited
for sleep.

*Julius stood outside the door of Marcus's house. It was incredibly cold out
that day, threatening to snow, yet he only had a thin t-shirt on and a light
pair of slacks. He was holding a paper bag in his left hand, but he didn't
know what its contents were. He rang the doorbell again and waited, and
made an attempt to peek into the window near him. He saw a figure behind*

the curtain moving toward the door, so he straightened himself for his reception.

The door opened and it was Austin, his oldest son. The look on his face was of disbelief, and although he was a grown man, he looked very much like the child Julius had left so long ago. Julius continued to look into his eyes until they squinted into a smile. Austin opened his arms, grabbed his father, and hugged him. "It's been too long, Dad," his son said, squeezing him tightly.

Julius tried to speak but could not. He thought at first that he was overcome by emotion, but it wasn't that. He tried to speak, but no words came out, just a tickling sensation in his throat that made him want to cough. Austin invited him in, showed him to a seat, and offered him something to drink. "I know it's been a long trip," he said. Julius just nodded his head and smiled. Austin disappeared into the kitchen, and Marcus came out. He walked into the room already smiling, as if Austin had told him that his father was sitting quietly in the living room, waiting for him.

Marcus walked over to Julius, coaxed him off the couch and hugged him just as energetically as his brother had. He pulled away to get a good look at his father. Marcus had a weird smile on his face.

"I was so mad that you left, that I thought I never wanted to see you again." He spoke as if he were speaking to a group of children. "I thought that I wouldn't have cared if you lived or died, but now . . . now that you're here, I realize how much I missed you and how much we need you in our lives. Isn't that right, Caleb?"

"That's right, big brother." Julius heard Caleb's voice from the other room. Then he saw his son. He entered skipping like a child, his mouth formed into a huge smile, but his eyes read anger.

"We've missed you so much, Dad, you could never imagine." He skipped up next to Marcus and threw his arms around Julius, holding him very tight.

"I never knew why you left," Caleb said. "I just remember standing there, crying my eyes out, looking up at you with those bags in your hands. You walked past me like I was a tree." Julius could feel Caleb's grip on him increasing in pressure. Julius tried to move, but Marcus and Caleb both were hugging him tightly and they wouldn't release him. Then he tried to speak, tried to explain why he had left, what happened that night, but nothing came but the tickling sensation, then a short episode of dry coughing.

"Don't worry, Dad. I have a drink for you right here to clear your throat." Austin came in holding a short, round glass, some of the contents swishing around and spilling to the carpet as he hurried to his father.

"I hope you like cognac. It's my favorite, besides, it's all I have." He held his father's neck, placed the glass to his lips, and tilted both his head and the glass back, letting the alcohol spill into Julius's mouth. The taste was extremely bitter. He closed his mouth, but Austin kept pouring.

"C'mon, you have to finish, or you won't get any dessert," he crooned in a patronizing voice. Julius shook his head violently from side to side, but Austin held his head tightly, continuing to feed him the bitter liquid even though it wasn't going in his father's mouth, but spilling over his lips and running down the side of his face and down his neck.

"How's that?" Austin asked after he was finished. Julius was breathing hard from the ordeal. When he opened his mouth and tried to speak, he didn't feel the sensation that was there before, and he didn't have the urge to cough. He still couldn't speak, but he did hear his own voice. It wasn't in the form of words but basic grunts and primary groans, as if he were an infant and did not know yet how to pronounce words.

"Good, that's good," Austin said, as he tossed the glass to a corner, where it shattered, startling Julius.

"We have missed you, Dad," Austin said, as he joined his brothers in smothering their father in a great mass hug, their arms intertwined and wrapped tightly around him. Julius grunted and groaned, trying to free himself.

"Don't, Dad," Caleb said, pressing his face against his father's shoulder. "We're just trying to show you how much we've missed you after you walked out on us, leaving us without a father. Not like it made any difference to me, because I never knew you anyway. You never spent time with me, never told me shit, never did nothing for me. But now you're back . . ."

"And we can't tell you how much we have missed you," Austin continued. "I went through life answering questions not with what I felt, but how I thought you'd feel, how I thought you'd answer the questions. I tried to live up to your expectations. I tried to be perfect because I felt that you left me because I fell so short of that. And now I wonder, are the problems that I'm experiencing even problems at all, or are they just problems because I'm comparing them to some overrated standard that you set for me? But now you're back!"

Julius tried again to answer his sons, but nothing came out again, not even the sound of his voice. They were still holding him, squeezing him even tighter. His back and arms hurt, and he knew that his body would be bruised like never before after this was all over.

"But that's okay, Dad," Marcus said. His voice came from somewhere in the crowd of his sons. "I remember you leaving that night after you beat mother up, but she was okay, and she never talked down about you after that. She always said you were a good man, the best man, and she would always love you. She said that it wasn't your fault that you had to go. Sometimes there are things in people that they can't control, and if it demands something of them, they must do it whether they like it or not. That's what she said, Dad. That you left because you weren't in control of that, and that you couldn't be blamed for it.

"So I believed her, and I respected that. But later on, Dad, she died. I'm telling you now, because I don't know if you heard. There's no way that I could know if you knew. It's not like you showed up to her funeral. It's not like you even called to tell us you were sorry. You did nothing, but let her die. It was the hardest thing I ever went through, Dad. It was something I'll never forget, seeing her on her deathbed like that. It haunts me to this day, and the thought of loving someone like that again and losing them scares me so much that I'm frightened by the idea of even becoming involved with a woman. So I spend my time by my damn self. But that's okay, Dad, because you're back. Isn't that right, guys?" Marcus asked of his brothers. They agreed and hugged Julius even tighter. So tightly that he could feel his air being cut off.

"We just love you so much," they said in unison, and they squeezed him tighter. Julius heard a loud snap and felt an excruciating pain in his side as one of his ribs broke. They were squeezing him so tightly that he could barely breathe, and he could feel himself becoming dizzy. Another rib broke and he cried out in pain, but not a sound came, just his face contorted in extreme agony. He was about to pass out when Marcus said, "We missed you so much. We all did, even Mom."

Then Julius's breathing stopped. He was still alive, but he was no longer breathing. And the pain—it was no longer there even though when he looked down, his sons were still squeezing him to death, and he could hear his bones snapping like dry twigs. He felt compelled to look toward the kitchen, and was shocked to see his wife walking toward him. It was Mary, the same as the day he left her, wearing the same nightgown. It was floating behind her as if filled with air. She walked toward him in what seemed to be slow motion. As she *came nearer a smile widened across her face. Her face was fully made up, her hair was curled, and it blew in the wind with her gown. She was beautiful standing before him, as beautiful as he could ever remember.*

She stepped very close to him, looked him in the face, then looked down to his left hand, carrying the bag. She pulled it from his grasp and reached into it, pulling something out, tossing the bag aside. It was a gun, and she smiled even wider as she pulled back the bolt to see that it was fully loaded. She looked drearily into his eyes for a long moment, as if there was something within him that could explain all her questions away. Then with both her hands around the gun she raised it, leveling it to the space between his eyes. Julius tried to squirm away, tried to fight his way out of the hold his sons had him in, but they were too strong. He tried to cry out but was overcome with violent coughs, hacking up spit, tears running from his squinted eyes. Mary took two steps closer, the tip of the gun's barrel resting against Julius's sweat-covered forehead. Julius shouted, "No! No!" His lips formed the words, but no sound was audible. Then while his sons held him tight, and while he struggled to free himself, the smile drained from Mary's face. "I'm sorry." She did not speak the words, just formed them with her lips, then pulled the trigger.

Julius sprang up in his bed. He was breathing at a frantic rate and was covered with sweat. His pajama top clung to his chest. He looked around in the dark, then smoothed his hand on the area he had been lying in and it was damp with sweat as well. He looked over to see if Cathy had been awakened, but she remained still, sleeping silently. Normally she would have been up by his side questioning him thoroughly, but she had been up with him so many late nights. He was glad that she had not been bothered.

Julius looked around the dark room, not knowing for what, maybe for the six-armed, six-legged monster his sons had become. All he knew was that he was pretty shaken up from the dream. He pulled himself from the bed, feeling a lot weaker than he was accustomed to, and walked through the dark room. He went into his closet, reached up to the top shelf, moved some things around, and felt for the photo.

He asked himself what the dream meant. Upon first thought, it was simple. Stay away from your sons. You would do more harm to them than good. But that was something that Julius didn't want to believe, for if he did, he would never see them again. He could never explain to them why he had left, and he would never know if they forgave him for the horrible thing he did.

In the den he sat on the floor in front of the coffee table. He turned on the small lamp that stood near him and laid his photo on the table. It was a torn, dog-eared snapshot of his sons, taken by one of the earliest Polaroid cameras. He could remember taking the picture, his sons crowding around him waiting for the the picture to develop before peeling off the strip of gummy paper. In the photo the three sat together on a bench, Austin and Marcus on the ends, Caleb smiling in the middle. It was winter, so they had on coats, hats, gloves, and rubber boots. Their sled was nearby, and Julius remembered how he took them out afterward, and took turns pushing them down a snow-covered hill.

His sons were the dearest thing to him, and he wondered, sitting there in the dark, why he had ever left.

He could've tolerated whatever it was that was bothering him, he could've learned to deal with it, and if he didn't—tough! You sacrifice things when you get married and have children, that's what it's all about. But obviously not for me, he told himself. I couldn't be in the position where I was expected to give of myself, where people depended on me, where I had to be the provider of almost everything for three children and a wife. "I couldn't do that," he told himself aloud. It was the last thing he was capable of back then. It seemed as though he would have rather died than stay another day in that house. But the way he felt now, he would give up all that he had lived over the last twenty or so years, just to be given the opportunity to have never left his family. Then again, that wouldn't be fair to Cathy. He loved her with all his heart, and thinking what he had just thought made it seem as though he would trade her as easily. That wasn't true, at least he didn't think it was.

He grabbed the picture and brought it very close to his face. He didn't know what he thought. It was torture to think about it at all. There was no way he could go back and change what had happened, and it was foolish to question his judgment now. He did what was best for him then, and that was all he could've done.

He stared at the picture some more in the dim light, and felt himself become dizzy. He was weak and shouldn't be out on the cold floor. He touched the picture with his finger and traced a line around each one of their faces, then brought it to his lips and kissed it. "I'll see you again."

THIRTEEN

After leaving his wife, Austin found himself driving around all night without anywhere to go. He drove around the city, watching the illuminated streetlights pass outside his window, not stopping, just driving, in anguish over what he had done. Was it the right thing to do or not? He was in a daze, not remembering the streets he drove on or where he was headed, just driving until sunlight slowly peeked through the clouds and lightened the day around him, something he had thought would never happen. His car started to sputter, forcing him to look down at his gas gauge. It was well past *E*. He shut off the car, looked around, and was surprised to see that he had landed in front of his brother's house. What brought him there, he didn't know.

He climbed the stairs and banged on Marcus's door. There was no immediate answer so he banged again until Marcus finally came.

"My car stopped outside. I just have to call a tow, then I'll be out of here, all right?" He walked past Marcus, not looking at him, heading straight for his phone.

"Yes, this is Austin Harris. My car is dead and I need some gas or a tow or something. I'm at—" He pulled the phone away from his mouth. "What's the address here?"

"5102 South Harper," Marcus said.

Austin repeated the information and told them to hurry.

"So what happened?" Marcus asked. Austin had known he would ask and didn't even bother to look up at him, let alone answer the question.

"I need some coffee," Austin said, dragging himself into the kitchen.

"I thought you didn't drink coffee," Marcus said, smiling a little.

"Just where is the coffee? I'm not in the mood for playing, so if you don't have any, then tell me." He stood in front of Marcus, a hand on the counter balancing himself so he wouldn't fall. He was still wearing the t-shirt and sweat pants he had put on the night before. He wore his light leather jacket over it. His hair was flattened to one side, and his face was covered with new beard growth.

"This is the worst I've seen you since we were kids, you know."

Austin frowned at the remark.

"But I do have coffee, and don't worry, I'll make it for you." Marcus began making the coffee while Austin slowly sat down in one of the kitchen chairs. His head was spinning a little, and it hurt like hell, just like the rest of his body. He felt filthy, and all he wanted to do was get a shower, shave, and crawl into bed and forget about the last day or two.

"So, Austin, you going to tell me what happened?" Marcus asked from the counter.

Austin was resting his head in his hands, his elbows on the table, wondering if it were possible to get decent sleep that way. "I don't know if I want to go into it right now, Marcus. I don't know if I feel like being preached to." His head was still in his hands, and he was talking down to the table.

"I'm not going to preach to you, I just want to know what happened. You look like crap. Really, like crap. You smell like alcohol and you can hardly walk. You come banging on my door early in the morning, and you aren't going to even tell me what happened."

"I don't want to hear anything from you, Marcus," Austin said, lifting his head, pointing a finger at him. Marcus nodded.

"I left Trace last night." It was all he said, nothing more. "Is the coffee ready yet?" he grunted.

Marcus stood, sugar in hand, mouth hanging slightly open. "What?" he said. "It sounded like you said you left Trace last night."

"That's what I said. Your hearing hasn't gone bad." Austin was looking Marcus directly in the eyes, waiting for him to get the look. The look right before he went into one of his sermons about how the world should be, and the idea of right and wrong, and all that other idealistic mess. "Don't," Austin said. "I told you, I don't want to hear it. I left and that's it. Now can I just have a cup of coffee and drink it in peace, please?" Marcus passed him a cup.

Mug in hand, Austin looked at his brother and knew he was dying to have his say, and knew he would go to any length to get it. "Go ahead, Marcus," Austin said. "Say what you want to say. It has to come out some time, but it won't make a bit of difference."

"I wasn't going to, but since you asked me, I will." He put his mug down, and the mock-innocent look drained from his face and was replaced with a much more serious stare. "Why did you leave her? What did she do wrong, Austin?"

Austin took a gulp from his coffee and swallowed hard. "She did some things wrong, all right?"

"What things? Tell me," Marcus said.

"Things. Things you wouldn't understand."

"Why not?"

"Because you wouldn't," Austin raised his voice over Marcus's. "You wouldn't because of who you are, because of how you see things, because you've never been married, let alone dated a woman in the last ten years!"

Marcus didn't answer right away. "And is that supposed to get to me?"

"Whatever, Marcus," Austin said.

"So why did you leave her? Was it you getting too good for everybody, again?"

"What is that supposed to mean?" Austin demanded.

"What do you think it means? It means nothing, Austin, absolutely nothing." Marcus just stared at Austin for a long moment after that. It was a judgmental stare. Austin knew, but he didn't give a damn. No one could stand in judgment of him, because they didn't know what he was going through, especially Marcus.

"So why did you leave her?" Marcus asked again.

"I told you, you wouldn't understand," Austin said.

"Well, try me." Marcus raised his voice.

"No."

"Austin! Why not? Who else are you going to talk—"

"No, all right? No!" Austin yelled. He paused for a moment, looking down into his coffee, rubbing a hand on the surface of the mug. He brought it up slowly to his mouth and took a drink. "You aren't my damn psychiatrist, all right?" He lowered his voice to normal. "I don't have to tell you everything that happens with me if I don't want to, and I won't fall apart if I don't."

"I'm just trying to help. I'm your brother," Marcus offered.

"I don't need your help all the damn time. Can't you get that, Marcus? Damn."

"I just don't think you should've left her, that's all," Marcus said, pushing his coffee away.

"Well, that's your opinion, and when you get married and have problems, you can handle it the way you want to. But until then, just mind your own damn business."

"But what about your children? Have you thought about them, or have you forgotten how it feels to lose your—"

"Don't you dare ask me that!" Austin yelled across the table as he stood straight up from his chair, sending the seat banging to the floor. "I thought about my children. They're the most important thing in the world to me. I thought about them, and I think about them every minute of the day, but I'm not going to let them see me miserable twenty-four hours a day. They don't deserve that, and I don't deserve to be miserable like that just so I can live under the same roof. Nothing is going to change. They'll understand that." Austin reached down to pick up the fallen chair.

"I bet you that's what Dad told Mother," Marcus said.

"What!"

"I said, I bet you that's what Dad told Mother," Marcus said, not backing down.

Austin looked over with fire in his eyes. "You take that back, Marcus." He let the chair fall again.

"Why? Situations are the same. Only a fool couldn't see it."

"Take that back," Austin said, moving around the table toward

Marcus. "I'm nothing like that man. I would never leave my family like he left us. Take it back."

"I'm not taking nothing back," he said, picking up his cup of coffee and taking a sip, not paying any attention as his brother moved right next to him.

"Take it back," Austin demanded, slapping the mug out of Marcus's hand to the floor where it broke into large, sharp sections, hot coffee splashing across the table. Austin grabbed him by the shirt, slammed him against the wall, and moved into his face.

Marcus stayed there, not resisting, not trying to free himself, but let out a short cough. "You had so much in common, you two were so much alike, isn't that what he always told you? So why wouldn't you do exactly what he did? To tell you the truth, I expected it. Surprised that it even took you this long," Marcus said.

Austin tightened his grip around Marcus's collar. He could tell by the way Marcus raised his head that he was struggling for air. "I ought to . . ."

"You ought to what?" Marcus said, gagging. His voice was thin and raspy, but still he didn't resist. "Why are you surprised that I would say you'd leave your family? You've already done it once."

Austin tightened the grip even more. He looked into his brother's eyes and they started to bulge a little; his skin was turning red. Austin released him. Marcus sank into a chair, taking large gulps of air, his chest expanding. Austin knew exactly what Marcus was talking about—the time he had left to go to school, just after their mother died. Even though he had his doubts, he had known it was something he had to do.

"That has nothing to do with this, and you know it," Austin said.

"Oh it doesn't? I think it has everything to do with this." Marcus straightened the collar of his shirt, still breathing irregularly. "Things were a little too intense for you so you left, plain and simple. And that's what you're doing now. Let's not make more of this than it is. You're very quick to abandon your family, just like our father was. You did it with me when you left to go to school."

"I had to go to school. Mother wanted me to do that, she even told me that's what she wanted," Austin retaliated.

"C'mon, Austin, what do you think she would've said? She knew how much you wanted to go to school. Do you think she would say,

'Stay home, Austin. Do the responsible thing, and stay with Marcus. Help him take care of the house and raise your younger brother'? She wouldn't have said that, even if that's what she was feeling."

All of a sudden, Austin felt regret and anxiety fall over him, as if he had just done something terrible and wondered if there was enough time to undo it. "Is that what she said? Is that what she wanted me to do?" He grabbed Marcus by the shoulder. "Did she tell you that?"

"No, she didn't. But she wanted me to keep us three together, and I don't think you going away to school is what she would've regarded as being together."

Austin turned his back to Marcus. He saw his mother lying in that bed, in that dark room, telling him to go to school. Make the most of himself, because that opportunity wouldn't come again. He hadn't really wanted to go, he was scared, but it seemed like it was her wish, so he went. But now, after hearing this, he felt betrayed. He felt his mother had lied to him, and he wondered if he could trust any of the things she had told him so long ago.

"You're like him." Marcus's voice seemed to be coming from far away, from down a long echoing hall. "It seems like family doesn't mean much to you. I call and call you, but we barely see each other. You don't even want to see Caleb. I don't care how you feel about him, he's still your brother.

"Sometimes you can be a selfish bastard," Marcus said. "I know how it feels to give, and not get back from you. I've known it for a long time, and it's not a good feeling, but I've accepted it because you're my brother. But I don't want you to put Trace through that. I don't want you to give up on your marriage for simple foolish reasons that can be resolved. You have so much more riding on this than whether or not someone sees you as average, or whether or not your wife is perfect or if she works, or went to school."

Austin turned to face Marcus. "Are you finished? Have you said everything that you're going to say?"

"Austin, I just want you to know—"

"Are you finished?" Austin yelled.

"I guess so," Marcus said.

Austin walked up to Marcus, stood very close to him, their bodies almost touching. "You don't have any idea what you're talking about.

What makes you think you can sit there and criticize me for doing something about *my* life? You don't know what it's like to be me, have my problems, my concerns, deal with what I deal with every day. It's very easy to sit there and give your damn advice when you have no obligations and no responsibilities, when all there is is you." He poked his finger into Marcus's chest.

"It's easy when you can work when you want to and not worry about a thing. Come and go as you please and not think about being anywhere except where you want to be. Not being expected to be a loving husband when you worked all day and don't feel like doing a damn thing but crawl in bed, hide your head under the covers, and hope no one finds you for a week. You don't have to hear from some woman that you're being inconsiderate, or selfish, or aloof, or stubborn. The only person you have to deal with is you. So don't tell me that sometimes I can be a selfish bastard. You're the bastard for not considering my situation before you open your mouth and try to instruct me on what I should do about my life."

Marcus stood there, looking blankly at Austin. He didn't say anything.

Austin stuck out his hand. "Give me the keys to your car."

"What?" Marcus said.

"Give me the keys to your car. I can't be here another minute, and I'm not about to walk." Marcus put his hand into his pocket, then hesitated.

"The truck is coming with gas. I'll leave my keys," Austin insisted. "You shouldn't be complaining. Mine is the Mercedes, you only have a Honda."

Marcus fished the keys out and Austin snatched them from him. "I'm not going to say thank you for what you said. You said a lot of stupid things without thinking like you always do, but then again I expected that from you, that's why I didn't want to get into this in the first place. I don't appreciate you comparing me with our father. I'm nothing like him, I know that, and if you don't then that's your problem.

"About me going away to school, I never told you this, but I really didn't want to go. Mother said she wanted me to, so I went because of her, not me. And my children . . . You often mention how we're brothers. I would've liked to think that you knew me well enough to know I would never do that to them, that I do remember what it was like to have Dad leave. It hurt then, and sometimes it still hurts now, and for you to think that I would deliberately put my children through the same hell, you must think very low of me. But, you know what, I don't care. I just don't care." Austin opened the front door. "I'll get your car back to you soon."

Austin drove around without knowing where it was he wanted to go. He wasn't going to work. He'd been in such a hurry to get out of the house last night that he hadn't packed anything appropriate, and it didn't matter to him anyway because he felt like shit. Fact was, he had no place to go. He had left his wife, given up his home, and now he was on his own.

Austin picked up Marcus's car phone and keyed in the number for his house. He didn't know why or what he'd say when his wife picked up, but he did it anyway, almost as if he had no control.

"Hello," Trace answered. Her voice was the same as it was all the time, but he could detect just a little sadness in it.

"Hello," she said again. Austin didn't answer. He was thinking of something to say, but nothing came to mind, and what little did was stupid, awkward, and without consideration of what had just happened.

"Hello . . . Austin, is that you?" Trace said, her voice filling with despair.

He was startled and frightened for some reason. As if he was doing something terribly wrong by being on the phone with his wife and not saying anything. He disconnected the call. His heart beat hard in his chest, a bead of sweat rolled down the side of his face. He had to know what was going on at his house. He had to know if his children were all right, if Trace was all right. Had she told them yet? He had to know these things. He found himself passing by the familiar stores and taking familiar turns toward his house. He parked his car a few houses down and sat there for ten minutes deciding what he would do.

He jumped out of the car and started down the street toward his house. He craned his head in every direction, making sure no one saw him. It really wouldn't have made a difference because he was only walking to his own house, but at that moment he felt as though he was trespassing on some secret government property. He walked across the lawn and toward the back of the house, moving light on his feet, still looking, making sure no one caught sight of him. He slid into some bushes surrounding the house, then edged his way to the living room window.

He didn't look in right away, just flattened his back against the house, trying to steady the rapid beating of his heart. When he had regained composure, he slowly turned and peered into the window. He saw his children, Bethany and Troy, playing, then quickly ducked his head back down for fear they had seen him. A few moments later, he lifted his head again, this time much slower. He caught sight of them again. They were playing on the floor, Troy with some GI Joe guy and Bethany with the orange Muppet thing. They looked as happy as they ever had, unaffected by the world around them, as if nothing had happened.

He placed his hand against the glass and moved his face right up to it so he could see better. His breath fogged the glass and obscured his vision so he moved back a little. They were so beautiful, he thought. He wanted to run in there, grab the two of them up, hold them so close and never let them go, never put them down. But how could he do that, then tell them he was leaving? He would only confuse them. He would only confuse himself. But it was so painful to see them there and not be able to do anything. They were playing as though their father not being there made no difference, as though he no longer existed or never did. It was like some weird scene from *It's a Wonderful Life*, but there was nothing wonderful about it at all.

He pulled himself away from the window and stayed against the side of the house. His heart sank. Trace obviously had not told them, and he didn't know how to feel about that. He was glad that they seemed to be happy, but he felt that maybe she didn't think it was important enough to tell them just yet. He looked in the window one final time and smiled as he saw them play, realizing that he would see them again.

He moved around to the other side of the house, expecting Trace to be in the family room. He could barely see through the curtains, but he could tell that she wasn't there. He moved toward the kitchen, stepping cautiously through the bushes, keeping his head low, making sure no one outside or inside the house saw him.

When he got to the kitchen window, he looked in and saw Trace.

There she was sitting at the table watching a small pot cooking over a flame on the stove. She stared at it without emotion. Austin could only see the side of her face, and even that was blocked by her left hand as it supported her chin.

Austin stood there for a while just looking at her, preparing to duck just in case she felt his stare and was moved to look in his direction. He had decided he would go when all of a sudden Trace slid her hand from her chin to her forehead. She moved her other hand to her eyes and he could see her body jerking. She laid her hands flat on the table and put her head on top of them. She was crying, he knew it, and he felt terrible.

She lifted her head and he could see the tears streaming down her face, but she didn't try to wipe them away, she just let them fall. She wrapped her arms around herself as she cried, her head shaking from side to side with grief. Austin saw all this. He wanted to go in there and talk to her, comfort her, but then he saw her head turn quickly toward the door. She brought her hands up and started to smear away the tears. Bethany walked in. Austin could tell she was asking why her mother was crying, but Trace just shook her head and gave her a strained smile. She lifted Bethany to her lap. The child wiped the tears away from her mother's eyes, then wrapped her arms around her neck.

It was all Austin had to see. He stepped away from the window and pushed his way through the bushes, straight through the bushes, not worrying if anyone saw him or not. He walked like a zombie, his eyes unblinking, in a trance of regret, remorse, and guilt. He trudged out to Marcus's car, got in, and drove off.

FOURTEEN

It had been days since Marcus had talked to Austin and he was becoming worried. Not about his well-being—he didn't think Austin would do anything foolish, the man was too rational for that. He just wanted to talk to him, make sure that the argument they had had was on the same level as the ones they had always had. The same ones they had as kids. The argument over the bike, or who gets to watch what on TV, or who gets to sit in the front seat on the way home from the store. He didn't want their relationship to be broken regardless of what had been said, or how hateful the argument seemed at the time. They were just words thrown between two brothers, words that only carried weight during the actual argument, but lost their power, their hateful meanings, after the stupid thing was over. That was how Marcus felt about it, and he hoped Austin felt the same.

Austin would carry the thing around in his head like a tape, rewinding it, playing it back, and going over it, trying to make sure what he said and did was right. Clarifying that he had made no mistake during the discussion, before he could finally get the thing out of his head and put his mind to rest. Marcus figured he was probably still somewhere going over the tape. Side A, the argument with his wife. Side B, the argument with Marcus. He hoped that wasn't the case because he didn't want him torturing himself like that, knowing he had no one to go to. The people he had argued with were more or less the only two he could trust.

Marcus picked up the phone and called Austin's firm.

"Austin Harris and Associates, this is Reecie speaking, how may I help you?" a sweet-sounding voice asked.

Reecie, Marcus thought. The name sounded familiar. "Is Austin Harris there, please?"

"I'm sorry, sir, he isn't. Chad Dubois is taking his calls if you need assistance."

"No, no. Do you know when he'll be back?" Marcus asked.

"No, I don't. But you can leave a message and I'll have him return your call promptly when he returns."

"Uh, that's okay." Marcus hesitated. "I'll just call back. Thank you." He hung up.

"Damn, where are you, man?" Marcus said aloud. He picked up the phone again and considered dialing Austin's house. It was worth a try.

"Hello." It was Trace on the phone. Her voice sounded a bit shaky and for a moment Marcus considered hanging up.

"Hello," she called again.

"Hi, Trace, this is Marcus," he finally said. "Would Austin happen to be around there, by any chance?"

"You know the answer to that question, Marcus," she answered.

"What do you mean?"

"Don't play dumb, Marcus. I know you were the first person he told."

Marcus paused for a moment and didn't say anything. Neither did Trace.

"So how are you doing?" Marcus asked.

"I'm doing okay, I guess. Making it, all things considered."

"Have you spoken to him?"

"Yes. He called a couple of days ago to speak to the kids, and to let me know he was all right and not to worry. How am I supposed to do that? I don't know where he is, Marcus. I don't know what he's doing, and worst of all, I don't know what he's going to do, about me, about the kids, about anything." Her voice was starting to fill with emotion, and Marcus recognized that as his cue to get off. Not that he didn't want to provide support for her, but he didn't want her to see him as being on her side. He had no side, that wasn't the way he saw things. But if he had to be mistaken for playing a side, it would have to be Austin's.

"He'll do the right thing," was the answer he provided her with. "Do you need anything? Are the kids all right?"

"Yes. We have plenty of money in the bank. We're fine, but thanks, Marcus," Trace said.

"Anytime. I'll call you back to check on you from time to time, all right?"

"Okay, and if you see him, would you please tell him to call me," Trace said. "Tell him I won't beg him to come back or anything, I know that's why he's not calling me. Tell him I just want to talk to him, know he's all right." Her voice sounded faint, trailing off, as if about to disappear altogether.

"I'll tell him. Bye, Trace." He hung up the phone and started pacing around the room. He felt helpless. He had tried every possibility he knew to contact his brother. He thought about jumping in the car and driving around, hoping to see him on the street. But that wouldn't do, that was the type of thing you did if your dog ran away, not your brother. Besides, he had Austin's Mercedes and he would feel funny about wheeling the big thing around town like it was his own.

The fact was, he didn't know what to do, had no clue, and would have to just sit and wait and hope that his hard-headed, over-thinking brother would call him or come by.

Marcus was in the kitchen when the doorbell rang. He ran to the door and opened it. Austin was standing there looking pathetic and rejected by the world. He was still wearing the leather jacket and the same pair of sweatpants, but he had managed to change his shirt to a red t-shirt with a hole torn in the belly. A full beard of a few days had grown on his face, and his hair could have used the serious attention of a comb.

"Damn, man, come in," Marcus said. "You look like hell."

"Considering what I'm going through, how am I supposed to look?" He gave Marcus his car keys back.

"Sit down," Marcus insisted. "Do you want some of my food? Are you hungry, or would you like some lemonade?"

Austin sat down and took off his jacket. "No food, just lemonade," he said.

Marcus went in the kitchen to get the lemonade. He was happy to see Austin, and even though his brother looked uncomfortable, he seemed fine. He didn't appear tired, he wasn't dragging, and there weren't any dark circles under his eyes or anything like that. Sure he needed a shave and maybe a change of clothes, but just like he said, it was to be expected.

"Here," Marcus said, passing the glass to his brother. Austin took it without saying thank you.

"So what's been up?" Austin asked.

"What do you mean, what's up? What's up with you? You all but disappeared off the face of the planet, and you act like nothing happened."

Austin took a sip of the lemonade, pulled it away from his lips, brought it back to his mouth and downed the rest of it in a few giant swallows. "Well, I had to find someplace to live. It took a couple of days, that's all." He set the glass down and leaned back on the sofa.

"Do you want some more?" Marcus asked eagerly.

"Uh-uh."

"So where are you staying?" Marcus asked, putting his glass down.

"Holiday Inn. It's just temporary," Austin said. He was looking around the room as if he had never been there.

"I see," Marcus said. He didn't know what to say next. There was a void in their conversation, and he couldn't seem to come up with anything that wouldn't sound like a bad attempt at small talk. They both looked at each other at the same time, then both looked away. Austin was tapping a finger on the back of the sofa.

"I'm sorry about the other day, man," Marcus said. "I said some pretty stupid things."

"Don't worry about it," Austin said, not looking in Marcus's direction.

"I just don't want you to—"

"I said, forget it," Austin said, focusing on Marcus. "It's no big deal. People get mad and things come out without them giving much thought to how it will affect the other person involved. Besides, I shouldn't have grabbed you and roughed you up like that." He looked away again.

"Well, I shouldn't have let you get away with grabbing me and roughing me up like that."

Austin looked blank. "What do you mean, let me get away with it?"

"I mean, you don't think I didn't do anything because I couldn't, do you?"

"I knew you couldn't. I grabbed you by the collar and swung you up against that wall like a rag doll," Austin said, illustrating the move for Marcus. "And that's just how you felt. Like a rag doll." Austin smiled briefly after the remark.

"Oh, you think so?" Marcus said. "If I wanted to, all I would've had to do was knock those Popsicle-stick arms out the way, grab you and toss you across the room into the kitchen sink, where you could've had a bath." Marcus shook his head, smiling at the thought. "And come to think of it, that wouldn't be that bad of an idea right now, because you're smelling bad."

"I'm smelling bad?" Austin said, getting up from the couch, and walking toward Marcus. "I'll have you know that I was in the shower for ten minutes this morning."

"Well, I forgot to tell you this, but sometimes you have to turn on the water for it to do any goooood!" Before he even finished his sentence, Austin was on him. He jumped at him, grabbed him by the collar again, and the chair tipped over, sending them both to the floor. Austin was on top of him, straddling him.

"Knock my Popsicle-stick arms away now, big man. Show me how tough you are." He smacked him lightly in the face a few times.

"You asked for it," Marcus said, raising his midsection, and bumping Austin off him. He rolled on top of Austin, but Austin was quicker and stronger than he had thought. Austin rolled on his stomach and raised up to all fours, lifting Marcus on his back, as if he was giving him a horseback ride. "Git along, doggeeeee!" Marcus said, waving a hand in the air as if he was riding a bull.

Austin raised up to his knees, sending his brother backwards to the floor. Austin fell down with him. Marcus had Austin in a headlock squeezing his neck, so Austin grabbed Marcus's leg and started to bend it up toward him, flexing the joint the wrong way.

"Oowwww!" Marcus cried out. "That hurts!"

"I know it hurts," Austin struggled to speak. "But I'm not going to let you go until you stop choking me, asshole."

"Asshole, huh." He squeezed his neck, which prompted Austin to pull a little harder on Marcus's leg.

"I told you that hurts!"

"Well . . . let go of my neck," Austin choked out.

"Let go of my leg," Marcus cried. They both lay struggling on the floor of Marcus's living room, their bodies twisted and contorted, each trying to gain the advantage.

"Okay, on three," Marcus said. "We'll let go at the same time. Okay."

Austin nodded his head.

"One two three!" They both counted, but neither one of them moved. "You were supposed to let go," Marcus said.

"So were you," Austin said, his air being cut off.

"This time on two. For real," Marcus said.

Austin grunted in agreement.

"One two!" They both let go. Austin rolled from atop his brother and grabbed for his neck, making loud breathing noises, sucking in gobs of air. Marcus bent down and rubbed his knee furiously, bending it slowly to make sure nothing was broken. "You almost maimed me for life," Marcus said.

"Well, you almost strangled me to death."

"Well, you just got a taste of your own medicine then, huh?" Marcus looked over at Austin. He was sitting on the carpet, his legs crossed, the neck of his t-shirt stretched all the way down to expose half of his chest, and his hair even more messed up than when he originally walked in. He looked like an overgrown third-grader that had gotten beaten up, then wrongly accused for starting the thing, and punished by half an hour in the corner. Marcus couldn't help but break up with laughter.

"What's so funny?" Austin said.

"You. You ought to see yourself," Marcus said, grabbing his knee.

Austin looked down at himself and started to laugh as well. "Well, you look pretty funny yourself, lying there like your leg has just been amputated."

They both laughed for a while, then lay across the carpet. It was just like when they were kids. They would wrestle first, and then when they were done, they would stretch out across the floor, still breathing hard, and look up at the ceiling and talk about anything and everything. Batman and Robin, which kind of cookie tasted better, what they would be when they grew up, things like that. Back when life gave them really nothing to worry about, or no serious things to talk about. Then they would always slap each other five after the conversation as a kind of formal closing.

"You ever think about Ma?" Marcus asked, speaking softly, still staring at the ceiling.

"Yeah. Sometimes. And sometimes I'll have dreams about her," Austin said. "It'll be like she never died, and then I'll wake up, and then I remember. I try and go back to sleep on those mornings."

"Yeah," Marcus said. He had similar dreams himself. They were the worst, because it was like having a second chance to do all the things he wanted to do for her, to tell her the things that he felt he didn't tell her before she died. But when he woke up, he realized that none of the things said made their way to his mother. It was all just a dream, foolish babbling in the night.

"Why do you think Dad left?" Marcus asked, looking over to his brother.

"I . . . I don't know."

"Do you think it was us?"

"I don't think so. I mean, I can't say for sure, but I really don't think so. And I don't think it was Ma either. I just think he had some personal problems that he had to deal with," Austin said in a dreamy voice.

"Well, I think that's all an excuse. Personal problems or not, that's no reason to just disappear without even keeping contact. We don't even know if he's dead or alive. Not that it'd make a difference to me."

Austin turned his head and looked in Marcus's direction.

"Would it matter to you?" Marcus asked.

"I don't know."

"If he came back and wanted you to forgive him, would you? I know I wouldn't."

Austin thought for a moment. "I don't know that either. It would depend on what his reason was, and if he was really sincere or not."

It didn't matter what Austin said, Marcus thought. He wouldn't take that man back, not after what he did, he just wouldn't. His father could come in claiming to have been abducted by aliens, it still wouldn't make one ounce of difference. And as far as sincerity went, the man probably didn't know what the word meant. It wasn't that Marcus thought his father was a liar among so many other things, but he did feel he was a coward, and negative traits like lying just seemed to walk hand in hand with cowardice. Marcus turned to see his brother staring out into space. He was pulling at the hole in his shirt, looking as though his mind was a million miles away. Marcus knew he was thinking about his family.

"About you and Trace, whatever you want to do, I'll stick with you, you know that, don't you?" Marcus said.

Austin came out of his dream state and looked over at Marcus. "I really don't know what I'm going to do, but I know that you'll be there for me. I know that." Austin stuck out his hand. "Give me five."

Marcus reached over and slapped Austin's hand with his own.

FIFTEEN

Caleb sat on a bench near his apartment. The sun was going down and he watched as it set slowly behind the building in which he lived. He wondered if some of its light made its way into his apartment and if Sonya saw it, making her feel better about the loser she had chosen as a mate.

He had been sitting out there all day picking pebbles from the ground, tossing them out a few feet in front of him, as though the space was a lake or the ocean. He would toss a pebble and imagine it being swallowed up by the blue water, see the ripples reverberate out into the vastness of the sea, and envision the pebble dropping for miles into the blackness of the deep water. It was what he did as a kid when he got in trouble and was told to disappear for a while.

Spilling milk across the carpet or scarring the walls with a red Crayola seemed to be such overwhelming problems at that time. How he wished for them now. He looked at his building again, and wondered if he should even go back there. It was obvious it didn't matter to Sonya either way; she had stopped caring about him. She had proved it the other night, and he wondered how long she had actually felt that way. He had wandered about the streets all day thinking about it. It was something that he felt he wasn't even capable of dealing with, because she was his entire life. He had told her on many occasions how much he loved her, but she just smiled and nodded her head, saying the same back, as though it was no big deal.

It might not have been to her, but to Caleb it was the biggest deal he could imagine. She was just the mother of his only child, the woman who had been there with him through all the trouble that he'd been in, and was there constantly to tell him that he was much more than a loser. The little confidence he had left was there because she kept him from losing it, from letting it go. It was why he loved her so much, more than even himself.

He didn't want to be without her, but he wondered, would it be better for her, would it be better for his son? He bent down, picked another pebble from the pavement, and tossed it into the deep blue cement ocean.

No. He wouldn't leave. Not just because it was a bad idea altogether, but because he just couldn't live without Sonya and Jahlil. They were all he had in his life. They were what gave him the reason to live. Without them, he would have surely been drunk in a gutter somewhere, or crumpled in a Dumpster, wearing filthy, torn clothing, a bullet swimming in his gut.

He got up from the bench, telling himself it was okay to go to his building. Sonya would still want to see him, even though he had failed on so many occasions. She would still love him and his son would still accept him as his father.

Caleb let himself in the apartment and closed the door behind him. He saw his son sitting at the kitchen table, Sonya spooning macaroni and cheese onto his plate. Sonya turned after Caleb closed the door. She dropped the spoon onto the red plastic plate and ran to Caleb and threw her arms around him. She squeezed him tight, then kissed him on the lips. Caleb was shocked.

"Where in the hell have you been all day?" Sonya said, stepping back.

Caleb didn't answer her, just walked past, his head bowed, knowing the hug and kiss thing had to have been a mistake.

"I'm talking to you, Caleb. Where have you been? I've been worried."

Caleb sat in the chair Sonya had been in. "Hey, Jahlil," he said in a less than enthused voice, patting the child on the head. "You didn't seem so worried the other night."

"What does that have to do with this?" she asked. She took the chair opposite his.

"When I needed to talk to you, when I needed you to listen, you didn't even care. You just lay in bed like it didn't make a difference to you either way. Like I don't matter. You know what I'm going through. You know that I'm trying. All I wanted was a little support from you and you couldn't even give me that."

"I . . . I . . ." Sonya tried forming words, but couldn't. "I don't believe you. First of all, I was asleep, all right? I was tired as hell because I worked all day. And when I was done with that, I picked up Jahlil, brought him home, cleaned up the house, made him dinner, played with him till he got tired, bathed him, then put him to sleep, and then did the same for my tired ass. Where were you?"

"I was out trying—"

"But that doesn't even matter," Sonya cut him off. "You say that I don't support you. There is no more support than what I give to you. Do you understand that?"

Caleb turned his nose up.

"Every time you lose a job, I tell you, don't worry, baby. It's not your fault, there will be another one. Every time you get your ass in trouble with the law, I come down there and bail you out, and curse out every fool walking in a blue uniform, telling them that you were wrongly accused." She got up from her chair and walked around in front of Caleb so he could see her. "Every time you're questioning yourself about whether you're a man or not, or whether you're supporting me and this child, I hold you up, I tell you that all you need to do is be here and keep on trying. Everything will work out fine sooner or later, don't worry. And you tell me I don't support you. I'm tired and sleepy one night, and that wipes away all the other times that I held your hand when you fell down off the swing and scraped your knee."

Caleb turned to her, looking her angrily in the eyes. "And what is that supposed to mean?"

"It means that you're acting like a child. No. A big grown-ass baby.

Caleb, I get tired sometimes. I can't be there every time you have something to tell me, and sometimes even if I am, I don't always want to hear about that depressing crap. How the man is holding you down, how they want you to trade your life for a nine to five. That stuff gets me down. It's depressing enough just living in this dump. Caleb, the world doesn't revolve around you."

Caleb was shocked by the remark, but he told himself he shouldn't have been. He looked over at her and she looked back at him as though she had said nothing at all wrong and had no intention of taking it back. There was silence for a long moment. Jahlil looked back and forth at them, then obviously bored with the discussion, yawned and stretched his arms out, one hand still holding his spoon.

"So what, should I leave?" Caleb asked.

Sonya's stare turned to him quickly, concern in her eyes. "What!"

"You heard me," Caleb said, standing. "Should I leave, since the world doesn't revolve around me?"

The tiny spoon Jahlil was holding dropped to the floor. The child was rubbing his eyes, overcome by sleep.

"You wait right there!" Sonya said, looking angered. She held a finger up, directing Caleb not to move an inch. "Let me put him to bed, and I'll be right back." She grabbed the child, hoisted him up to her shoulder. A long, thin line of drool stretched from the plate to the child's mouth as his head rolled limp with sleep about his neck. "I'll be right back," she said again, her voice quaking with emotion this time. Caleb had no idea what was up, and he was almost afraid to find out. He didn't think he had said anything that would get that kind of response out of her. He sat in the chair, crossed his legs trying to look carefree, then uncrossed them, feeling he appeared self-conscious.

Sonya came in the room looking more disturbed than when she had walked out.

"So that's what our relationship is worth to you. You want to leave because you aren't getting as much attention as you feel you should, is that right?"

Caleb didn't reply. He threw one leg over the other, crossed his arms, and looked to the ceiling to imply that nothing that she said mattered. It was how he felt she had treated him the other night.

"Shit, Caleb answer me!" She picked up Jahlil's plastic dish and sent it sailing past Caleb's head, where it crashed and spun in the corner in an explosion of cheese and macaroni curls. Caleb jumped out of his chair.

"What the hell was that?" he shouted.

"Is that all our relationship means to you? You don't get your damn way and you're ready to take off. After all we've been through, you're ready to leave me by myself. And what about your son? Huh, can you tell me what you're going to do about him?" She stood with her hands on her almost nonexistent hips. Her eyes were wide and her chest heaved up and down as she stared at Caleb, waiting for his response. She looked scared. Caleb had had no clue that he meant that much to her.

"I don't want to leave," he said under his breath.

"Speak up, I can't hear you," Sonya directed.

"I don't want to leave!" He raised his voice, almost yelling at her. "I thought you wanted me to." He rubbed his hands together, then stuck them in his pockets as though he was looking for something, brought them out again, and smoothed them over his jeans. He looked at Sonya for a brief moment, then looked away, sitting down again. "I let you down so many times that I thought you were tired of me. I thought you didn't want to hear any more excuses, regardless if they were my fault or not. I came in here last night feeling the world was falling apart, and I wanted to talk to you about it to ease my mind. But it seemed like you didn't care. I thought you were done, and it's not like I can blame you. I don't know why you allowed me to stay this long. I ain't shit but a loser."

After saying that, he found the courage to look up at Sonya. He felt weak, like a child. He wanted to cry and be held and be told not to worry, everything would be all right, but she had done that so many times for him in the past that he didn't know if it would work this time, or if she even cared to do it, or if he deserved it.

Sonya looked down on him, sympathy in her eyes. She walked over to him and stood in front of him. Caleb saw her feet near his; he could smell her perfume, and all he wanted to do was lose himself in it. Breathe her in, be smothered by it. He saw her hand dangling by her side. He reached out, caressed it, and gently pulled her closer to him. She didn't resist and he was grateful for that. She was standing right before him, her waist at the level of his face. He noticed how her shirt was pushed into the waist of her jeans. He reached for her with his other hand and laid it flat against her stomach. He pulled her closer still, close enough to place the side of his face against her belly like he used to do so long ago when she was pregnant with their son.

"I'm sorry," he admitted to her, but not just to her but to everyone. Everyone that came in contact with him and was disappointed by his behavior, and everyone he had wronged in one way or another, because there were so many.

Sonya dropped to her knees and wrapped herself around him, letting his face fall into her shoulder. "Why do you have to be so damn hard on yourself all the time?" She rubbed his hair and kissed him on his cheek. "Why can't you just say the hell with everybody, and everything, and just don't worry anymore."

"Because I can't. I have responsibilities." There was that word again, and he wished he had never learned its meaning.

Sonya pulled away from him slightly so she could look in his face. "We've always made it before. We'll do it again. I just don't like when you get like this."

"How are we going to make it this time?"

"What do you mean?" Sonya asked.

"You said the landlord came down here looking for the rent. I don't have any money and you don't get paid for two weeks. How are we going to make it this time?"

Sonya stood up from the floor and walked toward the sink. She turned her back on Caleb and started to rummage through the dirty dishes, cutting the water on, then off, and back on, then back off again. "Because I hit the numbers, that's how. I hit the lottery." She turned to Caleb, a smile on her face.

"You hit the lottery. Right," Caleb said, not believing a word. "You don't even play."

"I know, but I played the other day. I said, what the hell. I . . . I spent one dollar, my last dollar. I played and I won. One thousand dollars. So I paid this month's rent and next month's, and we even got a little money left. So you don't have to worry, at least for a couple of months. How about that?"

Caleb didn't know what to say. He looked at Sonya with skepticism, but she stuck to her story, so he believed her. Why would she lie? Besides, where would she get that kind of money if she didn't win it? Nowhere. That kind of money didn't normally make itself available to people like them.

Then something crept into Caleb's head.

"Marcus!" Caleb blurted, almost as if the name took him by surprise.

"What?" Sonya said, shocked.

"Tell me you didn't get money from my brother."

"Who?"

"Marcus. You know who." Caleb was angry at the possibility of her even considering taking a handout from his brother.

"No. I told you, I won the lottery."

Then Caleb walked over to her. Stood right in her face.

"Are you telling me the truth? Just tell me. I won't be mad and we'll give back the money, and that'll be the end of it."

Sonya didn't speak a word, just looked at him blankly.

"Did you take it?" Caleb asked again, and he was hoping that she didn't. God how he was hoping, because even though he had said he wouldn't be mad, if she had lied, he knew he would be furious. So with hope in his voice he asked Sonya one last time.

"You didn't get the money from Marcus, did you?"

Sonya looked directly into Caleb's eyes and said, "No."

Caleb looked at her, scrutinizing her for a moment, then all of a sudden, a huge smile appeared on his face.

"I knew you wouldn't do that to me, baby," he said, grabbing her face between the palms of his hands and giving her a quick kiss. Then he placed his hands around her waist. "And about the other night. You didn't give up on me?"

"No, I didn't give up on you. I was tired, Caleb, that's all." She kissed him on the lips. "Can't I be tired sometimes?"

"You won the lottery," Caleb said, smiling. "I still can't believe it."

"Yup," Sonya said.

"Our luck must be changing, huh?"

"Must be," Sonya agreed.

Caleb looked at her for a long moment, then kissed her on the forehead. "I love you, you know that?"

"Yeah, I do," Sonya said.

Caleb went into the bathroom, pulled back the shower curtain and started the water. He looked in the mirror and was almost astonished at the person looking back at him. It was not that he was surprised to see his own face, just surprised to see his face smiling. It was something that he had almost forgotten he was capable of doing. For some reason or another he was getting a break. The hard times seemed to be lightening up on him a little.

Before he stepped into the shower he called out to Sonya, "Hey, baby, did Marcus call me back today?"

"Ummm," she called back.

Caleb stepped into the shower, waiting for her answer. The warm water felt good running down his tired body.

"No, he didn't call, but some other guy did, I forgot to tell you."

Caleb barely heard her over the running water. "What did you say?" He stuck his head out from behind the shower curtain.

"Some guy called. I wrote it down." Sonya rummaged through a drawer where all the junk was stashed and came up with an envelope with a thousand messages scribbled across it. "Ummm, Mr. Benning called from Main Frame Software or something."

Caleb knew he had heard her right, but he wanted to make sure. He wanted to see the paper she wrote it on, wanted to hold it in his hand. He immediately cut off the shower water, jumped out of the tub, almost falling and banging his head against the toilet, wrapped the towel around him without drying off, and skipped to the kitchen on his toes dripping wet.

"You're dripping water all over the place," Sonya said. "Don't you know how to dry off?"

"Just show me the message," Caleb said. Sonya gave it to him. He scanned the envelope. She pointed to the scribble that was his message, and he read it aloud.

"Joseph Benning called, Main Frame Software, 12:45." He read it over again, twice to make sure he had it right. Benning had even left a phone number. "12:45, why didn't you tell me about this earlier. This is important!"

Sonya didn't turn away from the sudsy dishwater to answer him. "You weren't home, Caleb. How was I supposed to tell you?"

"What number is this?" Caleb asked.

"He said you have his work number, so he said if you come in after hours give him a call at home."

Caleb couldn't believe it. He was on a roll, and this would be the thing that would top off his incredible streak of good luck. "What time is it?"

"The clock is right there, like it's been for the past five years. What's wrong with you, Caleb? And who is that anyway?" she said, rinsing suds from her hands.

"Nobody, don't worry about it yet," he answered. "But if things work out the way I hope, he'll be the man to change my life."

SIXTEEN

Lately Marcus had noticed a huge void in his life. Something was missing. He was so bored that if he didn't get out and do something he would lose his mind. He thought only for a moment about going upstairs to his work. He had been doing that all day, and there was only so much illustrating a person could do in a lifetime. Besides, his characters could not do for him what they used to. Not that he cared any less for his work, but it could not compare to a warm body, an enticing smile, or pleasant conversation; it just could not compare.

He tried calling Caleb.

"Sorry, man. Me and the family are about to grab something to eat, but you're welcome to come over," he said.

Marcus thought about it for a moment, then turned him down.

"Naw," he said, feeling sorry for himself. "You guys go ahead. We'll get together some other time."

Marcus hung up the phone, then sat down on his sofa. He kicked his feet up on the table and thought about who else he could call. He thought for one moment, and that was all it took to realize that there was no one he knew. He had tried so hard for so long to distance himself from relationships that now when he needed just a friend to spend time with, he had no one. There was no one to call outside of his brother. How pathetic, he thought. Then he remembered something. He sprang from the sofa and climbed the stairs two at a time.

He went into his bedroom, swung open the closet door and yanked out his jacket, the same jacket he had worn when he met Austin for drinks. He went through the side pockets and came out with nothing. The inside pockets—nothing. He started to panic because he knew he hadn't thrown the thing away. He pushed his hand into the breast pocket and finally felt the tiny card that Austin had given him. He flipped it over and there it was, Austin's secretary's name and her number jotted across the back. There might be hope for him yet, he thought. Marcus didn't know her, but Austin had said he would tell her to expect his call and that was good enough for Marcus, considering how he was feeling at that moment.

He went to the phone with no hesitation.

"Hello," Reecie answered.

Immediately Marcus thought her voice sounded warm and sweet. And after they had talked for a while, he asked her out for that same night.

"That's kind of quick, don't you think? This is the first time I've ever spoken to you in my life," Reecie said.

"Well, I'm not really doing anything, and the night is so beautiful, I just thought I'd ask." She sounded as though she was hesitating, when Marcus said, "Look, it's not as though you're meeting a stranger. You work for my brother, so it's not as though you have to worry about me doing something crazy. If you're worried about how I look, I look like him, but better. If you want to know how I act, a little like him, but more personable, more caring, more talkative, and I have a better personality. So what do you think? We can meet at the outdoor cafe on Michigan. Neutral meeting place."

"I don't normally do this," she said.

At that point he knew he had her. "Well, give it a shot this one time. You never know what can come of it, and if it doesn't work out then you haven't lost anything for trying."

The night was even more beautiful than Marcus had imagined. The sky was clear and full of stars. The temperature was warm, and a steady breeze blew off the lake. He arrived late, because he had spent too much time getting dressed, but he wanted to make sure that he looked just right. He had on a pair of faded jeans, some loafers, a collarless shirt and a sport jacket. The outfit was relaxed, but he felt good, and he thought he looked good as well.

When he walked up to the restaurant, all the outdoor tables were taken by couples or larger parties except for one that was unoccupied and one that was taken by a beautiful woman. He was hoping that she was Reecie, but he wasn't sure. He didn't want to plop down next to her and have the woman yell rape and start beating on him with one of her shoes.

He sat down at the empty table. It was facing the woman so he figured he would just sit there for a while and admire her beauty, and wait for Reecie, if indeed that wasn't her. He ordered a sparkling water and sipped on it, occasionally looking up at the stars, breathing in the clean air from the lake, and once in a while looking over at the woman. She was truly beautiful. She had the biggest brown eyes and the prettiest lips he had seen on a woman. Her complexion was a flawless almond brown. Her hair was perfect, cut short just the way he liked on a woman. She was wearing a spring dress and matching sandals. Her legs were crossed and Marcus couldn't help but notice them, how smooth and shapely they were. She was perfect. Even her toes were perfectly manicured and painted with bright orange and yellow, a strip of glitter on her right big toe. He decided he would go over there, because this had to be her, and if it wasn't then tough, he would just have to disappoint Reecie when she came, and pretend he wasn't the man she had spoken to on the phone.

He picked up his drink and sauntered over, trying to be as cool and carefree as possible. He wanted to sit right down and ask her if she was the woman he was supposed to meet. It would make things easier on him if she was, but he knew he would blow his game wide open if she wasn't. So he coolly leaned against the chair opposite her and asked, "Is this seat taken?"

She looked up at him, seeming to approve of what she saw. "No, it's not. Would you like to sit down?"

"Yes, I would," Marcus said, accepting graciously. He pulled the seat out, sat down, and noticed that the woman was smiling at him. He took a sip of his water, looked over his shoulder, then back at her and she was still smiling in his face.

"So how are you doing?" he asked, not knowing what else to say.

"I'm doing fine," she said, still smiling. "And more importantly, how are you doing with your fine self?"

Marcus knew he didn't hear what he thought he did, so he asked her to repeat herself.

"I said, and how are you doing with your fine self?" She smiled slyly.

"Oh, I'm fine, I guess," Marcus answered, a bit shaken by her bluntness.

"You here by yourself, Daddy?"

"What did you call me?" Marcus asked.

"Daddy. Big papa, you know." She sipped at the glass of wine before her, then winked at him.

"Uh, yeah. I'm here by myself . . . I guess." This all seemed very strange to Marcus. He was sure that this woman was coming on to him, and he thought that she might have even been a prostitute. What a shame considering how beautiful she was.

"Well, that's good, Daddy, 'cause I'm here by myself too." She reached across the table and put her hand on top of his. "So would you like a date tonight?" she said in a sly seductive voice.

Marcus didn't move his hand although he wanted to, and he didn't say a word, just took another swig of his water, and almost gagged on it.

"How much you got, baby? You got to at least have a hundred for this, because this is the good stuff, you know what I'm talking about, Papa?"

Marcus snatched back his hand, then scooted his chair back from the table. "I don't know what you think this is, or who you think I am, but I'm not that person. I don't have to . . . to pay for sex." He gave the woman a look of disgust, looked around to make sure he hadn't made a scene, then walked away. He was walking through the tables of people eating, stepping around chairs, when he heard someone call him.

"Marcus." He stopped in his tracks, and looked around for where the voice was coming from. He didn't see anyone but the people sitting at their tables enjoying their meals, paying him no mind.

"Marcus, over here," the voice said again.

It was the woman who was calling him—the prostitute.

"I told you, I don't do that sort of thing," he called back, almost afraid to look back at her. When he did, he saw that she was grabbing her middle and laughing. She was bent over the table, tears falling from her eyes. She definitely had a problem. But how did she know his name? He hadn't told her. He walked over to her, a suspicious look on his face.

"Uh, excuse me, how did you know my name? I don't believe I told you," he said.

"Marcus . . ." she said through her laughter. She wiped her eyes. "It's me, Marcus. Reecie. You know, I spoke to you on the phone."

"You didn't say you were a prostitute."

"I'm not," she said, trying to compose herself.

"Then why did you say those things?" he asked.

"Because I knew you didn't know who I was by the way you were looking at me. And then you came over here trying to look so cool, I just couldn't resist."

"Well, how did you know it was me? You've never seen me before, just like I've never seen you."

She gave him a sarcastic look. "Marcus, you look just like your older brother. Did you really think I wouldn't be able to know you when I saw you?"

She had a point, Marcus thought. He felt a little silly, actually. He pulled out the chair he had been sitting in and sat down again. "You got me," he admitted.

She didn't say anything, just looked at him with a straight face, then all of a sudden doubled over with laughter again. "You should've seen your face! 'I don't have to . . . to pay for sex!'"

Yes, he had been fooled, and he felt a bit embarrassed, but he didn't mind. He just relaxed back in his chair and watched her as she had a good laugh. She was really very beautiful, he thought, and he could have done nothing but sit there and admire her for the rest of the night. He didn't even know her, but something told him that she was a very special woman, or maybe he just wanted her to be.

They spent the rest of the evening sitting out on the walk drinking wine, talking about their professions, their likes and dislikes, and why neither one of them was seriously involved.

When the night was over, Marcus walked Reecie to her car. He was brave enough to grab her hand when they crossed the street, and to his surprise, she held his hand back. It was a good feeling, something that he really hadn't felt before. Not a sexual feeling, nothing like that, but . . . unexplainable. All he knew was he was happy, and he had laughed more that night than he had in the last five years.

When they got to her car, she scooted up playfully on the hood as though she wasn't ready to leave.

"Nice car," Marcus said. "BMW. Maybe my brother pays you too much."

"Maybe, but he just gave me a raise," Reecie said, kicking her legs out playfully, her heels bumping against the tires.

"I'm definitely going to have to talk to him," Marcus said, joking. He was standing near her, but he took a step closer. She was smiling as he was, then both their smiles left, and they stared dreamily into each other's eyes. Marcus thought the whole thing felt sort of corny, like in those B movies, right before that oh-so-memorable first kiss is exchanged. She might have wanted him to kiss her, but he just couldn't see himself leaning his head in toward her in slow motion. Tilting his head slightly so their noses could fit like two puzzle pieces. Puckering up, preparing to taste her sweet lips, then closing his eyes with intense anticipation, then getting the hell slapped out of him, because she never wanted him to kiss her in the first place.

"I really enjoyed tonight," he said, staring at her red lips.

She took his hands in hers. "So did I. You're really a nice man. I'm glad your brother gave me your number."

"So that means we can go out again?" Marcus said, moving closer, his thighs touching her knees.

"No, that doesn't," she said. Then she leaned forward and kissed him on the lips.

"*That* does, okay?" She jumped off the hood, climbed in her car, waved good-bye, and drove away, all while Marcus stood there, a drunken expression on his face.

SEVENTEEN

The next day Caleb sat on the bench outside his apartment waiting for Joseph Benning. He would probably ring the doorbell, but Caleb didn't want the man to have to step into the building and see how bad the place looked. It would be just Caleb's luck that as Benning walked up the stairs, a rat would jump out and bite him on the ankle or something. The thought made him laugh a little, but just a little. The fact was it was sad. That was the reason he was sitting out on the bench like a child waiting for his mother to pick him up after school.

Caleb had his pants on again, but this time they were washed really well, and pressed with a lot of starch. He even had Sonya cut off the very bottoms of the pants legs and hem them, because they were all chewed up from being stepped on. He wore a plain white button-down shirt, but he wasn't wearing a tie. He had left it on the bus, and he regretted that because he felt a little underdressed.

He looked down at his watch. It was ten minutes past eleven o'clock, and Caleb figured Benning should be rolling down the street any minute in some huge car with horses pulling the thing forward, some guy on the hood tossing confetti in the air, and trumpeters marching in front. Caleb wondered exactly why the man wanted to even continue the conversation from the bus to begin with. Folks up top don't usually reach down and help pull the people beneath them up. Down isn't the direction they're going, so it's out of their way, and although Caleb didn't like it, he understood. He probably wouldn't be trying to help some loser on the street if he had all the money that Benning did. So why is he trying to help me? Caleb thought.

Caleb saw a large car rolling slowly toward his building. It was a Lexus, the biggest, most expensive one and it could've been no one else but Benning. Caleb stood up from the bench and waved him farther down to where he was standing. The car rolled to a stop in front of him and Caleb opened the door and jumped in.

"How are you doing, Caleb?" Benning asked, smiling from behind the steering wheel.

"Fine." Caleb's attention was stolen by the car. He had never been in such a nice car and it felt like he had stepped from one world into another in a matter of seconds. He rubbed his hands against the leather of his seat. He admired the wood that trimmed the dash, the design of the instruments, the wonderful sound of the expensive CD player coming softly through all the speakers.

"So are you ready to go?" Benning asked.

"Yeah, okay." Caleb nodded his head and they drove off. He looked out the window as he left the littered streets of his neighborhood behind. He would do that someday, and it would be for good, he told himself.

The two men ended up in a restaurant in Hyde Park, not too far from downtown. It wasn't too fancy, but a lot fancier than anywhere Caleb had ever been. They sat at a booth, a very large booth, with leather bench seats that could have accommodated at least six people.

"Are you sure I don't need a tie or nothing to be in here?" Caleb said, smoothing the area where his tie should have been.

"No. Everybody is just coming from work to have lunch, that's why they have ties on, but you don't have to wear one."

The waiter came and asked to take their orders. Caleb had been looking at the menu already. He didn't want to seem like he didn't get out much and was taking advantage of the situation by ordering something very expensive, but there were no prices on the menu. He was thinking about just asking for a hamburger.

"I'll have the grilled tuna," Mr. Benning said. "And a bottle of mineral water."

The waiter turned to Caleb. He looked up from behind the menu still with no idea. "I don't know."

"Would you mind if I select for you?" Benning said.

"No, I don't mind. No problem."

He told the waiter that Caleb would have a steak, grilled onions and mushrooms, baked potato, and corn. "Do you drink beer?" Benning asked him.

"Yeah!" Caleb said, a bit too enthusiastically, he thought.

"And a Heineken," Benning told the waiter.

Benning took off his suit jacket and laid it beside him. "Did I make a good choice?" he asked Caleb.

"Yeah, real good choice. Thanks a lot." Caleb felt a little uncomfortable. He was nervously playing with his napkin and when he noticed it, he pushed it away and folded his hands on the table. So here he was hanging out at an expensive restaurant with some rich black dude about to eat a meal of steak and potatoes and drink down a beer, a good beer. Not that domestic crap that's so cheap they can put it in forty-ounce bottles and charge less for it than what the other guys charge for twelve ounces.

"So how's the job hunting going?" Benning asked, reaching over for a piece of bread from the basket in the middle of the table.

"Not so hot. I ain't found nothing yet. There's nothing out there, but I told you that before."

"Yes, you did, and I'm sorry to hear that. Our society isn't very forgiving of our past." He buttered the bread and bit off a piece. Caleb didn't know what he meant, but he was sure he would elaborate when he was finished chewing.

"Did you finish high school?" he asked.

Caleb didn't answer right away. It was something that he wasn't proud of. Besides, that was pretty personal shit. "Why?" Caleb asked.

Benning lifted his glass of water and took a sip. "I thought we were supposed to be talking. That is why we came down here, correct?"

Caleb nodded hesitantly.

"We come from the same place, I told you that. I understand what happens there."

This man is full of bull, Caleb told himself. He didn't think he was from the same place, but if he wasn't, why would he be telling him that? What was his angle?

"Naw, I didn't finish high school, but I have my reasons."

"I know you do, and I'm sure they're perfectly sound reasons, but I don't care to hear them. I told you I understand."

"Then why did you ask me in the first place?" Caleb felt used.

"Because I figured you hadn't finished." Benning took another bite of bread.

"And what is that supposed to mean?" Caleb defended.

"I just figured, that's all. I know it when I see it. I didn't finish either," he said as though it was no big deal. "I mean, I did go back and get my equivalency, and went on to college, but no, I didn't finish high school either."

Caleb was shocked and could hardly believe it. "Why are you telling me this?"

"We're just talking, right?" Benning said.

"Yeah, just talking," Caleb said.

The waiter came with the food, set the plates in front of them, then left. Caleb watched as Benning took the cloth napkin, opened it, and laid it in his lap. Caleb did the same.

"Taste it, and let me know what you think," Benning told him.

Caleb cut into the meat and put a piece into his mouth. "It's good," he said.

"Good." Benning began eating as well. "So do you have any children?" he asked, still chewing the food.

"Yeah. One. A boy, his name is Jahlil." He answered the question even though it was just as personal as the first, but he felt just a little more comfortable this time.

"And are you with the mother?" Benning asked.

"Yeah, we're together," Caleb said, cutting into his baked potato.

"I'm glad to hear that. That's one of the reasons we're so encumbered with the problems we have today—lack of the right type of leadership, the right mentors. We need to understand that anyone can lead. Anyone can raise a child. Anyone can tell another what to do, and how to do it."

Benning was gesturing with his knife. "But will the leadership be good? Will the child be raised well, will the person listen to the one giving him instructions, and if so, will the instructions be correct? My mother raised me. My father had left her, so she did the best she could with my sister and me. She had no problem with my sister—she went on to do very well. She's a doctor in Atlanta. A surgeon no less." He smiled as he spoke of her. "Went straight through school without incident, but that's because my mother could relate to her. She was able to instill in my sister her knowledge, what she thought was important and how to achieve certain goals. My sister listened, and she is successful. It's very simple.

"But it wasn't that simple for me. For some reason or another, I couldn't hear what my mother was trying to tell me. And if I did hear it, maybe it translated into something entirely different. I thought about this for a long time, and the only thing I am able to come up with is that it didn't come from someone I could directly relate to. It's like listening to a speech on how to become a doctor given by a lawyer. Even if the information is sound, you still wouldn't be very quick to accept it. I like to tell myself that if that was my father telling me what to do, I would've listened. I would've seen myself in his image, and he would've seen himself in mine, and we could've worked together to shape my future into something we both wanted."

Benning scooped some of his rice onto his fork, stabbed a piece of tuna, and slid both into his mouth. He followed it with another swallow of his mineral water, then dabbed his mouth with his napkin.

"I'm not saying that my mother wasn't a good mother. She was the best. I just may have been a bad son. But whatever it was, I think our primary problem was that I couldn't or didn't want to relate. After a while she got tired of me disobeying her, doing what I wanted, and coming and going as I pleased. She tried to put restrictions on me, but being sixteen, I felt I was grown and should be exempt from such nonsense. So I left, and it was on very bad terms. I stayed with friends here and there for the first two weeks, then they could no longer put me up. I resorted to living on the streets, in alleys, in doorways on cold days, under porches, anywhere to get out of this strong Chicago wind. The funny part was, I lived within five blocks of the house I grew up in. I would see my house every day, I was so close. I just couldn't find it in myself to crawl back to my mother.

"There were some days during the winter when it was extremely cold. People were dying on the streets, I had even known a couple. I had to go somewhere, so I stayed in our garage. My mother didn't know about it, or at least I thought she didn't, but the garage door was always unlocked, and later on she told me she left it that way because she knew I might try there."

"So how did you go from that to this? You were living on the streets, and now you're making all that money." Caleb was sipping on his beer, but was held by the story Benning was telling.

"There was this older gentleman. He was trying to keep warm under a porch. I was looking for shelter for the night and he invited me to share his. But first you have to understand that the homeless are very territorial. If they have a spot, it is their home for the night, and just walking into that area uninvited is like breaking into a man's house. So it was a very kind gesture, his inviting me in, and it was so cold that neither of us could sleep that night. So we just sat there and talked, two black men, an older and a younger with common ties, kind of like us."

Benning smiled, and so did Caleb.

"The man was a wealth of knowledge, filled with experiences. He told me all he knew, his triumphs and of the many mistakes he made. He told me to always think positively, never treat a person any other way than the way you would want to be treated, and always put forth your best efforts. The advice sounded very simple. These things are taught on children's shows and sung on commercials, but how many people actually follow that advice, I mean really follow it and never sway? He told me things like that, but most important of all, he told me to never give up. Never give up! If there is something you want to do, you can do it if you just don't give up. 'A persistent, unswerving man is very hard to stop,' he said.

"He said if a man wanted to dig holes for a living, and he devoted his life to it, eventually he would be the best damn hole digger that ever lived and everyone would come to him to have their holes dug. He'd probably make millions doing it too. Eventually, he told me that I was too young to be throwing away my life like I was. He told me whatever problems I had with my mother to get over them, and do what I had to do. It was easy to live out on the street when you knew that your mama had a nice warm house for you when you got tired, but when you had nothing else but the cardboard box you were sleeping on, or the clothes on your back that used to be someone else's clothes, it became the hardest thing in the world, and it was something that you would never want to have to deal with. I looked at that man, looked in his eyes, and realized that I never wanted to be where he was. So I took his advice and went back home after six months."

"Every decision after that, I made with him in mind, because he was the one I could relate to; he was my mentor."

Benning pushed his plate aside, pulled his napkin from his lap, wiped his mouth with it and set it atop the remains of his food.

"You understand what I'm saying?"

"I guess I do. It was an interesting story." It was all Caleb could think of to say.

"All I'm saying is that the man changed my life. If it wasn't for him, I don't know where I'd be, and I realized that sometimes that's all it takes to make that change; someone to see promise in you, someone to tell you of their triumphs and their mistakes, someone to stick out their hand. I told myself that I would do that, and that's what I've been doing now that I have the opportunity. I helped a young man out in your situation about three years ago, by hiring him to work for me, but he's moving on to better things so I seem to have a vacancy. I think you're a good man, Caleb, who just got a little turned around for some reason and lost his way. I would like to offer you that position. What do you think?"

Caleb felt he had to be dreaming. Maybe the beer was too strong, and it made him delusional, maybe this was some fool his brother Austin hired to play a dirty trick on him, he didn't know, but it just never happened like that for him.

"Yeah . . . I want it!" The words dropped out his mouth awkwardly and without thought. "I mean, I'll take it."

"It doesn't make that much money, but it's—"

"It doesn't matter how much money it makes. I'll take it. I'll take it. I'll take it!" He was so happy and relieved, and all he could think of was getting back home and telling Sonya. He could finally prove to her that he wasn't a loser. He could prove it to her, he could prove it to his brothers, and most of all, he could prove it to himself.

EIGHTEEN

During the past month, Julius had gotten hold of Austin's phone number. Still in Chicago after all this time. So many years had passed that he didn't know if by dialing the number he would actually get in touch with his son; it could have been the wrong number or an old listing. It felt odd knowing how to contact his child, the child he had not seen in almost twenty years. It felt so odd that he didn't even inform Cathy that he had the number in his possession. Whenever she asked if he was making progress, he just shrugged his shoulders, made a stupid face, and said, "Not really."

One night while Cathy was out at the store, Julius sat in the dark for almost two hours trying to muster the courage to dial the number. He reached for the phone and listened to the dial tone for quite a while before dialing. He punched the buttons, knowing the number by heart, then waited while the phone rang. He could feel the phone slowly sliding in his sweat-covered palm. He switched hands and wiped the sweaty hand on his pants, then held it out before him and saw that it was shaking. His heart was beating like crazy in his chest, as if he had just climbed ten flights of stairs. He couldn't do it, he told himself, he was just too nervous. He gently hung up the phone, admitting defeat.

"It'll be all right. Julius, you can do it," he whispered to himself, try-ing to find some confidence. "Just hang in there."

He tried again. "Hello?" a voice asked.

Julius almost jumped when he heard it. He swallowed hard, and knew that the person on the other end had to have heard him.

"Hello," the voice came again.

Julius wanted to speak, even fixed his lips to form the words, but nothing came out. It was as if he had swallowed cement and his vocal cords were seized in stone.

"Is there anyone there?" the voice asked. It sounded harsh and in-timidating.

Julius couldn't do it. He hung up the phone and tried to regain his composure. He had never thought it would be that difficult to talk to his son, if that was him. He couldn't tell. He told himself there was no way in the world he could've been able to tell his son's voice from the voice of any other man his age. When he left, the boy's voice was still high-pitched, full of innocence, and couldn't have managed to be harsh or intimidating if he tried.

But this person was very close to being mean, as though he had a world of troubles. Julius wanted to find his son, but something in him almost didn't want this person to be him. There was too much . . . too much something in his voice that made him sound unhappy, and the last thing Julius wanted was for his sons to be unhappy, and even worse, for it to have been his fault.

He told himself he would try again in the morning. He would feel better, he had to, because there was no way he could feel worse. He went to his bedroom and retired for the night. It was only eight o'clock, and Cathy hadn't even walked in from the store yet, but he was feeling bad about what had happened. Hearing what might have been his son's voice made him think about the terrible way he had left them, without a word. Without even pulling the boys aside and kneeling down, ex-plaining the situation—nothing. It made him feel horrible and he just wanted to stop his brain from going back there. He needed to sleep.

He was feeling very weak. The weakness was coming and going lately, and he attributed it to the fact that he wasn't eating like he should or wasn't resting as much as he needed to. He had had a lot on his mind over the last month or so. Julius undressed and got into bed. He might have spoken to his son today, after twenty years, he might have actually spoken to him, Julius thought. And maybe he would see him again soon. See all of them, talk to them, and see how they had grown into fine young men.

He would see if they resembled him, see if they spoke like him, walked like him, had his odd sense of humor, as Cathy put it. He would do that, and it would be the best feeling in the world, and the only thing left in his life he had wished for would have been given to him.

Julius woke up sometime after three in the morning, feeling strange, Cathy beside him. He felt light-headed and when he tried to sit up, he felt as though the bed was picked up off the floor and spun in quick dizzying circles. He lay back down, his head on his pillow where he felt safe, where the room or the bed didn't spin any longer. Cathy was lying beside him, sleeping peacefully. He didn't want to wake her, but he felt betrayed by his body, not knowing what it would do next. He laid a soft hand on her shoulder and gently nudged her. "Cathy," he whispered. For some reason, the juices in his mouth began to flow heavily.

Julius swallowed, feeling as though if he didn't the saliva would begin to spill from his mouth, run down over his chin and wet the blankets. He felt sick to his stomach, about to vomit. He was getting nervous. He could feel his stomach churning and flipping, the fluid rolling around in there, threatening to come rumbling up and raging out of his mouth. He reached for Cathy but was overcome. He grabbed her shoulder, then threw his head over the side of the bed where he heaved violently onto the floor. Clear, foul-smelling fluid shot from his mouth onto the carpet, on the side of the bed, and speckled his face and hands. He tried to stop it, tried shutting off whatever valve inside him allowed the stuff to flow out of him, but he couldn't, it kept coming. He had a handful of the blanket and was squeezing it tightly.

He felt Cathy reaching over him to see what was wrong. She was rubbing his back with one hand, the other clutching his shoulder.

"It'll be all right, baby," he heard her say through his eruptions. "Don't worry, baby."

Julius eventually stopped throwing up and his body collapsed on the bed, his head hanging over the side, a thin line of vomit stretching to the floor. "I'm sorry," he said in an exhausted voice.

"Don't you dare. Don't you dare!" Cathy said, still rubbing his back. "Are you okay?" She grasped his chin and turned his face toward hers, wiping a tear from his eye.

"Yeah, I'm all right. Just give me a minute and I'll clean this up," he said.

"Don't be crazy, I'll get it. But first we have to get you cleaned up. You stay right here, okay?"

"Don't worry, I won't be going anywhere," Julius said, his voice still thin.

Cathy cleaned him off with a washcloth and a basin of warm soapy water. She washed his face, his chest and his hands, and changed him into some pajamas. She helped him to the nearby chair, then changed the sheets and blanket on the bed. She moved him back and allowed him to brush his teeth over the basin that she poured fresh cool water into, then she fed him a half a glass of ice water. He drank it slowly as she went about cleaning up the vomit that was on the floor.

She scrubbed the area with a brush, every so often asking him how he was doing.

"Feeling better," Julius replied, taking another slow sip from the water.

When she was finished, she slid under the covers with him, cuddled next to him, and placed a hand on his forehead to check his temperature. "What happened?" she asked, concern in her eyes.

"I don't know. I guess I shouldn't have had that three-foot submarine sandwich with extra peppers before I went to bed." He looked at Cathy, a slight smile on his face.

"So you don't know what happened."

"No. I just . . . just felt sick, that's all," he said.

"You haven't been eating right, you know that, right?" Cathy said.

"Yeah."

"And you haven't been sleeping as much as you should, either."

"Yes, I know that too," Julius said.

She shifted herself in bed to face him. "I don't know what you're trying to do. You can't act like this is no big deal, you have to take care of yourself. I don't know how many times someone has to tell you that."

RM Johnson

"I know that, but—"

"But nothing, Julius. Every time I try to tell you, you don't want to hear it. Every time I fix you something nutritious to eat, you turn your nose up at it. I know it's not a double cheeseburger, but it's something that you have to eat."

"I know that . . ." Julius said.

"No, Julius," Cathy said. "If you knew, you wouldn't fight me. If you knew, you'd just eat the damn food that I make for you. You aren't twenty-five anymore. You just can't do what you want and expect that it'll have no effect on your body. You have to start taking this thing seriously. Julius, you have cancer."

Julius looked at her, and didn't know what to say. He could barely see the look in her eyes; the only light entered from the bathroom through the cracked door.

"It's hard," he said in a quivering voice. "Sometimes I tell myself it's not me this is happening to. I tell myself that I don't have cancer, and I try to make myself believe it. But I know . . . I can almost feel it growing inside me, and it's the scariest feeling in the world. Before all this, when I got a pain in my back, I used to chuckle and say to myself, the old man is getting older. But now I wonder if it's the cancer spreading. I wonder if it's already deep in my spine eating it away, starting to cripple me, soon making it where I won't even be able to walk. It's hard knowing that you're going to die," he said, putting his fingers through Cathy's hair.

"I mean, we all know, but knowing that it's going to happen so soon. It's frightening." A tear rolled quickly down his face. "I'm going to lose you."

Julius caressed Cathy's face. She turned to kiss his palm.

"You'll never lose me. I'll always be yours, and I know you know that. Just as sure as I'm with you now, I will be with you after you pass, and someday, we will walk together in heaven. We will." She reached for his face in the dim light, and it was covered with tears. "You are the only man I truly loved. Do you know that?"

"Yes," he said faintly, not wanting her to hear the crying in his voice.

"And I will always love you," she said. She placed both her hands on his face and moved close to him to kiss him. Julius did the same and placed his quivering lips on hers. He could feel that her face was wet with tears as well. He kissed her and prayed that the moment would never end.

"I . . . I have his number," Julius admitted after kissing Cathy. He looked away from her as if ashamed of his lying.

"Whose?"

"My son's," he said, lying back in the bed.

"Did you call him yet?"

Julius thought about how he had acted when he heard what could have been Austin's voice. He remembered how nervous he had been and how he'd hung up the phone, afraid to see if his son even wanted to hear his old man's voice again.

"No. I haven't called him yet, but I will in the morning. I will."

NINETEEN

Caleb sat on the floor of the inventory room of the Main Frame Software Company. He was wearing a pair of new slacks, new shoes, a new shirt and a nice new brightly colored tie to replace the old one that he had thrown away. This one wasn't even clip-on. It was the real kind that you had to tie yourself. It took him about a million tries standing at the mirror before he got it, but he finally did, and it was just one more accomplishment that told him he was now capable of doing or obtaining anything he set his mind to. ·

He sat there, a large box of discs beside him. He pulled them out, one small box at a time, looked at the six-digit number at the top of the box, then filed them in the space they belonged in on the shelf. After doing that, he marked his clipboard with the information, so he could later enter it into the computer. That was more or less the description of his job, the job that paid him $6.35 per hour, and that was just for the first three months while he was on probation. After that, he would get a small raise, Benning had said, and then he'd get another raise after he had been working for a year. When he heard that, he almost turned a back flip right there in Benning's office. He had never made so much money. When he went back home to tell Sonya, she almost cried, she was so happy.

She told Caleb that she always knew he would come through. Caleb didn't know if she truly meant it or if she was just saying it because he finally got a job, but either way, those words meant the world to him.

He placed each box carefully, paying close attention to the numbers on the boxes and the numbers on the shelves they were to be placed on. He didn't want to make any mistakes, or any more. He had been there a month and had already managed to make his fair share of slip-ups. Putting the discs in the wrong place, counting inventory and coming up with the wrong number, entering the wrong information in the computer, things like that. But it hadn't gotten to him. He was determined to become proficient at his job.

One day Benning sat him down in his office to find out how he was doing. Benning was sitting behind his desk, not wearing a suit jacket, simply a shirt, a tie, and a pair of suspenders, the sleeves of the shirt rolled up around his forearms as if he was elbow-deep in some serious plumbing.

"So how are things working out, Mr. Harris?" he said, smiling because he used his name so formally.

"I'm sure I don't have to tell you. I'm sure you heard how I've been messing up. I'm sure Jim ran back and told you like he always does."

Jim was the person that Caleb worked with. He was a thin, nerdy-looking man, a few years younger than Caleb. He had been working there in the inventory room for four or five years, and by looking at him doing his work, punching the keys of the computer, interacting with it like they had a very special personal relationship, you could tell the work was his life. He looked like the standard-issue nerd. Buttoned-down short-sleeve shirt, pocket protector, high-water slacks, white socks, penny loafers, and thick black-framed glasses. As if he'd ordered the nerd kit complete in the mail. He said he was working on his master's degree in computer science, and that was the only reason he was there. Caleb could remember the first time meeting the man. His head had been glued to the computer monitor when Benning and Caleb walked in.

Benning called to Jim. Jim looked up as though he was being pulled away from sex right before ejaculation.

"I want you to meet Caleb Harris. He's going to be taking Martin's place."

Caleb stuck out a hand. Jim didn't take it, just looked him over from his shoes to his eyes. "You have any experience?" he said.

Caleb lowered his hand. "No," he said, looking into the man's eyes through his thick lenses, thinking how much of an asshole he was.

"Well, what else is new?" Jim said, a look of frustration on his face. "Good to meet you, but I have important things to do, so if you'll excuse me," he said in a voice that led Caleb to believe that it didn't matter to him if he was excused or not.

That was Jim, and immediately Caleb knew he would have problems with him.

Benning opened a thin folder, a few sheets of paper in it. Caleb figured it had to be his personnel folder.

"I spoke to Jim, and he says you made a couple of mistakes here and there, but that's to be expected, Caleb." Caleb looked disappointed at the news. "You can't get this overnight. I hope you're not thinking that you can," Benning said.

"No, but every time I make a damn mistake, he's there to point it out to me."

"Well, that's part of his job, Caleb. You can't blame him for doing that," Benning said. "He's just trying to help you so you don't do it again."

"But it's not like that. It's like he's waiting for me to make a mistake, like he's hoping I will, so he can blame me. Talking down at me like I'm some dog, like I'm some kid. I'm older than he is, I shouldn't have to take that." Caleb could feel himself getting angry, and just the thought of Jim's face made him want to find his frail behind and push him out of a window.

"Caleb, age has nothing to do with this. He has experience and you don't. That's what it comes down to right now. He has the knowledge and it's your job to obtain that knowledge." Benning put his pencil down and straightened up in his chair. "It's one of the things I pay you for. It's your job to learn. It may not be easy coming from him, but what in life worth anything is easy? Now you say he's talking down to you. I hope that's not the case, I hope to think that you were just a bit angry and it may have just felt like he was attacking you. I've never had that problem with him before, but if it happens again, let me know." Benning stood up from his chair, a smile on his face. He extended his hand.

Caleb stood and wondered what the man was so happy about, probably that he didn't have to deal with Jim. Caleb took his hand and they shook.

"You going to be all right?" Benning asked, holding onto his hand for the answer.

"Yeah, I'll be cool," Caleb said, smiling.

"Caleb!" Jim practically yelled. The sound of his voice made Caleb cringe.

"Yeah, what is it this time?" Caleb said, standing.

"That's right, this time. You made another mistake," he said, his arms folded, his eyebrows bunched down on top of his thick glasses.

"Well, what is it?"

"Just come with me." Jim led the way, walking very briskly, almost running as Caleb lagged behind him. Jim stopped at one of the computer terminals. He waited for Caleb to get there, then swiveled the screen over so he could see too.

"Did you process this shipment?" Jim said.

Caleb looked at the screen. Immediately he could tell that he did, but he looked it over, trying to find something that would tell him that he really didn't, that the mistake was made by someone else. He couldn't find what he was looking for, so he answered, "Yeah, I entered that stuff into the computer."

"That's what I meant when I said 'processed this shipment.' "

Caleb looked at the screen again. He didn't see anything wrong, and was actually beginning to get angry.

"Yeah, well, that's what I did. I did process this shipment. What's the problem?"

Jim turned the screen his way, examined it for a moment, then swiveled it back so they could both look at it again. "You don't see it. It's staring you right in the face."

Caleb looked again, looked very carefully this time. Looked over the number of boxes shipped, the type of boxes, the time of the shipment, even the name of the carrier. He flipped to the page on his clipboard, and everything checked, everything, just like he knew it would when he entered the crap into the computer.

"I don't see a thing wrong. Maybe *you* ought to take a better look!"

"Where did you send this shipment to?" Jim asked calmly.

Caleb referred back to his clipboard, then to the computer screen; they both read the same. "Washington," Caleb said, as though he was being kept from very important matters.

"Washington where, Einstein?" Jim said, reaching into a drawer and pulling out a pink sheet of paper.

"Washington, D.C., where do you expect?" Caleb returned.

Jim held the pink duplicate form and pointed to a tiny box in the top left-hand corner. In that box were tiny scribbled letters reading "Sea—Wa."

"So. What is that supposed to mean?" Caleb said.

"The shipment wasn't supposed to go to Washington, D.C. It was supposed to go to Seattle, Washington. If you were able to read you would've known that," Jim said, folding the paper and throwing it to the table. "Do you know how many boxes that was?"

Caleb knew, 250 boxes. Hell, he was the one that entered it. But he didn't answer. The question wasn't meant to be answered. The question was meant to make him feel lower than he already felt, and there would be more of that, he knew it.

"Now I have to try and repair this gross mistake you made." He began tapping on the keys feverishly at about a mile a minute. "I have to reroute the order to them, then place another order . . ." He was talking to himself as he worked at the station.

"So are you done with me? I would like to get the rest of those boxes filed," Caleb said.

Jim stopped what he was doing and looked up, his glasses hanging crooked on his face, a crazed look in his eyes.

"Are you serious? You stay right there while I finish this, then we're going in to see Mr. Benning." Then he went back to banging the keys again and talking to himself. "Let you get back to work. Hmph! You'll be lucky if you have work to get back to after we see Mr. Benning."

Benning was sitting on the corner of his desk. "C'mon in, Caleb. Have a seat."

Caleb sat down in one of the chairs in front of his desk. Jim didn't sit down, just hovered about the room.

"Jim tells me that you processed a shipment of discs to go to Washington, D.C., when they actually should've gone to Seattle. Is that correct?" asked Benning.

"Yeah, that's about what happened, Mr. Benning," Caleb said, still angry about the entire situation.

"Can you tell me what happened?" he asked.

"I don't know, I guess I saw Washington, and the first thing that popped in my head was D.C."

"No it wasn't, you just weren't paying attention," Jim said.

Caleb looked over at him, anger in his eyes. "I'm not saying I didn't do it. I even told him that it was my mistake."

"I'm not saying that you tried to deny it," Jim said in a high-pitched voice. "I'm just saying that you should understand this now."

"Can you just shut the hell up?" Caleb stood from his chair and was ready to leap at Jim.

"I don't have to do anything," Jim taunted. "I can't help it that you can't do what's required of you."

"Mr. Benning, he had his opportunity to tell his story uninterrupted while I sat outside the office. Can I have the same consideration?" Caleb asked.

"I think that's fair," Benning said. "Jim, have a seat outside, will you please."

"But, Mr. Benning . . ."

"Jim. Outside." Benning pointed toward the door. "Thank you."

Benning waited till the door closed, then stood from the desk, placed another chair facing Caleb, then sat in it.

"Now what happened?" he asked.

"Like I told you, I just messed up. And it's not like I wasn't paying attention. I was really watching what I was doing, almost too much. I don't know, I think I was just trying too hard or something." He looked into Benning's face, trying to read what he was thinking.

"It's a mistake, Caleb, and they do happen, but I'm going to ask you to try your best to limit them. It's understandable. It happens. Even Jim did the same thing when he was first hired, twice, so I don't understand why he's making such a huge deal out of this."

"I told you why. He has something against me," Caleb said. "He doesn't want me working here, and I can't understand that. And to tell you the truth, I wish he'd just leave me the hell alone."

"Well, Caleb, all I can say is, it's not up to him. He can't fire you, so don't let him make you believe he can, and don't let him get you so upset that you make more mistakes that will put you in the position where you can get fired. Just do what you've been doing. Take your time, work at your own pace, do what he tells you, within reason, and before you know it, things will be fine, all right?"

Caleb nodded his head, not feeling the issue had been resolved.

"Now, I wrote down that we had this talk, and I put down what I told you and what I expect of you by the time we meet for the three-month evaluation. All I need for you to do is to sign here." Benning pushed a form in front of him.

Caleb took the pen, preparing to sign on the line, then he looked up at Benning. "I'm doing the best I can."

"Caleb, I know that," Benning said. His voice was reassuring. "Mistakes will be made. You've only been here one month. All this form is saying is that I expect more of you after you've been here for three months, and that's going to happen. You'll pick up more, you'll become more confident, and you'll be able to handle the requirements without a problem, okay?" Benning gave him a slap on the back.

"All right." Caleb signed the page, then left the office. Jim was sitting in the hall. Caleb walked by him, not even looking in his direction.

Caleb checked his watch again. It read 5:31. He had gotten off work an hour ago, but he stood in an alley by the building waiting for Jim. He knew Jim had to walk by that point to get to the train station. Caleb saw him do it every day while he stood at the bus stop.

He was standing there hoping he would hurry up. They got off at the same time, but Jim liked to stick around just for the fun of doing extra work. That was probably cool with him because he had nothing else happening in his life, but Caleb had better things to do than wait around for the nerd all day. He was about to leave when he caught sight of Jim coming his way. Caleb stepped back into the shadows of the alley, waiting for him to pass.

When he did, Caleb snatched him by the back of his collar and dragged him further into the alley where no one would see them. Jim cried out like a stuck pig till he turned around and saw who was holding him.

"Caleb, what are you doing back here? You almost scared me half to death." He seemed to relax.

Caleb couldn't believe it. Here Jim was standing in a dark alley with a brother whose job he had just tried taking and couldn't see that it was possibly a dangerous situation.

"How you doing, Jim?" Caleb said coolly.

"That's none of your business." He straightened the glasses on his face.

"What was all that nonsense about at work today?" Caleb spoke in the same cool, calm voice.

"You're incompetent. That's what it was about. You don't pay attention to what you're doing and that makes my job harder. I'm not going to be repairing your mistakes all the time. Now if you don't mind." He readjusted the collar on his jean jacket, situated his book bag back on his shoulder, and prepared to leave.

Caleb watched him take two steps away from him, almost laughed, then snatched him back by the collar and threw him up against the wall again, this time with enough force to knock his glasses from his face.

"You just don't get it, do you, motherfucker?" Caleb said, holding him by the throat of the jacket. He was right up in his face, and when Caleb spoke, spittle flew into Jim's face. Caleb didn't know if he was squinting his eyes because he couldn't see or if he was trying to keep spit from flying into them. He was wiggling like a wet dog trying to get away from a bath, but he barely had the strength of a teenager.

"Hold your ass still, before I fuck you up! Now you can make this easy on yourself, or you can make it hard. Which do you want to do?"

Jim didn't say a word, just stood there, his face balled up, his jacket hiked up around his ears.

"Which do you want to fucking do!" Caleb ordered, slamming him into the wall again. He heard his head connect against the brick wall hard, and was almost inclined to apologize. He didn't want to hurt him, just scare him.

Jim looked dazed for a moment. His eyes whirled around in his head.

"I'm . . . I'm not scared of you," Jim managed to say, regaining his senses.

Caleb was stopped by this boy's foolishness. It took him a moment to know how to proceed next, because he wasn't expecting words like that to come out of Jim's mouth.

"You better be scared because I'll . . . I'll—" Caleb grabbed him by the throat again. "I'll fuck you up right here. Don't believe me, try me." He looked in Jim's eyes to see if he was shaken at all by the threats. He wasn't sure.

"Now, I just want to say I have nothing against you or any other white person, and I would like to think you feel the same way about me and my people. I think you might even be a decent person and there might be somebody out there crazy enough to care for your funny-looking ass, and if there is, you know how important it is to have that, to have people that care for you. Do you know that?"

Jim didn't answer, just stood there, letting Caleb hold him at the throat. His look was evil, Caleb thought, like he intended on really jacking Caleb up the moment he was released.

"I said, do you know that?" Caleb shook him.

"Yes, I know that," Jim said.

Caleb was still in his face, but he loosened his grip just a little.

"I have that. I have a girlfriend who is practically my wife, and we have the most adorable little guy you'd ever want to see. If I had a picture, I'd show you, but I don't, so you'll just have to take my word. What I'm trying to say is that they depend on me for a lot of shit. Shit that this job will provide. To cut to the chase, I'm saying I need this job. Do you understand? I need this job and I need it bad, and when you sat up there like a little bitch and complained when I made the same mistake you made twice, I wanted to fuck you up. And I mean fuck you up bad, you know what I'm saying?"

Jim nodded his head up and down.

"And if you try that shit again, I'll do it, and I mean it." He looked at Jim with as serious a face as he could make. "My family is everything

I have, Jim. If I lose them, I have nothing else to live for. So that ought to let you know that I'll jack you up without a second thought, do you understand me?"

Jim nodded his head again.

"No. I want to hear you say the words, motherfucker!"

"Yes . . . I understand," Jim said, his voice more steady than Caleb wanted it to be.

"Yes, you understand, who?" Caleb jerked him a little, careful not to bump his head again.

"Sir. I understand, sir," Jim said smugly.

"Good." Caleb released him, and even straightened out his jacket. He looked at him standing there, and was surprised that he wasn't hauling his ass down the alley fearing for his life. Jim stood there and looked defiantly into Caleb's eyes.

"What the fuck are you still doing here?" Caleb yelled at him.

"You just can't go muscling me around like that," Jim said.

"What did you say to me?" Caleb was wearing his crazed-man face, but it wasn't just for effect this time. He really was shocked by this suburban-living white boy's nerve.

"I said, you can't just go muscling me—"

"That's what I thought you said." Caleb grabbed him by the shoulders and bulldozed him to the wall. His head banged against the bricks again, but this time a lot harder. Caleb could tell by the cry the boy let out and the deep thud his head made against the solid surface that he was hurt. But Caleb didn't care. Jim wanted to act tough, now he had to be tough.

"You're a bad motherfucker, huh?" Caleb pounded him with a hard shot to the gut. The air blew out of Jim's body. He choked in pain and doubled over.

"I can't be muscling you, huh?" Caleb hit him again, to the gut, forcing Jim to fall on all fours. He was gagging and coughing when Caleb picked him up and looked in his eyes. Blood trickled from one of his nostrils, and there was saliva streaming out the sides of his mouth.

Caleb pushed right up to him, their bodies touching, the contours of their profiles almost fitting together like puzzle pieces. "I didn't want to fucking do this, I'm not a violent person, but you forced me, motherfucker. I need this job. Don't fuck with me. I mean it. I don't want us to have to come back here, all right?"

Jim pulled his head up. It wobbled around on his neck, as if the shots to his stomach had knocked a bolt loose in his neck. "Yes . . . sir," he said, coughing wildly after that. Caleb had to step back so he wouldn't be shot with spit.

"And don't let me hear that you told Mr. Benning about this, because if I do . . ." Caleb raised a fist high to Jim's head. "Now get the fuck out of here!"

Jim fell to his knees again, and smoothed his hands about the ground of the dark alley, looking for his glasses. When he found them, he placed them on his face, clumsily, with both hands. He stood, gave Caleb a long strange look, then turned and took off running.

TWENTY

Austin had been away from his family for roughly a month. He had gotten himself an apartment, a small two-bedroom, where the second bedroom doubled as a den. Just as he had wanted, he had his own space, his privacy, and the time to do with it what he wanted.

He had a large bookshelf in the living room. He put his recliner next to it, enabling him to just reach over, barely moving in his seat, to grab a book. A few magazines sat fanned on the coffee table. They had been that way since the last time he looked at them, and that was two weeks ago. One of the pleasures of living alone, he thought. If something is set one way, and you don't move it, it will remain that way forever. He wouldn't have to wonder on the way home from work if that last little bit of his favorite ice cream was left in the icebox. Hell, he could build a house of cards on the kitchen table, leave his apartment for a week, and when he came back, it would be standing there just as perfect as when he left it. No noises, no kids yelling, no wife nagging, just the gentle low droning of the refrigerator, or the occasional ringing of the telephone. It was so quiet sometimes, when he was sitting in his recliner, reading one of his books, he could hear the ticking of his wristwatch. It was eerie and sometimes Austin would find himself making noises, talking to himself, just to hear the sound of a voice.

Over the last month he had been fighting himself to try and stick with what he thought he wanted. There were times when he thought of just giving the whole thing up, packing up and going back home and forgetting everything. It would have been so easy, because during those times he was so lonely. It took everything he had just to think rationally, to tell himself that if things were worth going back to, he wouldn't have left to begin with. He didn't want to go back home and three days later feel trapped again, then have to go through that ordeal of leaving again.

What he missed most were his children. They were the sunshine in his world, and now without them, each and every day seemed black with despair. He missed them running up to him in the morning, his son sitting in his lap, yanking on his tie. He missed his daughter asking to climb his back or swing on his arm. He missed hearing their voices and smelling them after they just had their baths, when they would run into his bedroom and jump into bed with him and Trace. It was terrible to be away from them, and each day that passed, he knew he was missing so much of their lives.

He had only seen them twice since he had left. Once on a Saturday, and the last time, a Friday night. They came over and spent the night. They played together that night, and after their baths, the three of them lay in Austin's bed wearing their pajamas and talked. Troy talked about what happened on his favorite cartoons. He talked about the new ice cream his mom bought, and how he bit off the head of GI Joe, and now he had to get a new one. Austin didn't think he really understood what was going on. Maybe he didn't have a full grasp of time yet. Because of his age, he probably didn't quite notice the difference in seeing his father twice a month as opposed to every day, but felt that everything was the same as long as he still saw him. But Bethany was a little different. She waited till after her brother was sound asleep, snoring on his father's shoulder to ask the question.

"When are you coming back, Daddy?" The expression on her face was sad, the saddest look he had ever seen on his child. He wanted to tell her he would go home with them when they woke up in the morning, no, they would leave right then, but he couldn't.

"I don't know, sweetheart. I don't know when I'm coming home," he said, brushing some hair out of her face.

"Then why did you leave?" she asked, her face filled with emotion.

Austin didn't know exactly how to answer the question. He didn't know if she'd understand the need for space, and what one expected of his spouse, and things like that.

"You don't love Mommy anymore?" she said, sitting up to get a better look at her father's face.

"No, it's not that, sweetheart. It's just . . ."

"Mommy said you're just taking a time out." She cracked a little smile. "Just like kids get at school."

"And how does that work?" Austin asked.

"Like Jonathan Miller was playing when he wasn't supposed to be. He was supposed to be reading, so Mrs. Kramer gave him a time out. He had to lay down on the other side of the room, away from the rest of the kids, till his time out was over. But when it was over, he was able to come back and talk to us and play with us again. Just like you, Daddy," she said, touching a spot on Austin's face for no particular reason. "Mommy said when you're done with your time out, you'll come back home and everything will be better again. Is that true?"

Trace really has a way of explaining things to our children, he thought. He smiled at what he had just heard. "That's very true," he said to his daughter, touching her face the same way.

Was that what he was doing, taking a time out? The idea seemed so simple to him, he almost wanted it to be true. Could it be that all he needed was some time away from his family, like Jonathan Miller needing time away from the rest of the kids, to realize what he had done was wrong? That he wasn't appreciating what he had, so it had to be taken away so he could value it again? He thought about it and hoped that it was that simple. "That's very true," Austin said again, believing more this time.

·　　　·　　　·

Austin went to the phone, picked it up, and was going to call Trace and ask her if he could come over, then thought he didn't have to go through all that. They were still as much his children as they were hers. He grabbed his jacket and left.

As he drove, he thought about calling her. It would be the polite thing to do, and it wouldn't inconvenience him in the slightest; all he had to do was pick up his car phone, but he didn't. For two reasons. He continued to tell himself that he didn't have to because nothing had truly changed except their living arrangements. Second, because he wanted to make sure that Trace didn't happen to have any company over that he wouldn't approve of. He knew she wouldn't, she wasn't that type of woman, but he would stop by unannounced just to be sure, anyway.

He drove his Mercedes up to the house and cut off the engine. He sat out there for a while, the radio playing low, looking at the house as though something about it might have changed. Austin stepped up to the door, thought about knocking, then decided to use his key. He pushed open the door, stuck his head in, looked around, then yelled out, "Is anybody home?"

He heard footsteps above him making their way quickly to the stairs.

"Daddy!" His children ran down the stairs, then leaped into his arms. He scooped them up, and they wrapped their arms around his neck, hugging him tightly.

"How ya been, Daddy?" Bethany said. "You got something for me?"

"Yeah, you got something for me too?" Troy said.

"I got a big kiss for both of you." He kissed them, then squeezed them tight in his arms. It felt good to be with them again. It felt like old times, like he had never left.

"Where's your mother?"

"She's upstairs in the bathroom," Bethany said. "Mommeeeeeee!"

"So how have you two been doing?" Austin asked them.

Trace came down the stairs, and was standing before Austin before he even realized she was there. He looked up and was so surprised to see her that he almost dropped his son. The boy dug his little hands into Austin's shoulder to keep from falling.

"Sorry to startle you," Trace said, smiling. She was pulling a comb through her hair. It was done in a style Austin had never seen before.

"No, no. You didn't startle me. I just uh . . . uh, you look good. New hairstyle or something?" He tried to make it seem as though he wasn't paying much attention and just happened upon the right guess.

"Yeah, or something," she said. "I got it cut the other day. I got tired of it."

Austin nodded his head in approval. "And looks like you dropped a few pounds too."

"I don't know about that," Trace said, placing her hands on her hips and smoothing them down the sides of her tight-fitting jeans. "But I may have. I haven't been cooking as heavy as I used to."

"Well, it looks good on you," he admitted. And it really did, he thought. The woman was almost stunning standing there in her faded jeans and plain button down shirt. She was looking as good as when they had first met, and her mental state seemed in need of no repair either. Was she actually happy that he had left?

"And what are you doing here?" she asked.

"Oh, sorry I didn't call first. I was passing through and thought I'd stop by to see the kids."

"Yeah, Daddy stopped by to see us," Troy said.

"Mmm, I wish you would've called, because I'm taking them over to see their grandmother."

"When?" Austin asked.

"We should've been walking out the door five minutes ago. As a matter of fact, Bethany, take your brother upstairs so you two can get ready."

Bethany made a sad face and climbed down off her father. She pulled at Troy's arm, trying to release him.

"No!" Troy whined, "I'm staying with Daddy."

Austin couldn't help but smile. He looked over at Trace as if he was surprised that the boy had said such a thing. He wasn't though, and was actually glad that someone still seemed to be on his side.

"Go ahead with your sister, Troy. We'll hang out again, soon," Austin said, lowering him to the floor. He watched as Bethany took his hand, and they both plodded up the stairs.

"Why don't you sit down?" Trace walked over to the sofa and had a seat herself.

Austin sat down, but didn't make himself comfortable. "So why are you taking them over there?"

"I'm going out with some girlfriends tonight."

Austin didn't know exactly how to take that. He wanted to tell her that she didn't need to go out. He wanted to assert the rights he had as her husband, and he probably could have too, because he was still her husband, but that would really have been the wrong thing to do.

"We're just going out to have a couple of drinks, that's all," Trace said.

Austin knew she was offering that up to make him feel more secure, but it didn't work.

"Well, if you have to go out, I can keep the kids. It would be no problem, and I can bring them home sometime tomorrow afternoon. Might even take them to the zoo. I hear it's supposed to be nice tomorrow."

Trace rubbed her hands together nervously. "I don't think I can do that."

"Why not?"

"My mother was really looking forward to seeing them, and I wouldn't want to disappoint her at the last minute. You understand, don't you?" She went over and sat next to him, putting a hand on his knee. It wasn't an intimate hand, a sexual hand, not even a friendly hand, but a partner hand, an associate hand.

"Yeah, I understand," he said, trying to sound cheery.

"Next weekend will be fine," Trace offered.

"No . . . can't do it then. Uh . . . I'm going out next weekend," Austin lied.

"We'll work something out, I'm sure."

They both looked away from each other, not having anything else to say.

"Oh, you have to congratulate me," Trace said. She was now grabbing his hand, excited. "I got a job! Believe it or not."

"Where?" Austin asked, figuring she'd say at the local A&P.

"At McKenzie and Strohm. You know the law office on . . ."

"Yeah, I know who they are."

"I'll only be doing some clerical work, but it's a start," Trace said.

"A start at what?"

Trace hunched her shoulders. "I don't know, a career maybe. Or don't you think I'm capable of that?" she said, with edge in her voice.

Now wait a minute, Austin thought. During the entire time they were married all she wanted to do was sit around and take care of the kids and watch the soaps and go shopping. Now all of a sudden she'd turned into the unstoppable nineties woman. If he had known this was going to happen, he would've left a long time ago and would've already come back.

"I didn't mean anything by it. But if you were interested in that kind of work, why didn't you just come to me? You know you could've worked over at the firm."

She gave Austin a look. "I don't believe you said that. You don't want to see me at home, but you could tolerate me at work, is that it? Mmm. No, thanks." She shook her head. "Anyway, I had to know that I could get something on my own."

"Can I ask you one question?" Austin said. "Why the turnaround all of a sudden? I've been gone only a month, and in that time, you've gotten a new hairstyle, you've lost weight, you've gotten a job, and you're going out to clubs for drinks. Were you just waiting for me to leave?"

He really didn't want to ask the question, but he had to know, and he surely didn't want to hear the answer for fear that it would be yes.

Trace looked at him, a blank look on her face, then she smiled, then she frowned a little, then the smile returned again, but not quite. Something between a smile and a frown.

"It's very simple, Austin. When you left, you left me with nothing. Sure, I had the house and the kids, and I didn't really have to worry about money, but those things, with the exception of the kids, are yours. What I had was nothing, nothing that I can say that I earned. I thought that we'd be together till we both dropped off and died. I didn't think I had to worry about being on my own, and didn't know that I should've rigged a safety net just in case our marriage fell off that thin wire it was teetering on. But now I know, that's all. I don't ever want to be in that situation again. Deep down, I think there's a chance that we'll get back together, but if we don't I need to be able to take care of myself. And if we do, and you want to leave again, I need to know that I can provide for myself and the kids."

Austin didn't appreciate that last remark. She was making it seem as though he was fickle or as if this was just some silly phase he was going through. Like he was a child running away from home, then returning only after finding out meals weren't a given every day on the street. He didn't appreciate that one bit.

Austin had to get out of there. If he remained any longer, he risked saying something that he would regret.

At the apartment door, fishing for his keys, he heard his phone ringing. He quickly found his key, stuck it in the lock, and raced to the phone.

"Hello," Austin said. There was no answer. "Hello," he said again.

"Hello," a man's voice said timidly over the phone.

Austin didn't know who it was, but something sounded strangely familiar about the voice. He knew he had heard it before.

"Who is this?" Austin demanded. There was a long pause.

"Austin, this is your father."

TWENTY-ONE

It had been a month and a half since Marcus's first date with Reecie, and although he told himself he would try with everything he had not to get hooked on her, they had been close to inseparable ever since.

He realized that he was developing feelings for the woman even though it wasn't something that he was trying to do. She would come over every Thursday and stay late, letting Marcus know that Fridays were the easiest day of the week, and she could function with no problem on a little less sleep. She would stay the night on those Thursdays, not because Marcus suggested it, but because it just seemed the logical thing to do, and although Reecie didn't mention it, Marcus knew she wanted to stay as much as he wanted her to.

On those occasions, they never slept in the same bed. Marcus would put fresh linen on his bed for Reecie and he would let out the sofa bed in the living room for himself. They would sit in the dark on the bed, Indian style, eating popcorn, watching a video. The glow that came off the TV was actually quite romantic, Marcus thought. It was like a little slumber party, at least that's what Reecie said.

After the movie was over, they would sit and talk and laugh for a while. One particular evening, Marcus found it hard to let Reecie go upstairs to bed. He kept talking, hoping that she would get the hint that he wanted them to share the same bed. He threw his arm around her shoulder. "So what time do you have to be at work tomorrow?"

She looked at him and smiled. "The same time I have to be at work every day."

"Oh, I was just wondering, that's all," Marcus said.

"Well, I better be going upstairs to bed. Some of us don't have the pleasure of working at home." She grabbed the empty bowl of popcorn, kernels rolling around on the bottom, and started to get up from the bed.

"Do you want to do something this weekend?" Marcus said quickly.

"Sure, I would like that." She put one bare foot on the carpet.

"What do you want to do?" Marcus asked.

"I don't know, anything is fine. Surprise me, okay?" She bent over and kissed him quickly on the lips.

"But what if you don't like the surprise? Maybe we should talk about it, huh?"

"Marcus, we don't . . . ooohhh," Reecie laughed cleverly. "I know what you're doing. You're trying to keep me down here aren't you? Mr. Slick." She laughed a little. "I would stay, honey, but if I did, there would be no work for me tomorrow, if you know what I mean," she said, patting him affectionately on his thigh.

"Are you sure?" Marcus asked, wearing his best pathetic look.

"I'm sorry. Not even the puppy-dog face will do it this time. Besides, I just can't see myself jumping in bed with you for only an hour, then getting up and going upstairs. I just couldn't do it."

Marcus got off the bed and grabbed her hands. "Then stay down here, or I'll come up there with you."

Reecie rolled her eyes, looked toward the ceiling as if she was giving it some thought. "Sorry, Marcus. We'll have time, baby. Trust me, all right? Good night," she said quickly. She flashed him a smile, took the popcorn bowl in the kitchen, told him good night once more, then skipped up the stairs.

Marcus stood there in his t-shirt and his boxers, a tiny tepee erected in the front of his shorts. He looked down at himself. "Nothing for you tonight, fella." He clicked off the TV, then crawled in bed. He slid under the covers and made himself comfortable, figuring it would be a long sleepless night.

He wasn't angry at Reecie. He almost thought it was cute. He knew she was playing hard to get, and that was fine with him. They'd only known each other a month and a half, and even though he was dying to feel her bare body in his arms, to feel himself inside her, he had gone much longer without the feel of a woman, much much longer. He didn't feel the way he felt about her because of the possibility of her being a wonderful lover. He was attracted to her because she was a beautiful, intelligent, caring, selfless person, who always seemed to look at the positive side of things, and who always had a smile on her face. Those were terrific traits to find in a woman.

He remembered his mother used to say, "It's hard to be depressed when you have a smile on your face." And that was the truth. He thought about his mother, and thought that he would have liked her to meet Reecie. She would have liked her, and he could picture them sitting together, talking and laughing over coffee or something.

God, how he missed her, how he wanted her back. He knew she would have loved Reecie, but should he be letting himself get so involved with her? He knew he was falling. Whenever she was not with him, his thoughts were on her. He had to force himself to concentrate on his work half the time. Before he met her, that was all he thought about.

Marcus squeezed and bunched the pillow under his head till he was comfortable. He wouldn't think about it anymore. She was far too sweet a person to want to hurt him, he told himself. He pulled the covers up to his chin and prepared for sleep. Then he heard something. He sat up in bed, looked in the darkness before him, and could vaguely make out the shape of a woman. "I'm going to have to miss work tomorrow," Reecie said, standing before him. She let her nightgown drop to the floor and stood there stark naked.

Marcus couldn't speak, could barely breathe, and he immediately felt his body responding to what his eyes were seeing.

"Well?" Reecie said.

She was beautiful, every inch of her bare body. He had known she would look like that, had seen her a hundred times over in his dreams, in his fantasies.

She slowly walked over to him, and Marcus swung his legs out over the side of the mattress, spreading his knees, opening a space for her near his body. She moved into the space, her body smelling of flowers and citrus-scented lotion. She was right up against him now, her soft breast lightly grazing his chin. But Marcus didn't touch her, didn't wrap his arms tightly around her, didn't place his wanting mouth around the full breast that hung just inches from his lips. He didn't move, and not only because he felt he no longer controlled his cold, trembling hands. Plain and simple, he was scared.

And although not even half an hour ago he had tried to persuade Reecie to stay downstairs with him, expressly for this purpose, he hadn't figured that she would. And even if he had, he hadn't anticipated his own reaction.

Reecie placed her hands on Marcus's shoulders and moved just a little closer to him, pushing both her breasts into his cheeks. "So what are you going to do?" Reecie whispered seductively.

Nothing, Marcus thought, feeling like an adolescent who had always dreamed of this day, but now confronted with it, wanted nothing more than just to disappear.

It had been more than six months since the last time he had been with a woman, and even if he wanted Reecie more than anything else in the world, which he thought he did, he didn't know if his body would support him in that want, although there seemed to be no problem in that department at this point. He seemed to be rearing, and ready to go, and Reecie had reached within the slit of his boxers, pulled him out, and had her hand around him, slowly tugging at him.

"So whatcha you wanna do? So whatcha you wanna do?" she said softly into his ear each time she pulled up on him, and he felt the warmth of her breath against his ear, heard the moistness on her lips as they parted to speak. And at that point Marcus wanted so much to lift her up into that bed and make love to her, make love to her like she wouldn't believe. But something in the back of his mind was stopping him. It kept asking him, kept posing the question, what would making love to her do? How would it change this relationship?

And the answer was, it would probably make him fall in love with her, or at least set him on that course. And the relationship would definitely change. At this moment, Marcus knew that he could walk away from her if he felt he had to. He could walk away from her and not fall apart with the reality that she was out of his life. But if they made love, if he fell in love, he wouldn't be able to let go so easily. And even if things were going well between them, something would always be looming overhead. Something would always be trying to convince him that this relationship would end, that his heart would ultimately be broken, because it would have to be. Because that's how it always had been, and the way it always would be.

"Marcus, what's wrong?"

"Huh?" Marcus gasped.

"What's wrong with you?" Reecie placed her palm to his chest. "Your heart's beating like crazy. Are you all right?"

"Yeah, yeah. Just excited, I guess," Marcus said, his mind dizzy with what he should do.

"Then I want you to lay on top of me." Reecie yanked Marcus off the mattress, and lay down playfully on her back, reaching her hands out for him.

Marcus stood there, dumbfounded, staring down at her naked body.

"Well?"

Marcus made a move toward the bed.

"Aren't you going to take those off?" And Reecie was pointing to his boxers, Marcus's penis still sticking awkwardly out of the slit like the raised trunk of an excited elephant.

"Oh," he said, slid them off, and placed himself on top of her. He lay there, propping himself up slightly above her, with his elbows on either side of her ears. He was staring down at her, his eyes wide, as if he was staring in the face of a ghost, his heart still beating rapidly.

"Marcus!" Reecie said, frustration in her voice.

"Huh," and he sounded timid, like a child.

"What is wrong?"

"Oh. Nothing."

"Don't tell me that. By the way you're acting, you'd think I had the Ebola virus. You're acting like you're scared of me."

Marcus inhaled deeply, then exhaled, his body relaxing some on top of hers.

"I am scared, a little. What happens after this?"

"What do you mean?"

"What happens? Where does this relationship go?"

"What do you want to happen? Where do you want it to go?"

"I just want you to stay here for me, and not leave."

"I didn't think I was going anywhere," Reecie said, smiling. She played with the hair at the back of his neck. "So, Mr. Harris, would you like to make love to me?"

And there it was again, that question, about that action, and Marcus could feel himself becoming anxious. Feel himself wanting to run.

"Marcus?" Reecie said, reaching up and holding his face in her hands. "Something's telling me the answer is yes, but you seem as though you aren't sure."

"The answer is yes, but it's been so long and I don't know if things are working as good as they used to, if you know what I mean," and before Marcus even finished his statement, he could feel Reecie's hand around him again, checking him.

"Well, it seems in perfect working condition to me. And about how long it's been, it's just like riding a bike. You never forget how." And with that, Reecie parted her legs, wrapped her hands around Marcus's hips, and slowly pulled him in.

TWENTY-TWO

The next day at work, Caleb walked between the large floor-to-ceiling shelves taking inventory. As he slowly passed from one aisle into another, he glanced at Jim, just to see what he was up to. Jim hadn't said anything to him all day, and Caleb didn't mind that one bit. The less interaction the better.

"Caleb, I need you to enter what you have into the computer, now. We have a shipment coming in and we have to go down to make sure it's all there." Caleb looked up and Jim was right there in front of him.

"All right." Caleb walked over to his terminal, feeling a little weird about Jim. He seemed all right, but then again he could be on the brink of snapping, pulling out an automatic weapon and killing everyone on the floor.

"Now, Caleb," Jim said politely. "Do you think you can batch enter those?"

So that was his angle, Caleb thought. That was the way he was going to get him. Jim knew Caleb didn't know the first thing about batch entry. He had never gone over it with him, and now he wanted Caleb to prove that he was competent with it.

"I don't know how to do that," Caleb said, staring angrily at the terminal.

"Well, let me show you," Jim said. He punched a couple of numbers, worked the mouse around a little, then entered an entire column of information.

"This way you can do the work in half the time." Jim was talking to Caleb as though he really wanted him to pick the stuff up. He was pointing things out, making eye contact. "You got it?" Jim asked him.

Caleb tried, punching the same buttons, manipulating the mouse the same way.

"And move it right up here," Jim said. He placed his hand, his white hand, right on top of Caleb's and moved the mouse, directing the pointer into the right column.

"Now press enter."

Caleb did, and he was successful. He slowly turned his head toward Jim and Jim was smiling. Teeth showing, his eyes squinting behind the thick lenses of his glasses. It was a genuine smile.

"Thanks," Caleb said, unsure if that was the word he really should have been using.

"No problem," Jim said, slapping him on the back as if they were old fishing buddies. "Now let me show you something else." He reached behind the computer and switched it off, then turned it back on again.

"Now instead of waiting to punch in your log-on code, if you hit this button," he didn't touch it, "enter your first three log-on numbers, then hit this number and enter your last three, the computer brings you right to the main batching screen. We aren't supposed to know that because it makes our work easier, but I found out how to do it, and I just thought I'd share it with you." He poked Caleb in the ribs.

"Now let me show you. What's your log-on code?"

"I'm not supposed to give you that. That's my personal number, right?" Caleb said.

Jim looked at him as though he was behaving childishly. "Don't be stupid, everyone in here knows everyone else's log-ons. What is it? I want to show you how to do this."

Caleb seriously thought about telling him the code, but he didn't know exactly why. He wanted to think it was because it was what he was supposed to do. That, as Caleb remembered Mr. Benning saying, he was supposed to learn from Jim, and that would be exactly what Caleb would be doing.

But Caleb knew the truth was that he really wanted Jim's help, his knowledge, and possibly even his friendship. Jim was extending his hand to Caleb, offering to pull him up, and if Caleb didn't give Jim the code, he might think Caleb didn't trust him. He might even take offense, and go back to paying him no attention at all.

Caleb couldn't afford that. He realized he needed Jim's help, that it could make the difference in Caleb keeping this job or losing it. Besides, Jim seemed to be very sincere. Something about the expression on his face said honesty. The way he gently nudged Caleb with his elbow, saying, "Well?" as though suspicion was a waste of time, and just downright foolish.

So Caleb gave him the code, feeling unsure at first. But then Jim showed Caleb the process. Caleb tried it, and it worked just like it did for Jim. Caleb sat there, brimming with confidence, and beaming inside like a proud child experiencing his first success.

He had made the right decision, Caleb told himself. He knew that, and from now on, everything would be fine.

Caleb went out with Marcus that evening. They had a beer at a small neighborhood tavern.

"So, you're a hard person to catch up to nowadays. What happened to you? Find a new hobby?" Caleb asked, joking.

"You might want to say that," Marcus said, driving the car out of the tavern's parking lot.

"And the hobby?"

"I met a woman. A beautiful woman." Marcus looked over at Caleb, then back to the road.

"Ooohhh, I don't believe it. Big brother finally got himself a girl. I didn't want to say anything, but I was starting to worry about you," Caleb said, nudging Marcus in the ribs with his elbow.

"Well, you haven't been standing outside my front door either. Since you got that job, you haven't been able to stay in the house. And

I'm not saying that's bad, that's the way it's supposed to be. One of the reasons you make money is so you can enjoy some of the things that it can buy," Marcus said.

"I haven't been enjoying that much. I'm making some money, but it's not a whole lot, so I don't want to go out there and act a fool." Caleb adjusted the station on the radio, trying to find something decent to listen to.

"You don't have any bills, do you?" Marcus said.

"No. 'Cause I never had any money."

"So the money that you make goes straight to you, outside of rent, that is?"

"I guess. I'm just trying to save as much as I can," Caleb said, turning the volume up a little, then settling back into the seat.

"Save for what?"

"Just to save. Because it's nice just to know you have a little money, when it used to be the only things swimming around in my pocket were my fingers," Caleb said, smiling.

"But what are you saving for?" Marcus asked again. "You don't want anything now that you have a job? Now that you work forty hours a week, busting your butt, running along in the rat race like you said you'd never do. There's nothing that you want?"

Caleb thought for a moment, then smiled to himself. "I'm tired of taking the damn bus everywhere. If I were to buy something, it would be a car. Yeah, that's what I'd want is a car."

"Really," Marcus said.

"Yeah, really. Why, I can't have a car, or something?" Caleb said.

"No, I didn't say that. I think you should have one. You're thirty years old, have a family, and you work full time. You should definitely have a car. As a matter of fact, let's go get you one right now."

"What! What do you mean?" Caleb asked, a look of almost fear on his face.

"We're out, it's a nice evening for car shopping, and you just said you needed a car."

"I said I wanted a car. There's a difference."

"Well, we're going anyway." Marcus made a quick U-turn. "I know of a quality place, and the owner is a friend of mine."

．　　　．　　　．

"So what do you think?" Marcus said in the used car lot. Most of the cars were very nice, well maintained, and fairly new.

"I can't afford nothing like what's out here. Where do they keep the hoopties? They don't have any '73 Delta 88's with a busted taillight and a crack in the windshield out here? That's the only kind of car I can afford." Caleb spun in a circle, taking in all the beautiful shiny cars. Considering all he had been through, where he had spent the last ten years of his life, chewing on stale bread, cheap peanut butter and jelly in between, it was a big deal just for him to be on a car lot. And it was enough just to look and know one day, maybe, he might be able to afford one.

"Naw, Marcus. Let's get out of here, because the only thing that's happening is I'm getting pissed off." He saw a car and wandered over to it. Marcus followed behind him. Caleb examined the car, walking all the way around it. He cupped his hands and put his face up to the driver's side window to look inside. "That's nice," he said, not loud enough for Marcus to hear.

"So, this is the one you like, huh? Red, very inconspicuous." Marcus walked over and stood in the front of it. "How much is it?"

Caleb read the price off the sticker on the window. "This car is damn near seven thousand dollars. I can't buy this," Caleb said, frustrated. "Let's get out of here, all right?"

"That's why they give you a number of years to buy. Most people don't have that kind of money in their pockets," Marcus said, holding his brother from leaving.

"But I don't have any credit, and they probably wouldn't give me any because I just got the job not even a month ago," Caleb said, looking over the car again.

"Let's just go in and see what happens," Marcus said. He looked into the driver's side window and nodded his head. "It is nice."

"What do you mean, see what happens?" Caleb said.

"Look, I'll just co-sign for you, all right. I'll co-sign, and you'll have your car. It's really very simple. Let's just do it." He had a hand on Caleb's back and was trying to force him in the direction of the sales department.

"I told you, I don't have any money on me. Can we just get out of here? And why are you pressing so hard for me to get a car? Damn, do you get a commission or something?"

"Caleb, don't worry about the money. If there's a down payment, I got it covered. That's no problem, okay? And the reason I'm pushing is because I feel you should have it. I'm very proud of you. You've been through a lot of . . . well, a lot of everything since you were a kid. It wasn't easy and I know it, yet you still came out with your priorities straight, a woman that thinks the world of you, and a strong little son. You got this job, and I'm just proud of you. I want to give you a gift, that's all. So let's just say, the down payment on the car will be my gift to you," Marcus said, slugging him in the shoulder once. "What do you say, little brother?"

Caleb looked at the car, then at Marcus, then took another long look at the car.

"I can't, man. You know I can't take money from you. I have to do it on my own, that's just how it is."

"Why, Caleb? I'm telling you, it's not a problem. I have the money. Why is it such a big deal?"

"It just is!" Caleb said, raising his voice. "You just don't think I can do it on my own, that's all. I can get this, just like I got that stupid job. You never thought I could do that but I did." The anger Caleb was feeling was very clear on his face.

"I never said that."

"You never had to. Every time I was in a situation, you came around talking about 'let me help you, let me handle it, is there anything I can do?' You call my apartment like crazy, checking up on me like I can't survive day to day without your supervision. You're always on my back. 'Do you need some money? Are you looking for a job? Do you need me to call someone?' "

"Couldn't that be just because I care, Caleb?" Marcus said.

"No. You do all that because you told Ma you'd take care of me, and you thought you failed. You feel guilty, that's all. That's all that is." Caleb just stood there, his hands in his pockets, staring at his older brother. Marcus didn't say anything.

"Well, we're getting this car for you," Marcus said, looking up, as if the last part of the conversation had never taken place.

"Didn't you hear what I just said?"

"Yeah, I heard you, and I don't feel guilty. I wasn't sure, so I had to think about it. And no, I'm not guilty. I care for my younger brother, that's all, just like I said. Now if you don't want to take the money, then you don't have to. We can call it a loan, and you can pay me back, even with interest if you like. How's that?" Marcus said.

"The answer is still no, Marcus. Now can we go?"

Marcus looked oddly at Caleb as if he was thinking something. "Do you care for your family?" Marcus asked.

"Yeah, what kind of question is that?"

"Say it was three o'clock in the morning and Sonya got sick, or worse yet, Jahlil. How would you get them to the hospital? I know you wouldn't be on the bus stop waiting on a bus at three in the morning while your child is crying with extreme pain."

"I know what you're doing, Marcus, and I don't appreciate it," Caleb said.

"Say it was late out and Sonya had to go somewhere, I don't know where, but she had to go, and you happened to be out. You would want her out in those streets on public transportation? Anything can happen. I'm sorry, Caleb, but it's true," Marcus said.

"So you're saying, if something happens to my family it's my fault?" Caleb asked.

"No, I'm not saying that."

"You said if they had to be out on the street and something happened, it would be my fault because we don't have a car, or you're implying that." Caleb walked very close to Marcus, the volume of his voice increasing as he neared him. "But seeing that I don't have a car then you're actually saying that."

"Wake up, Caleb, and get that damn chip off your shoulder," Marcus yelled at him. An older woman walked by and looked in their direction. They both looked at her as if to tell her to mind her own business.

"I'm tired of your damn attitude. No one can do anything for poor Caleb because he wants to prove to the world that he can do it himself. Well, you know what, you can't. How's that?" Marcus said, crossing his arms, a smug look on his face. "No one can, Caleb, so stop your pouting. Now I understand you and respect you for wanting to do some things for yourself, but don't be a fool when someone is trying to help you a little. I told you it will be a loan. You will have to pay me back the money. It's something that you will have to do eventually. It's called getting credit. You might as well start with someone you trust. And if you don't want to see the car as something that I'm doing for you, just look at it as something that I'm doing for my nephew. Yeah, let's just say that I'm not helping you buy the car, I'm helping Jahlil buy it. It's going to be his car, all right? You'll just drive it till he's sixteen, then you'll have to give it up."

Caleb smiled a little at the remark. Everything he threw up to stop Marcus from helping him get the car, Marcus worked around. He guessed Marcus really wanted him to have it. Besides, a lot of what he said made sense. He was tired of being mad at the world for everything that had happened to him. Actually, he should be happy as hell, right? Lately things really seemed to be going his way. Too bad it took his brother to open his eyes, and he wasn't able to see it for himself.

"All right," Caleb said, breaking down. "It's a loan, and you're buying the car for Jahlil, okay. I'll just drive it till he's sixteen," Caleb said, as they walked toward the sales department.

After just a little haggling over price, and the signing of some papers, Caleb was in the car and driving home. It was the best feeling in the world. He had never owned a car, and now he had finally gotten one, and a nice one at that. A Honda Prelude. Kind of sporty, but still practical, having a back seat for the boy, a decent-size trunk and all that other stuff.

After thinking back to all the fuss he had put up about Marcus laying out the down payment and signing for the thing, he was glad that Marcus had been persistent and pushed for him to get it.

Caleb had the music going at a fairly high volume. He was testing how well it cornered by cutting the wheel hard around each turn and weaving in and out of traffic. He drove all over town, through neighborhoods he had never been to, and to places he had only heard about.

One house caught his attention and wouldn't let it go. Caleb pulled the car over and got out. He didn't know where he was but he knew it was far from where he lived. It was late in the evening and he heard not a single police or fire siren. As a matter of fact he heard nothing, nothing at all, except for maybe crickets and the distant sound of children laughing. He took a breath in and the air was fresh, with just a trace of freshly cut grass and the faint scent of barbecue.

He stepped up on the front lawn and the house sat about fifty to seventy-five feet away from him. That entire front lawn was theirs, he thought. The house was huge, and old, and there were curves and angles that he'd never seen on the housing in the inner city. The windows were cut into odd shapes, and refracted the late evening sunlight in a strange way, but it looked beautiful. There had to have been at least twenty or thirty rooms in that thing, and the garage was as big as the house Caleb grew up in.

Caleb stood out on the lawn and just looked up at the house for a long time. He was storing the image in his head, telling himself, if nothing else, this would be his inspiration. He would live in something like that one day. He made that pact with himself as the sun went down.

When he finally made his way home, Sonya was ready to have a fit, asking him if he'd reverted back to his old ways of staying out late and running the streets. But when Caleb told her what he had done, she ran down the stairs to see his shiny new red car. She insisted that he take her and Jahlil for a ride.

They slid Jahlil into the back seat without waking him. Sonya got in and said, "Oh, this is nice." Caleb didn't say anything, as though he was so used to nice things that something as simple as this car would never evoke such a response from him.

He drove them all about town that warm night. They drove over the bridge that crossed the Chicago River, and Sonya stuck her head out the window to look down in the dark water. He drove them under the tall skyscrapers and opened the sunroof so she could look straight up toward the tops of them, as the warm night air blew over her face.

They ended up parked at the lake, surrounded by nothing but a couple of other cars, darkness, and water that stretched out as far as they could see, then went black as if the sky had swallowed it up. Caleb didn't say a word, transfixed at the beauty of the lake, at how the stars sparkled off it as if millions of diamonds were floating on its waves. He turned his head toward Sonya. She was speechless as well. She turned to look at him, then slowly moved toward him to kiss him. She placed a hand on his cheek, and looked as though she wanted to say something, but didn't. She didn't have to. Caleb knew exactly what she was thinking and he felt the same way. He loved her, and he had wanted this moment for so long, and he never wanted it to end. At least he felt she was thinking something like that.

She let her hand fall and resumed gazing back at the lake. Caleb looked to the back seat and his son was still sound asleep. He wished that Jahlil was awake for this, but there would be many more times— many more times like these and many more opportunities to show his child what he should see, what he needed to see. To let him know that his father was a good man, one who could and should be respected by his son, and he should know that his father loved him. He should know these things, because for him to not know them would be so damaging. He didn't want that to happen to Jahlil, because it was a terrible thing, a hopeless situation, and if anyone knew, he did. He wouldn't do that to his child like it was done to him, never.

A week later Caleb was actually looking forward to going to work. As he drove his car in, he felt confident and purposeful. And even though there was bumper-to-bumper traffic, he felt relaxed, turning his radio from news to some rap. The sun was entering his eyes a little so he reached over in his glove compartment and slipped on his sunglasses, the brand-new ones he had bought the other day. They were rather expensive, forty dollars, but it wasn't a problem. He just put them on his store credit card. He had applied for it the day after he got his car, and to his surprise they gave it to him that same day, no previous credit and all. Along with the sunglasses he had bought a twenty-five-inch color TV and a VCR. The next day, he had applied for two more credit cards at different stores and got them. There he bought some clothes for work, a nice leather jacket for Sonya, and a video game with a lot of cartridges for Jahlil. It was all very easy. At first he was skeptical, but just like Marcus said, he would have to deal with credit sometime. He was working so he should experience nice things and have some of the things he wanted. He took a quick glimpse in the rearview mirror, straightened his tie, and admired himself.

At the rate he was driving he would never get to work on time, but that really didn't bother Caleb, because Jim would be understanding about it.

It was weird because Caleb was beginning to see Jim as a pretty decent guy, and he could even see the guy being his friend one day. When he told Blue how he felt, the brother almost went crazy.

"Have you been smoking that cheap shit again, man?" he said, a crazed look on his face.

"I ain't been smoking nothing lately," Caleb said. "I don't want to get caught on a piss test."

Blue shook his head and blew out a long sigh in disgust. "There it goes, already you starting to change. Don't want to do the things you grew up doing, don't want to hang around your old partners no more."

"I'm at work, Blue. I can't be hanging out during the middle of the day, sippin' malt liquor, like you and Ray Ray."

Blue walked over to him slowly, eyeing him up and down. "And what is that supposed to mean?"

"What?" Caleb said.

" 'Sippin' malt liquor like you and Ray Ray,' " Blue said, still circling Caleb. "You hear the way you said that? Like that's some shit that's beneath you. Like you all better than that now, so you can't be doing some low-life, black people shit like sippin' malt liquor all day with me and Ray Ray."

Caleb laughed a little. "That wasn't what I meant, man. I'm just saying that I got to be at work. You know the whole story. We went over this, so don't be talking that shit about me changing."

"You changed, man," Blue said.

"No I didn't," Caleb said, following Blue as he walked slowly about his room. "And sit your ass down, Blue, you're making me dizzy."

"You befriending some white motherfucker," he said, flopping down into a beat-up sofa. "The same motherfucker who tried to get you fired in the first place. What about that? You think shit like that just goes away?"

"I told you. I took care of that. I put the shit on the line so even he could understand, and he realized I wasn't playing so he cooled out. That's it," Caleb said.

"Oh, that's it, huh? You think because you, Caleb Harris, pulls him to a side and says 'If you don't stop fucking with me, I'm going to kick your ass,' he's going to change altogether? He's going to be a new motherfucker. Because you know that's all it really would've took to change white folks back in the sixties," Blue said sarcastically. "If each brother would've pulled a white boy aside and threatened him with a serious ass kicking, they would've changed their ways. They would've stopped burning crosses, they would've stopped breaking up our protest, by spraying us with high-powered water hoses, and letting dogs loose on us to tear into our legs, and they would've stopped choking us and beating us with them damn billy clubs, because we let them know that we'd fuck them up if they kept on, right?"

"I'm not saying that and you know it."

"What are you saying then, brotha?" Blue raised his voice and stood from the sofa. "Their beliefs about us don't change overnight. That shit has been bred into their asses since birth. They didn't want to stop us from voting just because it was something to do. They didn't want us to have a say in what happened around us. They didn't segregate bathrooms, and lunch halls and schools, because they needed the space for themselves. It was because they couldn't stand the sight of us, because they couldn't stomach the idea of us being so near to them, eating their food, sharing their space, breathing their air. Brotha, that's hate. Not that simple surfacey shit, but the deep-seated kind, the kind you take to your grave. One little skinny, two-buck brotha like yourself ain't going to change that with a discussion." Blue gave Caleb another one of those creepy looks, then fell back into the sofa as though he was exhausted from his speech.

"That was a long time ago, Blue. It ain't the same now," Caleb said, knowing that there was still racism about, but not of the same species.

"I can't believe you saying that. Listen, don't go believing that shit. The only thing that changed is the number of years that we been living with this shit and the number of black folks that been wronged. Just watch your back, that's all I'm telling you, all right? Because to them, you ain't shit, and you'll never be shit as long as they have something to say about it."

TWENTY-THREE

He wouldn't run, Marcus told himself as he sat at the table with Reecie, a chessboard between them, trying to avoid her stare. They were becoming very close, very serious, or at least she was. It had all begun after they started making love on a regular basis, and Marcus often asked himself why he ever went there.

Of course, the lovemaking was wonderful. Long sessions, full of passion and feelings. But that was what scared him the most, that love thing. It was the beginning of the end. Nothing could compare to the beginning of a relationship, the day a man tells a woman that he loves her. Every day in the relationship thereafter pales in comparison. And after a month or two the whole thing is in the toilet.

After each time they made love, Reecie would stare into his eyes. "I love you," she'd say, her voice sounding as sweet as ever. Marcus would wait a few seconds, try to persuade himself to say something, search around in his soul for whatever it is that makes men say such a thing, but he couldn't find it. Not that he didn't feel the same as she did; he did, but he wasn't sure if he actually wanted to admit that to her.

On those occasions he would just grab her tight and kiss her on the forehead or the lips, whichever was closer. It wasn't an admission of love, but it was a tiny gesture that she seemed to accept as that, or close enough to that for the moment.

Sometimes Marcus and Reecie would be talking about nothing in particular, and all of a sudden she would make some remark about the future. "Maybe next year we can plan a vacation to the islands," she would say as she poured herself a glass of water, or brushed her hair.

On these occasions, which were becoming more frequent, Marcus would only nod his head and agree with a simple "Sounds good, baby," not giving it any more thought than what he would have for dinner a year from then. But he realized what she was doing. Reecie was checking to see where his head was at, where she stood with him in the future. He didn't know why women played games like that. She would have been a lot better off, and things would have been a lot easier, if she just came right out and asked him, and he would have simply told her. He liked her a great deal, even loved her. Thought she was cute as a button and all that, but he just didn't know if they'd be sharing the same bathroom in a year or two or anytime in the future for that matter.

For quite a while she seemed to go along with his simple nods and his kisses on the forehead to avoid admission of love for her, and the generally casual attitude Marcus took toward their relationship. But lately Reecie had become a lot less patient.

Eventually she had invited Marcus to her parents' house for Sunday dinner. He had turned her down, and she all but lost her mind looking for the reason for his refusal.

"Because I just don't feel like driving all the way down to Indianapolis," Marcus said.

"Why not?"

"Because . . . because I have a lot of work to do, and I have a deadline." He was lying, but it sounded good as it came out, and as he turned his head so she couldn't read his face, he hoped she believed it. Reecie would have him sitting at her family table over dinner. Her mother would be smiling politely at Marcus, saying things like "Oh, what a handsome couple the two of you make." And her father would be staring at him suspiciously over his eyeglasses all during dinner, and afterward, Marcus knew, he would pull him aside, into the den, and the first thing out of his mouth would be, "So, young man, what are your inten-tions for my daughter?" Marcus just wasn't going to be bulldozed into any type of situation with Reecie.

"Bullshit, Marcus!" Reecie said, rejecting his excuse.

"What?" he said, knowing he was busted.

"You didn't tell me of any project you had going," Reecie said, look-ing into his face. "You just don't want to meet my parents. Why?"

Marcus squirmed uncomfortably for a moment. "Don't you think that's a pretty big step? We've only been dating for a few months."

"It's just meeting my parents. I'm not asking you to ask my father if you can have my hand in marriage."

"Oh, you're not, huh?"

"No. I'm not, and I don't even know why you're thinking that," Reecie said.

"Maybe because it's just the way I feel. I don't know about the par-ent thing. Can't we just postpone for maybe ten years?" Marcus said, smiling, hoping Reecie would follow. She didn't.

"I don't know what the big deal is. It's going to have to happen sometime if you're going to be with me. I don't know why you're scared."

"I'm not scared, all right?" Marcus said, taking offense. "I just don't feel like driving all the way out there to meet your people, that's all."

"Whatever you say, Marcus," Reecie said. She looked at him as though she didn't believe a word he said, but that didn't make a differ-ence to Marcus. He wasn't going to be pushed into anything, because relationships went bad nowadays. Once a man commits, the woman ei-ther tries to chain him to the plumbing under the kitchen sink so he can't move without her permission, or she starts to lose interest after having the man believe he means the world to her, and then she walks out. He wasn't having either one of those things happen to him, espe-cially the latter.

"You going to move him or not, Marcus?" Reecie said, aggravated, star-ing at the halted chess piece. Marcus had his hand on his rook and was just letting it sit there.

"Oh," he said, coming out of his daydreaming. He slid the piece across the board, looked at all Reecie's pieces, looked in her face to see no helpful hints, then hesitantly removed his hand from the piece.

Reecie shook her head. "Pitiful, pathetic move, Marcus. You must've wanted me to win." Reecie slid her queen across the board, knocking Marcus's rook over, snatching it off the board, then yelled, "Check! and checkmate!"

Marcus surveyed the board, and to his dismay saw the trap. Her queen had him from one angle, her bishop the other, and that damn knight, the final angle. It was always that damn horse that got him with that funky little L-shaped move.

Damn, Marcus thought to himself.

"You must've wanted me to win," Reecie said again, smiling.

But that was the farthest thing from the truth. It was his suggestion that they play, and he wanted the game to last as long as humanly possible, because just before the game she had gotten on the feelings conversation again.

Frustrated, Marcus cleared the board with a sweep of his hand. "Let's play again."

"No, I don't want to," Reecie said.

"C'mon, why not?"

"Because I don't want to. I want to talk," and that was the last thing Marcus wanted to hear.

Reecie pushed the chessboard aside and grabbed one of Marcus's hands. "How do you feel, Marcus?"

Marcus looked straight into her eyes, trying to find out where that question came from all of a sudden. "I feel fine. I've been taking my vitamins. No sign of a cold or a—"

"Stop it, already. You know what I'm talking about. I mean about me. How do you feel about me?"

Marcus swallowed hard. He could feel perspiration starting to build between their hands. "I think you're fine, you're cool. I like you a lot," he said.

"Well, thanks a lot. Thank you for going out on that emotional ledge for me. I know it took a great deal of bravery, but I always knew you had it in you." She pulled her hand away.

Marcus didn't say anything, just pondered what she had said, trying to find meaning in it, but all he could find was sarcasm.

"And that's how you feel about me? That's it?" Reecie said.

"What am I supposed to say?" Marcus said, trying to avoid her stare.

"Just what I asked you, how you feel," she said curtly.

"Well … I guess that's it," Marcus said, lowering his head.

"I guess that's going to have to do," Reecie said. She sounded disappointed. "You know that I love you. I told you a million times, how do you feel about that?"

Marcus sighed, tired of the inquisition. "I'm glad you love me. I'm glad."

"But you don't love me?"

"Reecie . . ." Marcus blew out another sigh filled with frustration. "Where is this going?"

"That's it. That's it right there," Reecie said, standing, pacing the floor in a short line in front of him.

"Where is this going, Marcus? That's what I want to know, too. Yes, we've only been dating for a few months, but I want to know if you intend on it being a few more, or if you want to be done, or if you have plans at all. I know you're not necessarily the sentimental type, but you've been just dishing out too many lukewarm receptions. I tell you that I love you and all you do is give me a kiss. What is that? I get the same thing from my dog when I tell him that I love him."

"What do you want from me, Reecie?" Marcus said.

"I just want you to be straight with me. I need that. It might not mean a lot to you, but when I tell you that I love you, I mean it. I'm not joking, it's not kid's stuff, and when I ask you how you feel about me, about us, I don't do it to torment you. I need you to let me know if I can continue loving you without being hurt."

"I would never hurt you, Reecie. I care too much about you."

"Oh. I see," she said, shaking her head, her arms crossed before her. "Then why can't you just tell me the truth about how you feel."

"Because I don't want to be hurt, okay? There! Everything I told you, about my family, about my mother, my father leaving, that obviously doesn't mean anything to you." Marcus lowered his head again, and ran his hands through his hair.

"Yes, it means something to me. It means that you've been hurt, and I'm sorry. I'm not trying to sound uncaring, but what does that have to do with me? I don't understand what that has to do with you telling me how you feel."

"Reecie," Marcus said, looking up at her. "I've just had too much experience with this. The minute I tell you I love you, the minute you become my best friend, mean so much to me that I can't live without you, you're going to leave. I know it."

"Marcus, I would never—" Reecie said, moving toward him.

"No. That's what they all say," Marcus said, putting his hand up to stop her from nearing him. "Did my father see himself walking out on me when he made my mother pregnant for the second time? Did my mother intend on dying, when she released me and watched as I walked across the floor for the first time by myself? Did either one of my brothers tell me that they would be leaving when I needed them the most? No. Not at all, and you won't either, Reecie. When everything is new, it's easy to say things that sound good, that make the other person feel safe, happy and content, but I can't . . . I can't risk that again."

Reecie walked near him and put her hand on Marcus's lowered head.

"I'm sorry for what happened to you, and I'm sorry that I can't take those things back, but you can't dwell on them forever. You have to get past that, Marcus. Bad things happen to all of us, but if we let them get us to the point where we can't take a step forward, we'll be trapped in that pain forever. Is that what you want, Marcus? Is that how you want to live your life?"

Marcus shook his head under the gentle weight of her hand.

"Look up at me, Marcus. I love you," she said, caressing his face. "I—love—you. And I never want to do anything to hurt you. Never. I just want to be here for you, love you, and have you love me. I don't think that's too much to ask, do you?"

He didn't say anything, but no, he thought. It wasn't too much to ask. She bent down and wrapped her arms around him. He hugged her back.

"I love you, Marcus," she said.

Marcus said nothing. He knew that she was probably hoping that the emotional pep talk would jar something in his heart and shake loose the admission, but it wasn't that simple. How he felt was how he felt and what he said, he meant. He just didn't want to get hurt, and openly admitting his love for someone seemed to make that reality all the more possible.

She stood there holding him in silence. Marcus felt his head gently rise and fall against her belly, and he felt that she was just waiting for him to finally come out and tell her.

"Marcus," Reecie said. "Should we stop seeing each other?"

Marcus gently pulled away from her, looking up to her face, not knowing what she was talking about.

"What?" he said, a disturbed look on his face.

"Should I go?" She pulled her hands from around him and let them hang at her sides. "Would you rather I not be with you? I don't want you to take this the wrong way, because I'm not threatening you, but I don't want to feel as though I'm pressuring you either."

"What are you talking about?" Marcus said. Why was she acting this way? Couldn't she tell that he loved her, that the last thing he wanted to do was lose her? No, he hadn't admitted it to her, but that didn't mean it wasn't true. He was sure, most of all, that he needed her to remain in his life.

"Why are you saying that?" Marcus said, standing to face her.

"I told you that I'm not threatening you," Reecie said.

"But you are. Can't you see that?" Marcus felt himself becoming angry, so angry that he wanted to grab her and shake her if she continued to play blind to what she was doing. "I told you I have problems expressing my feelings, and I told you why," Marcus said, raising his voice. "I've been perfectly honest with you, and now you talk about this! That's not fair, Reecie, and I didn't think you would take such a route to get what you wanted."

"Don't even say that, Marcus, because you act like I'm doing some great wrong. I'm just doing what you're doing, trying to protect myself from getting hurt."

"But that's not the way to do it!" Marcus yelled, very loud this time.

"Why the fuck not?" Reecie yelled back even louder.

They both stood in silent anger. Marcus looked away for a moment, then back up at Reecie, who had also turned away.

"Because I don't want you to leave, and I don't think I can handle being without you," Marcus said reluctantly, feeling that the words were tricked out of him.

"And why is that, Marcus? Why don't you think you can handle being without me?"

He knew what she was doing. He knew the point she was getting at and he had to tell her. She had him. Check! and checkmate! He could not hold back how he obviously felt about her.

"Because I love you," Marcus said softly. The admission slipped out of his mouth with as much pain as he had known there would be, but with that bit of pain also came relief. Something seemed to drop off his shoulders, and he knew it was the load of all the years he had tried so desperately to keep those words locked inside him. Well, they were out now, and there was nothing he could do about it but have faith.

Faith. The word almost seemed foreign to him. "Because I love you," Marcus said again.

Reecie walked back up to him and put her arms around him. "That's all I wanted to hear."

TWENTY-FOUR

The next day, Caleb walked in the office feeling as cheery as if nothing in the world was ever wrong.

"Good morning, Ms. Childress," he said merrily.

"Good morning, Mr. Harris," she returned.

Today was Friday, last day of the week, and he was able to look forward to the weekend. Marcus had said he and Reecie would keep Jahlil to give Caleb an opportunity to plan something with Sonya. He told her to pack a bag because they were going to drive up to Wisconsin and stay in a hotel for the weekend. He'd been looking forward to it the entire week, counting each day as it dragged by. But now it was here and he couldn't wait to get off work and head home.

He pulled his card and punched in. The clock read 8:23 A.M. He should have been there at 8:00. Caleb walked past it and thought nothing of it.

He put his bag in his locker and walked into the inventory room. Jim was standing by the door, wearing a tie. Caleb thought back and didn't remember him mentioning any special event.

"Who's getting married?" Caleb said, walking past him.

"Where were you?" Jim said dryly, looking down at his watch.

"Oh, sorry, man. Traffic was backed up out there. It won't happen again," Caleb said, paying it no mind. He sat at his terminal and logged on to his computer.

"That may be the least of your problems," Jim said. "Caleb, you need to come with me." He reached behind Caleb's computer and switched it off. Caleb saw the screen go black before him.

"What are you doing?" Caleb asked, truly baffled.

"I said you have to come with me. Mr. Benning wants to see you."

Caleb did not have the slightest idea what this was about, but one thing he did know was that Jim wasn't his same friendly self anymore. No more smiles and jokes. He looked at Caleb with firm, unflinching eyes and a stone face. They walked down the hall toward Benning's office, Caleb in front, Jim walking behind as if to stop him from running in the other direction.

Jim knocked once on the door, and Benning told them to come in.

"Morning," Benning said. No smile, no pleasant face, no nothing. He motioned with his hand for them to sit down. Caleb sat down, and he knew something was wrong.

Benning opened that folder again, the one that Caleb knew was his personnel folder. "Caleb, do you know why you're sitting in this office right now?" Benning said, his face blank.

Caleb squirmed a little in his chair. "No, sir, I don't."

Jim blew a sarcastic sigh. "Right," he said under his breath, but loud enough for everyone to hear.

"I have here some computer printouts, detailing aspects of our inventory." He held the papers in his hand, then threw them to the desk as if they reeked of something foul. "It lets me know what shipments are going where, how large the shipment is, and what time it leaves here and what time it arrives wherever it's going. These papers let me know what shipments I can expect, size, type, and so forth, and they also let me know how many boxes of discs are entered into the computer as being shelved and how many discs are actually shelved." He put emphasis on the point, giving Caleb a cold hard stare before looking away. Caleb had no idea what was going on. Benning sat quietly for a moment.

"Am I supposed to say something about that?" Caleb asked.

"Is there something you want to say?" Benning asked.

"Outside of saying I like the job, no." He looked at Jim. Jim turned his head away.

"I see," Benning said. He took a loud audible breath, then released it before clearing his throat. "I'm not accusing you of anything, Caleb. But these papers . . . these papers," he said again, picking them up and waving them in his hands. "They say that a number of boxes of discs were logged in as being shelved, but when I checked the cross reference, it says that the number is wrong. That all the boxes entered have not been shelved. Then when I check the shelves myself, I find the same thing, that we're short. Do you know what happened to the boxes that are missing, Caleb?"

"No," Caleb said, his heart beginning to beat faster. "I don't know why you're asking me."

"Well, who else should he ask? Me? I didn't take them," Jim said, squealing. "The only person it could've been was you."

"What! What are you talking about?" Caleb couldn't believe what he was hearing. He looked over at Jim. His face was red. That damn tie was probably cutting off the circulation to his head.

"Caleb, these printouts come from your terminal. You entered this false information," Benning said. "I want to know why you did that, and where are the other boxes?"

"I don't know what you're talking about. What boxes?"

"The other three hundred boxes of discs."

Caleb's eyes bulged wide. "What am I supposed to do with three hundred boxes of discs?"

"You could've sold them to some of your people on the street," Jim said.

Caleb shot up from his seat. "What the fuck is that supposed to mean? Huh, what does that mean?" He grabbed Jim by the tie and pulled. Jim's arms were flailing about as if he were furiously trying to fly away.

"Caleb!" Benning yelled. Caleb still had Jim by the tie. "Caleb!" he yelled louder in a thunderous voice. Caleb let Jim go. He fell to his seat and grasped at his throat.

"Jim, leave the room," Benning said. Jim pulled himself up and staggered out.

Benning pushed away from the desk where he could kick his legs out to the side of it. He leaned back in his chair, put his elbow on the desk and his hand to his forehead. "The boy told me about you hitting him," Benning said, sounding disappointed.

Caleb couldn't say or do a thing. But what he wanted to do was find Jim and strangle him with that tie.

"Why did you do it?"

"He was trying to make me lose my job. This is all I got, I can't lose it," Caleb said, leaning closer to Benning's desk.

"And what did you think threatening him would allow you to do, keep it? Caleb, you can't bring that stuff in here. It may work on the street, but it doesn't work like that in business. Now, I'm going to put it to you straight. These papers say that you stole or misplaced some three hundred boxes of discs. I say that because it comes from your terminal and the only person that can log on to your terminal is you. So I'm going to ask you straight out, did you steal these discs, and if not do you know where you might have misplaced them?"

His terminal. *His* terminal. How could this have happened at *his* terminal? Then he thought back to the day he gave Jim his log-on code. Jim had set him up. Jim fucking set him up!

"Hold it. He had my code. Jim has my log-on code, that's why it says that it's on my terminal," Caleb said, as though there might be hope for his situation.

"I thought when I gave you that code, that you weren't supposed to give or show that to anyone."

"I know that, but he has my code. He said he could show me how to—"

"It doesn't matter, because it doesn't prove that he set you up, it just proves that you gave him your code, which was something that you had no business doing in the first place. And if I asked him whether he has your code, do you think he'd tell me the truth if he actually did?"

Caleb knew he wouldn't. He would be giving away the only thing that pinned all the guilt on Caleb. "But I . . . " There was nothing to say and he knew it. "I didn't take anything. You know how much I need this job."

"What am I supposed to do?" Benning said. He looked distraught, as though he really felt sympathy for Caleb. "This paper says you had something to do with those discs."

"I didn't take nothing. You can't fire me just because he said that I did. That doesn't mean nothing. He set me up," Caleb said, coming close to tears. His heart was beating like crazy, his hands were shaking, and beads of perspiration started to form on his brow and soak through his shirt.

"Caleb, I'm not saying you took them," Benning said. "And to tell you the truth, I don't think you did, I'm almost sure that you didn't, but—"

"Doesn't that count for something?" Caleb said, desperately.

"Not necessarily. We still have three hundred boxes of discs missing off your log, and it's not as though they were all stolen at one time but over a period of about a month, starting just after you started work here."

"But you're the boss," Caleb pushed.

"But there's one more problem."

Benning reached in his desk and pulled out another folder. He lifted a sheet from Caleb's personnel folder and held it in front of Caleb. "What is this?" he asked.

"That's my application," he said, and immediately he knew what Benning was referring to.

"I did a background check, Caleb. Why didn't you tell me you've been convicted before?"

Caleb looked down at his hands. He felt ashamed of himself for lying to one of the only people that had tried to help him.

"Did you hear me, son?" Benning said. "Why didn't you tell me you were convicted of a crime? Stealing, no less!"

Caleb slowly looked up. "I didn't think you would have hired me if you knew. I needed this job."

"I would've hired you." Benning got up and paced around the room, the papers in his hands. "I would've hired you. I told you, I make the decisions on that. But it's not in my hands anymore. I don't think you stole those discs, but everything points to you. What am I supposed to do?" He walked over and stood right before Caleb. "I have a partner, and how would it look, me having you on after you physically abused an employee, are suspected of stealing after only being here a month, and have a criminal record that you neglected to inform us about? You've tied my hands."

He slumped down in the chair beside Caleb. Benning looked as though he was beaten badly, and Caleb felt it was his fault. He saw Benning as the rescuer of young black men from the streets, from poverty, from the trap that the white man set for them. And who was the one that stopped him from saving a young black man this time? Not some powerful white politician, or some racist cop, or some sheet-wearing Klan member, but the very brother that he was trying to save. Caleb almost felt worse for Benning than he did for himself. This was Benning's purpose, what he lived for, and he probably thought that Caleb didn't give a damn either way.

Caleb stood from his chair and placed a hand on Benning's shoulder. "I'm sorry."

Benning looked up. His face was filled with sympathy. "So am I," he said. "So am I."

Caleb went to clear out his locker. Benning didn't have to tell him he was fired; he was smart enough to know that with everything that was stacked against him, Benning had no other recourse but to let him go. Caleb stuffed all his belongings into his book bag. He was thinking about finding Jim and confronting him. He knew that Jim had set him up, acted as though he was a friend so he could get his log-on code.

He thought about closing the door on the inventory room and knocking Jim around for a while, and not just to frighten him but to hurt him, to spill blood and break his bones, and make him regret ever messing with him like that. But what good would that do? Caleb had already managed to lose his job that day; would going to jail make things any better? If anything, it would make things worse, because Sonya had said she would leave him the next time he ended up in there.

He stood just outside the doorway of the inventory room. He saw Jim sitting at his terminal, punching at the keys. Caleb looked at him for a long time, and he knew Jim could feel his stare, but the boy didn't look up. He was a coward. After all he did, he couldn't even face Caleb to tell him why he did it, but he didn't have to, because he had won. Caleb had thought he had him under control when he beat him in the alley, but for Jim that was probably just the beginning. That's when he probably put his plan into action, and Caleb was too stupid to realize it, too stupid to suspect some white boy.

He deserved to lose that job. He left the doorway, deciding to say nothing to Jim.

TWENTY-FIVE

Austin sat in his chair, his fingers intertwined, a blank look on his face. He had been like that for an hour after getting off the phone with the man who claimed to be his father. It was all he could do, because he was so stunned to hear from him. Their conversation was difficult, long, and full of questions. He didn't know what to say half the time and how to feel the other half. He didn't even know if the man he was talking to was really his father or if the whole thing was just some cruel joke. Either way, it didn't really matter. The man had left so long ago without even explaining himself. Austin laughed when the man on the phone said he wanted to see him.

Truthfully, from the moment he picked up the phone and heard the man say hello, he knew it was his father. He didn't know how he came to that conclusion, but he did. He felt it, and it was almost frightening.

His father explained to him why he had left, what forced him to do what he did, why he didn't have time to explain—all of that. There were times when he broke down during the conversation. Austin heard his voice weaken, and could tell that he was crying. Even though he wasn't supposed to feel for the man who had left him as a boy, Austin felt sorry for him, so he couldn't understand what had made him laugh. In some way he thought that was how he was supposed to react.

Part of Austin wanted to yell at his father, curse him, and tell him that he shouldn't have called, that the only thing he could do for Austin at that point was go to hell. But another part of him wouldn't let him. He had never stopped thinking about his father since the day he had left. The night his father left, Austin told himself that he would see his father again, no matter what. There had been times over the past twenty years when he had come close to doubting that belief, but he held on.

Many times Austin had thought about starting a search for this man. Digging up records, phone numbers, and old pictures, trying to imagine what his father would look like after so many years of aging. But he never did; it would have been too much work, and there was no way he could find a man that he hadn't seen or heard from in twenty years.

But that was just an excuse. The real reason Austin never tried to track down his father was—what if he did find him? What if after a year or two, or five, of searching for this man he loved and honored so much, he found him? And he excitedly rang his doorbell, waiting with years of anticipation to see this man, only to be met by a man who wanted nothing less than to see his son.

What if upon seeing Austin, his father said, "What the hell are you doing here? I left you, don't you remember? And if I wanted to see you again, don't you think I would've found you? Now get out of here! Go now! Go!"

Austin knew he wouldn't have been able to handle that. It was so much safer to dream that his father wanted to see him again someday, just as much as he wanted to see his father, than to end that fantasy, find out that it wasn't true.

After the phone call, Austin sat in his chair going over his life from the day his father walked out till the moment he left his own wife and children. He thought about the effect his father's absence had had on him, how, at times, he felt that his father left solely because of him, felt that his father might have even hated him. Austin realized he couldn't put his own children through that. He could not sacrifice his children for personal problems he had, or problems that he had with his wife, without considering how it would affect them.

But it wasn't just that. There was a tone of deep sadness and regret in his father's voice, and Austin knew it was because his father had been looking back and feeling he had made the biggest mistake of his life. But what was worse was knowing that there was nothing he could do about it now. And even though Austin still loved his father, he didn't want to see himself ending up like that. He had to know for sure that leaving his family was something that he *had* to do, not just wanted to do.

Austin went to bed, that being the last thing on his mind, and when he woke up the next morning, it was the first thing he thought about. He had to see Trace, he had to be sure.

Trace opened the door for Austin and he walked in.

"Thanks for calling this time," she said.

Austin didn't know how to feel about that remark, but he grunted, "You're welcome." She went in the kitchen and he followed. She offered him a seat and he took it while she finished whatever she was making on the stove.

Austin felt uncomfortable. By mistake he had sat in the same chair he was sitting in the night he left. He wanted to get up and change his seat, but before he could do that, Trace sat down at the table in the seat opposite, the same seat she was in that night. She looked at him, and he could tell she noticed it as well.

"So what brings you by today?" she asked. She wasn't in the same cheery mood she was in yesterday, although she looked as nice, if not better. "This is two days in a row. I'm surprised you haven't gotten sick of me by now."

That was quite a low blow, but Austin should have seen that coming.

"I'm sorry," she said, smiling a little. "I shouldn't have said that. Actually I'm glad to see you, a little. And it's too bad the kids aren't here because they really miss you," Trace said.

If they weren't always at her mother's house when he came by, he could have seen them sometimes, and they wouldn't have missed him so much.

"Well, I miss them, too," was all he said. He looked around the kitchen and everything seemed the same. Nothing out of place, nothing needing fixing. The house hadn't fallen apart since he was gone, and neither had his wife. She was fine, just like everything else was, and he was almost sorry that his absence wasn't immediately evident.

"So, you start your job tomorrow, huh?" Austin asked.

"Yeah. I'm looking forward to it," Trace said.

It was the hardest time Austin had ever had talking to his own wife. He considered telling her about the phone call from his father, but something told him not to. Something told him to just shut up and deal with his problems first, because he definitely had them. They could discuss what he should do about his father later. Austin looked over at her, and she was staring at him.

"You're thinking again," she said.

"Yeah, I have a lot on my mind." He rubbed a hand through his hair.

"You shouldn't let things bother you so much. Everything will be all right," Trace said.

Austin wondered whether she was referring to *his* problems or *their* problems. He looked in her eyes, trying to find the answer without coming right out and asking.

"Do you think so?" he said.

"Maybe. But even if they aren't, you shouldn't worry like that. It won't do you any good. It's nothing but wasted energy."

She was right, Austin thought. She was always right. And what she had just told him was nothing new. She had told him the same thing many times during the course of their marriage. Then Trace would take him in her arms and cradle his head on her breast, and tell him not to worry, that everything would be all right. He would fall asleep sometimes to the sound of her voice, and when he woke up, she was still there, looking lovingly into his eyes. He felt so safe at those times.

He didn't have that anymore. Austin felt he'd lost that bond with Trace. That connection that kept him strong, that steadied him when he was in danger of moving in the wrong direction.

"I'm sorry," he said.

"Sorry for what?"

"About . . ." Austin paused for a moment. "I'm just sorry."

Trace looked over at Austin and placed her hand on the table near him. He reached out and took it in his hands. "Don't be sorry. You did what you had to do. That's how you felt. You can't blame yourself for following your feelings," she said. He could tell she said it for his benefit. It wasn't how she really felt.

Austin moved his chair closer. He was still holding her hand but grabbed the other one and held it tight as well.

"Trace, something just happened to me to let me know that what I did may have been . . ." He paused again, not feeling comfortable with what he had to say, or how it would be perceived. He didn't want Trace thinking that he couldn't survive without her, he just wanted her to know that he would prefer her back in his life.

"That you may have been what, Austin?" Trace said.

"That I may have been wrong. Wrong about my decision to leave. You and the kids need me." He looked away from her, almost as if he was ashamed of what had come out of his mouth. He waited for a moment, expecting a response from his wife, but when he heard nothing, he slowly turned his face back in her direction.

"So, you don't have anything to say about that?" Austin asked.

"About what?"

"About what I just said."

"Oh, that. You didn't say anything, Austin," Trace said.

He released her hands and crossed his arms in front of him. "Yes, I did. I just said that I was sorry."

"Oooohhhhh," Trace blew. "And I'm supposed to do what, Austin? Break down and cry because I'm so happy and relieved that you apologized? Am I supposed to hop up in your lap, throw my arms around your neck and welcome you back into the family? Is that what I'm supposed to do because you forced a half-assed apology out of your mouth?"

"It was sincere," Austin mumbled. "I was wrong, okay? Is that what you want to hear over and over again?"

"Austin, I don't have to hear it over and over again. I knew you were wrong before you knew it yourself. Your admitting it doesn't improve anything, it doesn't change what I'm going—"

"I want to come back!" Austin said, raising his voice, cutting off whatever argument she was about to get into. It hurt to release those words because it felt as though he was giving in, felt as though he had lost whatever battle he was fighting and was crawling over to the side of the enemy to surrender, after being beaten and bloodied.

Trace paused for a moment, an incredulous look on her face, almost as if in shock. "I know," she said. "But I can't take you back, not now," Trace said.

Austin didn't speak, just clenched his jaws in anticipation of Trace's explanation.

"Austin, did you think about anything you told me before you left? When you were rehearsing your good-bye speech, did you think that you would feel the way that you're feeling right now?"

"What does that have to do with anything?" Austin asked.

"I just want to know," Trace said.

"No." He shook his head.

"I know. You just felt the way that you were feeling at that time, and acted on it. You didn't think about how you would feel later, what the consequences would be, nothing." Trace stood up from her chair and stood in front of him.

"Why should I think you're doing anything different now? Why should I think that you thought this through, and once I let you back in, you won't start feeling the exact same way you were feeling when you left. What if that happens? Are you going to leave me again? Austin, you don't know how I felt that night. Do you remember some of the things you said to me that night? You made me feel like I wasn't good enough for you. Like I wasn't worthy enough to be your wife. You said that I was wasting my potential, Austin. What happened to that?"

Austin didn't speak, just looked at his hands. "I was wrong."

"Damn right!" Trace said. "I told you that the night you said all that, remember, but you walked right out of here like it didn't make a difference to you if you ever saw me or the kids again. This was coming from my husband. The man who was supposed to love me more than anyone in the world." Trace folded her arms around herself. "I hated you that night. After you left, I cried the entire night, and I told myself I would never forgive you for doing that to me, for leaving me like that, for leaving our children. I begged God to make you come back here one day and ask for forgiveness so I could turn you down and spit in your face. That's how I felt about you, Austin."

She slowly sat back in her seat.

"You left for a reason, and at the time, in your mind, it had to be a good reason, so you have nothing to be sorry about. But I can't take you back now. I still love you, Austin, but I just want you to think about this some more. I want you to be sure that I'm *good* enough for you to be with, because the decision you make this time will be the last. Do you understand?"

Yeah, he understood. He understood perfectly, and he regretted even going over there in the first place. He drove his Mercedes through the Sunday afternoon traffic, wondering why he had gone. Trace wanted him back just as much as he wanted to be back; she was just making him wait, a personal form of punishment. But she shouldn't wait too long, Austin thought. Because if she did, he would just have to get over her, and start a new life. It wouldn't be something that he would want to do, but he would not be played with like a puppet.

Austin pulled up in front of Marcus's house. He had to tell his brother about their father's phone call. He needed to discuss this thing out in the open. He banged on the door and waited for a moment.

Marcus opened the door. "All right, where's the fire?"

Austin walked straight in and was surprised to see his legal secretary sitting on his brother's sofa, looking like she lived there.

"Hi, Mr. Harris," she said, looking relieved. She was eating ice cream out of a plastic container.

"You don't have to call him that," Marcus joked. "That's my brother."

Austin nodded in Reecie's direction. "Nice to see you, Reecie," he said, then grabbed Marcus's arm and pulled him into the kitchen.

"I want to thank you again for getting us together," Marcus said, grinning in his brother's face. "Things are working out perfectly."

"I'm glad to see that, but will you ask her to leave? I have something I want to talk to you about," Austin said.

Marcus took a step back and gave Austin a long look.

"What do you mean, ask her to leave? No. Just tell me what you have to talk about right now."

Austin was surprised by his brother's reaction. He had never put up such a stand in all the time he had known the twerp. It was in defense of the woman, he thought. They give men foolish courage like that, but he would forgive his brother's behavior this time.

"Marcus, listen to me. I have something very important to talk to you about. Now I want you to have Reecie leave, because if you don't, I will," Austin said.

"No you won't."

"Have it your way," Austin said. He walked out of the kitchen and into the living room. "Reecie, do you have a jacket?" Austin asked politely.

"Yes," Reecie said. "What's going on?"

"It's between brothers. It's really none of your business," Austin said, going to the closet. "What color?"

"It's red," she said hesitantly.

Austin went through the closet, found the red feminine-looking coat, and removed it from its hanger. "I'm sorry, Reecie, but you have to go. You two can play together some other time," Austin said, draping the jacket over her shoulders and taking the ice cream container out of her hands.

Marcus, behind him, said, "You don't have to go anywhere. What do you think you're doing, Austin? Have you lost your mind?"

"I'll see you at work tomorrow, Reecie," Austin said, prompting her toward the door with a gentle shove in the back. She walked slowly toward the door, looking back at Marcus, a worried look on her face.

"You don't have the right to tell my company to leave," Marcus said. He was moving toward Austin. Austin stepped to the side, waited for Marcus to walk right up on him, then let him have it with a quick punch to the gut. Marcus folded over to his knees. Reecie started to rush over to him, but Austin grabbed her, turning her back in the direction of the door.

"Don't worry. I just knocked the air out of him. He'll be all right," he assured her. "See you later." Austin escorted her out the door. As for Marcus, he was trying to make his way to his feet holding his gut.

"What's your fucking problem?" he yelled.

"I told you I had—"

"I don't care what you have to tell me. You don't come in here kicking my company out because you want my attention." He coughed a couple of times. "And when I catch my breath I'm going to kick your ass." He hobbled over to the couch and fell on it. "I don't believe you," he said, holding his stomach.

"Marcus," Austin said.

"You're going to come in my house and—"

"Marcus!" Austin called again, raising his voice.

"—make a fool out of me in front of—"

"*Marcus!*" Austin yelled at the top of his voice.

"*What?*" Marcus yelled back.

"Our father called me last night," Austin said very calmly.

Marcus started to chuckle through his coughing, and when Austin didn't join in, he stopped and his smile disappeared.

"What did you say?" Marcus said, swallowing hard, leaning forward on the couch.

"I said, our father called me last night." Austin spoke the words slowly and clearly.

Marcus settled back on the sofa. His face looked flushed. He looked ill, as if he was about to vomit. He tilted his head back, banging it by accident against the wall, but he didn't make any effort to comfort the area. "Damn!" Marcus said. "Are you sure it was him?"

"I'm sure. I spoke to the man for hours. It was him."

Marcus breathed heavily. "What did that bastard want?" he asked, not turning to look at Austin.

"He wanted a lot of things, but I guess, most importantly, he wanted to say he was sorry."

"Ha!" Marcus said, standing from the sofa. "Sorry! Sorry for what? For walking out on us? There is no sorry for that."

Austin had known Marcus would react like that. He would have to pick and choose the things he would tell him about their conversation.

"I can't believe that. I can't believe that bastard," Marcus said, marching around the living room, rubbing his head where he had hit it against the wall.

"Who gave him the nerve to call here talking about sorry? The nerve. That bastard!" Marcus yelled. "What else did he say?"

"He didn't say much, not much at all," Austin said.

"You said you talked to him for hours. You all just didn't breathe on the phone, did you?"

"No. We didn't just breathe on the phone. And you should sit your butt down and calm yourself," Austin said, tired of watching his brother pace the floor.

"Don't worry about me," Marcus said, still rubbing the knot on his head. "What else did he say?"

"He said he was sorry," Austin said.

"Yeah, yeah, I heard that part." Marcus waved him on. "What else?"

"He said he missed us, that he made a mistake in leaving, that he never stopped loving Ma."

"What!" Marcus stopped in mid-step. "He never stopped loving Ma, huh? That's probably why he didn't make it to her funeral, you think? Or that could be the reason he left her in the first place. Never sent her any money, never called, never did a damn thing, because he never stopped loving her. I don't believe him. He definitely has his nerve, doesn't he?"

Austin guessed he wanted him to participate with him in tearing down his father, but it wasn't something that he wanted to be part of.

"He called just to tell you that? I wonder what would make him do that after all these years, call just to say that he was sorry. I guess the guilt was finally getting to him. But I don't know what he thought a phone call would do."

"He also mentioned coming here to see us," Austin said. "He's in California. He wants to fly over here and see us."

"I don't believe this man. He has more nerve than I thought." Marcus sat back down on the sofa. "You told him hell no, right? You told him there was no way in hell that we'd want to see his face again in life, right?"

"I told him I had to discuss it with you and Caleb first," Austin said.

"Well, you got my answer, and I think I can vouch for Caleb as well. Tell him to drop dead next time he calls, okay?"

Austin didn't answer, just sat there looking at his brother.

"I don't think I'm going to do that. I think he deserves a chance to explain himself," Austin said.

Marcus sprang up from the sofa, waving his arms about. "He doesn't deserve a damn thing. Not a damn thing after what he did to us, or don't you remember? Or could it be that you're hoping I give him a second chance because you're hoping the same thing of your children when you go back begging them after you realize you made a mistake in leaving your own family?"

Austin didn't say a word for a moment. But one thing had nothing to do with the other, he told himself.

"This conversation is not about me," Austin said, disdain in his voice. "Whatever."

"People make mistakes, Marcus."

Marcus spun around in a frustrated circle and pumped his fist. "Austin, that's not a mistake. You lock your keys in your car, that's a mistake. You buy your wife the wrong size dress for her birthday, that's a fucking mistake. Leaving your children and not speaking to them for twenty years isn't a mistake. I don't care that he's our biological father. I don't care that you looked up to the man even though he walked out on our asses like we weren't even worth his time. You need to get some things straight in your head, big brother. Some things can't be that simply overlooked. Some people shouldn't be forgiven," Marcus said.

Austin didn't speak right away. He paused just to see if Marcus had anything left to say. "I didn't say that I was taking the man into my house to try and pick up where we left off. I didn't even say I thought it was a good idea for him to come down. All I'm saying is, maybe we ought to hear him out. Aren't you the least bit interested in why he walked out in the first place? I know you are because you asked me not long ago. This is your chance to find out. You don't have to do anything. You don't have to say a word to the man, all you have to do is listen, and when he's done, you can either walk out the door, just like he did to us, or you can finally let him have a piece of your mind. Let out all that frustration, all that anger you've been holding in for these twenty years. Wouldn't you like to do that?"

Marcus seemed to be running the idea over in his head. "I can't stand the man. I'm letting you know that. I can't stand the thought of him," he said.

"Yeah, I know that."

"But I would like to let him know what I think about his ass face to face." Marcus had a look of disgust on his face, as if he was chewing on the foulest thing edible and was dying to spit it out all over the carpet. "Besides, I know you want him to come."

He didn't know that for sure, Austin thought. There was an interest, though, and that was one of the reasons why he was trying so hard to convince his brother to agree with him. Austin knew his father didn't just walk off on them for no reason. He knew he wouldn't do that unless something pushed him away, or something happened that made him go.

TWENTY-SIX

After Caleb left his job, he didn't know what to do. He sat in his car, the car that he would have to give up soon because he had no way of paying for it. He wondered in which direction to point the thing because he definitely couldn't go home, and there would no way be any trip to Wisconsin. Maybe he should just run the thing off a cliff, with him in it. Crash the motherfucker right into some rocks a hundred feet down and hope he blacked out before the impact. Or maybe he should get on the highway, do about ninety miles an hour, and cross the median into oncoming traffic, take himself out and about ten or twelve other people. Make the news, have some rough mug shot shown all over TV. That was how Caleb felt, like he wasn't fit to live, and he wanted to punish himself for screwing up the way that he did.

He was a fool to think he could assimilate, and who would ever want to in the first place. "Don't chase the white man's dream," Blue had said. And he should've listened to what he was told.

Caleb stopped at a pay phone to call Sonya.

"You on your way home? 'Cause I got everything packed, and I'm ready to go," she said. She sounded excited, like she was jumping around with the phone in her hand.

"We ain't going, so calm down, okay?" Caleb said, not trying to spare her feelings.

"Why not?" she asked.

"It's a long story, so don't even ask. And I ain't coming home tonight so don't wait up. Bye." He heard her saying something as he hung up the phone, but he didn't care what it was. Whatever it was she had to say couldn't have helped him feel any better, or any worse for that matter, so why bother with it?

That night he got two bottles of wine and drove all around town. It was a warm night, a pretty night, too pretty to be thinking about how much of a failure he was. He drove around, his windows down, his sunroof open, volume turned full blast, drinking from the huge dark bottle of wine, not caring who saw. He pulled over and rolled up on the curb when he no longer felt like driving, climbed out of the car and sat on the hood, turning up the bottle again.

Occasionally an old guy down on his luck, or a young woman looking for a fix, or anyone just looking for conversation would stop at his car, and he would talk to them, even offer them a drink. They would take the bottle, suck down a swig, and pass it back, smiling. Caleb would dig in his pocket and toss them some change, or a dollar bill or a twenty, whatever he pulled out.

He could talk to those people, and he wasn't worried about nothing. About them having some alternative agenda, or them trying to pull a move on him. He didn't worry about that from them, because he was one of them, just as down on his luck as they were. He'd had an opportunity to pretend he wasn't, to make believe he was someone he wasn't. But that got him nowhere.

Caleb ended up at the lake. Not the same spot he took Sonya and Jahlil. Very far from that. He was lucky to have even gotten there, because he could barely see as he drove. His head was so full of wine that the road looked as though it was spiraling, and the streetlights looked like they were bouncing balls of fire, ricocheting all over the pavement. He drove more on instinct than on what he saw, and surprisingly enough, he made it to where he was trying to go.

He crawled into the back seat of his car, pushed the front seat forward and kicked his feet over it. That was where he was going to sleep. It was as good a place as any, and to tell the truth, in his mind he didn't deserve better. He deserved to be right there where he was, on the damn street, drunk out of his mind on cheap wine, not knowing whether he was coming or going, on the brink of killing himself and not giving a damn that no one cared and not a single person probably would've showed up to his funeral.

His head was spinning, and his mouth tasted of stale grapes. He was hot, but he wasn't sweating. He unbuttoned his shirt all the way down and opened it up. He pulled the tie from around his neck and tossed it out of the sunroof.

"Go find your friend," he said, his words slurred. He was referring to the tie he had abandoned on the bus.

His head fell back against the back seat, and he looked up at the stars; only slits of his eyes were open. I'm sorry, he thought. I'm sorry. But he didn't know who he was saying it to. That would have required too much thinking, and at that point he wasn't capable, nor did he care. But he did see his son's face pop into his head.

"I'm sorry," he said out loud. He was exhausted, and he was so drunk that his brain felt detached from the rest of his body. He could barely feel his limbs. He didn't try to get up, didn't try to move. He wasn't sure what was going to happen to him, staying there overnight. Someone could try to kill him and take the car. The keys were dangling right there in the ignition, the radio was humming low, even the parking lights were on to attract interested thieves like moths to a porch lamp.

But he thought if that's what happens, then so be it. If he didn't make it till the morning, it was only because he wasn't supposed to, and more likely than not, everyone that had any kind of link to him would be better off without him.

He didn't wake up till late morning. The sun was shining brightly into his eyes, the wind was blowing, and the waves of the lake were crashing hard against the rocks. He was curled up in a ball on the back seat. He pulled himself up wearily, feeling sharp jolts of pain in his head and his joints. The keys were still in the ignition, but the radio was no longer on and he knew that the battery must have gone dead. He would have to get a jump from someone.

.   .   .

He ended up at Marcus's house later that afternoon. He pulled up behind Austin's Mercedes and was sorry to see it there. He hadn't seen
him in quite a while, and he wouldn't have minded if he never saw him
again. Caleb stumbled out of the car, looking beaten. His shirt was still
open, his pants were falling off him, his hair was a mess, and his eyes
looked as though they had sunk two inches into his head. He knocked
on the door and Marcus let him in.

"Caleb, where the hell were you? Sonya called, sounding like she
was about to lose her mind with worry."

"Doesn't matter where I was," Caleb said, dragging himself in the
house. "I'm here now, so at least that means I'm not dead."

"Caleb, I just heard some news from Austin. Maybe you ought to sit
down."

Caleb just stood in front of Marcus looking tired enough to col-
lapse, but not wanting to sit. "Forget about the presentation and just
tell me, Marcus."

"Austin just told me that he heard from our father."

Caleb didn't know how to react to this news. He stood for a moment and let it sink in, waiting for a reaction to come out of him, but
there wasn't one.

"Did you hear what I said?" Marcus said.

"Yeah," Caleb said. "I don't give a fuck. I came to give you these."
He dropped the car keys into Marcus's hand.

Marcus examined them, saw that they were the keys to the car he
had just helped Caleb buy. "What are you talking about? Why are you
giving these to me?"

"Because I can't keep the car. I told you it was a dumb idea to get it
in the first place," Caleb said.

"Why can't you keep it? What happened?" Marcus asked, examining his brother's face as if he could find the answer without Caleb
telling him.

"Nothing happened, all right? I just can't keep it." Caleb turned his
back on Marcus, ready to walk out the door.

"But you were happy about it when we got it." Marcus walked
around to face his brother. "Something had to happen to make you
change your mind this quick."

"I got fired, okay? There it is, now you know," Caleb said.

Marcus stood and said nothing. He fumbled with the keys, looking down at them.

"I'm sorry," Marcus said.

"Well, I don't need your pity, all right? I'll talk—"

"How did you lose this job?" Austin interrupted. He had returned from the bathroom during the middle of the conversation, and was leaning casually against the wall.

"It's none of your damn business, okay? I just lost it," Caleb said.

"People don't just lose jobs. It's not something you misplace, or something that falls through a hole in your pocket," Austin said, sitting down on the sofa. "You have to work to lose your job, you have to do something that makes you deserving of losing it. I guess the question is, how did you *work* to lose your job this time?"

The only thing his brother could do for him, Caleb thought, was to find ways to put him down. It was like he lived for it, like he looked forward to it and took great pleasure in it. "It wasn't my fault," Caleb said, clenching his jaws.

"Well, whose fault was it, Caleb?" Austin said, a smug look on his face.

"Why don't you ease up on him, Austin?" Marcus said.

"Ease up from what? I'm not doing a thing," Austin said, innocently. "Whose fault was it, Caleb?" Austin raised his voice. "The white man's fault again? Was it a conspiracy? Was it the bus driver's fault for always making you late? Or maybe the guy at the liquor store for making you buy that cheap-ass bottle of wine, or could it have possibly been, maybe, your fault? Do you think, Caleb? Huh?" Austin looked very comfortable stretched out on the couch now. His legs were crossed, his arms were spread out, and it sounded like he was questioning a defendant that was guilty as hell in a case Austin couldn't possibly lose.

Caleb looked over at him and hated his very existence. "Why do you have to come at me like that? What have I done to you, Austin?"

"I was just asking you a question," Austin said.

"No, I want to know what I've done to you. What the fuck have I ever done to you to deserve the way you treat me?" Caleb was trembling and so angry that tears almost came to his eyes.

Marcus put an arm around his shoulder. Caleb batted it away. "No, I want to hear this, and he's going to tell me," Caleb said, still staring furiously at Austin.

Austin pulled his arms in, uncrossed his legs and assumed a more professional position. The expression on his face changed from careless to serious.

"When did you decide to quit?" Austin said.

Caleb didn't know what the hell he was talking about, but Austin continued to stare at him, waiting for him to answer. "Quit what?" Caleb asked, becoming more angry at the stupid question.

"Life, Caleb. When did you decide to quit life? I figure it was very early on, when we were kids, maybe even earlier. You just weren't enthused about anything, never took anything serious. You did lousy in school even though I tried to help you. Do you remember that? Staying up late trying to teach you multiplication tables. Scribbling out flash cards so you could better understand. Do you remember any of that? How you acted, like you were doing me a favor just to sit there and pay attention? I always tried to help you with your homework, but you never paid attention and you got pitiful grades because of it."

"Some people aren't cut out for school like you are. Sorry," Caleb said. It was a sad-ass excuse and he knew it, but it was the only thing he could think of at the time.

"It has nothing to do with whether or not you're cut out for school," Austin said, standing from the sofa. "I said nothing about that. If you would've simply tried, it wouldn't have mattered if you got all F's. At least I would've known you gave it your all, instead of giving up like you did."

"I did give it my all! I didn't get it, all right? I just didn't get it, so shoot me!" Caleb said.

"Whatever, Caleb. You had a piss-poor attitude about everything, and I got tired of wasting my time on you. You weren't going to learn anything anyway. Not because you couldn't, but because you didn't want to. I gave you your little space, I stopped hounding you, stopped playing the older brother like you asked, and let you try to do things for yourself. And look what you've done for yourself over the years. Exactly what I thought you would do. Not a damn thing. I knew you were going to be a loser the moment I let you do what you wanted." Austin had walked very near to Caleb and was standing before him, looking him up and down. Marcus stood off to the side listening, looking very tense.

"That's so easy for you to say," Caleb said to Austin's face, "for you to criticize someone when you had someone to show you, to teach you. There were times when I wanted to ask you something, when I was ready to try learning that shit, but you were off with our old man, like you always were. You were off somewhere that he only wanted to take you to, but wouldn't think about taking me. How do you think that made me feel? What kind of effect do you think that had on me?"

"He's right, Austin," Marcus said.

"You can't talk, Marcus," Caleb said, turning in his direction. "You were always up under Ma, like she didn't have any other children, like she couldn't give attention to anyone else while you were around. Nobody had time for me, so what I did, I had to do on my own. What I learned, I had to learn by myself. I didn't have anyone to guide me. I had to make my mistakes on my own and just learn from that."

Austin still stood in front of Caleb. He crossed his arms and looked at Caleb as if he didn't believe a word. "Save the melodrama, Caleb. Just save it, because I heard it all before. It's just you trying to put the blame on someone or something else for your shortcomings. It's what you always do to try and explain how pitifully you failed in life."

"Maybe you should hold it right there," Marcus said, holding a hand up before Austin.

"No, no. He wanted to hear this, he should hear it all," Austin said.

"That's right," Caleb said, stepping just a little closer to Austin. "Let him say what he's going to say."

Austin cleared his throat. "After you went out on your own, what did you accomplish? Nothing. Not a damn thing. Never spent a single day in college, never finished high school for that matter. Jumped around from one whore's bed to the next just so you could have someplace to lay your head. You got put in jail for stealing, and from an old lady, for Christ's sake. You have never held a job longer than six months, and at the rate you're going, it doesn't seem as though you will. You have a decent woman that carries you like dead weight, and a child that you can barely afford to raise, and I don't even know if that matters to you."

He had crossed the line, Caleb thought. He could talk about Caleb all he wanted, say anything he wanted, but for him to bring Jahlil into it, to say that Caleb wasn't able to raise him, that he might not even care—he was really asking for it. Caleb could feel the anger in him threatening to erupt, his heart pounding hard in his chest.

"And you ask me why I treat you the way I do," Austin said. "Look at you. You look and speak just like a common street thug. What I'm trying to say is that you disappoint me, plain and simple." Austin was looking down on Caleb. He was only a couple of inches taller, but he had a way of looking at Caleb that made him feel as though his brother was standing high on a building peering down at him. "That's all I have to say to you." Austin turned his back on Caleb and took a step toward the sofa.

Caleb was red-hot with anger. At that moment he hated Austin more than he could ever remember. He hated his arrogance, the way he belittled him in front of Marcus, the way he talked down to him, the way he looked at him with that pompous smirk, Caleb hated it all. Especially the remarks about his family, his child. Caleb felt his breathing come more rapidly, his heart pound quicker. He grabbed Austin's jacket by the shoulder and yanked him around, then reared back and, with all he had, sent a punch flying into Austin's jaw. Caleb's knuckles solidly connected into his brother's face with a dull thud. It hurt like hell, but he didn't care. Seeing Austin crumple to the floor seemed to make the pain disappear. Austin looked up, grabbing his jaw, a look of shock on his face that quickly turned to anger.

"I hate you! I hate you!" Caleb yelled.

Marcus grabbed Caleb from behind. "What in the hell is wrong with you? Have you lost your damn mind?" He had Caleb's shirt balled up in his fist and he was shaking Caleb, trying to get the answer out of him.

"Just let me go, so I can get out of here," Caleb said, trying to release Marcus's hands from his shirt.

"I don't know what's gotten into you, Caleb, but you better get it together. Get it together quick," Marcus warned. He pushed Caleb in the direction of the door, where he almost tripped and fell. Marcus rushed over to help Austin up.

"That's right. Go help his sorry ass. Stick with him like you always did," Caleb said. "'Cause I don't need him, or you. I don't need no damn body. I don't need nobody, and I don't need nothing." He pulled open the door and walked out, feeling sorry for himself, not bothering to look back.

Caleb walked in the door of his apartment looking and feeling like garbage. After leaving Marcus's he had wandered around the streets, not knowing where he was going. He felt something else bad was about to happen, but he didn't know what.

"Sonya," he called out, but there was no answer and he was grateful. He couldn't take seeing her at that moment, and he didn't want her to see him, not in the condition he was in. He had to clean up, look presentable. He had lost his job, but he didn't have to look like he did. He didn't want her to be able to walk in the place and immediately say, "I can tell by the beard on your face and the million and one wrinkles that have crumpled your clothes that you lost your job again. Is that right, or what?"

He walked out of his clothes and left them straggled across the living room floor. He got a shower, shaved, and fixed himself something to eat. He was about to dig into a steaming bowl of franks and beans when he heard keys outside the door. Caleb cursed under his breath.

Sonya walked in with a bag of groceries, Jahlil trailing behind, amused by a toy. She walked past Caleb at the table and started putting away the things she had purchased without saying a word.

"Hi, Daddy," Jahlil said, pulling out a chair and climbing into it.

"Hi, son, how are you today?"

"I'm okay. Give me some." He reached out toward the bowl with the hand that wasn't holding onto the motorcycle reptile guy.

Caleb slid him the bowl, and Jahlil went to spooning from it.

Caleb turned his chair to face Sonya. "Mad at me?" he asked.

Sonya didn't answer.

"Would it help if I said I was sorry? Would that help at all?" Caleb asked.

Sonya opened up the fridge and stuck something in it, still paying no mind to Caleb.

"What can I do?" Caleb asked, standing up and putting himself in between Sonya and the bag of groceries.

Sonya turned around and looked Caleb in the face. "I was really looking forward to getting out of here, and having a little time away from your son." Sonya nodded in Jahlil's direction. He was floating the spoon in the air like an odd-shaped spaceship.

"You said we were going and I made all the arrangements so Jahlil would be taken care of. I packed all my things, I even bought some new stuff, and you call me on the day that we're supposed to be going and tell me that we aren't. And when I ask, you just blow me off and hang up in my face. I think I'm supposed to be mad, and if I wasn't there would be something wrong with me. Now if you'd let me by." She pushed Caleb off and tried to get past him. He wrapped his arms around her waist and pulled her back in.

"I had my reasons, all right?" Caleb said, looking in her eyes.

"Well, obviously, they're secret reasons, because you didn't tell me. Now let me go so I can finish."

He dropped his arms, and she walked out of his space and began to put away the last of the groceries.

"Sonya, there is really a reason why we couldn't go," Caleb said, picking up a jar of pickles from the bag, pretending it had something interesting written on it.

"And what was that?" Sonya said in a skeptical tone. Her head was buried in the fridge, as she stuck some fruit in the crisper.

"I lost my job," Caleb said, still fiddling with the jar of pickles.

Sonya didn't say anything, just stepped back from the refrigerator and closed the door. She turned to Caleb and just stared at him. Caleb knew exactly what that look said, he could read it as plain as if the words raced across her forehead in flashing lights.

You finally got a decent job, and you couldn't even keep it for two months. We were finally able to get ahead in the bills, and buy a couple of nice things. Now what? I'm tired of you getting jobs and losing them. I'm tired of carrying you, paying most of the bills, while you're out there screwing around. You can never stick with anything. You're always making excuses. You're worthless.

Sonya looked at him for about a minute longer, then she grabbed her keys off the kitchen table and started for the door.

Caleb grabbed her by the arm. "Where are you going?"

She spun on Caleb, fury in her eyes. "Let me go," she spat.

"But where are you going?"

"I need some time to think." That was all she said, looking down at Caleb's hand as if waiting to be released.

Caleb let go of her, and she was out the door.

The next couple of weeks were as Caleb had expected they would be. Sonya didn't have much to say to him at all. When she got home from work, she'd dodge him at all costs, and watch TV to avoid conversation. On occasion she would tell him "good night" or "goodbye."

He wondered what was happening with her. He thought about just coming out and asking her what the deal was, but decided not to. She was probably waiting for just that moment so she could let him have it. Tell him that her bags were packed, and there was a bus ticket in the side pocket of one of those bags, and she and the child would be leaving in the morning, forever. That was something that crossed his mind once or twice and it scared him.

For some reason or another it seemed the credit card people, the electricity people, the gas people, or whoever he owed money to knew exactly when to send out those bills—when he had no money at all. The bills came for the new TV and VCR, the clothes that he had bought, the things he had purchased for Sonya and for Jahlil. And the payment book for the car came. He pulled it out of the envelope and fanned through it. Nothing but what seemed an endless number of duplicate slips telling him that he owed those people $311.00 every month, and the first payment was very close to being overdue.

Caleb came in one afternoon from looking for another job, with of course no luck at all. Sonya was sitting on the sofa riffling through all those bills. She was surrounded by a small pile of statements, torn envelopes, and little advertisements that were slipped in with the statement, as though the money these companies were getting from people wasn't already enough.

When Caleb walked in, she turned to him, a haggard expression on her face, a crumpled statement clutched in her hand. "What are we going to do about all this?"

"I'm trying to find a job, all right?" Caleb said, throwing his book bag in the corner of the room.

"You're always trying to find a job, Caleb. But once you get one you have this incredible knack for losing it," Sonya said. "You had a job when you created all these bills, when you were out there spending money like you never had to pay it back."

"Some of those things I bought for you." Caleb raised his voice. "You weren't complaining then, were you?"

"I never asked you for those things. You didn't have to buy me anything, all I would've liked for you to do was keep your job for a change. Would that have been too hard?"

"It wasn't my fault," he said, more to himself than to her. He sat down in a chair, crossed his arms and sank his face into his chest.

"It's never your fault. Ever. Dammit, you have a family to take care of! Jahlil needs things. We have expenses, and sometimes you have to just deal with the little problems you're having. I don't care if you don't like your job, or the people hate you, or whatever excuses you use. You think I like my job? You think I like going down to the unemployment office every day, and seeing all those poor folks down there, with their babies in their laps, begging for jobs, looking pathetic when I tell them what they already know, that there's nothing out there? I don't like that shit, but I do it anyway, because I have responsibilities. It wasn't your fault, huh? You think the people who send us these bills will buy that?" she said, grabbing a handful of the bills and waving them around.

"Maybe I should just take a pencil and write that on each one of them." She picked up a pencil and tapped the lead against her tongue, and proceeded to write on them as she spoke. "Sorry, can't pay you right now, but it's not Caleb's fault."

"Very nice," Caleb said, feeling lower than he had ever felt in her presence.

"No, it's not very nice," Sonya yelled as Caleb walked out of the apartment. "It's not nice at all!"

Caleb had to get away from her, had to get out of her face, because if he remained there any longer he wouldn't be responsible for what he might do.

Caleb sat down on a bench outside. The day was ugly, just the way he was feeling. The clouds were gray and heavy and hung low. Fall, clouds, he commanded. Fall on top of my head and smash me to death, because there's nothing else that could happen to me.

A car pulled up to the curb and parked in front of Caleb's apartment. It was the landlord's car, and he was the last person that Caleb wanted to see.

He got out of the car and walked up to Caleb. "You got my rent?" he said.

"Naw, I don't have your rent, not yet," Caleb said, turning in disgust from the foul smell of his breath.

"The rent's due today. You gonna have it today?" he said.

Caleb looked at him, the thin strands of hair pushed over to cover the white skin of his head. Specks of food clung to his face, probably left over from last night's dinner. Caleb just wished the fat man would turn and roll away.

"I don't think I'll have it today, I really don't think so," Caleb said.

"Whatever," the man said and slowly walked off.

Caleb didn't know what was going on; he had never accepted it so well, no threats or anything.

"I'll just have to go to your brother again," the landlord said.

His face was away from Caleb, so Caleb didn't hear him very well. All he heard was brother, and that was enough to make Caleb question the man.

"What did you say?"

The landlord stopped, turned and told him. "I said I'll just have to go to your brother again, because your sorry ass don't have the money. But it's no big deal because I knew you wouldn't." He chuckled a little.

"What are you talking about? What brother?" Caleb asked.

The landlord pulled a fat little leather wallet out of his pants and thumbed through it for a moment, then pulled out a card. "Marcus Harris, Commercial Artist. That brother," the fat landlord said. "He paid your rent for the last two months and told me to call him when you were too broke to pay up which is all the time."

"He didn't give you anything. Sonya won the lottery. She paid you with that money so how did Marcus give you anything?" Caleb said.

The old dirty man cracked a smile, then let out a loud belly laugh.

"She won the lottery, huh? That's what she told you?" He was rubbing his belly and pointing mockingly at Caleb. "That's a laugh." His laughter calmed down and he straightened up a little. "Look, you didn't win shit, and your little woman didn't win shit. Your brother paid me the rent because I told him I was going to put you, your little wife or girlfriend or whatever she is, and that little chocolate kid of yours out on the street if the rent wasn't paid up. Now I don't know what goes on between you two, but obviously she has no problem lying to you, probably because she knows you'll believe anything. The lottery!" He let out another gut laugh and turned and went on his way.

Caleb sat for a moment, wondering what he should do. He should approach it rationally. He should look at this from her point of view and try to understand why she would do something like that to him. But he couldn't understand, he'd have to hear it from her.

Caleb took the stairs, skipping two and three as he hurled himself up to the third floor. He busted in the door, and slammed it hard enough behind him to almost send Sonya to the floor.

"Where did you get the money to pay the rent?" Caleb yelled. He was huffing, and his chest was heaving from the run up the stairs. His eyes looked crazy, sweat covered his forehead and was running down his face.

"I told you . . . I . . . won the lottery," Sonya said in a meek voice.

"Really, where's the ticket?" Caleb said.

"You have to turn it in when you collect the money."

"Where's the receipt? I know they gave you a receipt. They wouldn't just hand you over cash like that and not give you a receipt, so where is it?"

Sonya didn't answer, just sat there looking stupid.

"Where is it?" Caleb yelled, walking over to the stacked pile of papers and sweeping them off the table, sending them floating all over the floor.

"I . . . I threw it away," she said.

"Bullshit! You never won any money. You didn't win a damn thing. You got the money from Marcus. You went begging to my brother like a damn street whore for money that you knew we could never pay back. You know how I feel about that. You know that I would rather live on the damn street than have to take money from him. I've tried all my life to be independent of them, take care of myself. It's the only thing I have, it's the only thing I can be proud of in myself, but you took that away from me," Caleb said, his voice still loud enough for people down the street to hear.

Jahlil stood by his bedroom, a large t-shirt hanging off his small body, wiping sleep from his eyes with a tiny fist. "Mommy, can I have some juice?" he said.

Caleb turned quickly toward him. "No! Now go back to bed, we're talking."

Jahlil looked very surprised as he looked at his father, then turned toward his mother.

"You heard what I said, looking at her won't do you any good. Get back to bed, now!" Caleb yelled, pointing in the direction of his bed, as if he didn't know where it was.

Jahlil's face crumpled up, his mouth slowly opened, letting out a long screeching whine, then he turned and went back into his room.

"Like I was—" Caleb started.

"What the hell is wrong with you?" Sonya interrupted. "The child has done nothing and you rip his head off just because he asks for some juice."

"We aren't talking about him right now, we're talking about this," Caleb said.

"The hell with this!" Sonya yelled.

Caleb was taken aback, then walked up and stuck a finger between Sonya's eyes. "No! Not the hell with this. We're talking about this and that's what we're going to continue to talk about."

Sonya looked angry, very angry. Her hands were on her hips, her eyes were bulging, and she was blowing air harder than Caleb had been when he entered the room. "Okay, we can talk about this. Fine! I didn't win the damn money. And you're right, I got it from your brother, but no I didn't ask. He offered it to me," Sonya said, stabbing herself in the chest with her finger.

"I was going to turn him down, but he convinced me to take it. And he was right. You said you'd rather sleep on the street than take money from him. Well guess what, I wouldn't, and I'm sure not going to have Jahlil on nobody's street corner living in no box!"

"How could you have done that?" Caleb said. "I asked you. Asked you specifically, 'Did you take money from my brother?' And you said no. You stood there in my face and lied. Lied to me as if I was some stranger on the damn street."

Sonya didn't speak, just looked at Caleb as if she was justified in her dishonesty.

Something about the smug look on Sonya's face made Caleb snap. He put his hands on her and shook her violently.

"Why did you lie to me? Why did you lie?" And he shook her a moment longer.

"How else would we have gotten the money?" Sonya replied, not seeming rattled at all.

"I would've came up with the money," Caleb said, deflated.

"Really? How, Caleb? How would you have come up with the money when we're already late? What were you going to do, rob a fucking bank? You weren't going to do shit. You should feel lucky that you have a brother that is willing to help you out when you can't do it for yourself. But all you're worried about is your stupid ego. If I didn't take that money, that ego would've had us on the street with nowhere to live and nothing to eat, but that would've been okay with you, right, because you didn't want to take money from your brother. What do you think family is for? He was just trying to help and you act like he was trying to take money *out* of your pocket. He was kind enough to you, but not just you, but me and your child. *Your* child. It seems sometimes he thinks more about Jahlil than you do."

"What!" Caleb couldn't believe what she had said. "What did you say?"

"You heard me, you just said you wouldn't have cared if we ended up on the street. At least Marcus cared enough so that wouldn't happen," Sonya said.

Caleb rushed at her and grabbed her by her shirt. He pulled her in, staring right in her eyes. He could feel her trembling in his grasp, but the look in her eyes didn't read fear. "I can't believe you said that to me, I can't believe it. I would do anything for the two of you, I would die for that boy. I love him."

Sonya didn't try to free herself from Caleb, just stood there limp and allowed herself to be handled. "Caleb, sometimes love isn't enough," she said through a tight jaw. "Love don't buy food. Love don't pay the bills or the rent, Caleb. Money does, all right? We don't need you to die, we don't want you to die, we just need you to make some money. Some money, Caleb!"

He was so angry that he contemplated raising his hand and slapping her face hard. The sound it would make, the stinging against his hand, would make him feel better, but it wouldn't accomplish a damn thing, nothing. Instead he tossed her down hard to the sofa. She fell like a rag doll, and he left her there.

TWENTY-SEVEN

Here I am again, Julius thought as he sat in the doctor's office waiting for the man to come in and no doubt give him more bad news. It was all he was good for, it was probably what he went to school for. To give people the type of news that would ruin the rest of their lives and get paid hundreds of thousands of dollars to do it. He had hated the doctor when he first diagnosed him with cancer and he hated him still.

"Your cancer is a bit more radical than I thought. It has seemed to spread to some of your pelvic lymph nodes and and it has invaded the lower region of your spine." The doctor spoke the words without emotion, without much of anything, almost as if he was reading the news from a cue card. "Because of that you may have only twelve months left, possibly a few more."

Julius sat very still in his chair, not moving an inch. The expression on his face didn't change, his breathing didn't change, nothing. He felt Cathy's grip tighten on his hand but he did not respond to it.

"I thought you said I had two years or more," Julius said calmly, as if he had been lied to about the time.

"At that time that's what I thought, Mr. Harris," the doctor explained.

"You thought. That's what you thought! You're a damn doctor. You went to school all that time so you could just think. Hell, I can think, but you're supposed to know," Julius said, standing from his chair. "And if you don't know for sure then you shouldn't say that you do. You told me two years and that's what the hell I was planning on. And now you tell me this. What am I supposed to do now?"

The doctor didn't respond to the question, just sat there stupidly as if it wasn't asked of him.

"I said, what am I supposed to do now?"

"I ... I don't know, Mr. Harris," the doctor said.

"Well, you seemed to know everything when you diagnosed me with cancer. You seemed to know how much time I had, but you were wrong. And now you tell me I have less. Maybe I should come back in a month and then you can tell me that I have even less time. Would you like that, Doctor?" Julius said, pushing himself right up to the desk, wanting to climb over it and strangle the old man. The doctor didn't say a thing, didn't react, just looked up at him as though he was used to his patients going ballistic at the news he told them, because he probably shortened people's lives like this every day.

Julius leaned over the desk, and moved as close to the doctor's face as possible.

"I hope to God that you never come down with cancer and have to rely on someone like you to try and cure it, because if that happens, you'll surely die. You will surely die."

On their way home, Cathy was driving a lot slower than she should have been. She kept looking over in Julius's direction, then turning her head quickly back to the road.

"Will you stop doing that, before you run us off a cliff and we'll both end up dead."

Cathy just looked at him, the longest she had since they got in the car, then turned back to the road again.

"Well, I really told him, didn't I?" Julius said, feeling as though he could have been a little less harsh.

"We can always get another opinion," Cathy said.

"No. I'm done. I'm done with opinions. I'm done with doctors and those white coats, done with getting my weight taken, getting poked with needles, getting my blood pressure taken. I'm done with all that."

"But maybe you—" Cathy said.

"No, Cathy. I'm done. No one really knows how long I have. He doesn't know, trust me. I could see it in his face. He was guessing just like I could guess. I'm not going to put any more faith in that doctor, okay? I'm just going to pick a time smack in the middle of the two and say that I have eighteen more months to live, and I'm going to do everything I can in that time, and not worry about a thing. That's what I'm going to do," Julius said. The last few words came out a little shaky.

She wasn't looking at him, but stared straight out at the road, both hands on the steering wheel. Her face was already lined with tear tracks, and she was blinking her eyelids to try and stop them from falling.

"I'm just going to have to hurry things a little," Julius said, his voice still quivering. "I'm going to have to do everything that I wanted to do, but . . . but sooner. You know what I mean."

Cathy reached over and grabbed his hand. "I know, sweetheart. I know."

When they got home, Julius went straight into the house and dialed Austin's number, with the express purpose of telling him that he was going to come to Chicago to see them whether he liked it or not. But Austin wasn't home. He tried a half hour later, and every hour on the hour after that.

At 9 P.M. Julius was sitting in his chair staring at the television. He had the phone by him, but had decided to give up calling his son for the night.

"Are you hungry?" Cathy asked, walking up behind him, massaging his shoulders.

"No."

"Well, are you sleepy?" she asked.

"No. I'm not sleepy, either," Julius said, fidgeting around in the chair.

Cathy came around the chair and kneeled down next to him, putting her head in his lap. "Is it about today? Do you want to talk about it?"

Julius didn't answer immediately; he had to think a moment to be sure of exactly what it was. "The way I'm feeling has nothing to do with today, or at least I think it doesn't. I just need to see my sons, and need to see them soon. No, not soon. I need to see them now. Right now."

"Maybe you should call Austin again. Maybe he's home now," Cathy suggested.

"I don't want to call anymore. Calling won't do anything," Julius said, frustrated.

"Well, what's his number? I'll call him, and I bet you he'll be home," Cathy said. Julius told her the number and she called. She held the phone to her ear, a hopeful look on her face. Julius knew he wouldn't be home, even though he hoped he would be wrong. But after Cathy waited for a moment he knew he was right.

"He'll be home in the morning, Julius. We'll call him then, all right?" she said, patting his hands.

"I don't want to call him then. I don't want to wait till the morning," Julius said. "You heard what the doctor said, I don't have as much time as I thought I did. I can't just sit back and wait any longer." Julius excused himself, and went over to the window where he looked out onto the dark street. "If I have something to do, I have to do it now. No more waiting."

"So what are you saying?" Cathy asked.

"I'm saying that I want us to go up those stairs, pull out our suitcases, fill them full of clothes, and get on a plane to Chicago, tonight. That's what I'm saying." Julius turned away from the window to see what Cathy thought of the idea.

"You don't even know if they have a flight out tonight," Cathy said.

"They do. I called earlier."

"But we don't know where your son lives."

"We'll call him in the morning and find out then." He walked over to Cathy and helped her stand. "Let's go. Just come with me, and we'll figure it out once we get there. All I want to do is see my boys. If I can do that I'll be happy. Please say you'll come. Please." He was holding Cathy's hands, looking in her eyes, trying to will her to say yes without asking her again.

"Jay, are you sure this is what you want to do?" she asked.

"I've never been more sure of anything in my life," Julius said.

TWENTY-EIGHT

Caleb stood in Blue's apartment, not knowing why he was actually there. All he knew was that something made him get on the bus and sent him to that destination. He didn't know if it was anger, frustration, or the fact that the floor was falling out from under him, everything falling down around him, and there was not a damn thing he could about it.

After finding out that Sonya had betrayed him, Caleb had gone straight to his landlord's apartment. He had banged on the door furiously, and when he heard the big man slowly dragging his feet across the floor, Caleb banged even harder and louder. When the landlord finally opened the door, an evil scowl on his face, Caleb was on him before he could belch out his first obcenity. He grabbed the man by the neck of his food-soiled t-shirt and pushed him back, forcing him to backpedal across the floor of his filthy apartment. The big man was off guard, his arms flailing, spinning in big circles, trying to keep himself on his feet as Caleb continued to force him back. Then the man hit the sofa on the far wall, fell onto it, and Caleb was on top of him, now with his hand buried in the landlord's throat.

Caleb's face was hideous with rage, a sheen of sweat building on his forehead, and he pressed his hand into the fat of the man's throat, cutting off his air.

"I live in this hellhole of an apartment building, not my brother!" Caleb spat. "If you ever go behind my back, begging him for money, I swear you'll regret it. I swear it!" Caleb pressed his hand deeper into the man's throat. He could see him struggling, hear him gag and gurgle, see his face turn pink, then crimson, then fringe on purple, but Caleb kept on with the pressure. And it wasn't just that he didn't want to take his hand away. It felt as though he couldn't. Wasn't physically able to do it, because this was a strike against more than just his landlord. This was payment for everything and everyone. Every obstacle that ever got in Caleb's way, every person that ever denied him something that he shoud have had.

The man was beating his fat fist into the sofa, struggling with the last of his energy, and his head looked like a huge blood vessel about to pop. Caleb yanked his hand from the man's throat and watched as the landlord threw his hands around his neck, taking in air as if he had just been saved from drowning.

Caleb wanted to spit on him. "Don't call my brother," he said, drained of emotion.

The landlord hacked and coughed, rolling around on the beatup sofa, then managed to speak in between his breathing fits.

"You don't have to worry about me calling your brother," he yelled, coughing as if he was about to choke up his insides. "Because you're fucking out of here! You get all your shit, your whore, and your bastard son, and get the hell out of here. You hear me?"

Of course he did. Caleb was standing in the doorway, his back turned toward the man, about to leave, when he heard what he said about his family. Caleb was grabbing the doorknob, angry enough to rip the thing off, go back and make the bastard eat it. But he controlled himself, let the anger drain from him as much as possible, then left.

How pathetic, Caleb thought, looking at himself now, standing in front of his friends Blue and Ray Ray. He didn't have the money to keep his family in an apartment, and now he had managed to get them kicked out. He was going to really have to come up with some money now so he could move them, and he would have to do it soon, because he didn't know how long it would take for his landlord to be able to legally evict him.

"I knew you'd come to your senses sooner or later, brotha. I was betting you couldn't have stood being kicked around too much longer," Blue said, smiling a sly smile. He had a toothpick in his mouth and was twirling it around with his fingers. "Now what seems to be the problem, man?"

"They got me," Caleb said, disgusted. "Just like you said they would. The guy at my job worked a scheme on me and got me fired, and there ain't shit I can do about it."

"Daaamn!" Ray Ray said, poking at his hair with an afro comb.

"I hate to say it, but I told you so," Blue said. "You can't trust them motherfuckers for shit. They always on your ass trying to get you to the point where you can't even support yourself, then they whining about there shouldn't be any welfare. Sometimes I just ask myself, what do they want?" Blue looked as though his mind was gone for a moment, possibly on the question he had posed to himself, then he redirected his attention to Caleb.

"How is your girl dealing with it?"

Caleb pulled a chair over and slumped in it. "She's *not* dealing with it. We had it out. It was fucked up, the worst we ever had. She's questioning whether I can even take care of them."

"That's fucked up, man. She's doubting your manhood, brother," Ray Ray said. "And once that goes, there ain't nothing else. Nothing else." He shook his head.

"So what you want to do? You want to find the chump who made you lose your job and jack his ass up, for real this time?" Blue said, looking serious.

Caleb actually thought about it, just like he had about a million times before, but he realized it wouldn't do any good. It would only put him in deeper trouble. He could wind up in jail, and he would never go there again, never.

"Naw, man," Caleb said.

"You sure?" Blue said, standing. "We could do him." He picked up the empty beer bottle off the table and slapped it against the palm of his hand. "He'll learn not to be pulling no tricks like that again."

"Naw, just forget about him. I got bigger problems," Caleb said, lowering his head.

"Well, what you need, man? You know whatever it is I'm here, I got your back," Blue said.

"I got bills like crazy, and I got to come up with some money in a hurry to move my family."

"Move? Hold it, hold it. What are you talking about?" Blue said, disbelief on his face.

"It ain't important right now," Caleb said. "I fucked up again is all, and I need to know if you have some extra ends you could loan me, just for a little while?" Caleb felt ashamed. He didn't like the idea of begging, but he had to get it from somewhere and he sure as hell wasn't going to go to his brothers. Blue was his last hope.

"How much you need, man," Blue said going into his baggy blue jeans pocket and pulling out his wallet.

"Like, four hundred, man. I need like four hundred," Caleb said.

"Oh ho ho," Blue said, tossing his wallet behind him. "I got twenty dollars, maybe I can come up with twenty-five if I dig up under the couch cushions. But I don't have no money like you talking about. Do you?" Blue asked, looking at Ray Ray.

"Man, I got six dollars," Ray Ray said. "And I ain't trying to give that to no one."

Caleb hung his head even lower than it was. "I understand. I don't even know why I asked. I'm going home."

"Caleb," Blue said, grabbing him by the arm and sitting him back in his seat. Blue pulled up a seat next to him, and threw his arm around Caleb's shoulder. He pulled his face in very close to Caleb's. He looked in his eyes a moment without saying a word, then smiled, showing his gold tooth.

"How long we been friends, Caleb?"

Caleb looked up at Blue, not interested in his question.

"Come on now, come along with me for a minute," Blue said.

"We've been friends for ten or twelve years," Caleb said.

"Fourteen years," Blue corrected. "We been friends fourteen years, man. Best friends. And during that time, whenever I gave you advice, was it wrong?"

Caleb didn't answer.

"Was it?" Blue asked again, giving him a little nudge with his shoulder.

"A couple of times," Caleb said.

"Well, over fourteen years a couple of times ain't bad, is it?"

Caleb nodded his head, agreeing with Blue.

"So the advice that I'm about to give you now is going to be right," he said, softening his voice so only the two of them could hear. He leaned his head forward a little more so their foreheads were very close to touching and their eyes were meeting straight on. "You in a bad situation, Caleb. You in a bad situation because the man is trying to wreck your life, and he's about to succeed. He's been fucking with you since you were born, black man, and all you've been doing was absorbing the blows, turning the other cheek, stupid shit like that. Now it's time to strike back, it's time to launch the offensive, time to get some 'get-back.' You know what I'm saying?"

Caleb really didn't have a clue. He knew he was talking about some racial shit, but Blue always talked about that. Only thing he knew for sure was that Blue was tripping him out, spooking him a bit with his behavior. All he wanted to do was borrow some money to pay his rent. "Naw, I don't know what you're saying, Blue," Caleb said, their foreheads still pressed together.

"They took your money, man. You got to take it back. I know this store—"

"Naw, naw, naw," Caleb said, pulling back from Blue. It was all he had to hear to know where Blue was going, and know that he didn't want anything to do with it. "I ain't going there, man. I ain't putting myself back in that situation. You know I did time already."

"So the fuck what?" Blue said, yelling, standing from his chair. "You did time because you had to. You needed money and you did what you had to do. And you need money now and you going to do what you have to do."

"No, I'm not. That's wrong," Caleb said, shaking his head.

"It was wrong for the white man to come take this land from the Indians, but he did that shit, didn't he? It was wrong for him to trap us like animals and drag our black asses over here, but he did that didn't he? It was wrong for him to keep us from voting, not allow us to walk where he walked, eat where he ate and live where he lived, but he did that shit, didn't he? And he did it because he had to. Because he felt that if he didn't we would do harm to his family, or we would take his jobs, putting him out of work, or whatever other crazy shit he thought. But bottom line was they did a lot of the crazy shit they did because they felt they had to, and that made it right in their mind." Blue moved back closer to Caleb. "That's what you have to do. You have to get it right in your mind," he said, sticking a finger to the center of Caleb's forehead.

"I . . . I don't know if I can do that," Caleb said.

"What the fuck is it going to take?" Blue grabbed him by the shirt with both hands. "Is it going to take your family out on the street for you to realize that you been done wrong? Is it going to take your damn child starving? Are you going to be digging in garbage cans for your dinner? What, motherfucker, what? Sometimes you just got to do what the fuck you got to do, all right?" Blue pushed him back, as if the sight of Caleb disgusted him and he could no longer stand to touch him.

"You know he right, don't you?" Ray Ray said.

Caleb looked at Ray Ray with an evil glare, but he did know that. Blue was right like he usually was, even though his idea was radical, very radical. But there was no doubt, he had to do something, and he could see no other way to get the kind of money he needed by the time he needed it. He just didn't want to fuck up again. But he sure as hell wasn't going to let anything happen to his family, and he sure as hell didn't want them to think they couldn't depend on him when they really needed to. Maybe this would buy him some time. Maybe if he pulled this off and got enough money to pay his rent and take care of the bills, that would buy him some time to get another job, and it would renew Sonya's faith in him. It would let her know that he could come through when he needed to. And he wouldn't even have to tell her where the money came from, and knowing her, she wouldn't even ask, and if she did, he would tell her he won the damn lottery.

"All right, man. I'll do it," Caleb said, still unsure as to whether he was making the right decision.

Blue turned around smiling, his eyes bright, gold tooth sparkling. "That's my motherfucker!" he said, throwing his arm back around Caleb. "You in, Ray Ray?"

"Oh yeah, and you know it!" Ray Ray said, rubbing his hands together like he was about to sit down to a home-cooked meal.

·   ·   ·

Ray Ray's car sat on a dark street outside a liquor store. Ray Ray was smoking a joint, while Blue informed Caleb about what was going to happen.

"This old white motherfucker been making money off this store for I don't know how long. Taking our money from us and driving back to the 'burbs and living in a fat-ass house," Blue said. "I always told myself it would just be a matter of time before I hit him up."

Caleb was in the back seat, scared, his heart beating like crazy. His eyes were wide, trying to see Blue's black face in the dark.

"So what is the plan?" Caleb managed to say, clutching the back seat with his shaking hands.

"He's about to close the store in five minutes," Blue said, looking in the direction of the store. "He's going to waddle his old ass over to the door and try and lock it, before he counts his money from the day. But when he does that, we going to bust in on him, clean him out and jet. That simple. It won't take ten minutes," Blue said, a crazed look in his eyes. Caleb could tell he was excited about what was going to happen; he just hoped that he wouldn't get too excited and slip up because of it.

"And he's just going to give up his money to us?" Caleb asked. "Just like that? He ain't going to say nothing about us trying to take it?"

"What are you looking for, the man's written permission? It ain't going to happen. What the fuck is wrong with you?" Blue said.

"I just . . . I just don't want this to go down the wrong way, that's all."

"Well, it will if you keep acting like this."

"Like what?" Caleb asked.

"Like a little bitch! That's what!"

"I ain't acting like that!" Caleb yelled back, taking offense at the remark.

"You acting like something. You ain't sure of yourself, and—"

"I am!"

"You ain't, motherfucker, you ain't!" Blue said. He settled down after a moment. "I'm trying to help you, man," he said, his voice now normal. "I'm sorry, man, that it ain't exactly the way you'd want, but I'm still trying. Now you got to let me know if you trying to do this. You got to fucking let me know, now."

Caleb saw the seriousness in Blue's eyes. He was giving him an opportunity to get out, run like crazy, and the whole thing might not ever be mentioned again, but he knew Blue would always remember how Caleb punked out, how Caleb refused to do what he had to do when his family was faced with hardship given to him by the white man, how Caleb couldn't hold up under pressure and fight the four-hundred-year battle that needed to be fought. Caleb turned and looked out his window toward the store. He could see the plump old man shuffling around in there. He didn't want to do it, but what choice did he have? There was nothing else he could do. "All right," Caleb said, barely able to get the words of his dry throat.

"Good," Blue said softly. He tapped Ray Ray in the area of his breast pocket, and Ray Ray came out with a black shiny handgun and passed it to Blue. Blue cocked it with a loud click-clack, then held it out to Caleb.

Caleb shook his head, not having to say that he didn't want to touch the thing for Blue to understand what was going on.

"It don't matter because Ray Ray's the gunman anyway," Blue said, pulling the gun back.

"That's right," Ray Ray said, taking the gun.

Blue looked in the direction of the store, then looked back at Caleb one last time. Caleb knew he was checking that Caleb's head was in the right place. Caleb just returned the look with a stone stare of his own. Blue smiled a little, then looked away.

"Put that shit in your pocket," he told Ray Ray. Blue said the word, and they started to empty out the car.

Blue ran lightly across the street on tiptoes, his back hunched, trying to avoid being seen. Ray Ray did the same, holding his hand against his breast pocket to stop the gun from jumping around. Caleb followed and they all ended up pressed up against the side of the building right by the door. Ray Ray was on one side, holding the gun to the side of his face, and Blue was on the other side, Caleb standing behind him.

Blue was motioning something to Ray Ray. Caleb couldn't see exactly but he knew it was to do with how they would bust in on the old man.

The old man walked up to the door, the key between his fingers. Blue turned to look at Caleb, a weird smile on his face, a strange look in his eyes, then turned to Ray Ray and motioned with a sweep of his hand. Ray Ray forced the door open on the man, hitting him in the head, sending him to the floor yelling. He fell hard, flat on his back, his body springing up a bit from the fat that coated him. The keys jumped out of his hand and slid across the floor. Ray Ray retrieved the keys, tossing them to Blue. Blue tossed them to Caleb. Caleb locked the door and left the keys swinging there.

Blue turned to the man, an angry scowl on his face. "Get the fuck up!" he yelled, louder than Caleb had ever heard him yell in his life. Blue grabbed the man by the back of the collar and was tugging at him like a bag of trash, forcing him in the direction of the register.

Ray Ray had a hold on the gun with both hands, stabbing the thing in the direction of the man's head.

Blue's actions were quick and forceful. He seemed to know exactly what he was doing. "Get the fuck over there and get the money," he said, pushing the large man against the counter.

The old man looked at Blue, and the look in his face was fear and disbelief. A thin stream of blood ran down his bald head, over his eye, and into his mouth from the wound he had taken when the door hit him. He continued to lean against the counter, a dumb scared look on his face, like a pig about to get slaughtered.

"What the fuck are you looking at? Don't look at me, you sorry motherfucker," Blue yelled. "Just reach in there and get the money!"

He motioned for Ray Ray. "Give him some incentive," Blue said.

Ray Ray rushed forward a few steps, dropped the barrel of the gun to the old man's head. "Move, you old bastard!" Ray Ray said. Caleb stood by the front door. His heart was racing so fast then, he was afraid it would jump out of his mouth. He looked out the window to make sure no one was coming, then went back to watching the old man. Don't think about it. Don't let it get to you, he told himself. He was trying to steady himself. Just trying to make it through all of it, because it would be over soon, and they would have the money, and everything would be fine, just fine.

"Get behind the counter and get the money, now! Do you want to fucking die?" Blue said.

The old man mumbled something. It was understood as a definite no. He shuffled back behind the counter toward the register.

"Move faster, motherfucker!" Blue yelled. Sweat started to run from his forehead. He was turning his head this way and that, staring wide-eyed in every direction.

"I don't want any trouble," the man mumbled in a heavy Jewish accent. He was mumbling and sobbing at the same time. It was pathetic, Caleb thought.

"I don't want any trouble," he said again, looking at Blue.

"I heard you the first time. Now stop fucking stalling and give up the cash."

The old man looked at Caleb, and there was something in his eyes that Caleb caught. It was as though he was pleading with his eyes, trying to appeal to some side of Caleb, hoping that he would do something to stop what was going on. That was exactly what he was doing, and it made Caleb mad. It angered him to think that the old man saw something in *him* to suggest that he was the weak link, that he wasn't just as much in on this as the rest of them.

"What the hell are you looking at, old man?" Caleb shouted. His voice cracked. Caleb reached to a nearby shelf and picked up a bottle and threw it at the man. It hit him in the chest and he clutched at the place, looking as though he was about to cry. "You heard what he said, get the fucking money!" God, how Caleb didn't want to do that.

"Now that's what I'm talking about!" Blue yelled, beating his fist on the counter.

Caleb turned his head toward the window, feeling as though he was going to vomit all over it.

Just then a police car came around the corner. Caleb could feel himself freezing. He stood there, his eyes wide open, staring at the car as it made its way toward the store. Caleb lowered his head, trying not to be seen. He wanted to warn Blue and Ray Ray, but he couldn't speak, he couldn't move, he couldn't even turn his head. He just froze there, helpless, and watched as the police car rolled right up in front of the store, slowed down, and halted for a moment. Caleb was yelling, screaming on the inside, but on the outside his body sat like a rock, unable to move. Then the car picked up speed and moved along.

Caleb could breathe again, as if someone had stepped off his chest. The old man was pulling money out of the register and Blue was stuffing it in his pocket. Ray Ray was a few feet away from him, the gun still aimed at the old man's bleeding forehead.

Caleb was about to warn them that the pigs were wandering outside when he heard a noise. It came from the back, and when he turned he saw an old white-haired woman stepping into the room. After that, everything moved in slow motion.

"Murray!" the woman yelled.

Ray Ray was the first to respond, taking the gun off the man and aiming at the woman. Blue's head snapped in her direction.

Caleb was praying that Ray Ray wouldn't shoot her, but he knew he would, he just knew it, and he figured the old man thought the same thing. As soon as the gun was taken off him the old guy bent down and blindly pulled out a huge shotgun.

"*Blue!*" Caleb yelled. "Watch out!" Caleb threw himself to the floor.

Blue turned, his eyes wide, the gun staring him right in the face, the old man's finger pulling the trigger.

Blue dropped to the floor and scrambled wildly up against the counter, but Ray Ray was left standing trying to move his gun as quickly as his eyes moved, trying to aim at the man and kill him before he was killed.

The shotgun went off, and a huge hole opened up in Ray Ray's gut. The force of the shot picked him off the floor like a gust of wind and sent him flying back, slamming against a wall of shelves, bottles toppling over him. His body slowly crumpled to the floor, leaving parts of the shelves painted red.

Blue sprang up from in front of the counter, catching the old man off guard. Blue grabbed the shotgun out of his hands and lunged at him with the butt of it, hitting the old man in the face. There was a loud crack from the impact and blood squirted freely from the man's nostrils. The man fell to the floor, and Blue leaped over the counter after him, furiously jabbing him in the gut, pounding his body with the butt of the gun, kicking him in the head and chest.

"You motherfucker!" Blue yelled, still beating the man with the shotgun.

Caleb ran over to Blue and grabbed him. "Come on, get off him before you kill him! Get off him!"

Blue was still swinging in a mad rage. The man was squealing and whimpering, his arms up trying to block the blows. Blue was mumbling something crazily.

"Come on, Blue, you're going to fucking kill him!" Caleb said, dragging him off the man. Caleb threw Blue to the side and looked to see if the man was still moving. He was. He was beaten horribly, his clothes soaked with blood, his body lying in a puddle of it, but he was moving.

The old woman rushed over to the man, and Blue stumbled over to Ray Ray. He pressed up against him and took his face in his hands. Ray Ray was barely alive. He was choking on blood and vomit and whatever else forced its way up his throat.

"C'mon, man, you're going to be all right," Blue said. Tears were running from his eyes. "You're going to fucking be all right."

Caleb looked around and saw the two bodies covered in blood. He knew it would happen, he just knew it. And for what? For a few hundred dollars of blood-stained money. It wasn't worth it, he knew it, and now it was too late. Now the only thing he could do was try to save their asses so everything wouldn't be lost.

"We got to go, man," he urged Blue, grabbing him under the arms.

Blue was sitting on the floor, Ray Ray's head in his lap. His shirt, his hands and his arms were covered with blood. "I ain't leaving him here by himself," Blue said. "That ain't right. I ain't going to leave him."

"Blue, he's going to die, he's probably dead right now. You got to get up so we can go. The police will be here any minute so get your ass up and let's get the fuck out of here!" Just as he said that, he heard sirens in the far distance. Something clicked in him, and he was thrown back to the last time he heard sirens and had known they were for him.

"We got to go. Now get the fuck up, now! Get the fuck up!" He yanked Blue up by the shoulders and dragged him kicking out the front door. Caleb threw him up against the wall, grabbed him by his shirt and quickly pulled his forehead into his. "We got to, all right? We got to fucking go. Now I'm sorry about Ray Ray, but we accepted that this shit could happen when we decided to do it. Now we got to go and that's all there is to it. Are you with me?"

Tears were streaming down Blue's face, and Caleb could hear the sirens moving closer, but he had to get Blue's head straight or he would just fall there to be captured by the police, and Caleb wasn't leaving his best friend.

"Now we're going to run because that's what we have to do. You have to get it in your head that that's right, can you do that?" Caleb was looking dead in his eyes and he could see that Blue seemed to accept what was being asked of him. Blue nodded.

"Good, now let's get the hell out of here." Caleb took a last look in the store to see Ray Ray's body lying in a puddle of blood, his eyes staring off into nowhere.

Caleb jumped in the car on the driver's side, Blue fell in on the passenger's. As Caleb sped off he heard the sirens all around him. He knew they were closing, but he also knew they didn't know who he was or what he was driving, or what had even happened for that matter. He raced the car around a corner and into an alley. His body was wet with sweat and he had that same fear in him that he had had the last time he was running from the police—the fear of death. And that's when it hit him, that he could have been the one lying in that puddle of blood. Goddammit, he thought, banging the steering wheel, right back where he said he would never end up. But he would get out of it. He looked over at his best friend in the seat next to him. *They* were going to get out of it.

The sirens sounded closer, as though they were all around him, coming from no particular direction, but from every direction. He sped down an alley. He came out the other end and took a left that should put him clear, but he thought he heard a car racing up behind him. He panicked, craned his neck around to see, but they weren't there. He blew out a tight sigh of relief, but when he turned back around, a police car was sitting right in front of him, blocking the exit from the alley. He slammed on the brakes, digging his foot into the floor of the car, grabbing the wheel with all he had to keep the thing from spinning, but it did no good. The wheels locked but the car continued to move, sliding ten feet, crashing head-on into the police car.

TWENTY-NINE

Austin was on his back playing with his children. He was at his house, or at least the place he used to know as his house before he left it. After leaving Marcus's house the day before, Austin had gone back to his apartment. He'd sat down, clicked on the television, flipped the channels several times, then clicked it off. He reached for a book, opened it up, and found out that that wouldn't keep his interest either.

There was entirely too much on his mind, with his father calling and the new desire to reconcile with his wife. He couldn't just sit and entertain himself with a book, or a mindless television show.

Austin went back to see his wife late that night. He knocked on the door and she came to answer it in a robe.

"What do you want?" she asked him as though he were a total stranger.

"I . . . I came to see the kids," he lied.

"It's ten-thirty, don't you think it's a little late for that?" Trace said, pulling her robe together, covering herself.

Austin looked down at his watch although he knew exactly what time it was. "I'm sorry, I didn't know it was that late." He stood there waiting for his wife to say something. She didn't, just gave him an odd look.

"So do you think I can come in, since I'm here, or do you have company?" he asked.

"Yeah, Austin, I have company," Trace said sarcastically. "Come in." She stood in the living room, holding her robe together, looking very unnatural. There were no lights on so the two of them stood in the dark.

"What are you doing?" Austin asked.

"What?" Trace said.

"You weren't standing here in the dark before I came, were you? I hear the TV going upstairs, so why are we standing down here?"

Trace smiled a little. "Because that's upstairs. That's my bedroom, and it's off limits to you."

Austin walked over to the stairs, looked up toward the bedroom as if he was inspecting the place, then came back to Trace. "You know both our names are still on this house, so that makes it our bedroom."

"But, because you left and took your things, and because there isn't one single solitary piece of clothing that is yours in that room, that makes it just my bedroom, and it's off limits to you." She folded her arms over her chest.

"I'm still your husband, Trace. I'm not a stranger. I haven't been gone that long to where you'd forget that."

She didn't say anything but Austin could tell that he had her thinking.

"I miss you, Trace," he said, moving next to her but not touching her. "You must miss me too. You must."

She took a step back, but Austin grabbed her arms and pulled her closer.

"You don't miss me? Are you telling me that? Because if you are, I'll leave. Tell me that you don't miss me as much as I miss you and I'll walk out that door." It was dramatic crap, stuff found in the movies. He had no intention of actually walking out, but he knew she'd believe him.

"I'm not going to say that I don't miss you, Austin. But I'm not going to tell you that I do, either," Trace said.

"Then what is it?"

"You aren't entitled to that. I thought you understood that last time we talked. You can't expect that things would be the same between us. Did you think that you would have free rein to come and go as you please, to have open access to me and my thoughts as if we were still married?"

"We are still married," Austin said coolly.

"Not like that we aren't," Trace said, walking away from him.

"Well, I want us to be married *like that* again, Trace. You're the one that's stopping that," Austin said, walking around to face her.

"You know that's not even true," she said.

"If it's not, then let me stay. Just forget about the last few months and let me stay and we'll start out new, right now, starting tonight. I'll move my things tomorrow."

"I don't think so, Austin. It's just not that simple. I just can't let you back in like that. There's so many things that I have to work out, get straight in my own head," Trace said.

"Get straight in your head, huh?"

"That's right," Trace answered.

"Well, how about your heart?"

Trace was silent. She readjusted her robe and ran a nervous hand through her hair.

Austin gave her a long look, then stepped toward the door. "If you don't want me to move back in, then you just don't. I'm not going to force myself on you," Austin said, opening the door, about to step out.

"You can stay the night," Trace blurted out.

Austin turned, the doorknob still in his hand. "What did you say?"

"I mean, it's late, and since you're here, you might as well stay the night . . . so . . . so you can see the children in the morning."

It was all he had to hear. He closed the door.

She allowed him to stay in their bedroom, allowed him to shower with her like old times, even allowed him to make love to her. But she cried the entire time. He didn't know if it was because she was glad that he was there, that he was making love to her again, or because she felt so bad about going back on the word she had given to herself. He didn't know, but that night he felt the most love he had felt for her in a long time. His heart was aching as much as hers, he was sure. When they were done she showered again, and then she came out with towels for Austin.

"You can take these downstairs and shower in the bathroom down there." She stood presenting the towels to him as if they were gifts.

Austin didn't know where she was coming from with the remark. He was stretched out across the bed, worn out, half asleep. "What do you mean?"

"You can't sleep with me," she said plainly. "You can sleep on the couch. You know where the linen is."

"I don't understand," Austin said, sitting up in bed.

"I just can't have you sleeping with me, not yet, all right?"

"But we just made love," Austin protested.

"So, you shouldn't have anything to complain about," Trace said, shoving the towels in his hands and sending him downstairs.

The next morning the children woke him. They were on the couch, jumping on him, pulling his blankets off, begging him to wake up. It was the best awakening he could remember in a long time.

Trace had to go and start her new job, but she said she would let the children stay home from school so they could be with Austin, if he was planning on staying home from work himself. There was no question in his mind.

"Thank you," he said, as Troy wrapped his arms around Austin's neck and Bethany jumped on his stomach.

Before Trace left, she said she would come home for lunch to see how they were doing.

It was 12:15 when Trace came in from work. Austin was in the kitchen preparing bologna sandwiches for the kids who were watching afternoon cartoons in the living room.

Trace came in the kitchen and put her briefcase down in a chair. "Now that's what I like to see, a man in the kitchen."

Austin turned around, a knife in his hand with mayonnaise on the end of it. "How was the first day?" he said.

"Like any first day at work. How was your day with the kids?" she said, walking over to him.

"Perfect. Couldn't be better."

"Getting right back in the groove, I see. Still the master chef."

Austin leaned in near her. "Can I have a kiss?"

Trace looked at him oddly. "I don't know, can you?"

"I'm asking," Austin said.

"I guess," she said reluctantly.

Austin moved to kiss her. He was aiming for her lips, but she turned her head and he ended up kissing her on the cheek.

"Very cute," he said.

"I thought so," Trace said, smiling.

"You're going to have to decide what you want to do," Austin said, not at all amused by Trace's maneuver.

"I will, Austin," she said. "Just give me time, all right?"

The phone rang.

"Do you want me to get it, Mommy?" Bethany called from the living room.

"No, let me," Trace called back, smiling at Austin.

He didn't find anything funny. She should be jumping at the chance to welcome him back into the house. Allow their children to have their father back full time, allow him not to have to eat sandwiches for dinner every day of the week anymore. He would give her just a little more time, a few days, a week at most to play her little game. But after that if she hadn't decided, then the option would no longer be open.

"Austin, it's for you. It's Marcus," Trace said.

Austin walked to the phone, irritated, wondering why Marcus seemed to bother him wherever he went.

"How did you know to call me here, Marcus?"

"It's Caleb. He's in jail, and somebody got shot. We got to get down there," Marcus said, not even addressing Austin's question.

Austin was shocked. For a moment he felt disoriented, wondering what to do.

"Okay, stand out in front of your house, I'll be right there."

Austin put the phone down, a bewildered look on his face.

"What's wrong?" Trace asked, putting a hand on his shoulder.

"Can you keep the kids? Will it be a problem?" Austin asked, moving toward the closet for his jacket. "Caleb's in jail again, and I think this time it's serious."

"Yes, yes, just go. We'll be fine," Trace said. She pulled him near her and kissed him good-bye.

Austin looked at her for a long moment, gave her an appreciative smile, then left.

.   .   .

"Dammit! Dammit, dammit!" Austin yelled within the confines of his speeding Mercedes. He blew past traffic lights as if their only purpose was to add color to the streets.

It was his fault. It was his fault that Caleb was in jail and he knew it. He was too hard on him. Talking to him like that, belittling him. One day it had to take its toll and now he was seeing the day. It wasn't supposed to work like that though, he told himself as he took a sharp turn, almost riding up on the curb. Such talks were only supposed to make him realize that he wasn't taking care of his business like he was supposed to. They were only designed to make him take a look at himself and maybe ask for help, ask how he could stop being considered lazy, how he could stop being considered irresponsible, how he could stop losing his jobs. But it hadn't worked the way Austin had planned. It had backfired, and because of Austin's big mouth his brother was in jail, somewhere he never wanted to see him again.

He didn't belong there, because he wasn't that kind of person. He wasn't the type of person that wasn't able to do for himself, that had to go out and steal. It was just that he had bad luck. Austin knew Caleb could do better for himself, he knew Caleb had potential. When he found out that Caleb had a job, dealing with computers no less, he was so happy for the man. He was proud of him, that after all that he had been through he was still able to land a decent job and take care of his family. He wanted to call him, congratulate him, tell him how proud he was of him back then, but he couldn't. Austin didn't know why, but he just felt that he would sound stupid, or insincere, or worse, just sound like he was lying, because they never spoke like that. They never really said things outside of childish, critical remarks to cause the other pain, but now Austin wished he had done what he felt like doing. He wished he had complimented his brother. Maybe the boy wouldn't have gotten caught up in the mess that he was in now. He wouldn't have felt that there was nowhere else to turn.

THIRTY

Austin picked Marcus up and the entire ride to the police station, Marcus was wondering aloud why Caleb was in jail, what had happened to put him there. He didn't come right out and say it, but he kept on hinting that Austin's and Caleb's argument might have had something to do with it.

Austin gripped the steering wheel tightly, trying not to let Marcus's ranting bother him. All he wanted to do was get there and get Caleb out of jail, but Marcus kept quizzing himself aloud.

"Would you just say it already, and be done with it!" Austin blurted out.

"What are you talking about?" Marcus said, turning his attention to Austin as though he had been woken up out of a sound sleep.

"You think it was me, don't you? You think because of that argument Caleb and I had, that's the reason he's in jail right now, don't you?"

Marcus looked at him strangely. "I never said that."

"You didn't say exactly that," Austin said, whipping the car around a corner. "But that's the point you're getting at. If you think I'm the reason, just come out and say it or shut up and let me drive."

"I don't think you're the reason, but you didn't have to be so hard on him. You didn't have to talk to him like that. What would you expect him to do after being treated like that?"

"I didn't expect him to commit a crime. I told him how I felt, and if he goes out and harms someone because I state my opinion, that's no fault of mine," Austin said, trying to make it sound as believable as possible.

"I said, I didn't think it was your fault, Austin, but your attitude— you don't give a damn either way. I know you didn't tell Caleb to go commit a crime, I know you didn't put a gun to his head and force him to do it, but the words you said, the thoughtless way you treated him, may have pushed him in that direction, and you don't care. So if you think I'm blaming you for something, I am. It's for not giving a damn." Marcus turned away from his brother, and made more than the effort needed to look out the passenger-side window.

Moments later Austin and Marcus arrived at the police station. At the front desk an older police officer, his shirt fitting tightly around the large load he carried in front of him, was writing something in a log book.

"Excuse me," Austin said, tapping on the desk impatiently.

"What is it?" the officer said, not looking up from the work he was doing.

"I need to see Caleb Harris. I need to see him now, please."

"When did he come in?" he said, still not looking up from the book.

"I don't know when he came in," Austin said, his temper beginning to flare. "He's here, shouldn't you people know what time he came in?"

The officer gave Austin a long stare without saying a word.

"Well, are you going to sit there and stare at me or are you going—"

"I'm sorry, Officer," Marcus said, pushing Austin aside. "Our brother was brought in sometime last night. His name is Caleb Harris, and we're pretty worried about him, so my brother's temper is a little out of control. Please forgive him."

The officer looked at Austin as if he wanted to drag him over the counter by his shirt collar, but instead grunted an acceptance of the apology Marcus offered. "Sit over there, and I'll find the detective working on it."

Marcus and Austin waited on a bench. After fifteen minutes a tall man walked up to them wearing a cheap suit and a loud tie. He was in bad need of a haircut and possibly a few hours of sleep, judging by the dark circles under his eyes.

"You here to see the Harris boy?" he said.

Austin stood up immediately. "His name is Caleb Harris, not the Harris boy, and yes, we're here to see him."

"Well, I'm Detective Hadly. You can follow me."

They followed him through a large room lined with desks and file cabinets. Uniformed police officers were weaving in and out of the spaces between the desks; some were typing on typewriters, some talking to arrestees sitting handcuffed at their desks.

They moved into a smaller room, and from that room into yet a smaller room where Caleb was being watched by a guard. When the three men entered the room, the young guard immediately stood up and walked out. Caleb was at a table placed in the middle of the room. Two chairs were pushed up next to it, and a bright light burned down on Caleb's head.

Caleb was lying across the table, his elbows out and his hands cuffed at the wrists. He was sleeping or at least he looked that way, and the first thing that went through Austin's head was that he hoped his brother was not lying there dead. Marcus rushed over to him, pulled up a chair beside him, and shook him.

Caleb didn't respond at first, so Marcus shook him harder. Finally Caleb woke up and when he brought his head up, he looked horrible. His eyes were blood-red, and he looked as though he had been beaten by the way he could barely keep his head up and eyes open. He was exhausted and had probably been through hell last night, Austin thought, and wondered why he was still sitting in this room, forced to sleep in that hard wooden chair. Austin pulled the detective aside.

"What the hell is he doing here? When was he brought in?"

"Sometime after midnight last night," Detective Hadly said, as if none of it made any difference to him.

"Sometime after midnight," Austin repeated. He looked down at his watch and it was just after one. "He's been in this room almost twelve hours."

"We had to question him. He wasn't saying nothing so we kept him here."

"He doesn't have to say anything!" Austin said, infuriated. "It's his damn right. I want him out of here, and I want him out of here right now."

"And who are you?"

"I'm his brother."

"Well, I'm sorry, but—"

"And his lawyer, and I want him out."

The detective looked at Austin oddly and readjusted his demeanor to a more professional one. "I'm sorry, we can't do that."

"Where is your supervisor?" Austin said, tired of dealing with this peon who obviously had no power to make the type of decisions Austin needed made.

"We can't—" the detective tried to explain.

"Your supervisor. I'm not dealing with you anymore. Get your supervisor."

The detective looked slighted but slowly turned and walked out of the room. Austin walked over to the table where Caleb was talking to Marcus.

"So what did you go and do this time?" Austin said in an unforgiving voice.

"It's none of your damn business, all right?" Caleb said, looking up at Austin with pain in his eyes, then looking away.

"I'm sorry, I didn't mean for it to come out that way," Austin said.

"Then what way was it supposed to come out?"

"I'm just upset to see you here like this," Austin said.

"I bet you are, Austin. Just tell the truth. This is what you expected of me, isn't it? Don't try and act surprised. This is exactly what you knew would happen sooner or later," Caleb said, gesturing with his cuffed hands. "Did you come down here to throw it in my face? Did you come down here because you weren't done with the last conversation, and you just wanted to put me down just a little more? What is it, Austin?"

"I just want to help get you out of here," Austin said. "Can you tell me what happened?"

"We robbed a store, and we got caught."

"Who is we?"

"Does it matter?" Caleb said. "They caught us, and I'm in here."

"It does matter," Austin said.

"He was with his best friend, Blue, and another guy named Ray Ray. Ray Ray was shot and killed by the owner," Marcus said. "Is that right, Caleb?" Caleb nodded, an evil look on his face.

"And what's that on your arms?" Austin asked. Caleb's arms were stained from his fingernails up to his elbows, spotting his shirtsleeves.

"It's blood, what does it look like?" Caleb said, planting his elbows on the table, his hands sticking straight up in the air so Austin could see the dried blood.

"And that is from this Ray Ray, I assume," Austin said.

"Yeah," Caleb's voice was low; his mind seemed to have taken off elsewhere. "It was from Ray Ray."

Austin could tell that his little brother was shaken by the loss of his friend. He didn't want to push him anymore on that point. He pulled out a chair and sat down across from Caleb.

"Did you tell them any of this? Anything?"

"No. I didn't tell them nothing, that's why they still got me in here," Caleb said, scratching the side of his head, having to use both hands because of the cuffs.

"Are you sure?" Austin questioned.

"Yeah, I told you I didn't tell them nothing. I told them I wanted to see a lawyer first. They said they'd get me a public defender, but he hasn't got here yet."

"Well, don't worry about that," Austin said.

"And why not?"

"Because I'll defend you."

Caleb didn't respond immediately, just gave him an odd look, then said, "Whatever. I just want to get out of here. I'm tired and I just want to go home."

The door opened and Detective Hadly walked in; a black man in a dark suit and glasses followed him. Austin jumped up.

"I'm Austin Harris, Caleb Harris's attorney. He needs to be let out of here, and let out right now," Austin said, stepping up very close to the man with glasses.

"Well, it's good to meet you too," the black man said. "I'm Lieutenant Coleman, and if you'd step outside we can talk about this."

"My client has been sitting in that room for twelve hours. I want to know why," Austin said, once outside the room.

The lieutenant turned to Detective Hadly.

"We were waiting to take a statement from him. He said he would give us one, and that's what we were waiting on, that's all," Detective Hadly said.

"That's a lie!" Austin yelled. "He never said such a thing and you know it."

"And how do you know?" Hadly remarked.

"Because he told me he didn't."

"Well, he broke into that old man's store, took his money and damn near killed him. He can do that, but he'd never fucking lie, right?" The detective stepped right in Austin's face, as if daring him to do something in retaliation. Austin clenched his jaw and tried with everything in him to suppress the urge to try and knock the man's teeth out of his head.

"Hadly, get the hell out of here," the lieutenant ordered.

Hadly gave Austin one more look, then walked away.

"I'm sorry about that. He has a bit of a temperament problem."

"Well, maybe you ought to have him get it fixed before someone fixes it for him," Austin said, still eyeing the man across the room.

"Mr. Harris, I don't know why your client has been in that room for so long, but I will find out, and I'll let you know."

"That's not going to do any good for me right now. What I want is for him to be released. I want you to let him out, and I'll follow up with you later," Austin said.

"How's that?" the lieutenant said, chuckling.

"I said, I want him to be released and I will follow up with you later."

"You're not a criminal attorney, are you, Mr. Harris?"

"No," Austin, replied, feeling self-conscious at the moment.

"I didn't think so, because we don't just let people out and then follow up with their lawyer at their convenience, especially those people who break into stores, beat the owners senseless, and steal their money. And it definitely doesn't help that he has a previous conviction. What I'm trying to say, Mr. Harris, is that we'll move him from that room, but the only place he's going is to a jail cell, over at the county. Do you understand that, counselor?" the lieutenant said, stressing the last word as if Austin had no business trying to pass himself off as a lawyer.

"Yes, I understand," Austin said. "I understand completely."

THIRTY-ONE

Caleb sat on the floor within the cold confines of his jail cell. They had taken him there, to the county jail, three days ago and processed him. Mug shots, fingerprints, loads of paperwork and all the shouting, cursing, and degrading one person could take from the guards. It was supposed to make him feel as though he deserved to be there, like he deserved to be caged up and given trash to eat, and a mattress that felt worse than the concrete the bed sat on. It was supposed to make him feel like he didn't deserve respect, or even to be treated on the same level as an animal. He was supposed to feel like that, so when he was treated like that it wouldn't come as any surprise, and he wouldn't gripe, or complain, or try and fight the guards for rights that he felt he should've received.

It was the same, Caleb thought, as the last time he had gone through it, and he was sorry that nothing had changed, not in the jail but in him. Nothing had changed. He hadn't learned a damn thing, hadn't realized that he couldn't do stupid things like rob a store and not expect to pay some sort of price.

They issued him some clothing: a standard county jail jumpsuit, the inmate number stenciled right on the breast pocket so everyone could see. He was a number again, nothing more.

They allowed him to make a phone call before they locked him up. He didn't want to, but he called Sonya. He felt he had to let her know what had happened because he knew she would be worried half to death. He told her that he was in the county jail and she almost lost her mind. She started cursing at him, ranting and raving about what would happen now that he was in trouble again. It was all too much for him to take, so he told her he was being forced off the phone by one of the guards, which was a lie. He told her to come down as soon as she could, and they would talk about it. He hung up the phone, feeling as though he had been separated from the rest of the world, and the rest of his life.

That was three days ago, and she had not come yet. He figured she had just given up on him like she said she would. He was hoping, praying for that not to be the case because he didn't know what he would do without her, do without his child, and he realized he would probably just die.

It was 10 P.M. The lights had just gone out and it was damn near pitch-black in his cell, save for some dull light that trickled in the window from a faraway spotlight. Caleb sat on the cold, hard cement floor, his knees pulled in tight to his chest, his hands clasped around them. Although he was tired, he didn't want to lie on that bed. It was disgusting.

He thought about all the men who had spent time on that bed. The criminals who came in off the street. The men who refused to shower, the dirt from weeks and months caked to their bodies. He saw them lying down, turning on the beaten mattress, the dead flakes of skin falling from their flesh, their mouths hanging open, allowing saliva to flow freely from their lips, being absorbed by the filthy skin of the bed.

Caleb couldn't knowingly lie in that. So he would sit on that cold floor, in the dark, staring at the little bit of light that found him, trying to stay awake until he could continue no longer. He would sit until he was so exhausted that he could no longer keep his head from falling limp onto his chest, until his eyes would no longer stay open without him holding them with his fingers and thumb. Then he would crawl over to the bed, climb up on it and pull himself into a ball, trying to minimize his contact with the disgusting thing. He would do that, as he had done the last few nights, but until then he would just sit and think.

The next evening, Caleb was allowed a short phone break along with the rest of the inmates. He called Sonya again to find out why she hadn't come to see him. He let the phone ring more than ten times but no one picked up. She should be home from work by now, he thought. He gave up the phone to the next person in line, and walked to the end of the long line, hoping she would be home next time he called.

On the second attempt, he let the phone ring twice as many times, but still no one picked up. He went back to his cell, saddened and distraught, hoping that she didn't answer because she was actually on her way up there to see him. He had told her that Wednesday was visitors' day, and it was Wednesday. But something told him that she wasn't on her way there. Something told him, as he sat on the floor of his cell, that she might be gone, might have left their apartment, never to return, and if she was there, she was letting the phone ring. She would be there, knowing it was him as she threw all her belongings into plastic bags and pillowcases. While he called, she was throwing Jahlil's jacket on him, pulling a hat over his head, and preparing for them to leave him forever.

Caleb told himself not to think of that happening, because all it would do was drive him crazy, but he couldn't help it. He turned to look out his cell, grabbing the bars with both hands. A guard walked by, and Caleb thought maybe if he asked the guard, he would let him out of there so he could run home, just to make sure that Sonya wasn't taking his child away from him, taking all of Jahlil's things from what used to be their home, and moving them elsewhere, a place where she intended him to grow up with nothing to remind him of his father. The thought angered Caleb, and he squeezed the bars tightly in his hands. They did not give.

"Harris," a guard said, looking down at him through the cell bars.

Caleb looked up.

"You got a visitor."

Caleb was let out of his cell, and walked down a long corridor leading to the visitors' room. He knew it would be Sonya. He knew she would be there, and that made him feel both better and worse. He would be glad to see her, but he didn't want to hear what she had to say. She might be thinking of walking out on him, and he wouldn't be able to take that, he just wouldn't.

Caleb was moved into the visiting area and sat down at a table. Across from him sat Sonya, looking very plain, no makeup on her face, showing no expression, her hair pulled back with a rubber band. Her hands were crossed before her, and an old beat-up purse lay beside her on the table.

Caleb felt strange, scared. A nervous feeling ran around inside him. He felt his heart beating a little quicker than it should have, a queasy feeling in his stomach.

"I'm glad to see you could make it down here," Caleb said softly. "I was starting to worry that you didn't want to see me."

Sonya just nodded her head and looked down at her hands.

"How you been?" Caleb said, trying to start a conversation.

"Fine," Sonya answered.

"I see, I see," Caleb nodded his head in an animated way, as if he was very interested that she was feeling fine. "And Jahlil, he's okay, too?"

"Yeah," Sonya said.

Caleb bobbed his head again in silence. "You know I was—"

"Why did you do it?" Sonya interrupted, her face filled with emotion.

"Do what?" Caleb said.

"Don't do that, Caleb. Don't play games with me. Why did you rob that store?" Caleb was stopped by the question, not able to answer it right away. He looked at her and chuckled pathetically. "Well, can't you at least say hello, ask me how I'm doing first?"

"Fuck a hello, Caleb! I want to know what made you lose your damn mind and run out there and try and rob a store."

"I needed the money, all right?" Caleb said solemnly, his head lowered in shame.

"For what?"

"For the bills, for the rent, for food, for things that you and Jahlil would need. Isn't that what you were saying? Didn't you say that you needed for me to bring some money into the house? Well, that's what I was trying to do."

"Oh, so you're trying to blame it on me," Sonya said. "We need money, Caleb, but I didn't tell you to be a fool and try and take it. I told you to get a damn job, Caleb! Why couldn't you just get a job like everybody else?"

"Because there ain't no jobs! How many times I got to tell you that? I shouldn't have to tell you of all people, you know how tight it is, you see them folks trying to get jobs every day. There ain't nothing out there."

"That don't make it right what you did. You weren't thinking. You just go out there and do, and worry about what happens later. Now look at you. You got yourself thrown in jail again, and now what are we supposed to do? I can't afford all those bills, and the rent, and the things Jahlil needs by myself. How am I supposed to manage all that without you?" Sonya said, bringing her face down into her hands.

It made Caleb feel terrible. All he was trying to do was help, and all he managed was to put them in a worse situation than they started in.

"You're just so selfish sometimes, Caleb," Sonya said, pulling her face from her hands.

"Selfish! What do you mean? I was thinking of the two of you. I tried to get that money for you. How can you say I'm selfish?"

"Because you weren't thinking about us, you were thinking about yourself. You were thinking about your damn pride, and your fucking ego. Marcus gave us some money before, and he would've given us some more to pay those bills if you just would've asked him, but you had too much pride for that. You could've just asked him for the money, and you would've never tried to rob that store and you would've never been in here. You're selfish, because you didn't think about what Jahlil and I would do if you got caught. You didn't think about how we would make it. How I would feel not to have you around, how it would be for Jahlil not to have his father there for him. Did you think about those things before you came up with the bright idea to rob that store?"

Caleb didn't say anything. He retreated back into his mind, searching his memory to see if he had given it any thought.

"Did you, Caleb?" Sonya yelled at him.

She knew the answer, Caleb thought. And even if she was wrong, she would assume she was right.

"No," Caleb said, his voice barely audible. "I didn't think about it."

He lowered his head again, and focused his attention on a scratch in the table. He was ashamed to look at her again, because he had no defense against her stone stare, against her accusations of selfishness, of thinking only about himself. Priding himself on taking care of situations without the help of his brother, feeling confident that he could always pull them through somehow or another. He was wrong. He needed Marcus to pay the rent for them or they would have been out on the street, and he couldn't count all the other things Marcus had done for them. And as far as pulling them through bad situations, that was a joke. It was just a matter of time before he and Sonya both realized that he wasn't capable of managing his own hardships, taking care of his own life, not to mention trying to handle the burden of a family. Caleb continued running his index finger over the scratch in the table, hoping he would never have to look up and confront Sonya again.

"I . . . I don't know if I can do this any longer," Sonya said, her voice soft but committed.

"What?" Caleb said, his attention snatched away from the table.

"I don't think I'll be able to continue to do this."

"Do what?" Caleb asked, knowing exactly what she was referring to. She was talking about leaving him, as she had threatened she would the next time he got into trouble like this. She was talking about packing up her things and leaving their home and going somewhere he would never be able to find her. She was talking about taking herself away from him, not allowing him to know her anymore. He would be left alone, and if he was found guilty and locked up, there would be no letters, no phone calls, nothing to look forward to. No release date to hold in his heart, giving him incentive to wake up every morning. But worst of all, she would be taking his son. She would take what meant the world to him, and Jahlil would be gone. Just gone, and it would be like her reaching into his chest and yanking out his heart, smashing it with the heel of her shoe right in front of his face. That's what she meant by her not being able to continue any longer, but he couldn't allow that, he wouldn't. He looked down, saw her hand resting on the table and reached for it, covering it with his hand.

"Maybe you ought to think about it a little more, baby," he said.

"I did all the thinking I had to do," Sonya said, pulling her hand away, cradling it in the other, as if it might be injured from his touch.

"But you can't do that. You just can't up and take our son and decide that you're leaving," Caleb said, fidgeting around in his chair.

"Well, what am I supposed to do, Caleb? Stay there, and what? Wait around for you to get out of jail, or are you going to take care of us from in here?" she said, the sadness that had been in her face now replaced with determination. "I'm taking him and I'm leaving because I have no other choice."

"You aren't taking him! That's not going to be good for him to be away from his father," Caleb said, his heart beating faster.

"Where do you think he is now? He's already away from his father, Caleb. And that's nobody's fault but your own. I'm leaving, and he's going with me, but we know where you are. I'll have him write you or something."

That was a lie. That was a damn lie, and Caleb knew it, could see it in her face. He wouldn't let her take his son away, because once that happened he would never see him again, he just knew it.

Sonya stood up. "Good-bye, Caleb. I'll try and get through on the phone or something."

That was it? That was all she had to say after the years they had spent together, after all that he had tried to give her? She couldn't leave him like that, not right now. She reached down for the purse on the table, and Caleb grabbed her around the wrist.

"You can't take him like this," he said.

Her eyes opened wide, and she tried to yank away from him, which made him close his grip tighter on her.

"Let go of me, Caleb!" she screamed, beating at his wrist with her other hand, trying desperately to pull away.

Other inmates and visitors looked in their direction, and a guard came running, his nightstick unholstered, making his way through the crowd that was forming around Caleb.

"Let's just talk about this!" Caleb yelled, grabbing her with both hands, pulling her in closer to him, as she continued to fight and scream.

Why was she yelling like that, why was she fighting him? All he wanted to do was talk to her, tell her that he still loved her and that he couldn't live without the two of them. All he wanted to do was ask her to stay, but she was running from him, hitting him, trying to kick him, as if he was some stranger trying to rape her. He wasn't that. He was the man that, not one week ago, she had said she loved, the man that had taken her and their child riding the streets of Chicago, the man she had kissed passionately beside the lake. He was that man, Caleb thought, when all of a sudden he felt the guard's nightstick thrown across his neck and smashed against his windpipe. He didn't know what was happening, why the guard was trying to choke him, but he continued to hold onto Sonya with all his might. He could hear her clothes starting to rip, feel the fabric tear off in his hands.

Another guard came through the crowd and started to jab Caleb in the gut with the butt of his nightstick. The guard hit him hard countless times, and it felt like small explosions in his stomach, but Caleb held on, trying to speak to Sonya as she continued to fight in his grasp, tears spilling from her eyes, a horrified look on her face. He tried to tell her all that he was feeling, tried to hang on to her, but the beating to his stomach and the dizziness from the lack of oxygen got to him. He felt himself blacking out, and fell limp in the arms of the guards. Sonya pulled away, disappearing into the crowd of people around him. The two guards grabbed Caleb's arms and started to drag him away.

"Sonya!" Caleb called. His head was whipping back and forth, scanning the crowd, trying to find her face to make sure she was all right, make sure she hadn't been swallowed up and hurt by the crowd of criminals.

"Sonya!" he called out again, coughing violently from the choking he had received. He was very close to being dragged out of the room. When he looked around feverishly one last time, knowing it might be the last time he saw her, he spotted her face looking over someone's shoulder. She no longer looked frightened, or angered. She just looked out from within the crowd, her shirt stretched and torn around her neck. She looked at Caleb and if there was an expression of any sort Caleb saw on her face, it was sympathy.

He saw that look, and told himself to burn it into his brain, because he might not see it from her again. "I love you, Sonya!" he called out, his throat still burning from the strangling. "I love you!"

THIRTY-TWO

"The facts are, Caleb was caught by the police driving the getaway car not two blocks from where the robbery took place. Blue was in the passenger seat, a pocket full of money that the store owner says was taken from him. That same person was half beaten to death with his own shotgun, and he identified Blue as the one who did it. He also pointed out Caleb as being there. Ray Ray's blood was found all over the both of them and so there's no claiming that they were being mistaken for two other black men, because the blood put them both there. All these facts are stacked up against your brother, Austin," William Lansford said. The well-dressed, white-haired criminal attorney was Austin's friend and mentor, and Austin had asked him to take the case.

"I spoke to the prosecuting attorney," William said, sitting in the large leather executive chair, behind his oak desk. "She happens to be a good friend of mine. If your brother pleads guilty, they'll give him five and the possibility of parole after three. If he's tried and convicted, they'll go for ten to fifteen. What do you think, Austin?"

Austin didn't know what to think. All he knew was that any way he looked at it, his brother was going to spend time in jail, and he didn't like that at all.

"I . . . I don't know what to do," Austin admitted, feeling helpless.

"Austin, I've known you from when you were in law school, so let me speak freely," William said. "There is an enormous amount of evidence stacked up against your brother, and the way things have been going lately, people are fed up with being abused by criminals. They're demanding that offenders be put behind bars and the key thrown away, and these prosecutors are working their asses off to give them what they want. If you haven't been following me so far, I don't think he has a chance if he goes to trial," William said, a sympathetic look on his face.

Austin didn't need the old man to tell him, any fool could see that. All the same, he sat there, a blank look on his face, feeling overwhelmed.

"Would you like for me to inform your brother of his options?"

"No," Austin said softly. "I think I ought to be the one that does that."

It was too late to go and see Caleb so Austin drove home to think about how he would explain to him what William had said.

He got out of his car and dragged himself up the stairs into his apartment. He hadn't been there in a couple of days. It felt good to be back, good to have someplace where he could be alone to sort out his feelings about everything that was happening to him.

He went to the kitchen cabinet and poured himself a glass of cognac. He pulled it to his nose and just the smell was enough to relax him a little. He looked over to the corner of the room and saw that the little red light on the answering machine was blinking like crazy. He went over, stood before it, and asked himself if he really wanted to push the button that would release, God only knows, what type of new problems on him. He kicked the glass of cognac back, coughed a little after swallowing all the contents, then punched the button.

Marcus had called twice just to find out what was going on; Trace had done the same. Someone had called asking for Roberto, which he assumed was a wrong number, and the next five messages were all hang-ups, which was strange. He was about to step away from the machine, assuming the final call would be a hang-up as well, when he heard the voice. "Hello, Austin, how are you doing? This is your father. I've been trying to call you off and on for the past couple of days but I haven't been able to catch you at home, so I didn't want to bother you with a hundred messages on your machine. I wanted to see how you were doing and if you thought about what I said. Oh, yeah, and I have a surprise for you. I'm here. I'm here in the city. I'm staying in room 220 at the Radisson, downtown. I would like you to call me, Austin. I was hoping I could see you. You know, talk about some things, maybe even the future. Call me when you can, I'll be looking forward to hearing from you. Bye."

That bastard, Austin thought. Why did he fly down here when he wasn't even invited? Austin sat on the bed feeling burdened. One more problem to add to the pile he was balancing. One more decision to make. He thought that he might have wanted to see his father, but there was just too much going on now. He would have to call him some other time, when things settled down, when he could think straight.

Austin made it to the county jail sometime around 8:30 A.M. He told the officer that he was Caleb's lawyer and wanted to see him in a private room; he didn't want to speak of their private matters among a crowd of inmates and their visitors.

Austin was sitting at the table going through some notes when a guard brought Caleb in. He was in his uniform still, a thin beard starting to cover his face. He walked freely, no shackles around his ankles or handcuffs around his wrists. He sat down in front of Austin and smiled a bit, but only with his mouth, not with his eyes.

"How are you doing?" Austin said to his brother.

"As well as can be expected, I guess," Caleb said glumly.

Austin shuffled his notes so he wouldn't have to look into his brother's eyes. "So, I see you're trying to grow a beard," he said.

"No, I'm not trying to grow one, it's just growing. I'm not trying to stop it is what it is. What's the point when I'm locked up in here?" Caleb said.

Austin didn't know how to take the remark, didn't know how to respond to it.

"But it itches a lot," Caleb said, scratching under his chin, smiling a bit.

Austin felt more comfortable and smiled in return.

"So I know you're not here just to visit, so what's the news?"

"Why don't you think I'm here just to visit?" Austin said.

Caleb laughed sarcastically.

"What?" Austin smiled uneasily. "Yes, I'm your lawyer, but I'm also your brother."

"Austin, stop it, man."

"Stop what?" Austin said.

"You're feeling guilty. You think I'm in here because of you. You're thinking because you treated me like shit all the time we were growing up that it had some type of effect on me that made me go out and rob that guy, or you're thinking the argument we had, the things you said weighed so heavy on my mind that I had no other choice than to go and commit a crime. Well, do me a favor and get over it, all right? It had nothing to do with you."

"I was just saying that I can come down here just to see how you're doing, that's all," Austin said.

"I said don't, man. You can't stand me. I know that, and you know that. You never once visited me at my place when I wasn't in jail. Why the change all of a sudden? I'd appreciate it if you just keep the caring act in your briefcase, okay?" Caleb said, slumping in his chair.

"But I do care," Austin said. "Why do you think I'm here? Why do you think I'm taking off work and helping to represent you for free?"

"For free, huh?" Caleb said. "You're doing it because you feel guilty. I already told you that. Now if you don't mind, can you tell me what's happening?"

"Not until you understand that I do care what happens to you," Austin said.

Caleb sat up straight. "Austin, you just don't get it, do you? I don't care either way, all right? Why should it matter to me now if you care? Why should things change when things were going along so well just the way they were, neither of us giving a damn?" Caleb said. "All I want you to do is get me out of here. When you come to see me, tell me what's going on. Tell me what you've learned from your little law books, tell me what you have hiding in the magic bag of tricks there, and how all of that can get me out of here. That's all you have to do. Save the small talk, brotherly love stuff for Marcus."

Caleb slumped back down in his seat. "So if we can pass all that and get on with it, what is the news?"

THIRTY-THREE

The room was dark save for the small amount of light that made its way from the streetlamp through the curtain of Reecie's bedroom. She and Marcus had just finished making love and Marcus was on top of her, but his mind wasn't where it should have been—on her. He kissed her on the cheek, then raised himself and walked over to the window.

She watched as the dark silhouette of his body moved through the room and was illuminated partially by the light coming in through the curtain. Marcus leaned against the windowpane and stared blankly out into the street, his body still coated with sweat from their exhaustive lovemaking.

Reecie walked up behind him, contouring her body to his, wrapping her arms around him. "What's wrong, baby?" she asked.

He turned his head and gave her a look almost as if he didn't recognize her. "Huh . . . oh, nothing. Nothing's wrong, sweetheart." He leaned toward her and gave her an absent kiss on the lips, then went back to staring out the window.

"Marcus, c'mon, I've known you long enough to know when there's something on your mind. Don't tell me nothing when there's something bothering you. What is it?" Reecie asked.

"Nothing," Marcus said in a blank tone, as if he hadn't heard a word she had said.

Reecie turned him around to see his face. "Will you talk to me?" she said.

Marcus didn't respond.

"Marcus, tell me what's going on."

He pulled away from her and walked back to the bed and sat down. "It's everything. It's just everything. Life, motherfucking life." He sank his chin into his hands.

Reecie walked over and sat behind him, draping her arms around his neck. "What do you mean by that?"

"It's just . . . it's just things have never been the way I wanted them to be—never. My parents break up, and I'm left without a father, but I deal with it. I tell myself things could always be worse. Then my mother gets sick and dies, but I still remain optimistic. I have a younger brother to take care of, I can't fall to pieces, I tell myself. He leaves only a year after my older brother, and who do I have—no one.

"I put myself through school, work in the profession I love, I'm happy with my accomplishments, but have no one to share them with. Over the years I'm able to build some type of relationship with my brothers again, so I have my family back, but I have no one I can love, that I can plan for the future with. I tell myself that's all I need and my life would be what I want it to be, but I'm too damn chicken to put my heart on the line. And then when I finally find you, I'm faced with losing my brother to prison."

Marcus turned to look in Reecie's eyes. He wanted her to see the pain he was feeling. "I'm just tired of things not going right, and tired of fighting to make them right."

"Marcus, he's not gone yet. You can't say that he's going to get convicted for sure," Reecie said.

"Really, why not? What's going to stop them from convicting him? Reecie, he's guilty. He robbed that store. They caught him red-handed, the money in their pockets, the blood on their hands. The damn thing shouldn't even go to trial, because there's nothing to try. He's guilty as hell and everybody knows it. Everybody! What a fucking fool he is."

Marcus was short with her, and he probably hurt her feelings, but at that point he was hurting too much to care.

Marcus thought about the day Caleb wanted to move away from the house. He had already dropped out of high school and no longer wanted to remain under Marcus's supervision. Marcus was in the kitchen trying to cook dinner, watch TV and work a crossword puzzle all at the same time when Caleb came in to give the news.

"Marcus, I'm going to leave now." He said it like he was going on an ice cream run.

"Where are you going? Dinner is going to be ready in a minute," Marcus said, the pencil in his teeth, his attention on the television.

"I'm not going to make it to dinner tonight. I'm leaving."

Marcus turned to see Caleb, and the pencil fell from his mouth. Caleb was standing in the kitchen doorway, a torn sports bag at his feet, a bag lunch in his hand. Marcus flashed back for a moment to when his father left, then shook the thought out of his head. No, it's different, he told himself.

"What do you mean, where do you think you're going?"

"I'm just going," Caleb said. "I can't take it no more. I can't take being in this house with you. I'm a grown man, and I can't be taking orders no more."

"You're not a grown man, you're seventeen years old. And you'll take orders if you have to. I'm your older brother, someone has to be in charge. You know that's what Ma would say."

"That's another reason I got to go. You always talking about Ma, Ma this and Ma that. You're acting like she's in the next room, talking about her like she's going to give me an ass-whooping if I don't clean my room. She's gone, man. Ma is dead," Caleb said, no emotion whatsoever on his face.

The remark shook Marcus. He never liked to look at it like that, and never said those words.

"She's only been gone for five years, Caleb."

"How long does it take? I loved her just as much as you did. I miss her just as much. But how am I supposed to get over her if you're always acting like she never died? I can't do it, Marcus. I just can't." He shouldered his bag and walked farther into the kitchen. "I got to go," he said, holding out an open hand.

Marcus sat there on the countertop, his feet in a chair, staring at his younger brother telling him he was going to leave. Going to go out in the world, not knowing exactly where, but he was going to go out there and make a life for himself. He had no idea of what he was doing.

"I can't let you go, Caleb. You know that," Marcus said, not taking his hand.

"You can't stop me, Marcus. I'm not staying. I've thought about this a long time and this is what I need to do. I got plans. I got somewhere to stay, and I'll call you when I'm settled. You don't have to worry, I'll be all right. Now are you going to shake my hand or not?" he said, his hand still floating before him.

Marcus hopped down from the counter and gave his brother a hug. He didn't know exactly what was happening at that moment. It didn't seem real. All he knew was that the last of his family was leaving him, and he would be alone.

"I got to go now, man," Caleb said, gently pulling away. He looked in Marcus's eyes. "You going to be all right?"

Marcus tried not to betray himself by letting his emotions show. "Yeah, yeah. There's just going to be more dinner for me—every day," he said.

Caleb smirked at the remark, turned his back and left. Marcus stood there in the middle of the kitchen, his head down, the TV droning on, the pots on the stove boiling over, his puzzle unfinished. He didn't want to let him leave. He felt that he was Caleb's last and only protector from the rest of the world, that he was the net that kept him from falling to the hard surface of the world below. But Caleb was slipping, falling through the small holes, and Marcus knew if Caleb fell, it would be so hard that he could not just get up and brush himself off.

That was how Marcus had felt then, and he felt the exact same way as he stood with his back toward Reecie. Somehow, a hole was opening up in the net that he had managed to re-rig under Caleb and he was falling, and there was no way Marcus could catch him.

"I have to go see him tomorrow," Marcus said, turning toward Reecie, barely seeing her in the shadows. "And I'm almost afraid to because there's nothing I can do for him."

Reecie brought Marcus in closer to her, wrapping her arms around him, comforting him in her embrace.

The next afternoon Marcus sat in the chair at a long table in the room reserved for inmates and their visitors. He felt odd and unsure of himself. He looked around nervously at other visitors and at a few of the inmates, and when they returned his stare, he quickly looked away. He fidgeted with his car keys as he waited for the guard to bring Caleb out of his cell.

Act natural, he told himself. Act as though you're having a normal conversation with your little brother, that's it. He took a deep breath in, then exhaled, preparing himself to speak to his brother.

The guard escorted Caleb in, and he sat down. Marcus could tell that he had lost some weight. His face looked a bit gaunt, his cheekbones protruding a little more than they had before. What caught Marcus's attention next was the blue-blackness and swelling that partially closed Caleb's left eye.

"What happened to you?" Marcus said.

"I can't get a 'How's it going' first?" Caleb said, looking haggard. "I'm glad you decided to finally come and see me, I was beginning to wonder about you."

"It took me a little while to get my head straight with it, you know what I mean?" Marcus said apologetically.

"I understand. It's no big deal. I mean, you're here now, right?" Caleb said in a melancholy tone.

"Yeah, I'm here now," Marcus agreed. "Can you tell me what happened to your eye?"

"Oh, that." Caleb touched it gently, poking at the puffiness. "Got in a fight. There's a couple of people that don't like me here, but that can be expected. I mean it's jail, right?"

"Are you okay? Is there anything I can do? Are they still bothering you?"

Caleb shook his head, touched the swollen eye once more, and let out a chuckle.

"There's nothing you can do, not this time, Marcus, and I know that's probably eating you alive, huh?"

Marcus didn't say anything, just looked down at his car keys.

"Don't worry, man, there ain't nothing I can do either. That's the whole idea behind jail, they want you helpless."

"I'm sorry, Caleb," Marcus finally admitted.

"For what?"

"For you being in here, for all of this happening," Marcus said.

"So you think it's your fault, too? Austin came here with that same nonsense. He tried to be the brother that he never was because he was feeling guilty. I told him he didn't have to worry about it. I think he was actually relieved to hear that. What do you think?"

Marcus didn't answer, just displayed that same sympathetic look.

"Look," Caleb said. "It's not your fault, so stop looking like that. I can make it all right. I don't blame you."

They sat there in silence for a few moments.

"Are you all right?" Marcus said.

"Yeah," Caleb said. "I just have something on my mind."

"Like what?"

Caleb thought for a moment. "Why did you give Sonya that money?"

"What?" Marcus said.

"Why did you give Sonya that money? You knew the last thing I wanted to do was take money from you."

Marcus was surprised. He didn't know how his brother found out, but he figured Sonya told him.

"Because you needed it. You were going to get thrown out of your apartment, and you needed to pay the rent so I paid it."

"You knew I wouldn't have wanted you to do that, but you did it anyway. You gave her that money like I wasn't able to. Like I couldn't take care of my own family. How do you think that made me look?" Caleb said.

"I don't know, Caleb. But I wasn't really thinking about how you would look, I just wanted you to have someplace to live. Is that a crime?" Marcus asked, his voice becoming firm.

"Yes, it's a crime. It's a crime against me and my family. It made me look like a punk, like a worthless loser. Sonya had to come to you for money when—"

"She didn't ask for it, all right? I made her take it. She didn't come to me. I found out on my own. She only acted with the interest of you and your son in mind."

"Well, I could've gotten it," Caleb said, his voice softening as if in contemplation.

"How, Caleb? By robbing someone?" Marcus spoke the words and didn't even realize what he had said until after it was too late, until after Caleb's face contorted in reaction. "I'm sorry. I didn't mean to say that."

"Really, what did you mean to say? 'What a fool you are, Caleb. Haven't you learned your lesson yet, Caleb? You deserve to be right where you are, Caleb.' Is that what you meant to say?"

"I didn't come here to argue with you," Marcus said.

"Well, it's what we're doing, isn't it?"

Marcus looked away, caught the eye of another inmate. The man was old, his face wrinkled, his body bent over with age.

"Did Austin tell you anything yet?" Marcus said, trying to change the subject.

"I don't want to talk about that right now."

"Why not, what's wrong?" Marcus asked.

"Nothing's wrong. I just don't want to talk about it."

"You have to tell me something. You can't keep what's going on a secret."

"Let's just say I got a decision to make, okay? I got to go." He got up from his chair and walked toward the guard. At the door he turned around and walked back over to the table.

"Thanks for the money," Caleb said, as though he had been forced by someone else to show his brother gratitude. He gave Marcus a long look, as if he'd never see him again.

"I got to go," Caleb said again.

THIRTY-FOUR

It was all very odd, Caleb thought as he looked at the suit Austin had bought him to wear for the preliminary hearing. It was an ugly color of gray in Caleb's opinion, but it really didn't matter what color it was because it was a suit either way. He remembered when he was on the bus, searching for a job, how he had laughed at the men who had to wander around in those things, not having the say to wear what they wanted. He told himself then he didn't have to wear those suits, and he was happy about it. No, he wasn't making their money, but he at least had his freedom. Now look at him, he had to wear the ugly thing just to get his freedom taken away. It was never supposed to be this bad, he thought, as he took off the uniform and started putting on the suit.

He had made up his mind what he was going to do, what he had to do, and he had spent the entire night, sleepless, on the floor of his cell, trying to accept it. It was a hard-fought battle, but he felt that he had come to grips with it. He needed to because he didn't want to break down and cry when he told the judge what he wanted. He didn't want his brothers to see him fall to pieces, be overcome with grief, lose his spine in the face of imprisonment and fall to the floor like a whimpering child.

He didn't want to look over and see Sonya there, a look of pathetic disgust on her face, as if she was questioning why she had ever involved herself with him in the first place, that is if she even showed. He had spoken to her on the phone the other day, apologized and told her what he had decided. She didn't respond to what he was saying, and sounded as though she wasn't even listening.

"I'm sorry about what happened when you came," he said softly. "I was just . . . just . . . "

"Whatever, Caleb," she said. She didn't say much else, but did bother to ask him why he hadn't considered her in his decision, and he told her that he couldn't. He just couldn't. It was the only explanation he gave her, and in his mind, it would have to be enough. She told him she wasn't sure if she would come or not, then she hung up, simply hung up in his face, as if he were not in prison but at his brother's place and could call her right back.

He pulled the trousers up and buttoned them. They were too long. He understood. Austin wouldn't have gotten them hemmed before he brought them. He didn't even know Caleb's length; besides, where he'd be going, he didn't have to worry about looking good wearing a suit, at least not that kind. Caleb bent down and rolled the pants over twice in wide cuffs to fit his length.

The night before, Austin had told him everything he needed to know and told him whatever decision he made, he would support him in it. If he wanted to plead guilty, he would understand, or if he wanted to go to trial, Austin assured him he would do everything possible to win the case, no matter how much it took.

It gave Caleb some reassurance to hear him speak like that. He wasn't sure if it was still the guilt that Austin was feeling, but his recent treatment of Caleb seemed fairly genuine and Caleb decided to stop guessing about him. He was one of the only people really trying to help him, so he would take his hand and follow him without question.

After Caleb finished dressing himself, he looked in the mirror. It wasn't actually a mirror, but one of those reflective metal jobs, bolted to the wall, that always reminded him of a fun house mirror. He saw himself in a suit and tie for the first time in his life, and he thought that he didn't look that bad, and they weren't as uncomfortable as he had figured them to be. A funny time to find out, he thought.

It happened to be a clear sunny day, and Caleb looked up and felt the warm sun on his face as the guard walked him across the street to the courthouse. There wasn't a single cloud up in the sky, and it was almost as if nature was mocking him, teasing him, letting him know that there would always be sunny days, even while he was behind bars.

For a moment Caleb saw an image of himself in the gray suit running through the crowded streets, through the congested traffic of cars and trucks, handcuffs dangling about his wrist. He was running for his freedom, like a well-dressed slave a hundred and some years after slavery had been abolished.

He cleared the thought out of his mind as he climbed the stairs to the court house, trying to convince himself that the sunny days wouldn't run out before he was released.

He was put in a room, a room where he was supposed to meet Austin and the other attorney so they could run over last-minute things. He was told that Blue would be there too, since they were to be together at the hearing. He wanted to see how his friend was handling life in jail.

The door opened and Blue walked in beside a guard. He wore a dark blue suit, the cuffs of the sleeves and pants hanging higher on him than they should have.

"Black man!" he said, smiling. He gave Caleb a hug, then pulled away to take a look at him. "You looking good, even if it is during the last hour. How you making it?"

"I'm making it, that's all," Caleb said. "You're looking good yourself, man."

Caleb sat down at the table.

"Man, this piece of shit," Blue said, tugging at the sleeve. "I haven't worn this thing in years. It's way too small, but I don't give a damn. I ain't trying to look good for no motherfuckers who just trying to hang me. But anyway, I've been talking to my lawyer. He's a public defender, but he's good—a brother. He's going to get me off. I'm going to walk up out of here, I'm telling you," Blue said, leaning over the table, filled with a fidgety childlike energy.

"I heard your brother and some white guy are representing you. They been pulling strings, I know. I'm surprised you still in here."

"Don't be," Caleb said.

"Your brother's going to get you out, right?" Blue asked.

"I'm not letting it go to trial," Caleb said, feeling his heart sink.

"What!" Blue said. "You ain't letting it go to trial. What are you going to do then?"

"I'm pleading guilty."

Blue got up from the table and spun around in a circle, his hands on his head like he was dying from an aneurysm. "Who told you to do that? Who's been fucking talking to you?"

"I just know what my options are, all right? This is the best thing for me to do," Caleb said, as though he had memorized the lines in an attempt to convince himself of their truth.

"The best thing for you to do is take this shit to trial and try to get off like I'm doing." Blue pulled his chair up and sat it right in front of Caleb. "How much time they talking if you lay down?"

"Five years, possible parole after three," Caleb said.

"Damn!" Blue put his hand to his face again, as if the words were causing him extreme agony. "Don't you know that's exactly what the white man wants from you, for you to take the first thing he offers you? He wants to see you in jail, behind bars like a damn animal. He doesn't want you to fight for your freedom. Don't do that shit! Don't do it, man!" He reached out and grabbed Caleb by the arm. "I ain't doing it. Just come with me."

Come with him, Caleb thought. That was the reason he was there in the first place. "I can't do what you're doing," Caleb said.

"Why not?"

"If I get convicted, I'm looking at ten to fifteen. I can't do that. I have a woman that I want to marry someday. I have a son that I want to see grow up. I take the guilty plea and I'm out of here maybe by the time he's eight years old. I can live with that," Caleb said.

"You can live with that! Caleb, you can't tell yourself that shit," Blue said, pointing a finger in Caleb's face. "You can't live with it. Five years is a long time to be locked up behind bars, Caleb. To have your damn freedom taken away. You're going to be locked up like a . . . a fucking slave!"

Caleb said nothing.

"Fuck that, Caleb, you're pleading innocent. That's it!"

"What are you talking about?" Caleb asked, seeing the distraught look on his friend's face.

Blue walked up to Caleb and grabbed him with both hands by the shoulders. "You can't just lay down for them, man. One more brother locked up behind bars, one more brother rotting away like some damn lab monkey that they feed and shelter every day just so they can experiment on it!"

"Blue, you ain't making any sense," Caleb said, moving to push Blue's hands off his shoulders.

Blue didn't let go, and almost looked offended.

"I'm making sense, you just don't understand. They're trying to take your life from you, and you just going to hand it over. No fight, no nothing. Ain't going to do—"

"But we're guilty, Blue!" Caleb said, louder than he should have. "We're guilty," he said again, this time lowering his voice.

There was silence. Blue's hands slowly fell from Caleb's shoulders. He turned away.

"That's where you're wrong, man. We ain't guilty. We did what we had to do." Blue turned around to face Caleb again. There was a solemn expression on his face, one that Caleb had never seen in all the years of knowing him.

"We ain't guilty, 'cause we did what we had to do to survive, and to me, there ain't no guilt in that."

Caleb sat in the courtroom, Austin beside him; the other guy, Caleb thought his name was Lansford, was sitting next to Austin. The room was only sparsely filled. It gave Caleb an indication of how important he was to the rest of the people in the world. He looked around and saw Marcus and a woman sitting together in the back of the room. Marcus had a look on his face like *he* was the one on trial, like *he* was about to trade his freedom for imprisonment. It was only because he cared, Caleb told himself. He scanned the room again, looking for Sonya. He didn't see her. He looked over it again, slower than before, checking every seat, but still there was no sign of her. But she had to be there; he knew she cared for him at least enough to want to find out what would happen to him, what would happen to them.

He heard the deep voice of the judge enter his brain. "Will the defendants rise." He was still looking for Sonya, looking at the door, hoping she would walk in. He felt Austin's hand around his arm, pulling him up.

"You have to stand, Caleb," Austin whispered in his ear. "You have to get up." He stood and Caleb stood with him. Sonya wasn't there. She wasn't there for him so that should let him know where she stood. There could be no greater statement made than the one she seemed to be making at that moment.

"How do you plead?" the judge asked.

The question was directed to Caleb, he knew that, because the big man with the huge white beard was staring right at him, but Caleb couldn't speak.

He turned his face to see Blue standing at a table beside him. Blue had a meek expression on his face; he barely resembled the brave, loud-mouthed, opinionated young man he had known for so long. He didn't wink at Caleb, made no gesture, no hint of strength somehow being transferred. Blue just turned his head slowly and looked at him, almost in pity.

"How do you plead?" the judge said, his voice booming even louder than before.

Caleb looked over the room one last time. He looked to the doors; still there was no Sonya. He saw Marcus and pulled what strength he could from what his brother meant to him. He looked to his side and saw Austin, the older brother that he had really never known, at least not the way he should have, but who was there for him now.

"Guilty, your honor." Caleb said the words softly, his head bowed in sadness. When he said those words, the realization that he would go to prison, lose his girlfriend and probably his son, slipped into his brain and all but killed him. But he didn't break down. He stood there, his eyes glazed over, a dizzy feeling in his head, finally telling himself that his life was all but over.

THIRTY-FIVE

The bedroom of the hotel suite was dark, the curtains were drawn closed so no light could get in. Julius sat up quickly in bed, his head whipping from side to side.

"What?" Cathy said, in a groggy morning voice. She was still very much asleep.

"Did you hear the phone ring? I heard the phone ring," Julius said.

"No, baby. Go back to sleep. It's . . ." Cathy reached blindly for the alarm clock on the nightstand and turned it toward her, ". . . six in the morning, honey."

"Oh," Julius said, regretting waking her up. He reached for the phone, pulled the receiver over and put it to his ear just to make sure. There was nothing but the long steady drone of the dial tone. He was expecting a call from his son. It had been days since he had left his last message and he knew Austin should have gotten it by now.

He had asked Austin to call him back, that was it. There were no other favors, except maybe having a little talk, but he didn't think that was too much to ask. Not at all. Julius settled back down in bed and pulled the covers back over him, trying not to think about it. Austin will call, Julius told himself. He will call and it will probably be today. But he had told himself that yesterday, and he had told himself that the day before and the day before that, but there was never a call from his son.

Julius sat back up in bed. Did he give him the wrong hotel? Could Austin have been trying to call somewhere else, looking for his father, thinking that Julius had left him again, after saying he would wait for his call? But then he remembered without a doubt telling Austin the Radisson.

Julius fell back into bed again, trying to think of any other reasons why Austin hadn't phoned him, but the only thing he could think of was that the boy didn't care anymore. Julius rolled over on his stomach, and tried to force himself to sleep.

He had been there in Chicago almost two weeks waiting to speak to his son, tell him how he felt and why he had left. Julius sat up in bed again and swung his feet out onto the carpet.

"What's wrong, Jay? Are you all right?" Cathy said.

"Not really," he said, anger in his voice.

"What's the matter?"

Julius walked across the room to the windows and yanked the curtains open. Sunlight blasted in. Cathy shut her eyes and disappeared back under the covers.

"C'mon, we're leaving," Julius said, pulling their suitcases out of the closet. He set them open on the floor and started pulling garments off the closet rack and tossing them into the suitcases, the hangers still in most of the clothes.

"What are you doing?" Cathy said. She had gotten out of bed and was standing behind him, still squinting against the sunlight.

"I told you, we're leaving. I'm sick of this."

"Sick of what?"

Julius didn't answer, just continued tossing the clothes toward the suitcases. He walked over to the dresser, pulled out one of the drawers and held it upside down over the suitcase, all of his belongings falling out onto the scattered clothing.

"Sick of what, Julius?" Cathy asked again. "Sick of what?"

Julius stopped, turned around and almost bumped into Cathy.

"Sick of waiting for my son to call here. Sick of trying to be patient, of trying to convince myself that he would want to see me, that we could actually be a—a—"

Julius tried turning and walking away to do more packing, but Cathy caught him by the arm.

"Be a what, Julius?"

"Be a family again." Julius forced the words out. "He doesn't want to see me, Cathy. I knew that after the first couple of days we were here and he didn't call, but like a fool, I stayed as long as I did hoping he'd change his mind."

"I don't think you're a fool, I'm just so sad that this didn't work out the way you wanted it to. I know how much you were looking forward to seeing them, and I know it must be hurting you."

Julius pulled away from her and began packing again.

Half an hour later they were on the road. Julius was trying to find his way to the highway so they could go to the airport, but he had managed to get lost in the dizzying bundle of streets that tangled through the inner city. He was driving around Chicago, getting cut off by cabs, getting stopped by red lights and held up by pedestrians who obviously felt they could stand the impact of a large car plowing into them. Each time he was stopped, he blew out a frustrated sigh and banged his fist on the steering wheel. He was angry as hell at what had happened, but more at himself for letting it happen. All he wanted to do was get out of Chicago, and forget about ever trying to reconcile with his sons.

The car was halted at a red light, and just as it turned green a huge white hearse drove into the intersection followed by a long line of cars, their lights on, little orange stickers on their windshields reading, "Funeral."

"Damn!" Julius shouted. "No one wants me to get out of here. Even the dead are trying to stop me."

"Julius, pull over," Cathy said.

"What?"

"I said, pull over! Turn right here."

Julius turned the car down an alley, came out the other side and pulled the car over.

"Can you park?" Cathy said, a perturbed look on her face.

Julius threw the car in park. He turned to look at Cathy; the same look was on her face.

"Can you turn it off, Julius?"

"Why?"

"Because I asked you, that's why," she said.

Julius reluctantly shut off the car and pulled the keys out of the ignition.

"What is your problem, Julius?" Cathy asked, speaking as though she were scolding a child.

"I don't know what you're talking about. All I want to do is get to the airport so we can get out of here," he said, both his hands on the steering wheel, as if he was just waiting for permission to start it up and race back on the road.

"That's not all you want to do. And you know what I think, I don't think you want to do that at all. I think you still want to try and see your son, but because you think he doesn't want to see you, you're getting upset, you're pouting and you want to run."

"I don't pout, and I'm not running?" Julius said, turning to face her, then looking away.

"What is it then?"

"I told you, I'm just tired."

"Tired of what? Tired of wanting? Because you sure aren't *doing* anything," Cathy said. "I'm just letting you know what I see is going on. You're acting like there's nothing else you can do. Why haven't you tried to contact either one of your other sons? If Austin doesn't want to see you, go through Marcus, or Caleb."

Julius saw an image of Marcus in his mind, standing before him the night Julius left them. He was in his pajamas, but he was full-grown. He was a full-grown man, giving him the most evil look, then he ran to his mother. She was sprawled out on the bedroom floor. Caleb was there, too. He stood there in front of him as well, except this time he wasn't crying, he was just there, staring into his father's eyes, a hateful look on his face.

"No. I can't contact them," Julius said, coming out of the daydream.

"Why not?"

"I just can't. I have my reasons, all right?" he snapped.

Cathy didn't say anything after that and neither did Julius, both staring out the windshield in front of them. When Julius turned to look at Cathy, he was looking at the side of her face because she wouldn't turn around.

"Well, I'm going to start the car now," he said, already moving his hand toward the ignition.

The car roared to a start. "I'm putting the car in drive, and I'm about to pull away from the curb, all right?"

Cathy didn't answer, just crossed her arms, her lips tightening.

Julius pulled the car away, took a turn, then made his way back onto a main street.

"And I'm going to drive us to the airport, where we will be getting on a plane and going back to California." Julius spoke as if he was explaining difficult instructions to a fool.

"All right, I get the picture," Cathy said. "We're leaving since you did all you could do to get back with your sons. I mean, there really is nothing else for us to do but leave, since you've exhausted all possibilities, right, Julius?"

Julius pulled the car over hard to the curb and threw it in park again.

"What are you talking about now, Cathy?" he said, not looking at her, but at himself in the rearview mirror.

"You want to see your sons, so why are you leaving?"

"I told you they don't want to see me. How many times have I called Austin?"

Cathy didn't answer.

"A lot," Julius answered for her. "Too many. He called me not one time. That says something to me, and when I think about it, really think about it, I can't blame him. That's why I'm leaving."

"Julius." Cathy turned toward him. "I don't mean to tell you something that you already know, but you've been gone twenty years. That's a long time not to talk to someone, and you think a phone call is enough to make him just want to jump in your arms and go see a ball game? Did you just expect him to come on down the moment he heard your voice on the other end of the phone?"

"No, but he could've at least called me back," Julius said.

"But he didn't. So you're going to leave because of it? You're going to get on that plane, and tell yourself that you'll never see your sons again for the rest of your life. The rest of your life," she said again, stressing the last word.

Julius considered the possibility. He had never thought about it that way, even though he saw himself leaving, saw himself on the plane. He had not gotten as far as imagining himself dying without seeing his sons at least one last time. He heard Cathy's voice outside his daydreaming, trying to convince him.

"I don't care what you have to do to see them, at least you'll know, when you do leave here, that you've tried, that you made some attempt, that you let them know all you wanted them to and told them that you loved them. You have to do that, Jay. I know it, and you know it, because if you don't you will never forgive yourself. Julius," Cathy called, but Julius's mind was elsewhere. She moved closer to him, looked into his eyes. "Julius?" she said, shaking him a little.

"Yeah, I'm here," he said. He reached into his pants pocket, pulled out his wallet, and took out a small piece of paper.

"I have this." He gave it to Cathy.

"What is it?" she said.

"Austin's phone number . . . and address."

THIRTY-SIX

"How do you plead?" Austin remembered hearing the judge ask his brother. Austin was trembling, shaking nervously, but trying to conceal it, especially from Caleb. He couldn't remember a time in his life when he felt quite like that. Standing there in front of the judge he was holding onto Caleb's arm. He didn't know why; he had just never let it go after pulling him up. He kept it there on him, in an attempt to let Caleb know he was there for him—more than just standing there next to him physically, but in mind and soul and in their connection as brothers.

He noticed Caleb looking around the room for something. He didn't know what, but whatever he was searching for, Austin hoped that he would find it.

"How do you plead?" the judge asked Caleb again, this time with more force. Caleb was staring glassy-eyed at the judge, seeming to prepare his mouth to say the word.

Austin had no idea what that word was going to be. Caleb had not told him yet, and he almost preferred it that way. But as he stood there, holding his brother's arm, feeling how terrified they both were, something inside him was hoping Caleb would say "innocent." Plead innocent, Caleb. Innocent! Austin said in his mind. He was guilty as all hell, Austin knew that, and there was probably no way in the world they would be able to get him off, but at least they would have a chance. Something could happen, somebody or something could be introduced that would cast doubt on whether or not he was truly guilty. And even if they didn't win the case, and free Caleb from spending time behind bars, at least they'd have hope for just a little longer.

Austin felt that Caleb was about to speak, and he felt himself about to lean over and stop him, cup his hand beside Caleb's head and whisper in his ear. Tell him whatever he did, not to plead guilty, because there just might be hope. But Austin didn't. He stood there, even closed his eyes, waiting for his brother to speak.

"Guilty," he heard Caleb say. His voice was soft but steady, even though his body felt weak and near collapsing in Austin's grasp.

Something in Austin's heart fell. He slowly turned to look at his brother. He was standing there, his eyes glazed over, his face displaying no emotion.

I'm sorry, Caleb, Austin thought. I'm sorry.

All that had happened only yesterday, even though it felt like such a long time ago to Austin. After the hearing, Marcus had asked him if he wanted to do something with him and Reecie. Austin told them no. Marcus would have wanted to talk about everything that had happened, but Austin needed to be alone with his feelings, with his guilt, his anger, his sadness. He didn't want anyone to be witness to his outbreak of emotion, not even his brother, because he didn't know how it would manifest itself.

Austin ended up in a small, dimly lit, smoke-filled blues club. He sat at a small table by himself, a glass and a full bottle of cognac sitting before him which he didn't touch. He just sat watching the old black men on stage, rhythmically craning and turning their heads with the music in the odd way that musicians do, their eyes closed at times, as they made their instruments cry out in sorrowful agony.

The music was beautiful, and it cut Austin down to his soul. It was filled with torment, suffering and misery, similar to what he had been through all his life. He wanted to cup his face in his hands and cry right there. Or better yet, cry right out in the open, let the old men on stage and the people around him see the tears spilling from his eyes, hear the pain in his cries. People would come up to him and ask him why he was crying and he would turn to them, not even wiping the tears from his face, and tell them it was for his brother. It would be his way of making sure that his brother didn't go to prison without anyone knowing or caring.

But Austin didn't do that. He remained in the chair, his back straight, his hands in his lap, listening to the music, showing no hint of the emotional turmoil he was feeling in his heart.

The place closed at five in the morning, and Austin wandered out with the band and one other spectator who obviously had no other place to go. He was exhausted, but found himself in an all-night grocery store, walking the aisles of the brightly lit place, pushing a squeaky cart in front of him, because he still didn't feel like being alone. He walked through the place not shopping, not looking at anything in particular, not putting anything in his cart, just pushing the empty, squeaky, wire-framed thing in front of him.

After a while he didn't have more than the ounce of energy it took to get himself home, crawl in his bed and fall off into a deep sleep. He didn't want to be awake a moment longer than he had to, to think or to worry.

When he stepped into his bedroom, the red fluorescence of the alarm clock read 7:37 A.M. He looked over at his answering machine, and it wasn't blinking. He was grateful for that, even though he wouldn't have listened to the recordings anyway.

He undid his tie, and figured his father had finally given up on calling him. He undressed and slipped under the covers, and took another quick glance at the answering machine, then rolled over to fall asleep.

THIRTY-SEVEN

"I don't know if I want to go up there," Julius told Cathy. They were parked outside the apartment they believed to be Austin's. Julius was looking at the place like a child about to be sent off into a school unknown to him for his first day of class.

"Then what are you going to do?" Cathy said.

"There's nothing else I can do, I guess." He looked away from the building at Cathy. "I just don't want to go up there."

"That's understandable, Jay." She placed a hand on his, and squeezed it tightly.

He blew out a nervous sigh, looking back toward the building. "I guess I should probably go up there now, you think?"

"I think so," Cathy said.

"You don't think it's too early, do you? He might not even be home. He may have gone to work already." Julius looked down at his watch. It read 7:45. "Yeah, he's probably gone already. Maybe I should just—"

"Jay. Do you want me to go up there with you?" Cathy interrupted.

He looked back to the building, and realized he was acting like a child.

"No, I can handle it," he told her, sounding more sure of himself. He leaned over and gave her a kiss on the lips. "I love you."

"I love you too, and good luck."

He stepped out of the car and closed the door. "I'm going to need it," he said to himself.

He took slow steps to the building, feeling as though he was being marched, blindfolded, to his place in front of a firing squad. Payment for the debt of leaving his children to grow up without a father, without love, without the knowledge that he even cared. He turned his head and looked back toward the car at Cathy. Her eyes were glued on him, just as he had known they'd be. There was no turning back at this point, he knew that. No matter how much he wanted to run, he couldn't. The thought of dealing with his cowardice in the future was too much for him. He would handle the fear that he'd been escaping for twenty years, now.

Julius stepped up to the door, took the handle in his hand and squeezed, but the door didn't open. It was locked. It was one of those security doors that always stayed locked, because this was one of those security apartments, Julius thought. He looked to his left, at the long list of names and buttons, no doubt leading to an intercom in each apartment. He was almost glad seeing what he did, because it gave him another excuse to tuck tail and run, but he told himself he wouldn't do that.

He looked over the list, searching for Harris. He found it—apartment 756—and moved to press the button beside it, then paused for a moment. What would happen when his son asked who was calling? What would Austin say if he told him it was his father wanting to see him? He might not even let him up. He might tell him to go to hell over the intercom. Julius wouldn't even get a chance to see his son at all. He looked over the list again, chose a button at random, and pushed it.

"Hello," a voice came crackling over the small speaker.

"Hello," Julius said. "Uh, sorry to bother you. This is Austin Harris in apartment—" he looked down for his son's number again. "—756. I misplaced my key. Can you buzz me in please?"

"Hey, Austin," the voice said. "How are things?" Julius was caught off guard. Of all the buzzers he could have pushed, he had chosen some-one his son knew. "Uh, fine, but I'm really in a hurry, so if you could . . ."

"Sure . . . uh, take it easy, Austin." The buzzer sounded.

Julius walked in the door, through another security door, and over to the elevators. He moved to pushed the up button, then held his fin-ger just an inch from it, hovering there.

He felt a cough coming on. It started as a thin cough, a tingling in his throat, but it persisted, impossible to stop, till he was bent over, al-most heaving. He put his fist up to his mouth to try to quiet the hack-ing, but the noise just pushed past the attempt and echoed throughout the hallway. When the coughing finally subsided he pulled his fist away and opened his palm to see if there was anything there. He was expect-ing to see saliva and blood spilling through his fingers, something to do with the cancer, but there was nothing. He was relieved, a bit shaken, but relieved. Without giving it another thought, Julius pushed the but-ton and stepped onto the elevator.

THIRTY-EIGHT

Austin tossed and turned in bed, the covers tangled in between his legs. He was exhausted but he could not fall asleep. Maybe because he was too tired. The thought crossed his mind as his eyelids hung slightly open.

He flipped over onto his stomach, telling himself that he would fall asleep, when he heard a faint tapping outside his bedroom. He didn't know where it was coming from for sure, but figured it had to be his front door. He didn't get up immediately, questioning whether it could be his mind playing tricks on him—the deprivation of sleep manifesting itself as strange sounds floating about his head.

He heard the knocking again. Austin pulled himself up in bed, threw his legs over the side, and waited. He told himself if the knocking persisted, he would take the noise as reality and investigate.

Another knock, louder this time, and Austin was out of bed, slipping on his trousers and walking to the door. He wasn't angry but aggravated. His business could never just be finished, he thought. He didn't bother looking through the peephole to see who was knocking at eight in the morning, because whoever it was was going to really hear about it.

He grabbed the doorknob and flung the door open, a chosen obscenity waiting on the tip of his tongue, until he saw who was standing in front of him. Austin was frozen, felt as though he could not even breathe, when he saw the man he had not seen in twenty years.

"How are you doing, Austin?" the man said, as if they had spoken just yesterday.

Austin didn't answer. He couldn't because whatever it was that controlled his voice wasn't there or wasn't working. He wanted to say something, but he didn't know what. All his emotions were clashing, bumping into one another, making it difficult for him to simply think one thing.

"Well," his father said, smiling uncomfortably. "Aren't you going to say something?"

The man was talking to him again, and Austin could feel himself becoming angry. It was because his father was standing in front of him, at his door so early in the morning, with this simple grin on his face, like a flowerpot dropped from the sky, crashing onto his head, making him forget about the last twenty years. "How are you?" Austin said in an unenthused, barely audible voice.

"I'm fine," his father said, fidgeting around. "I tried calling you, did you get my messages?"

Austin nodded his head. "I was busy," he said in the same bland tone, almost regretting it. He owed him no explanation. But the fact that Julius was still his father made him feel as though he did.

"Since you weren't answering my messages, I just thought I'd stop by." The smile disappeared from Julius's face. "I needed to see you, Austin."

Austin looked his father up and down. The nerve of him, he thought. He wanted to let him have it, let him know how he felt to be left and not spoken to for so long.

"Well, you just can't go knocking on doors whenever you want," Austin said, summoning as much anger as possible. "Especially after twenty years. You don't know what I have going on in my life right now. Call me tomorrow and we'll talk," Austin said. That was his stand. That was Austin telling his father off for walking out on him, for leaving him without explanation, for making him suffer through countless experiences that would have been much easier to suffer through with the aid of his father. And that was all he could come up with. Austin tried closing the door on him, but his father stopped the door with his hand.

"I'm leaving today, Austin, that's why I stopped by," Julius said from behind the half-closed door.

Austin slowly opened the door.

"I figured you not calling me back was letting me know that you weren't interested in speaking, so I decided to go. Am I right about that?"

Austin didn't answer. He couldn't answer because he wasn't sure what was going on in his head, how he felt about anything. He was far past tired, and standing there without falling to the floor took enough energy without having to make decisions about his father that would impact the rest of his life.

"That's what I thought," his father said. "This was a bad idea from the beginning. I shouldn't have assumed anything, and I shouldn't have come all the way out here just to pester you. I'm sorry, Austin. Good-bye."

His father turned, looking saddened. Austin didn't react at all. He didn't know if it was because he was too tired to move, or if it was because he just didn't want to move.

Austin looked on as his father slowly made his way down the hallway. He tried to quickly think, tried to assess how he really felt about the man, tried to decide if he should take him back into his life or just let him walk out as he had done so many years before.

Austin stepped out into the hallway. His father was waiting by the elevator, looking overcome with grief, appearing just as beaten and tired as Austin. Austin just stood there for a moment, not alerting the man to his presence. He just stared at him, realizing that it really was him, the man he had loved so much, looked up to for so many years, had known would come back to him one day. And there he was.

"Dad," Austin called, just loud enough for him to hear. The word was not awkward or strange coming out of his mouth, but then he had never thought it would be.

His father's head turned slowly, a pitiful look on his face.

"Can you come back down for a minute so we can talk?" Austin said.

THIRTY-NINE

"**D**on't you think you should've told Marcus that you were bringing us with you over there to his house?" Julius asked, as he drove the rental.

"I don't think so. I didn't want to get into all of that over the phone. It'd be best if we just all meet face to face, and see what develops," Austin said.

But that was the thing that Julius was most afraid of. Austin had told him that of all his sons, Marcus was the most angry at him. He was hatefully bitter, Austin had told him, and that was something that Julius was not looking forward to experiencing. But he would deal with it. He had to, and just to see another one of his sons would make it worth going through.

Austin had also told him that Caleb was going to prison. "They're really going to lock him up," Austin said, a melancholy look on his face.

Julius hadn't answered. He didn't know what to say. He just took the responsibility for Caleb being there, and told himself he would have to go there to see him.

"Make a left at the next light," Austin said, pointing ahead of them.

Julius took the turn, then stole a quick glance at his son. His son who looked almost just the way he did so many years ago. His son who had become a successful lawyer with his own firm. The son who had given him two grandchildren, whom Austin had said Julius would see soon. It was so good to see him, and to think that he felt the same way.

Julius looked in the rearview mirror and caught Cathy looking up at him. She was smiling and he knew she knew how he felt at that moment. He couldn't wait to get her alone and tell her how happy he was with how everything was going, and how much he loved her, appreciated her for doing all the things she'd done for him over the years, especially pushing him to see his sons.

There was not much conversation to be had on the trip to Marcus's house. Julius had already told Austin he didn't want to get into explanations of why he left and how he'd felt over the years about leaving and not seeing his sons. He told Austin he wanted both him and Marcus to be there for that. He wanted them to talk it over as a family. *Family.* The word sounded good coming out, and he wasn't sure, but he thought he saw a small smile emerging on Austin's face when he said it.

"All right, pull up right there. This is his house right here," Austin said.

Julius parked the car. He was nervous as he'd ever been, and all he wanted to do was get in there, take the abuse he was sure he was going to get, and get it over with. He just wanted to tell his sons what he had to say so they could get past all the ill feelings that had grown over the years and start enjoying their time together, now that they had found each other.

Austin got out of the car and walked around to Julius's window.

"I'm going to go up there and talk to him first, okay? I think I'll tell him that you're here so he'll at least have time to prepare himself," Austin said.

Julius didn't say anything, just looked at his son nervously.

"It's going to be all right," Austin said, sticking a hand in the window and squeezing his father's shoulder. "I just don't want to pop in on him. I know how he is. It'll be better this way."

Even though Cathy was in the car with him, Julius felt alone and vulnerable at that moment. He'd only been in the company of his son for a couple of hours and already he'd developed a dependence of sorts, as though they'd never separated.

"I'm hoping everything will be all right," he said to Cathy as he watched Austin ring the doorbell. He saw the door open. He tried to get a look at Marcus, but Austin stepped in the way. Julius knew it was intentional, probably blocking Marcus's view until he told him that his father was out in the car waiting to speak to him.

They talked up there for what seemed like hours. Julius looked intently, his hands starting to coat with nervous sweat, waiting for some sign to know that the news had been broken. Then all of a sudden it came. Marcus practically pushed Austin to the ground to get a look straight at the car. He stared right through the window, right into Julius's eyes. Julius wanted to duck, or cover his face with his hands, but he told himself not to. The look in Marcus's eyes was shock, then disbelief, then something that bordered on hatred. But Julius didn't look away, just stared into his son's eyes as long as his son stared at him. Marcus eventually turned away.

Julius saw his sons' mouths moving, the gestures of their hands and arms. Marcus's were wild, full of emotion, Austin's were controlled and calming. Clearly Marcus wasn't taking the news well.

Austin walked back to the car, his face betraying no information. He walked around to the driver's side window again.

"Everything is fine. If you're ready, we'll go in now."

Everything didn't look fine. It didn't look fine at all, and Julius wanted to ask Austin what the hell was said up there, but he figured his son knew Marcus better than he did, and if he felt things would be fine, then they would be.

They stood on the doorstep, Austin in front, Julius behind him, Cathy holding tightly onto Julius's hand. Austin knocked on the door, looked back at Julius for a moment, then walked in.

FORTY

Marcus didn't know what to think as he stood in the middle of his living room, his jaw locked, his teeth grinding together, feeling anger that threatened to set his entire body on fire. He told himself to stand there and try to stay composed, and watch as the man who had deserted him so long ago tried to step back into his life. He held his fists clenched to his sides, the fingers starting to ache. He would plant one fist in his father's face, he told himself. He would hit him in the mouth, or in the eye, upon entering his house, and he would watch him fall, and that would be the end of their fucking reunion.

"What's happening, Marcus?" Reecie asked him. She was sitting on the sofa, quiet, bewildered. A moment ago, Marcus had pulled her out of the bathroom, her hair half curled, and dragged her downstairs and sat her on the sofa. "Just don't move," he said. "You should be here for this."

"For what?" she asked, trying to hold the curls together with her fingers.

"Just don't move," Marcus said, pointing a finger at her. "You'll see."

She sat there obediently, and when she asked him again what was happening, he didn't turn around, did not say a word.

There was a knock at the door, and everything inside Marcus seemed to tighten up. He felt both anger and fear as he stood there, staring at the door, knowing that this man whom he hadn't spoken to in twenty years, his so-called father, was standing just behind it. Marcus knew that all the hatred and the years of questioning would come down on him, knew that there would be no way he could think objectively, as he figured his father would ask him. He was biased. And he knew his father wouldn't understand that. He wasn't there to know how his walking out affected his family, sent his wife into a downward spiral of grief and pain, which is what Marcus knew eventually killed her. He wasn't there to know how Marcus felt, having a piece of him snatched away like an arm from his body, and then trying to accomplish things without it, to live a normal life as though he had never been born with that arm—as though he had never had a father.

Marcus tried to steady himself, tried to breathe deeply, telling himself it would make a difference, but it didn't. His heart was still pounding, his pulse still racing, and the many devastating thoughts were still spinning, revolving around in his head like some sick family movie. The unforgettable night his father left, the day his mother died, the funeral, the day Austin boarded the bus for law school, leaving him there to be Caleb's father and mother, and the day Caleb decided the task was too much for Marcus and figured he'd better care for himself.

Then the long days and nights Marcus had sat by himself in the house that everyone he loved used to lived in. The house everyone he loved had left him in, one way or the other. He sat in that house for weeks, crying once in a while, wondering most of the time was it him that drove them away? Was it his fault that his father left, was it because of him that his mother truly died? It had to be, he told himself then. He could have taken better care of her. He could have been there for her more, exhausted every possibility, and he thought he had, but for some reason, something told him he hadn't.

The door was pushed open and Austin came in. By the look on Austin's face, he was trying to tell Marcus to behave himself, but Marcus didn't acknowledge him. His attention was on the man behind him, and the woman that he had in tow by the hand. The three of them walked into Marcus's house and stood there by the door. Austin closed it behind them.

There he was, Marcus thought, Julius Wilson Harris. The man who had destroyed their family, and the man who was supposed to be his father. He looked strangely the same to Marcus. His hair had grayed some, his skin had wrinkled just a little, and he had lost some weight, but for the most part he looked the same as the day he left. He looked the same, not broken down and distraught with pain and guilt, not burned by fire, leaving his face scarred and disfigured for life, or his eyes blind from a horrible accident involving hot acid, as Marcus thought should have happened, considering what he had done. How unfair, Marcus thought.

But he would give him a reason to feel pain, he thought as he walked right up on him, right up in his face. Marcus held his aching, tightly clenched fists at his side, poised, ready to swing wildly in the direction of the man, to hit whatever, to break his father's bones, retrieve his fists to find blood all over them. But Marcus didn't move. He just stood there, stood strangely still in front of his father, looking him dead in the eyes, his father looking back.

Then Marcus turned and walked away, just left, feeling disgusted, feeling sickened as though he would vomit. He pushed his way into the kitchen and fell onto the counter. He just had to get out of there, had to get away from that man for fear of what he might do to him, what he might say.

"What the hell was that?" Austin said a moment later, coming into the kitchen.

Marcus pulled himself up from the counter. "I want him out of here."

"What are you talking about? You didn't even say one word to him."

"That's because I'm not going to say a word to him. He doesn't deserve it. I want him out," Marcus said.

"Marcus, the man flew all the way from—"

"I don't care. I want him out!" Marcus yelled.

"Shhhh," Austin said, rushing over to Marcus. "They're going to hear you out there."

"I don't care, Austin. You had no right bringing him over here in the first place without telling me. That wasn't fair."

"Forget about fair, Marcus. Just forget about it this one time, all right? The man wants to talk to you. Go out there and have a conversation with him. Is that too much to ask?"

Marcus paused for a moment. "Who's asking?"

"And what is that supposed to mean?" Austin said.

"You seem to want this more than he does."

"Just go out there and talk to the man."

"I'm not going out there," Marcus said.

"Why not?" Austin raised his voice.

"Why? So he can fill my ears with some bullshit that he made up on the way down here? So he can try to explain the reason he walked out? Austin, there is no reason. There just isn't, can't you understand that?"

"And how do you know if you're too much of a coward to go out there and listen to what he has to say?"

"I'm not the coward here, Austin. I think you know that."

"Well, go out there and hear what he has to say. Prove your point to me," Austin said, crossing his arms.

"I don't have to prove anything to you or anybody else."

"How about to yourself?" Austin said.

Marcus looked at his brother strongly, not saying a word.

"You say you don't want him back, but how can you say that till you hear him out?"

Marcus still didn't respond. Austin was staring at him. Marcus stared right back at him.

"I'll be in there in a minute," Marcus said to his brother.

Austin gave him a studied look, as if he was wondering if Marcus would climb the kitchen sink and jump out the window just to get away from the confrontation.

"I said I'll be in there, all right?" Marcus said.

Austin left. He was a traitor, Marcus thought. He was a traitor and a sell-out to his family, the family that mattered, the family that was there for him. And whom did he sell his family out to? To the worthless piece of crap standing in his living room, soiling Marcus's carpet like fresh puppy shit. Marcus didn't want to go back out there, not because he was scared, but because he felt there was nothing more to talk about. All statements were made the night his father walked out, and they were only reinforced each time something bad happened to Marcus, and there were so many things.

Talking to him would be like discounting those things, like acting as though he had gotten over them, as though he wasn't still angry that Caleb would rot in jail for the next so many years, as though he didn't miss his mother each and every day. Talking to his father would be a sign of disrespect for his mother, and considering taking him back would be like spitting on her grave.

Marcus pushed his way back out into the living room, and saw his father.

Marcus stepped right up into his face. "I'm sorry, I had to step out, I was so angry that I was about to take a shot at you."

"Well, I'm glad you considered me and didn't do it," Julius said, smiling thinly.

"That's not what I did. I didn't consider you," Marcus said. "Not at all."

"I see." The smile disappeared from Julius's face.

"Why are you here?" Marcus asked, not finding any reason to prolong the conversation.

"What?" Julius said.

"I said, why are you here?"

"You needed to know why I left. I needed to tell you," Julius said. He looked over to Austin, and Austin gave him a reassuring look. Marcus didn't even know why his brother was there. He sure as hell wasn't there to listen to what had to be said, because he was already convinced that he wanted his father to come back. Marcus wasn't sure of how long they had spoken, or what they had talked about before that moment, but one thing he was sure of was that they had things all ironed out. They were already a family reunited again, fucking father and son, after all those years. How sweet.

The thought sickened him and angered him at the same time. He wouldn't be able to talk to the man, at least not while Austin was there. It would just complicate things. It would interfere with Marcus telling him just where he could go and why. Austin would try to step in and defend his father, being the lawyer that he was. He would fight for him like he was an innocent man wrongly accused, but he would fight like he never had before, because his emotional attachment was so strong. Marcus couldn't have that.

"I can't do this."

"What do you mean, you can't do this?" Austin said.

"I just can't," Marcus said, turning his back.

"What do you mean by that? You're here, all you have to do is talk."

"It's not *me* being here that's the problem. It's you."

Austin looked himself over, then directed a questioning stare at his father.

"If I'm going to talk to you," Marcus told his father, "I'm not going to do it around Austin."

"Why can't you? I'm just—"

"It's nothing against you, Austin, but it seems to me that the two of you have already done your talking."

Austin and their father just turned and looked at one another, almost as if agreeing.

Marcus and Julius ended up outside by the lake, very near to where Marcus lived. He thought it was the perfect place for them to talk because if he no longer wanted to listen to the web of lies his father weaved, he would just stare out on the water, and wait till the lies ran out.

The two of them sat on the rocks looking out. Marcus thought he should have felt uncomfortable there after not seeing his father for twenty years, but he didn't feel uncomfortable at all. He didn't feel anything.

Marcus waited for his father to speak. It wasn't himself that had the story to tell, that had the explanations to give for what he did so long ago. He would wait patiently for his father to start the conversation, and until then Marcus would just stare out onto the water as if the man was not there, as if he did not even exist.

"I like to do this, sometimes," his father said.

"What's that?" Marcus said, not bothering to look in the man's direction.

"Come out to the water, and just sit for a while, but we have an ocean in California. It's beautiful, especially when the sun is going down."

"I can imagine," Marcus said, not caring, but all the same trying to see it in his mind.

"Not that this is bad. This is actually quite nice, you know?" Julius looked over at his son. Marcus felt his stare and returned his glance briefly, then looked away.

"Yeah, I know," Marcus replied. "I used to come out here a lot when I was in school. When I was stressed out by tests, and felt that I would never finish. I would just come out here and lay a blanket out on the grass and look out on the water or up at the sky and watch it turn from light blue to purple to black. I would stay out here for hours sometimes, because I didn't want to go home. I knew there would be no one there, with Austin being away at school, and Caleb being gone and Ma . . ." Marcus chose not to finish the sentence. It wasn't something he wanted to go into. It would make him angry at the man sitting beside him, and Marcus was trying to avoid that. He was trying just to hear him out, talk to him without any bias, and when it was time to turn him down, send him on his way. He wanted to make the decision solely on the fact that it would not be feasible to take him back, and that alone. Not because he felt he was getting revenge for what his father did to his mother, or for leaving them in the first place.

Marcus picked up a small pebble and tossed it out toward the water.

"I'm sorry about that," Julius said.

He was trying to apologize for what he had done to Marcus's mother, but it was too late. "Don't worry about it," Marcus said, searching the ground around him for another pebble.

"By the time I found out it was too late to—"

"I said don't worry about it," Marcus said, raising his voice. "There's nothing that can be done about it now."

"So, you married?" Julius asked after a moment.

"Not yet."

"You planning on it?"

"No," Marcus answered sharply.

"I see. So, what do you do for a living?"

"I'm a commercial artist."

"You draw for a living, huh? You were always good at that," Julius said, smiling.

"And how would you know?"

"I remember when you used to scribble on every piece of paper you could get your hands on. I still have a picture you drew me for Father's Day when you were in first grade. Remember when you gave that to me? I wish I would've brought it with me."

"And what good would that have done?" Marcus said, squinting at his father, the sun shining in his eyes.

"None, I guess. I just wish I would've brought it with me, that's all." Julius paused. "Marcus?"

"Yeah," Marcus answered, without turning.

"Marcus?" his father called again.

Marcus turned to look at him.

"I'm sorry, really. I'm sorry about everything," Julius said.

Marcus chuckled. "Yeah, well, whatever. It's okay."

"It's not okay. I did a terrible thing twenty years ago, and I'm apologizing for it. I don't expect you to act like it's no big deal."

"Well, it's not a big deal, not anymore."

"Don't you even want to know why I left?"

"Not if you're just telling me to try and come back, to try and change my mind about how I really feel about you," Marcus said, picking up another pebble and rubbing it between his fingers.

"I am telling you because I feel you should know. That's all," Julius said.

"Fine, then tell me. Why did you leave?"

Julius took a deep breath in, then exhaled. "I was overwhelmed. I thought I was ready for marriage, for a wife, for you guys. Thought I was ready for the house note, and the bills, and all the time that was taken away from me, the time that I used to do things I needed to do for me. I tried to fight it, the urge to leave, but I just couldn't do it any longer. There were times when your mother and I were lying in bed watching TV and all I wanted to do was get out of there, pack my things and leave. I don't expect you to understand, but I felt trapped. I felt like I had no life of my own anymore, like I lost my identity. I was no longer Julius Harris, but Mary's husband, and your father, not that that was a terrible thing, but I just couldn't handle it.

"I tried to hang in there, telling myself that the feeling would pass, that everything would be all right. I waited six years for it to pass, and when it never did, I knew that I didn't belong there anymore."

"So you just decided to pick up and leave," Marcus said.

"That's what I did," Julius said. "I told myself that I needed to find myself again. That I needed to get out and try and recapture what I lost. For some reason I felt that there was an entire world of things happening out there, while I was in the house being the dedicated father and husband. I couldn't allow those things to take place anymore without me being there to witness them, to take part in them, and feel like I belonged in that world."

Marcus didn't comment on what his father had said. It sounded like a bunch of nonsense. Like the dreams of a starry-eyed child, and it didn't make sense for a man with such responsibilities to have felt that way, and made even less sense for him to have acted on it.

"And what about us? You didn't even tell us you were going. You just walked right past us, and didn't say a thing. Ma had to tell us you were leaving us."

"She wouldn't let me. She was trying to stop me from waking you and your brothers, that's why we argued. I was going to tell you before I left, but when I opened the door, you guys were right there."

"Then why didn't you tell us then?" Marcus said, now staring at his father, remembering how he saw him that night.

"Tell you then, yeah. I had suitcases in my hands, and your mother was lying on the floor, and you would've understood when I told you I was leaving after seeing that? You probably don't remember the look you gave me, but it was the most evil thing I've ever seen on a child's face. After all these years, I haven't forgotten it. As a matter of fact, it's almost the identical look you're giving me right now."

Marcus made a quick attempt to change the expression on his face, but he knew it had no effect; the muscles that formed his stare were not budging. He didn't remember exactly what he looked like that night, but he remembered how he felt. Like he had been sold. No, more like given away or left for dead, and he vowed never to forgive his father for that feeling that he introduced him to so long ago.

"You still could've said something. I would've listened," Marcus said.

"No you wouldn't have."

"Yes I would've. You weren't the one standing there watching your father walk out. You weren't the one that was awakened in the middle